MW00576993

BOOK 1.5:

HELL TO PAY

LUKE
CHMILENKO

AETHERWORLD
PRODUCTIONS

ASCEND ONLINE: HELL TO PAY

Editor: Tom Shute
Proofer: Evan Mears
Cover Illustration: Yongjae Choi
Cover Design and Interior Layout: STK•Kreations

Hardcover ISBN: 978-1-7752413-8-6
Trade paperback ISBN: 978-1-7752413-9-3
Ebook ISBN: 978-0-9953378-4-8
Worldwide Rights.

2nd Edition, April 2020

Published by Aetherworld Productions Inc.
www.lukechmilenko.com

To my loving wife, family and friends.
Thank you for all of your constant support and the willingness to listen to me ramble about my story ideas. This book wouldn't be what it is today without all of your help.

FOREWORD

Before you start reading this book I'd like to make special mention that while it isn't explicitly necessary, this book assumes that you have read the first book in the Ascend Online series as it helps build the foundation for the rest of the world that this book refers to and without it, you may end up being a little bit confused!

If you haven't read book one, I highly recommend that you go read it then return to this one!

Thank you all so much for reading my book and I hope you enjoy the story!

Luke

ONE

Saturday, February 23rd, 2047
Unknown House in Eberia

I AWOKE ON MY BACK TO an intense, searing pain digging deep into the left side of my chest, burning as if someone had poured molten metal on my bare flesh. My body arched wildly, trying to tear itself away from the unknown source of pain, my mouth open in a silent scream.

Driven wild by the agony, instinct screamed at me to use my hands to brush away whatever was touching my skin, but the moment I tried to move them, I found them stopped by thick leather bands wrapped around my wrists. Panicking, I kicked my feet in desperation, feeling the bite of similar bindings keeping my legs from moving.

What's happening? The thought slammed into my head with nearly the same intensity as the pain shooting through my breast. *Where am I?*

The sickly-sweet smell of burning flesh reached my nose just as the pain ceased, leaving me gasping and covered in a cold sweat.

How did I get here? Where are my clothes? I craned my head upward and found myself strapped onto a stone table, completely naked, my olive-tinted skin gleaming with sweat. The last thing I remembered was checking over my gear, getting ready for the heist…then everything faded to black. The movement made my head spin, forcing me to lay it back down on the table, feeling cool stone on the back of my cleanly shaven head as I stared up at the wooden ceiling above me. *Damn, my head…*

As I waited for my head to clear, the realization that I was still logged in to Ascend Online gradually penetrated my consciousness, my heavy breathing slowly returning to normal. A quest notification flashed urgently in the corner of my vision, desperately trying to catch my attention.

Choosing to ignore the alert for the time being, I risked glancing around the dimly lit room once again, at least as best as I could with my head's limited range of motion.

Thanks to my elven ancestry, my eyes easily pierced through the gloom as I craned my head to the left, seeing four similar stone tables filling the room. As my vision adjusted, I noticed a fully clothed body lying on the stone table furthest from me, streaks of dried blood having coated the sides of the table. From the angle that I could see, it almost looked like something had viciously torn out the person's chest, leaving the ribs splayed wide open.

"*Fuck,*" I cursed to myself as I shifted my glance away from the body, doing my best to ignore the smell of death and rot in the air. *Where the hell is the rest of the team? Where the hell am I?*

Twisting my head in the opposite direction, I found myself staring at a large tray an arm's length away from my table. The tray was filled with an array of sharp tools, complete with a ragged-looking bone saw, jagged knives, and a wicked pair of pliers that sent my heart into a panic.

Get your shit together, Lazarus, this is just a game, remember? I scolded myself, as I closed my eyes and laid my head back on the cool table once again, feeling my heart hammer wildly in my chest. I took a breath to help steady my sudden nerves before reopening my eyes and bringing up the alert I had seen desperately calling for my attention.

QUEST UPDATED! THE HEIST! *(Chain-Quest) (Evolving Quest) (Criminal Quest)*

Something has gone terribly wrong with the heist you planned last night! You've just awoken to find yourself strapped to a table with a strange sigil burned into your chest and your memories of the previous night missing!

Escape from the torture chamber: 0/1

Find party members - Molly, Ransom, and Edith: 0/3

(Optional) Recover Memory: 0/1

Difficulty: Hard

Reward: Experience & Infamy

Note: Player Messaging has been temporarily blocked.

What the hell happened yesterday? I swallowed hard as I read the quest update, taking special note that I couldn't just directly message my party members and that the group we had formed had been disbanded. I couldn't even remember what we had set out to steal yesterday.

I paused to reread the quest update. *Wait, sigil? Is that what was burning me?*

Pulling against my bindings, I pushed myself upwards in a half-crunch, spotting bright orange lines glowing just below my left breast and moving down towards my ribs. After staring at the glowing sigil for a handful of seconds, a prompt appeared in my vision.

You have gained the Trait: ***Sigil of Rage***

> ***Sigil of Rage*** *– A magical sigil written in the Primal Tongue has been carved deep into your flesh, causing it to pulse with an unfathomable torrent of energy. When activated, Primal Rage suffuses your body, granting you +10 to Strength and Agility. While this ability is active, you are consumed by pure rage as your body is burned from within, dealing 10 points of damage per second. This ability scales per level.*

"Sigil of Rage?" My dry throat couldn't help but whisper. "Seriously, what the *hell* happened to me? I need to fucking get out of here."

I feel like I'm back in college again, I thought to myself as I started to pull against the leather bindings, feeling them strain under my strength, *and I just woke up hungover on a park bench with a tattoo I never remembered getting. Except this park bench is a fucking torture dungeon, and I don't have a stitch of clothes on me!*

I let out a low grunt as I curled my bicep, feeling the muscles in my arm struggle to stretch the heavy leather bindings to the point of breaking. *Come on, giant side, don't let me down…*

When I had created my character in Ascend Online several weeks ago, I had decided to embrace the game's flexibility in racial options, choosing a rather unorthodox race combination.

Half giant, half elf.

Mixing the thinner and agile build of a full-blooded elf with that of the bulky and powerful build of a giant, I had created a sleek, yet heavily muscled form that worked well to blend both races' strengths, giving me the speed and agility that elves were renowned for, while also channeling the raw strength and power of a giant.

Though what I desperately needed right now was my giant side to shine through and help me get the *hell* off this table before anyone realized I was awake.

"What's making noise out here?" I heard a voice echo from the hallway adjoining the torture chamber, followed by quick footsteps.

Ah, shit! I cursed again, pulling even harder against the leather bindings, feeling them starting to cut into my wrists. *Had to jinx myself!*

Coming around the corner appeared a tall, thin man, his cleanly shaven head glistening with sweat, despite the cool air in the room. He took a look across the room before his eyes landed on me, his expression filling with fear.

"Oh, fuck, the drugs wore off!" the man shouted, pulling a dagger from his waist and rushing towards me.

As the dark-haired man approached, a tag appeared in my vision, labelling him as a *[Torturer] – Level 11*, followed by a second prompt that filled my vision with burning red letters.

*Do you wish to activate the **Sigil of Rage?***

To my credit, I only hesitated for a heartbeat before accepting the prompt.

The second the prompt vanished, my vision blurred red as burning energy shot through my body, my heart thundering in my chest. It felt like molten metal was coursing through my veins, slowly consuming me from within. I locked eyes with the torturer, feeling a wave of pure rage wash through my mind.

HOW DARE HE DO THIS TO ME? The words pounded through my head as my rage-fueled strength finally tore through the binding holding my right arm to the table.

Past the point of no return, I saw the torturer's fearful expression shift to one of pure terror as his momentum brought himself within the range of my now-free arm. Shifting his charge into an awkward lunge in an attempt to stay clear of my reach, the torturer thrust his dagger towards my face, intent on burying the shiny length of metal in my throat.

Shifting my body as best I could to avoid the thrust, I lashed out with my free hand, slamming my fist into the torturer's stomach at the same instant his dagger carved a wickedly long line across my chest before imbedding itself just under my collarbone. The blow sent the torturer sprawling as the air left his body, his free arm instinctively reaching out to catch himself on the table.

Pulling my arm free from under the retching man, I hammered my fist into the side of his head, distantly hearing bones crack under the savage impact. Stunned by my vicious blow, the torturer's legs gave out from under him and he began to slide off the table.

"NO!" I heard my rage-filled voice snarl as I grabbed the man by the side of the head. "I'M NOT DONE WITH YOU!"

Digging my nails into the man's head, I slammed it directly into the stone table with a heavy, satisfying crunch, before pulling my hand back and doing it again, and again. Blood sprayed everywhere from the repeated impacts, coating the table and my body in crimson gore.

The sound of rushing feet finally pierced through my rage-filled consciousness as three similarly dressed men burst into the torture chamber, weapons at hand. A simple tag appeared in my vision, identifying each of them as a *[Thug] – Level 9.* Their eyes immediately snapping onto me, then the near headless remains of the torturer in my hand.

"Gods, he *is* awake again!" one of them shouted, his voice breaking as he spoke, slowly trying to back away into the hallway. "And he's killed Pawel!"

"Where are you going, Raiz?" The man at the rear of the group shoved the first man forward. "Hurry up and kill him before he gets free!"

"You think I want to get close to that monster? You fucking do it, Joel!" Raiz barked, taking a second step backward. "You saw what he did to the others!"

"Fucking coward!" Joel shouted, his bluster doing little to conceal the fear in his voice. He took a hesitant step forward, elbowing the third man beside him. "Karl! Wit—"

"ENOUGH TALK!" I bellowed, a distant part of my consciousness finally catching up and identifying the group of men as members of the Undertaker street gang. I felt the sigil pulse with energy, sending another wave of burning rage through my body, allowing me to tear through the leather strap holding my left arm down.

Through my crimson-filled vision, I saw the three thugs recoil in horror as I threw the body of the torturer in their direction. The torturer tumbled lifelessly across the floor, forcing the trio to scatter to avoid being hit by the body, giving me the time I needed to free myself.

Sitting up, I grabbed hold of the heavy leather straps holding me on the table. With a massive heave, I ripped through the bonds as if they were paper and leaped straight off the table. I felt my bare feet splash into the torturer's hot blood on the floor as I launched myself forward, shouting incomprehensibly.

I quickly closed into melee range, focusing my charge on the closest thug, Karl. With my momentum fully behind me, I led with a heavy haymaker punch, slamming my fist straight into the terrified gang member's face. I felt delicate bones shatter under the impact as his head rebounded from my fist and smashed into the wall with a sickening crunch.

The rest of my body followed a heartbeat behind, crashing into the stunned thug with a brutal tackle as I slammed him to the wall. Shaking off the impact, my fist began thundering repeatedly into Karl's face, which began to deform under the ferocity of my blows.

A screaming shout caused my head to swivel towards the noise, seeing a scything blade descending from high above towards my head. Instinctively, my arm shot out to protect my face, causing the blade to brutally chop into my forearm.

Everything paused for a split second as I looked at the sword grinding against the bones in my arm. I felt a distant pain bloom somewhere beyond the crimson haze, overshadowed by the boiling blood that rushed through my veins. My eyes traveled along the edge of the sword, down to the hand that held it, then continuing until I met the eyes of the thug wielding it.

Terror was written across Joel's face, his bright blue eyes staring directly into mine for a heartbeat, then shifting to the blade imbedded in my arm. He began to pull on the blade, desperately trying to wrench it free. With a vicious snarl, I forced the blade deeper into my arm as I twisted my body away from Karl's broken body, not allowing the panicking gangster the chance to regroup.

My left hand shot out as I turned, sending a short but savage jab towards Joel's throat. The sound of crunching cartilage echoed through the air as my knuckles crushed his windpipe. Immediately, the man let go of his sword, both hands moving to grasp his ruined throat as he attempted to retreat.

Following the thug as he staggered backwards, I hopped forward on the balls of my feet and launched a brutal kick towards his knee, sending him sprawling onto the ground, writhing in pain. Rushing forward, I wound up for a second kick, this time connecting with the side of the fallen man's head, a snapping sound filled the air as the thug's head lolled at an unnatural angle.

Rage still burning through my body, I glanced up from the dead Undertaker, my crimson gaze spotting the last standing gang member wheeling to run back down the hall.

"COWARD!" I bellowed as moved to chase the fleeing gangster down the hall, jumping over the Torturer's body. "FIGHT ME!"

"N-No! I-I surr—" The man's words were cut off as I tackled him from behind, riding him to a stop as he slid across the floor.

Straddling the man, I wasted no time in beginning to pummel him, my rage-driven fists lashing out repeatedly. It took me half a dozen blows before I realized that the sword was still imbedded in my arm, the distant pain of the metal grating against my bone buried under the sigil's rage.

Grasping the hilt of the blade awkwardly with my left hand, I wrenched the blade free from my arm and held it high in the air before twisting in my hand and plunging it deep into the bandit's back, feeling it bite into the stone floor underneath me. The man's body shuddered briefly as I twisted the blade, then went limp.

It's over. The realization hit me as the crimson tint to my vision faded and my body began screaming in pain from all the wounds that I had taken during the fight. *That sigil's power is...terrifying.*

An intense throbbing pain in my chest threatened to overwhelm me, forcing me to look down, spotting the torturer's dagger sticking out from just under my collarbone. Blood wept from around the blade, having covered my chest during all the fighting.

I think I'm going to be sick. I felt my gorge rise as I shakily lifted my wounded arm and caught a glimpse of white bone in between the rent flesh. Closing my eyes, I changed hands, reaching for the small blade buried in my chest with my uninjured arm. Grasping the hilt tightly, I pulled it free with a gasp and immediately threw it to the ground.

Standing up, I stepped away from the body, the bloody sword I had killed the thug with still sticking out of his back. Turning my head away from the sight, I looked back down the hall, my eyes landing on the pile of bodies I had left in my wake.

Oh fuck, I thought to myself, feeling my stomach twist at the sight.

Then I threw up.

TWO

I PLUNGED MY HEAD INTO A bucket of water I had filled from a basin, my hands urgently scrubbing to clean the blood from my face. Pulling my head free, I took a single deep breath before grabbing the bucket and spilling its contents over my body. I shuddered as the cold water splashed over me, watching it turn crimson as it washed the blood off my skin.

Grabbing the cleanest cloth I could find, I wiped myself down, feeling the shock beginning to fade from my mind as the game started working its eerie magic on soothing my ragged psyche.

I hope the game completely erases that fight from my memory, I thought to myself while panting. The sigil had filled me with such an addictive, yet powerful rush of energy. It felt like I could do anything while it was active.

With a shake of my head, I pushed past the recent fight, choosing to look around the room and focus on immediate concerns.

Like just where the hell I was.

After violently retching from the carnage I had caused, I lay stunned for a moment as my wounds slowly regenerated before staggering down the hallway I had seen the torturer and other guards appear from, coming to a pair of adjoining rooms. The first was filled with a single stone table fixed in the center of the chamber, similar to the one I had awoken on. Unlike the main torture chamber, however, this one had even more torture tools stored inside it, along with a disturbing-looking pile of leather that a prompt in the corner of my vision told me was *[Human Skin]*.

Recoiling from the room, I immediately felt slightly less guilty of what I had done to the torturer and his companions.

Thankfully, the other room, the one I currently found myself in, was free of torture implements and other disturbing devices. Instead, it was filled with a number of crates, in addition to a small table with a pair of chairs set beside a large water basin. Judging from the bits of food left on the table, I figured the space was a rest and cleanup area.

Guess even torturers need to take a break sometimes, I told myself grimly as I grabbed an uneaten loaf of bread and forced it down while eagerly searching the room, checking the crates stashed in there. The last thing I needed was for my body to go into starvation mode and prevent itself from regenerating after combat. *Gods, I hope my gear is somewhere around here…*

Ransacking the crates, at first I found nothing but clothes, some ranging from the simplest of rags that only the poorest commoners would wear to finely crafted tunics that wouldn't look out of place on a merchant prince or one of the nobility.

The Undertakers definitely live up to their name. I scowled as I continued to scour the crates looking for my gear, breathing in the faint earthy smell of dirt.

Considered to be the lowest and most disreputable of all the street gangs in Eberia, the Undertakers didn't earn their living through *respectable* criminal means such as blackmail, burglary, or racketeering. Instead, they truly embraced their namesake, preying upon targets that couldn't fight back, as they chose to invade their victim's final rest, robbing their graves for whatever trinkets that had been buried with them.

But yet despite their ill reputation, they remained a prominent force within Eberia's criminal underworld, for the twin reasons that they had the ability to make a body disappear as if it had never existed, as well as being able to acquire all types of body parts or ingredients needed for necromantic rites.

Which was why my guild put up with them, though given how I had just ended up in one of their torture chambers, I had a feeling that was about to change.

I guess the old saying is true...there really is no honor among thieves, I thought to myself bitterly.

I happened to be one of the few players that had decided to fully embrace the criminal path that Ascend Online offered, choosing to shy away from the grand adventure that the majority of the other adventurers embarked on as they left the cities behind, looking to make their fortunes the honest way out in the wilderness.

While other adventurers trudged through the wild for days on end where a single untimely death could undo days of playtime, I stayed within the relative safety within the city walls, happily enjoying the fruits of civilization. What was the point in going out looking for adventure out in the wild when there was plenty to do here in the city?

Well, as long as you didn't have trivial things like morals holding you back and weren't afraid of taking mind-bogglingly dangerous risks.

"Ah! Here it is!" I exclaimed while opening the last crate in the room, revealing my gear tightly packed inside. I quickly began pulling out the set of black-dyed leather armor that had been given to me the day I had been formally accepted into my guild, the Grim Shadows.

Laying out the armor out on the ground, I was relieved to find that none of the pieces from the armor set had gone missing, the set description appearing in my vision.

Grim Shadow Initiate Armor Set
Slots: Arm, Chest, Feet, Hands, Legs, Head, Shoulders
Item Class: Magical
Item Quality: Good (+15%)
Armor: 195
Set Bonus: (7/7)
Strength: +5
Agility: +5
Constitution: +5
Armor Type: Light
Weight: 7 kg
Favored Class: Any Martial
Softened Leather: +10% bonus to Stealth to avoid being heard or spotted.
Level: 12

Grabbing a basic set of clothes from one of the other boxes to wear underneath, I dressed myself in the dark leather armor, feeling my confidence rebuild itself with every single piece I equipped. With the final piece on and the last strap tightened, I glanced inside the crate, looking for my weapons.

"Shit, no sign of my lockpicks, crossbow, or my daggers." I cursed quietly to myself after a quick glance inside the crate revealed it to be empty. As I looked up, however, a glimmer of metal caught my eye, revealing a hilt trapped between the wall and the floor. Reaching, my hand grabbed hold of the hilt and pulled free a long, scabbarded greatsword from behind the crate. "Ah! Found my sword, though!"

I hefted the heavy weapon in both my hands, checking it over for damage. Seeing nothing that looked out of the ordinary, I called up the item description.

Heavy Iron Greatsword
Slot: Main Hand and Offhand
Item Class: Magical
Item Quality: Good (+15%)
Damage 25-55 (Slashing)
Strength: +5
Durability: 120/120
Base Material: Iron
Weight: 2 kg
Class: Any Martial
Level: 12

It was a plain, if serviceable weapon, with obvious signs of having been repaired throughout its lifetime, having enjoyed a wide variety of owners before it had found its way into my hands. Likely decades old, I was fairly confident that this blade had been forged to help fight in the endless stalemate that was the war.

Which made it all the more the pity when I had first spotted the blade in a greedy merchant's shop, half hidden under a pile of ragged carpets. I was fairly confident that the merchant had long since forgotten about it and never even knew I had stolen it.

Damn shame, since this is a pretty decent sword! I grabbed the hilt tightly, feeling the familiar leather grip mesh to my hand. Looking around one more time, I tried to find a hiding spot where my crossbow could have been stashed but came up empty. *Damn…I guess it's not here.*

"Okay, time to get moving," I whispered to myself as I mentally brought up my character sheet. "But first we need to make sure nothing serious has changed."

LAZARUS CAIN – LEVEL 12 BRUISER

Half-Giant/Half-Elf Male

Statistics:

HP: 439/710

Stamina: 534/710

Mana: 255/255

Experience to next level: 19637/25200

Attributes:

Strength: 75 (85)

Agility: 63 (68)

Constitution: 42 (47)

Intelligence: 10

Willpower: 10

Abilities:

***Sneak Attack II** (Passive) – Attacks made before the target is aware of you automatically deal weapon damage +35.*

Bleeding Attack I (Passive) – Enemies who take sneak attack damage will continue to bleed for 5 seconds, taking 40% of the sneak attack damage dealt.

***Power Attack II** (Active: 50 Stamina) – You slash viciously at the target, putting extra strength behind the blow. Deal weapon damage +25.*

***Ambush** I (Active: 60 Stamina) – You ambush your target, striking them in vulnerable location. Deals weapon damage +125. This ability can only be used on a target unaware of you.*

***Kick** (Active: 20 Stamina) – You kick your enemy for 10-20 points of damage and knock them back 1-2 yards. Depending on your Strength/Agility score, you may also knock down the target.*

***Shoulder Tackle** (Active: 40 Stamina) – Stun enemy for 1-2 seconds with chance to knock enemy down based on Strength and/or Agility attribute.*

***Deadly Throw I** (Active: 30 Stamina) – Throw a weapon with extra strength behind it. Deals weapon damage +15. This ability has a chance to interrupt spellcasting if thrown at the target's head, force them to drop their weapon if thrown at target's hands, or slow their movement if thrown at target's legs.*

Skills:

Weapons:

Unarmed Combat – Level 12 – 11% (Increases knowledge of Hand-to-Hand fighting and improves related Abilities.)

Swords – Level 12 – 75% (Increases knowledge of Sword fighting and improves related Abilities.)

Daggers – Level 11 – 43% (Increases knowledge of Dagger fighting and improves related Abilities.)

Crossbows – Level 12 – 22% (Increases knowledge of Crossbows and improves related Abilities.)

Throwing – Level 10 – 10% (Increases knowledge of Throwing Weapons and improves related Abilities.)

Other:

Stealth – Level 12 – 82% (Decreases chance of being detected while attempting to stay hidden. Improves related Abilities.)

Lockpicking – Level 12 – 89% (Increases knowledge of lock mechanics, allowing you to pick harder locks.)

Wordplay – Level 12 – 84% (Increases chance to persuade others, resolve differences, and/or get information.)

Perception - Level 12 - 95% (You are skilled in spotting hidden creatures and places. Depending on your skill level, hidden creatures and places will be highlighted in red.)

Tradeskills:

Blacksmithing – Level 11 – 12%

Cooking – Level 10 – 34%
Alchemy – Level 12 – 11%
Leatherworking – Level 12 – 17%

Racial Ability:

***Titan's Might** (Giant) (Passive) – Your giant ancestry has given you the ability to wield large weapons in with exceptional strength. All damage dealt by two-handed weapons is increased by 3%.*

***Keen Sight** (Elf) (Passive) – Your elven ancestry has given you exceptional eyesight, granting you the ability to see twice as far as normal in all lighting conditions. This ability also grants you Darkvision.*

***Darkvision** (Elf) (Passive) – While in total darkness, your vision will have near daylight clarity up to 100 ft.*

Traits:

***Sigil of Rage** – A magical sigil written in the Primal Tongue has been carved deep into your flesh, causing it to pulse with an unfathomable torrent of energy. When activated, Primal Rage suffuses your body granting you +10 to Strength and Agility. While this ability is active, you are consumed by pure rage as your body is burned from within, dealing 10 points of damage per second. This ability scales per level.*

Scanning over the sheet, I noted that I hadn't completely yet regenerated from my earlier fight, still feeling pain and fatigue throughout my body, but I couldn't afford to sit around and wait for it to completely heal itself. I had to get myself moving in case someone else came down to check on the guards posted down here or had heard the noise from the earlier battle and decided to investigate.

Reaching the bottom of the sheet, I focused on the new trait entry and reread the sigil's ability once more, which left me shaking my head and wondering what had happened during the heist that cost me my memory and separated me from my groupmates.

Dismissing the sheet from my vision, I looked towards a heavy wooden door leading out of the room, then shifted my glance back towards the torture chamber where I had left the bodies of the Undertakers and the one unknown body I had seen lying on the table.

I have to go back and see who it is, I resignedly told myself as my feet shifted back towards the hallway. *The Undertakers are up to something beyond just robbing graves; otherwise, I wouldn't have ended up here.*

Walking quickly, I found the bodies of the Undertakers lying where I had left them, sprawled out on the ground staring blankly into nothingness. One of the first lessons a criminal player usually learned was that unlike creatures in the wild or other players, sentient NPCs within cities didn't just dissolve into nothingness, conveniently cleaning up after themselves after a few minutes of death. They either had to be burned to ashes or physically carted away and buried for at least seven consecutive days before they vanished from the world.

This added yet another layer of danger to those who chose to play the game on the opposite side of the law, forcing them to choose between lethal violence and the trouble of disposing a body, lest their crimes be found out and traced back to them, or finding a nonlethal way to remove an NPC from play.

Steeling myself, I stepped over the bodies, walking with purpose as I moved deeper into the torture chamber. My eyes found the unknown body I had seen earlier, still lying on the stone table with its chest rent wide open. The smell of burnt flesh still filled the air on this side of the room, forcing me to take a deep breath before stepping closer to the corpse. I paused for a moment to gather my will and continued moving forward, hoping to identify the body as quickly as possible and leave.

Unfortunately, it seemed like the game had other plans.

I felt a spike shoot through my heart the moment I saw the body's face, my breath leaving my chest as I recognized the dead man as Fairfax Grimm.

My mentor and a thief lord of Eberia.

"Shit!" I gasped, gagging as I breathed in the foul air. Coughing wildly, I looked down at the rest of the body, seeing it covered in wickedly long cuts that appeared to have been cauterized almost instantly after being dealt. I couldn't help but stare at the thief lord's chest, wincing as I inspected the massive wound that had killed the man who had brought me into a life of crime.

As I finished my inspection of the body, a chime echoed in my ears. The same moment, a quest appeared in my vision.

>**NEW QUEST! NO HONOR AMONG THIEVES!** *(Criminal Quest) (Evolving Quest) (Unique Quest)*
>*You have discovered the body of Thief Lord Fairfax Grimm, one of the five thief lords that rule the Eberian underworld. You have no idea how his body ended up here or who killed him, but judging from his appearance, he did not go peacefully. As his loyal follower, will you seek revenge? Or will you sell out your former master to another? Perhaps this is an opportunity to take advantage of the power void for yourself?*
>*Inform the Grim Shadows that Thief Lord Fairfax has been killed: 0/1*
>*Inform another Thieves Guild that Thief Lord Fairfax has been killed: 0/1*
>*Difficulty: Hard*
>*Reward: Experience & Infamy*

Damn criminal quests. I scowled at the quest description, mentally dismissing it from my vision. They almost always portrayed themselves as having multiple solutions to finishing the quest, while also encouraging the player to be as selfish as possible.

"What happened, Fairfax?" I whispered at the thief lord's body.

"How did you end up here with me?"

Not expecting a reply from the dead thief lord, I stifled another cough before I started rifling through the man's pockets, remembering the lessons that he had taught me just a few days prior. With any luck, I might find a clue to what may have happened to him, something I could take back to the rest of the guild and ensure that he was properly avenged.

"I know you wouldn't take this personally," I told the corpse softly as I shifted the body, checking for the hidden pockets I knew every thief worth their salt had. "But *sorry*, just in case."

"Here's something," I muttered to myself after a few minutes of searching, feeling my fingers touch something hard and round sewn into Fairfax's shirt. Pinching the cloth, I tore the fabric apart, causing an oversized silver coin to fall into my hand.

"Eh?" I couldn't help but be taken by surprise as I inspected the coin, finding it to be nearly twice the size of regular currency. As I looked closer at the minting of the coin, I was shocked to find Fairfax's profile emblazoned on both sides, a tag unhelpfully identifying it as a *[Strange Coin]*.

"Huh, guess this might be something to figure out later," I said to myself as I pocketed the coin, and finished my search of Fairfax's body, finding nothing else of interest. Shifting my mentor onto his back once more, I did my best to arrange him into a dignified position. "All right, Fairfax, time for me to go."

I turned to walk away from the body, feeling a spark of anger kindle in my heart.

"Don't worry, though, I'll find out who did this to you. And make them *pay*."

THREE

MY DISCOVERY OF THE CRIMINAl path in Ascend Online was a pure accident, in which what I truly mean is that it was because of a woman.

It all began on launch day, the very first day that Ascend Online was released to the public. I was walking through the market, still star struck by the authenticity of the game, when a sudden horde of adventurers pushed past me and descended on a blacksmith's stall. Within seconds, they had grabbed everything that the smith had on display, each of them breaking off into different directions to evade the immediate pursuit by the city guards posted in the market.

Well-practiced at the art, the guards easily intercepted the would-be thieves, easily subduing them and returning their ill-gotten gains back to the understandably irate smith. But while everyone's attention shifted to the fleeing adventurers, no one saw a lithe, dark-haired woman approach the distracted blacksmith and deftly pluck a key from his pocket in the chaos.

At least, no one except me.

Moving naturally, without even the slightest bit of hesitation, the pale-skinned adventurer then walked straight through the gathered crowds and out of the market, casually leaving the scene of the crime behind without a care in the world.

Instantly realizing what the woman had done, I moved to follow her, stunned to see how effortlessly she had gotten away with her crime and intrigued to see what she would do with the blacksmith's key. Weaving through the crowds of milling adventurers, I was hard pressed to keep up with her as she crossed the city with the easy familiarity of a local, then brazenly walked into a tavern that I wouldn't have even considered entering without at least half a dozen friends behind me, had it been in reality.

Surprised by the woman's choice, I remembered hesitating for a moment before I managed to push my reservations aside and follow the mystery woman inside.

Fortunately for me, my delay didn't cost me anything, as the tavern was completely empty and I was able to spot the woman just as she was handing over the blacksmith's key to a red-haired man. Unfortunately, my entry was obvious enough for her and the man to instantly spot me. I remembered the woman's face reddening in embarrassment, contrasting with the man's sudden smile.

Before I could figure out exactly what I had just walked into, the man wordlessly kicked out a chair and beckoned me over. I remembered crossing the room and nervously taking the proffered seat, chancing a glance at the dark-haired woman, who refused to meet my eye, then back towards the smiling red-haired man. He said nothing for the longest time, staring intently at me before he posed a single question.

"Are you interested in a challenge?"

I still recalled my confused nod and how the man's smile had grown even wider. The man introduced himself as Fairfax Grimm and the woman I had followed as Molly. Then, without another word, he returned the stolen key to the woman while he nodded his head towards me, then promptly got up and left.

What followed after that proved to be some of the most trying and exciting days of my life.

Fairfax put one challenge after another before Molly and me, the dark-haired woman eventually warming to my presence. Looking back at it now, it was clear that every challenge that Fairfax sent Molly and me was designed to build off of the one before it and push us both to our limits.

It took a special kind of player to want to experience the game as a criminal, and it was a path not easily recovered from should there be any second thoughts or doubts. For obvious reasons, the criminal life was much more difficult than the regular path that the majority of adventurers chose, filled with even higher levels of violence, risk, and stress. The game wanted to be absolutely sure that we were cut out for a life of crime and weed us out early if we weren't.

In short, playing as a criminal in Ascend Online was like playing the game on hard mode. You had little margin for error, and God forbid, if you somehow managed to screw up, you were punished. *Brutally.*

With that being said, Fairfax's approach wasn't to simply throw us into deep water and hope we learned how to swim, but instead he started us off with minor challenges, tasks such as petty theft, bribery, or gathering reasonably easy-to-get information. Then as Molly's and my own skills improved, the challenges grew in difficulty, eventually becoming burglaries, muggings, and blackmail.

There was next to no rest during our brutal initiation into the criminal underworld under Fairfax's tutelage. He had us working for nearly sixteen hours a day for nine consecutive days, filling us with every single shred of information and ability that we would need in order to survive. Then, on our last day, when we would be forced to log off and rest in the real world to reset our play cycle, Fairfax extended an offer.

To fully commit to the Eberian underworld and join his guild, the Grim Shadows, as initiates.

Needless to say, Molly and I didn't even hesitate at the offer.

Which is how I ended up here, I thought to myself morbidly as I slowly eased open the heavy wooden door that led out of the torture chambers and began creeping up the stairs behind it with my great-sword in hand, still lost in thought as I moved.

It was only after we'd joined the guild that the veil had finally been lifted from our eyes and we were shown how the underworld was run. There were five guilds that controlled the underworld in Eberia, each one based within a different district of the city and responsible for maintaining order among the street gangs. Of those guilds, each guild leader was referred to by a special title: *Thief Lord.* Together, all five thief lords made up the Council of Thieves, a formal group that directed and controlled all criminal activity in Eberia.

I knew that the moment that Fairfax's death leaked out, a massive power struggle would erupt within the underworld. Fearing treachery, the thief lords and their guilds would retreat from sight, burying themselves deep inside their hideouts. Which would then be noticed by disgruntled or ambitious street gangs, who would then begin acting without restraint, settling old scores or preying on the populace in ways that were normally forbidden or held in check.

The streets would be filled with chaos in no time. Bodies would begin to pile up. It would be only a matter of time before the city guard intervened.

Who would profit from Fairfax's death? I asked myself, pausing halfway up the stairs to listen for any sound of movement. There were only half a dozen criminal players within Eberia that I knew of, three of them being Molly, Edith, and Ransom. Though to be fair, even out of those three, Molly was the only one I was *sure* hadn't killed Fairfax. *No, this seems too big for a single adventurer to do. A rival faction or gang has to be involved. But which one? Can we really afford a witch hunt once this all comes to light?*

I shook my head to banish that train of thought, focusing on my current task. The best thing I could do right now was to collect whatever clues I could get my hands on. If I could get enough evidence to find out who had killed Fairfax, then it *might* just be possible to keep the underworld from breaking out into open war.

Given that I had awoken inside an Undertaker torture chamber, that meant paying a visit to the leader of the gang, Cayden Onyxbone, who I was almost certain would be somewhere inside this building.

Having earned a legendary reputation within the underworld as a neurotic control freak, Cayden actively suppressed ambition and initiative in his subordinates, preferring dull, disposable minions that would do exactly what he told them to. Which had me fairly confident that since both Fairfax and I had ended up in one of his torture chambers that he not only damned well knew about it, but was likely involved right up to his eyes.

Gripping the hilt of my sword tightly, I continued prowling up the stone stairs, gradually ascending out of what I now knew to be the basement of the building. At the top of the stairs, I was met by a second heavy door, more than thick enough to block out even the most desperate cries from those trapped below. Trying the handle, I found the door to be unlocked and opened it ever so slightly to peer through the crack.

The overpowering scent of lavender wafted through the door, as I found myself peering into a richly appointed hallway. From my vantage point, I could see several paintings of flowers and nature hanging on cream-colored walls, with a soft red carpet covering the floors, creating a quiet, soothing environment. A stark contrast from what I had seen in the basement below.

Pushing open the door more, it swung silently on its well-oiled hinges as I risked a quick glance past it.

It's a funeral home, I realized after spotting three caskets standing propped against the nearby wall. *Of course the Undertakers would find themselves in the business of running one.*

Listening carefully, I strained my ears for any sign of anyone else being in the building, counting on my Perception skill to alert me to any noises. Hearing nothing, I crept carefully out from behind the door and closed it behind me. Three long strides allowed me to cross the hallway as I continued my exploration of the area.

This place is completely deserted. I couldn't help but frown as I stealthily skulked through the building, bypassing three empty visitation rooms and stopping just shy of the main hall. Carefully peering into the room, I saw an ornate staircase leading to an upper level with a seating area adjacent to it, likely intended for visitors and the bereaved to sit at. Set directly opposite of the room, I spotted a door to the outside, the absence of light telling me that the sun had already gone down. *How long have I been he—*

A smashing sound echoed through the air, causing me to flinch in panic. A red directional prompt appeared in my vision pointing straight above me, informing me of the sound's direction. A heartbeat later, a second, more vicious crunch followed the first, the sound of a man's cursing ringing out.

"—you two are fucking useless!" the man's voice screamed. "Get the fuck out of my office and back on the streets! Don't come back until you have something useful to tell me!"

The sound of rushing feet echoed from the floor above, followed by a heavy door being slammed shut. I heard multiple footsteps stomp across the hallway above me, moving towards the stairs.

Gotta move. I darted forward into the main hall, making the split-second decision to move further into the room and take cover beside the stairs. Had I chosen to stay where I was, whoever was coming down the stairs would have clearly seen me standing in the hallway. At least here beside the stairs, the railing and elevation would give me chance to remain hidden if they chose to go directly outside.

"Dat bastard Cayden, actin' all fucking high 'n' mighty," a voice grumbled from above me. "We spent da last day scouring da streets, wit' nothin' to show fer it. Least he could do is let us catch a wink."

"Boy, your momma musta dropped you on your head one too many times when you were a li'l gremlin," a second, older voice replied. "Cayden ain't bein' an ass, he just hella terrified, is all."

"That corpselighter?" the first voice answered with surprise as feet started descending down the stairs. "The way he acts about it, I never thought he knew what fear even was."

"Take it from an old fart," the second voice replied sagely. "He's putting us on to *show* he ain't 'fraid."

I heard the two men reach the bottom of the stairs, barely more than ten feet away from me as I pressed myself up the staircase, hoping that they would go straight outside. If they turned around, I would have no choice but to attack.

"Huh, I guess I missed dat," I heard the first voice grunt thoughtfully. "Anyway, you wanna grab a bite 'fore we start questionin' again?"

I eagerly leaned forward, hoping that the second man would take the first up on his offer and walk straight out of the building.

"Yeah, we can," the second voice answered, followed by the sound of shifting feet towards me. "Gonna check on the boys in the basement first, though; they've musta had a twitchy night babysittin' that *demon.*"

Awww, damn it! I charged out from beside the staircase, spotting a silver-haired human slowly turning away from his half-orc companion.

Bracing my greatsword against my hip, I took a powerful lunge forward as I thrust the large blade through the aging human's back. A trio of flashing messages instantly appeared in my vision as the sword burst through his chest.

You critically [Ambush I] a [Human Thug] for 594 points of damage!
You have slain a [Human Thug!]
You have gained Experience!

Driving my blade right up into the hilt, I slammed into the thug's body and lifted it straight off the ground as my momentum carried me right into the half-orc. The protruding blade caught the second thug high in the shoulder as he twisted to meet my attack. The sharp point of the sword easily bit through the half-orc's thin leather armor as I thrust the blade deeper into his body, sending the surprised thug backpedaling wildly as he tried to free himself from my blade.

With a crunch, the half-orc ran out of space to retreat, slamming into the wall behind him with a grunt of pain. That gave me the chance to fully drive my blade through his shoulder and into the wall behind him, pinning him and his now-dead companion in place.

Panic filling his face, the half-orc sucked in a deep breath as he readied himself to call for help but found one of my hands wrapped around his throat, stifling his cry before it could even start. Wasting no time, I let go of my sword, letting it hang in the air as I flicked my hand down sharply. The motion sent a hidden dagger to fall into my palm, the very same dagger the torturer had stabbed me with a few minutes earlier.

Shifting my grip on the tiny blade, I viciously thrust the dagger into the trapped half-orc's eye, completely burying it up to the hilt, and twisted sharply. I felt the thug's body stiffen in shock before falling limp as two prompts appeared in my vision.

You have slain a [Half-Orc Thug!]
You have gained Experience!

I hope that wasn't too loud. I held my breath as I let go of the half-orc's neck and took a step backwards, watching the two bodies hang from the wall grotesquely, still pinned in place by my sword. Pausing for moment, I listened carefully for any sounds from the upstairs. Hearing nothing out of the ordinary, I let out a deep sigh of relief and grabbed the hilt of my blade.

That could have been messy, I told myself as I carefully pulled my blade free and guided the two bodies to the floor with a minimal amount of noise. Moving with purpose, I carried the two thugs away from the stairway and out of easy view from anyone who entered the building, unceremoniously dumping their bodies behind a couch in the waiting area beside the stairway.

That should buy me some time in case anyone comes inside and doesn't look around too closely. I scanned the area, silently thanking whoever had designed this place for the red carpeting and how easily it hid spilled blood. *Time to go pay a visit to Cayden.*

Gliding up the stairs, I retraced the steps I had heard the two thugs take, passing a pair of empty sitting rooms filled with comfortable-looking seats and couches, likely additional spaces for the bereaved to sit and process their grief if they didn't want to sit downstairs. Not seeing anything else of interest in the two rooms, I continued down the hall, eventually finding a sign labeled "Only Staff Beyond This Point."

Bingo. I carefully crept down the hallway until I arrived at a thick oak door, hearing the soft patter of feet behind the door. *This has to be Cayden's office.*

Reaching out carefully, I gently grabbed the doorknob and twisted, feeling the handle shift ever so slightly before stopping.

Damn it, it's locked! I cursed silently, wishing that my lockpicks hadn't gone missing with the rest of my gear. *Looks like we're going to have to do this the hard way.*

FOUR

THE DOOR PRACTICALLY EXPLODED OFF of its hinges as my kick shattered the lock and sent it slamming into the wall behind it. Half a second behind the door, I burst into the swelteringly hot room, my eyes drinking in every detail as they searched for Cayden. Designed in a completely different style from the rest of the building, the office was dark and bare, save for countless books lining the walls, the smell of rot finally overpowering the lavender that filled every other room. A large fireplace blazed on the far side of the office, its orange flames the only source of light.

Caught standing in the center of the room with a wine bottle in hand, a jaundiced dwarf wearing a dark black robe gaped at my explosive entrance, his expression a cross between surprise and anger.

Angling my charge across the office, I quickly crossed the distance, bringing my greatsword down in a vicious chop intending to split the man in two.

Reacting instinctively, the dwarf dropped the wine bottle, letting it smash on the floor as he raised a single hand upwards, conjuring a small wall of force. My sword slammed into the invisible shield and was deflected straight towards the ground with a loud crash.

"Cain!" the dwarf shouted in surprise, his voice carrying a note of fear. "How did you get loose?"

"What the fuck were you thinking, Cayden?" I shouted back at the gang leader, ignoring his question as I shifted my weight and landed a weak kick in his stomach. "You killed a thief lord!"

"You think I'm that stup—oof!" Cayden wheezed as he staggered backward from my blow, losing control of his force shield and causing it to wink out of existence.

"Yea—" My reply was cut off as a pair massive hands grabbed me from behind and lifted me up off the ground as if I weighed nothing. Before I could even make sense of what was happening, I found myself sailing through the air and crashing into a bookshelf.

Books fell all around me as my weight completely shattered the shelving, leaving me dizzy and disoriented as several large tomes fell directly on my head. Looking up, I gradually began to regain my senses and spotted a massive figure slowly striding towards me.

"You don't understand!" I heard Cayden shout as my head stopped spinning. "I had no choice!"

Oh, fucking hell, I swore as I struggled to stand up, happy that I had managed to maintain a strong grip on my sword. *Of course a control freak like Cayden would be a pet-based necromancer.*

The smell of rotting flesh intensified as the figure drew closer, the flickering flames of the fire casting the massive, seven-and-a-half-foot-tall zombie in an eerie light. Catching sight of the creature's face as it lumbered across the room, a distant part of my brain identified the zombie as once being an ogre, death having done little to improve its appearance.

Its rotted and dissected hands reached out for me as it came into range, forcing me to step backwards, and I felt my back bump into the remains of the bookshelf. *I can't get trapped fighting this thing; Cayden is the real threat.*

"What the hell don't I understand, Cayden?" I called back, while watching the zombie approach. "That you're trying to start a *war*?"

"War is coming no matter what we do!" Cayden barked. "I'm just making sure *I'm* one of the survivors!"

Waiting for the zombie to commit itself, I ducked under its outstretched hands and rolled between the creature's legs, springing up behind it, then rushing towards Cayden. Unfortunately for me, the dwarf hadn't been wasting his time while his zombie had trapped me in the corner. A purple ball of energy slammed into my chest, sending a wave of freezing cold pain through my body.

Cayden Onyxbone's [Spirit Bolt] hits you for 45 points of damage!

Forcing myself through the pain, I dodged a second Spirit Bolt as I closed with the necromancer, the purple missile of energy exploding harmlessly on the wall behind me. Lunging forward, I used my blade's longer reach and swung it in a wide arc in front of me, slicing a line open on Cayden's chest as he leaped backwards and crashed into the desk behind him. With a yelp of pain, he flailed his arm wildly to catch his balance, grabbing on to a large box on the desk to steady himself. Having likely fought his way up the ranks to gain control of his gang, he had more than enough combat experience to know that if he fell to the ground, his chances of survival were as good as none.

"Why did you do it, Cayden?" I chopped my blade down at Cayden's head, only to be stopped again by a glimmering force shield.

The dwarf simply sneered at me as his free hand began glowing with a sickly green aura and a thin ray shot out, hitting me in the arm.

Cayden hits you with [Ray of Sickness]!

You have been afflicted with intense nausea!

Instantly a wave of sickness passed over me, causing my stomach and bowels to roil. I tried to summon every bit of willpower I had to keep myself from doubling over but failed. Retching uncontrollably, I fell to one knee, my stomach clenching viciously as it reacted to the spell's magic. I slashed weakly at Cayden as he danced around me, easily evading my attack.

Fighting through the sickness, I managed two staggering steps before Cayden's zombie grabbed me once more. But, instead of throwing me this time, the undead creature slammed his rotting fist into my face, causing my vision to blur in an explosion of pain which made me drop my sword with a heavy thud.

The zombie landed two more hits by the time I was able to regain my senses and free myself from its rotting grip, which allowed me to dodge a brutal, slow-moving punch that would have certainly killed me. With nowhere else to go, I forced my way inside the zombie's reach, fighting down an entirely new wave of nausea as the creature's putrid stench threatened to overwhelm me.

What now, Lazarus? I asked myself, staring up at the massive wall of decaying flesh before me with nowhere to escape to.

Caught hesitating too long, the zombie's arms enveloped me in massive hug and begun slowly crushing me against its rotting chest. Feeling my face sink deep into the wet, necrotic flesh, I began to panic, my hands pulling chunks of weeping flesh free from the zombie's body as I tried to escape.

A suffocation alert appeared in the corner of my vision and gradually began to count down as my body began to thirst for air, my heart thrashing wildly in my chest. I felt my ribs begin to crack as the pressure intensified, driving my face even deeper into the zombie's body.

I'm out of options, I thought to myself resignedly, not having accounted for Cayden having such a powerful minion at his disposal. If he were still alive, I knew Fairfax would have skinned me alive for making such an amateur mistake and rushing in without proper reconnaissance or support.

The thought of my dead mentor flashed before my eyes as I pictured him lying on a table somewhere below me. I felt a surge of rage pulse from the sigil on my chest, reminding me of its presence, begging to be released.

If I'm going down—I felt the rage well up inside me as I activated the sigil once again and embraced the torrent of energy that surged through my body—*I'm going to take the house down with me!*

Charged with a newfound strength, I thrashed in the ogre's grip, fighting against its unholy strength as I tried to free myself. Surprised by my sudden increase in strength, the zombie's grip slipped, allowing me a chance to catch a single, glorious, rot-filled breath of air. Revitalized, I used the opportunity to attack the creature, digging my hands deep into its abdomen, ripping and tearing at everything I could find.

Bloated and rotting intestines fell on the ground as I tore through the zombie's soft stomach, rending a massive hole in its gut. I heard Cayden shouting something that my rage-filled state couldn't comprehend, focused entirely on disemboweling the zombie. Liquid fire coursed through my veins as I ripped chunks of flesh from the zombie's body, barely feeling the creature regain its grip around me.

As I dug through the zombie's insides, I felt my fingers hit its hip bone and immediately forced them even deeper, a desperate and daring plan forming in my mind.

Grabbing the bone firmly, I began to pull upwards, gradually lifting the hulking zombie off the ground. I felt its legs sway under me in confusion as the magic powering its undead brain simply couldn't comprehend what exactly was happening to it. Maintaining my grip, I leaned backwards, letting the zombie's weight tip me over as I arched my back.

Leading the creature straight over my body, I completed the lethal suplex with an earthshattering crunch and an explosion of gore as its head smashed into the ground.

Twisting my body, I allowed the once again lifeless corpse of the ogre to fall to the side. Wasting no time, I launched myself up to my feet, grabbing my fallen sword as I stood and scanned the room for Cayden. I spotted the dwarf a short distance away, staring at me with a completely terrified expression. I shot forward and swung the blade in a vicious arc with every single ounce of rage-filled strength I possessed.

Eyes widening at my sudden attack, Cayden thrust his arm out, desperately trying to conjure yet another force shield in an attempt to block my sword.

This time, however, he was just too slow.

Catching him before the spell could fully form, my sword sliced straight through the jaundiced dwarf's wrist, sending his hand falling uselessly to the floor. A spurt of blood gushed from the stump as Cayden pulled it to his chest.

"Ahhh, my hand!" I distantly heard his voice penetrate the wall of rage that clouded my vision.

Not letting up in my assault, I smashed the hilt of my sword into the wounded dwarf's mouth, watching a pair of teeth sail into the air as his head reeled backwards and slammed into the wall behind him. I followed up with a vicious knee to the stomach, bending the crime lord over as he gasped for air.

Grabbing a fistful of hair, I yanked Cayden away from the wall and pressed my sword into his neck, preparing myself to saw straight through it. Rage filled every fiber of my being, demanding revenge for

Fairfax's death. I felt my hand tremble as blood began to weep from a shallow cut on Cayden's throat.

N-No. I tried to push the sigil's rage away, feeling the energy flowing through my body begin to slow. *I need to question him, I need to find out what happened here.*

Gradually, my crimson vision began to clear, leaving me standing in the dull orange light of the room, looking down at Cayden's bloody face.

"I can sheee now why she wanted that ssstupid sigil," the broken dwarf whispered, slurring through his shattered teeth. "It makess you into a *monster.*"

"*She?*" I demanded, my eyes widening in surprise. "Who the hell are you talking about?"

"You don't remember? *Of course you don't!*" Cayden chuckled morbidly. "Why elssse would you be wasting your time here with me?"

"What happened, Cayden?" I demanded, shaking the dwarf violently. "How did Fairfax and I end up here?"

"Fuck you," Cayden hissed. "You killed nearly half my gang…more if you made it out of the basement. Why ssshould I tell you anything?"

I killed nearly half his gang? How much happened to me last night? The thoughts swirled around in my head as I scowled at the crime lord, staring deep into his eyes. I saw defiance, mixed in with the faintest glint of fear. *He's afraid of me, but afraid of this woman even more.*

That just won't do.

Gritting my teeth, I backhanded the dwarf, sending him sprawling across the ground and crashing into the desk. The impact sent the box sitting on the desk falling, causing it to land right on top of Cayden and bounce off before breaking open and spilling a wide variety of items to the floor.

Half a dozen gleaming daggers and crossbow bolts bounced everywhere, followed by the heavy, rattling clatter of a familiar shape I had thought lost.

My crossbow.

"You had it!" I barked at the stunned dwarf, scooping down to pick up my beloved weapon. I couldn't help but check it over, having dearly missed its comforting weight on my side.

Irontwine Crossbow
Slot: Main Hand and Offhand
Item Class: Magical
Item Quality: Good (+15%)
Damage 30-35 (Piercing)
Agility: +6
Durability: 120/120
Base Material: Iron
Weight: 1.3 kg
Class: Any Martial
Level: 12

Setting my sword against the wall, I grabbed the string and cocked the crossbow in one smooth motion while nocking a bolt in place, my strength more than enough to reload the device without needing to brace it against the ground.

I saw Cayden slowly regaining his senses after his collision with the desk, his eyes landing on the crossbow in my hand. Before he could say anything, I took careful aim and fired a bolt straight through his knee.

"Aaaaah!" the dwarf screamed as the bolt shattered the joint and imbedded itself deep into his leg.

"Who is *she*, Cayden?" I asked the dwarf menacingly as I reloaded the crossbow and pointed it towards his other knee.

"Aaah! Stop! Stop!" Cayden gasped, waving his remaining hand in the air. "I'll talk!"

I nodded, smiling grimly as I motioned with the crossbow. "I'm listening."

"Ssshe's a new player in the city, an adventurer like you," Cayden hissed through his broken teeth. "Wears a massk around her face, so I can't tell you more. She was alone, though; don't think she's had time to set up a network just yet."

"That doesn't help me very much, Cayden," I warned the man, shifting my aim towards his crotch. "Do you have anything actually *useful* to tell me about her?"

"She brought you in!" Cayden practically shouted as he realized what I was pointing at. "I have no idea what happened to you, but you were completely worked over. Cut, beaten, bruised, burned, the works! You should have been dead!"

I frowned for a moment, before motioning for the dwarf to continue.

"She said that you had stolen something from her, and pointed to the sigil on your chest," Cayden continued. "She paid me twenty gold to cut that stupid thing from your chest and give it to her."

Twenty gold? I tried to not let the surprise show on my face. There were very few players in Eberia that would be able to afford that much at this early stage in the game. Unless they had substantial backing from another NPC faction.

"So why didn't you?" I waved a hand at a nearby window, indicating the time of day. "I'm pretty sure I've been out for an entire day, yet the sigil is still on my chest."

"We *tried.*" Cayden shook his head, his eyes taking on a faraway look. "The moment we tried to carve that sigil from your chest…you went *berserk.*"

Cayden looked right at me. "You killed *nine* of my men before my pet was able to beat you back to unconsciousness. After that, we kept you fed and drugged. Our plan was to stuff you in a coffin and throw you in to the harbor later tonight."

"How *nice*," I replied sarcastically, even if I did completely understand Cayden's reasoning. "What about Fairfax? You should have known that the death of a thief lord wouldn't go over easily in the city."

"You think I don't know that?" Cayden retorted hotly. "*Ssshe* fucking brought him too! An hour after she dropped you off!"

"And you just accepted it?" I asked incredulously, my voice echoing my disbelief. "Why didn't you tell her to fuck the hell off when you knew who Fairfax was?"

"I *tried* to," Cayden explained. "But she insisted, and when I tried to get her to leave...she *disintegrated* my other pet as easy as day."

I couldn't help but look over at the massive mound of rotting flesh on the ground, silently imagining having to fight *two* of them at the same time.

"You should have gone to *your* thief lord, then," I told the dwarf. "Then turned her in."

"And what would that have gotten me?" Cayden asked. "She had already killed Fairfax and was an adventurer like you! Dying means something completely different to your kind! I wasn't about to get on her bad side by pissssing her off."

Shaking my head at the dwarf, I asked one final question. "What were you supposed to do after cutting the sigil from my chest?"

"Take it to Stone Sailor's Pier tonight," Cayden answered quickly, sensing that the questioning was about to come to a close. "After midnight."

QUEST UPDATED! THE HEIST!

After a brutal interrogation, Cayden has revealed to you that a mysterious woman was responsible for bringing you to the Undertaker headquarters in hopes of removing the Sigil of Rage from your body but has no clue to her real identity. Once he removed the sigil, Cayden was supposed to bring it to Stone Sailor's Pier, tonight.

Meet the mysterious woman: 0/1

Find party members - Molly, Ransom, and Edith: 0/3

(Optional) Recover Memory: 0/1

I scanned the quest update before dismissing it from my vision. *At least I have a lead to follow now, even if it seems that the Undertakers weren't directly involved in whatever happened to me and Fairfax.*

I sighed, looking down at Cayden's bleeding form. "Seems to me like this was all a terrible misunderstanding, then, *if* what you're saying is true. You *really* didn't have a choice but to do whatever this woman wanted."

"Hell of a misunderstanding," Cayden agreed, waving the stump of his arm at me. "But I'm willing to let it pass."

"You know what I hate more than misunderstandings, though?" I asked thoughtfully, cocking my head.

"Eh?" The dwarf's voice sounded nervous. "What's that?"

"Loose ends," I replied as I shot Cayden in the throat.

FIVE

I KNELT ON A NEARBY ROOFTOP a short distance away from the Undertaker funeral home, watching orange flames dancing into the night sky as fire began to consume the building. After killing Cayden, I recovered my throwing daggers, spare crossbow bolts, and lockpick set that had spilled from the knocked-over box. Then set about ransacking the office.

Well aware of all the tactics thieves and criminal used to hide things, it didn't take me long to discover a secret compartment in the necromancer's desk, containing a booklet written in Cayden's steady hand. Scanning through it briefly, I realized that it outlined the entirety of the gang's activities, including transactions, profits, safe houses, and a list of fences that were always open to buy and sell the various items that the Undertakers acquired. A nearly priceless item, considering the information it held, and one that wasn't likely to change with the Undertaker gang effectively destroyed.

Molly or one of the other guild members would be better suited to make complete sense of all the information the booklet contained, but a cursory look on the last few pages of the booklet had a list of transactions that caught my eye.

Two dozen Seraphinite Crystals – Deliver to HP.
Eight yards of both Silver and Gold Filament – Deliver to HP.
Three intact skeletons, two Human, one Elf. Dry and clean – Deliver to HP.
Twenty yards of Human or Elf Skin, cut in one yard increments. Needs to be fresh – Deliver to HP.

I had no idea who *HP* was, or why they needed such an exotic list of items, but I was hesitant to believe that Cayden had told me everything. Whoever this woman was, she clearly knew her way around the Eberian underworld, and it wouldn't have surprised me if she had prior contact with Cayden before dumping mine and Fairfax's bodies there.

Another avenue to investigate if the pier doesn't pan out, I told myself as I patted the chest pocket containing the booklet.

The booklet wasn't the only thing that I had found, though. Secured in the same secret compartment, I had discovered a stash of coins containing twenty-nine gold pieces, eight silver pieces, and thirty copper pieces, the sum of which nearly quadrupled my total net worth in raw coinage. As if that weren't enough, however, I had pried a plain gold ring from Cayden's severed hand and was lucky to find that it happened to be enchanted. Looking down at my hand, where I had put the ring on for the time being, I brought up the item's description.

Ring of Willpower
Slot: Ring

Item Class: Magical
Item Quality: Good (+15%)
Willpower: +2
Base Material: Gold
Weight: 0.0 kg
Class: Any
Level: 12

Not a very useful item for me, I thought with a shrug, shifting my glance away from the ring and towards the burning funeral home. *But probably worth two or three gold to a caster.*

The sound of shouts and rushing feet from the street alerted me to the arrival of the fire brigade, a team of specialized mages that used both water and ice spells to put out fires, or at the very least keep them under control.

I frowned slightly as the mages set about blasting the now raging fire with torrents of water and ice. I had hoped for the fire I'd set to have more time to burn and destroy the building entirely.

Giving Fairfax some semblance of a burial while destroying the evidence, I thought to myself as I turned to leave, then heard several loud cracks echo through the air. Wheeling back towards the building, I saw the structure sag as something critical inside gave up, then began to collapse in on itself. The mages below me retreated away from the building as the flames suddenly rose even higher into the air, sending a massive plume of smoke into the night sky.

"Rest in peace, Grimm," I whispered, feeling a strange sense of loss fall upon me as I turned away from the fire. The thief lord may have only been a digital entity within the game, but in the few weeks that I had been playing Ascend Online, he had made a lasting impression on me. Despite being one of the lowest-ranking members of his guild, he made it a point to treat both Molly and I as valuable members, taking the time to train and mentor us.

Swallowing hard, I buried my grief as I left the rooftop and began my trek across the city, choosing to avoid the streets for the time being. I still didn't have a clear picture of what had happened to me yesterday, but at least now I had a few leads to follow. After traveling a block away from the fire, I was surprised to see a prompt and a mail symbol appear in the corner of my vision.

Player Messaging has been unblocked. You have pending messages from: Molly.

My eyes widened at the prompt, and I immediately opened the pending message as I ducked into a small alcove on the roof I was crossing. A trail of messages from Molly appeared in my vision, each separated by an unknown period of time.

Molly: Lazarus, what happened? Something just killed me, and I was dropped from the group! I'm trying to make my way back!

Molly: Damn it! The window has been sealed again! I can't get back in! Message me when you can!

Molly: I know my messages must be going into a queue at this point, but I still haven't heard from any of the others. I'm assuming something went wrong with the heist and they tried to cut us out. If you see this, meet me at the blue safe house or send me a message.

I reread the messages several times before dismissing them from my vision, leaning my back against the wall while I closed my eyes in thought.

So whatever happened to me started back at the heist, I concluded, probing at the completely blank spot in my memories, feeling greatly unsettled that the game was capable of manipulating my memory in such a way.

The realism in Ascend Online was unparalleled, putting every other game humanity had ever created to shame and proving to be the reason for its incredible success. But when it started to play with your very memory, treating it like just another variable to be adjusted and controlled, it made me feel like the game was going too far.

Is it any different than what we would read in a story, or have played in other games, though? I couldn't help but ask myself. *This game is pure imagination come true. Anything and everything we can think of can actually happen. Be it good or bad.*

I opened my eyes and looked up into the night sky, spotting the twin full moons, Eris and Ananke, in the distance. Notably larger than its sister moon, Eris shone dominant with a bright crimson light, contrasting with Ananke's pale azure hue as the two began their ascent into the sky.

The night's still young, I thought to myself, pushing away from the alcove and beginning to make my way towards the safe house Molly had mentioned. *Maybe she'll have more answers for me.*

HALF AN HOUR LATER, I had crossed the city with the speed and familiarity only a well-practiced local could achieve, and I was carefully looking out at the safe house Molly had mentioned to me.

Set within the market quarter on the opposite end of the city, the safe house was actually a small room that had been blocked off from easy access in a three-story apartment building, with the only entrance being through a skylight on the very roof of the structure.

At least that was what I had told Molly.

Seeing nothing suspicious, I crossed the street with purpose and entered the tall stone building, taking the stairs to the second floor.

But instead of continuing to climb to the roof, I darted down the hallway, passing by several apartments until I arrived at a small closet that I knew to be directly under the safe house. Checking the door to ensure that it was still locked, I pulled out my lockpicks, and had the simple lock open in a heartbeat.

Pulling the closet door open, I stepped inside the small space, quietly pushing a pair of brooms and buckets to the side, then closed and relocked the door behind me. Craning my head straight up at the ceiling, I grabbed a thick iron handle set into the wall as I braced my feet on the sides of the closet and began pulling myself upwards.

Secret trapdoors are always handy, if you're the only one who knows that they're there. I couldn't help but smile to myself as I triggered a hidden latch set into the ceiling of the closet, causing it to swing downwards silently.

Climbing upwards through the trapdoor, I pulled myself into the safe house's closet, carefully closing the hidden entrance under me. Light gleamed all around the edges of the closet door, followed by a steady rustle of activity in the room beyond. I knew Molly wasn't one to pace, especially in such a small room as the safe house, but she did have a tendency to grind her foot against the ground when she was lost in thought or working on something intensive.

Pushing the closet door open ever so slightly, I peered through the gap, spotting Molly sitting at the sole table in the room with her back towards me. Dressed in a white linen shirt, her long, curly black hair cascaded down her back, shifting from side to side as she shook her head at something in front of her. Looking down, I saw she was wearing dark leather pants, complete with calf-high boots.

Shifting the door open a little further, I spotted her leather armor hanging from a peg on the wall, my eyes picking out a large bloodstain marring its otherwise immaculate appearance.

Looks like she was telling the truth, I noted after seeing the stain, remembering Molly's earlier message that she had been killed. While I trusted Molly implicitly, Fairfax had made sure to drive the concept of excessive paranoia home, teaching us to expect betrayal from anyone at any time.

Even close friends.

Especially close friends.

Checking one last time to make sure that Molly was the only person in the room, I stepped out of the closet, silently closing the door behind me. A careful glance around the room showed nothing out of place, though I couldn't help but notice that the bed directly beside the closet didn't appear to be slept in at all, leading me to think that Molly had spent the last two days awake.

She was worried. I felt a strange feeling come over me as I looked towards the woman sitting on the other side of the room.

"Molly," I called her name softly, hoping not to startle her too badly.

Unfortunately, it didn't help.

With a shout of surprise, Molly launched herself out of her chair like a startled cat, her dark hair billowing wildly in the air as she spun to face me. An orb of pure darkness filled one of her hands as she pointed a heavy sabre straight at me.

A devout follower of Azmus, the God of Secrets, I knew that Molly was more than capable of defending herself, and if she chose to throw it at me, the inky black orb that she held would temporarily render me blind and deaf, giving her more than enough time to put her sword to use.

"Gavin!" she exclaimed after a second, calling me by my real name as her blue eyes went wide.

The orb faded from her hand, followed by the sabre clattering to the ground as she rushed across the room and wrapped her arms around me tightly, pushing her head into my chest.

"How the hell did you get in here?" she asked while staring up at me with tired eyes. "I didn't hear you come in through the sky—*wait,* there's another way in and out of here, isn't there?"

"In the closet," I admitted, knowing that Molly wouldn't let the issue rest unless I told her, or until she tore the place apart and found it.

"What *happened*, Lazarus?" Molly asked, refusing to let go of me. "I haven't heard from you or the others in over a day! Did Edith and Ransom cut us out? Were you caught?"

"I don't know," I replied hesitantly, motioning for the two of us to sit down on the bed as I tried to find the words to explain what happened.

"What do you mean, you don't know?" Molly pressed, taking a seat on the bed beside me. "Where have you been for the last day? What exactly happened inside the Arcaneum?"

We broke into the Arcaneum? Surprise flashed across my face as I wondered what the hell I had been thinking to even dare to attempt to break into the Mages Guild building. Breaking into the Arcaneum was more suicidal than attempting to break into the royal chambers.

"I don't know," I repeated with a shake of my head as I held up a hand to indicate I had more to say. "Until you mentioned it just now, I didn't even know that we broke into the Arcaneum. The last thing I remember from yesterday was getting ready for a heist...then after that, *nothing*."

"Nothing?" Molly gave me a look that was mixed with both confusion and concern. "Gavin, are you feeling okay? Have you had any headaches or vision problems that you can remember?"

"What?" It was my turn to look at Molly in confusion. "What are you talking about?"

"A stroke," Molly clarified as she reached out to touch my face. "Do you think you may have had a stroke?"

"*What?*" I replied, completely surprised that she would jump to that conclusion. "No, it wasn't a stroke. When I awoke, I saw a quest alert telling me that my memories had been blocked by something that had happened the day before."

"The game is blocking your memories?" Molly practically shouted in disbelief as she reached out to grab my hand. "How can it can do that? Is that even *legal?*"

"It must be if the game allowed it to happened," I told Molly with a shrug.

"Okay," she said slowly as an uneasy expression crossed her face. "So that terrifying fact aside…what happened to you? You said you woke up somewhere?"

"Yeah," I began, trying to figure out where the best place to start. "Two hours ago, I woke up strapped to a table in Cayden Onyxbone's personal torture chamber, with Fairfax's body right beside me."

"*What?*" Shock and surprise filled Molly's expression, causing her to lean backwards away from me. "Fairfax is…dead?"

"He is," I affirmed with a sigh. "And Cayden didn't kill him."

"How can you be sure?" Molly asked, her hand gripping mine tightly as she spoke.

"Because I asked him, right before I put a bolt in his throat," I replied, an angry expression crossing my face. "He said someone else did, another adventurer. A woman."

"Anyone we know?" Molly's voice took a hard edge to it as she asked.

"He never saw her face, nor did she give him a name." I paused to take a deep breath as I summarized everything that Cayden had told me, making sure to hand her the ledger that I had stolen.

"Fuck," Molly cursed as she rubbed her eyes with a hand. "This is going to light the underworld on fire as soon as the word gets out."

"I know," I said softly while looking into her eyes and seeing the same sadness I had felt earlier reflected in them. "But unfortunately, that's not everything that happened. When I woke up, I had some sort of new ability linked to a sigil burned into my chest, and I have no idea how I got it."

"A sigil?" Molly repeated with curiosity. "Can you show it to me?"

"Sure," I replied, standing up from the bed and loosening the straps on my armor, eventually pulling it free and taking my shirt off.

"I've never seen anything like it," Molly whispered, reaching out to running her hand across the sigil. "It almost seems like it's divine in nature, but also not..."

"Your guess is better than mine, seeing as you're an actual *priestess,*" I said, feeling my skin tingle as Molly's hand touched my chest. "From the description of the ability, it mentions that it's written in the Primal Tongue, but I'm not a lore expert, so I have no idea what exactly that means within the context of the game."

"Me neither," Molly replied with a shrug. "Makes me wonder what happened in the Arcaneum."

"What were we after?" I asked while grabbing my shirt after Molly finished with her inspection. "Pretty much everything to do with the heist is a black hole in my memory. I have no idea why we even attempted a break-in. The place is a deathtrap."

"We were after an artifact, no idea what kind. All we had was a drawing of it and a rough location of where it was stored in," Molly replied, eyeing my chest as I pulled my shirt on. "As for how we got in, we had an inside man...or at least, Ransom and Edith did.

"I don't know how he managed it, but their mole managed to somehow key us all into the security wards in the building and even unlocked a window to let us inside," Molly continued, motioning to herself. "But the only catch was that every few minutes, a secondary ward activated, which would automatically relock the window and cut off our only way out. I had to stay behind to constantly disrupt the ward while the rest of you searched for the artifact."

I nodded to show that I was following along. As a priestess of

Azmus, Molly had the unique ability to be able to temporarily obscure an object or single person, essentially blurring them from the world for a short period of time. It wasn't something that could turn a person or object completely invisible but would instead cause eyes to glance over the object or person as if it wasn't something worth noticing. Given our profession as criminals and thieves, it was an extremely useful and powerful ability. Though, given my lack of magical expertise, I really wasn't sure how that ability directly interacted with the wards in the Arcaneum.

"Everything seemed to be going according to plan." Molly's eyes glazed over as she recalled yesterday's events. "I had a vague sense of you three moving through the building via the party sense, and it was reasonably easy work keeping the ward from seeing the window, but after a while...something *happened.* I suddenly lost party sense, and before I realized what was happening, I felt a quick flash of pain in my back, and then I was at my bind spot."

"Damn," I replied, shaking my head slowly.

"I tried to get back before the wards relocked..." Molly trailed off with a shrug. "But there was really no chance of that happening. I waited around for a while in case you guys found another exit out, but eventually, I gave up. I've holed myself up in here working while waiting...*hoping* that you'd eventually make contact. I've only left twice to go check my drops and speak to my contacts."

"You did the best you could," I told Molly with an empathetic nod. "Have you been able to figure out who hired us?"

"No." Molly shook her head with obvious frustration. "I did my best to find out before the mission started, and even after everything went to hell, but Edith and Ransom held the deal pretty close to their chest. They were pretty clear that they just wanted us for our talents and muscle, not to actually be involved in dealing with the client."

"Hm," I mused. Given the risk for betrayal, it wasn't uncommon for criminal players to keep their clients, contacts, and fences to themselves, refusing to reveal their identities to anyone. A good client or fence usually took a long time to cultivate, and no one wanted to have one stolen out from under them.

But what really concerned me about this particular situation was that Molly hadn't been able to find anything out about the mystery buyer, or what had happened to me or the rest of the group once the heist went bust.

People always had something to say in the criminal underworld, especially when a big heist went down, and if Molly of all people couldn't find or figure out at least the barest details of someone's plans, then there was something seriously wrong.

"What were they offering for our help?" I asked after thinking for a moment.

"Four-way split of the artifact's sale, which Edith expected to be around three hundred gold pieces," Molly answered.

"Yeah, that'd definitely have to be an NPC buyer." I shook my head at the staggering sum of money. With that amount of gold being offered for a single item, it almost had to be one of the major factions in the city that was buying the item. "Either that or the buyer just planned to take it from her."

Molly and I stared at one another quietly for a moment, silently thinking of the implications.

"You think they got thrown into the Tower of Atonement?" Molly asked after a moment, referring to the massive prison tower in Eberia that troublesome adventurers found themselves locked in. "After I hadn't heard from any of you, I'd started thinking the worst."

"I don't know," I said, frustration entering my voice. I had hoped that Molly would have had been able to uncover more information, but unfortunately it seemed like she was just in the dark as I was. Clearly someone had tried very hard to make sure that anything we did yesterday wouldn't easily be traced. "I wasn't, which makes me think Edit and Ransom weren't either. But at this point, anything is possible; maybe Edith and Ransom double crossed us, or maybe they've gone to ground like you did."

"A lot has happened in the last day, Lazarus," Molly commented, taking a deep breath and letting it out slowly. "When I checked my drops yesterday after the heist, there was word from Isabella ordering me and every other guild member to go dark. She didn't give any reason why."

"Damn, what the hell is going on?" I felt my heart quicken, realizing that Molly and I were on our own. "If everyone's gone into hiding, we can't go to the guild to ask for help."

Isabella was another NPC within the guild and was considered to be Fairfax's right-hand woman. Her responsibilities tended to lean more towards the organizational aspects of the guild, but given that Fairfax had been killed, she was the lead candidate likely to replace him as thief lord.

"Our guild isn't the only one that's gone dark," Molly continued speaking, nodding with me in agreement. "All of the major players have gone to ground over the last twenty-four hours, and a good chunk of my sources and informants are long overdue in checking in with me. I have no idea what's happening out and have been struggling to piece together even the barest picture of what's going on out there."

"Oh?" I asked, nodding towards the table where Molly had been sitting at. "Is that what you were working on earlier?"

"Yeah." She nodded. "I've been correlating every bit of information I've been able to beg, buy, or threaten out of the contacts that have even bothered to reply back to me. Based on what they've told me, there seems to have been a sudden drop in criminal activity all throughout the city."

"What do they know that we don't?" I asked out loud. "Do you think the thief lords might have started moving against one another?"

"If you'd asked me yesterday, I'd have said no, but after Fairfax... anything's possible," Molly replied with a shrug, then waved down at Cayden's ledger that lay on the bed between us. "The information you recovered from Cayden's office might help me paint a clearer picture on what's happening throughout the city, but that's going to take some time to piece together. We might even have to wait and bring it to Isabella. She would have a bigger picture of what's happening in the city than I do."

"Time that I don't have," I said with a sigh, looking up towards the partly covered skylight. "Not if I want to make it to Cayden's meeting in time."

"Are you sure that's even a good idea?" Molly asked, giving me an annoyed look. "You set Cayden's place on *fire*; if they had eyes on the place, you could be walking right into a trap."

"I didn't feel I had any other choice," I replied with a fatalistic shrug. "If word got out about Fairfax's death before we can get ahead of it..."

"Fair enough," Molly said, her expression shifting slowly and nodding at me in understanding. "What's your plan for the meeting?"

"Hadn't thought too much about it," I admitted. "I was going to hide out there and pretend to be Cayden's representative."

"And what are you going to do when they ask to see the sigil?" Molly asked me pointedly. "Lift up your shirt?"

"My first thought was to hit them, actually," I answered hesitantly, realizing that maybe I hadn't quite thought *everything* through. "You have something else in mind?"

"Well, hitting and maybe some stabbing is definitely high on my list," Molly admitted with a devilish smile. "But we can get around to that later. What we need the most is information, and to find out exactly what happened to both you and Fairfax. *Before* things get violent."

"I'm open to suggestions." I held my hands open to show that I didn't have any other ideas. "We don't have that much time, though."

"That's not a problem," Molly said while moving to grab her hanging leather armor. "There's a butcher shop not far from here; we can grab everything we need there."

"A butcher shop?" I echoed, completely confused. "What could we possibly need at a butcher shop?"

Molly grinned as she slipped her leather tunic over her head. "You'll see."

SIX

"ALMOST DONE," MOLLY WHISPERED TO me as a faintly wet, squishing sound filled the air. "Just adding in the last few details and waiting for the ink to dry."

"You think this will really make a difference?" I asked, while looking over Molly's shoulder, my elven eyes easily allowing me to see through the darkness.

"Should buy you a few seconds, if nothing else," the priestess replied while recasting an enchantment to allow her to see in the dark. "Now shush while I finish this, I need to concentrate."

Leaving Molly to her work, I carefully shifted away, peering over the edge of the balcony that we had taken cover on, and carefully scanned the area for threats, turning my nose up at the smell that wafted up from below. After stopping at the butcher shop to pick up supplies for Molly's idea, we had made our way into the Harbor District and towards Stone Sailor's Pier.

Set deep in what once used to be the most productive district of the city, it was obvious that both the pier and the rest of the harbor had seen better days. Mounds of garbage and refuse littered the streets, piling high into alleyways to the point where they had become impassable, lest one wish to disrupt hordes of rats and other vermin. Buried in the filth were also countless abandoned and dilapidated buildings, their owners long having left with the changing tides of fortune.

Hard to believe that this place once supplied almost all of Eberia's food. I looked out at the waterline, seeing the jutting shapes of sunken boats sticking free of the water.

During the war, a conflict during which countless orc tribes had besieged Eberia for nearly four decades, the harbor and the bounty it provided was the only thing that had kept the city from starving. But as the war had worn on, constant overfishing had eventually taken its toll, leaving the surrounding ocean barren of life. With the fishing devastated and no other commercial reasons for keeping the harbor open, the noble houses had allowed it to flounder and decay as they turned their energy and coffers elsewhere.

Today, the Harbor District was only used by those too desperate—or too poor—to go anywhere else. A place that the city guard paid little attention to, save for the rare patrol pretending otherwise. Instead, the gangs and other criminals had moved in, using the harbor as a transitory place to store goods, people, or conduct meetings with little chance of interference from an outside party.

"That should be good enough," Molly whispered a few minutes later, carefully folding up her project and putting it into a leather bag. She quietly moved over towards me and handed the bag over before leaning into my shoulder, staring out towards the pier.

"That statue was once a beacon used by the sailors and fishermen to know that they had come home," Molly breathed, pointing out to a large stone statue of a man with open arms facing out towards the ocean. "It was supposed to be the first thing they'd see, reminding them of how important they were to the city."

"Until the food stopped coming," I replied sadly, seeing that the once-proud statue now stood dirty and stained.

"Yeah," Molly agreed, shifting her head to look out towards the ocean. We stood together silently for a while, biding our time until we had to get into position for the meeting, watching for any sign of movement below.

Both experience and Fairfax's tutelage had taught us better than to continue talking despite the concealment of the night. Excessive noise or movement while staking out a place was a good way to end up being spotted.

And being spotted was a good way to end up with a dagger between your ribs.

Seeing nothing of concern cross our vision during our vigil, I eventually grabbed a thick cloak I had brought with me and threw it over my shoulders as I descended back down towards street level, while Molly maintained her watch from above. Once I safely made it into position, she would obscure herself with her class ability and climb straight down from the balcony, then take up position somewhere nearby.

Pulling up the mask built into my armor's hood as I walked, I ensured that my face was covered and made my way out onto the pier. Combined with the cloak's presence, I hoped that it would provide me with enough anonymity to keep the mystery woman from recognizing me.

At least long enough for me to get what I needed out of her.

It smells even worse out here. I grimaced under the mask as the stench of the fetid water wafted up towards me. Long before the garbage and refuse had begun to litter the streets, much of it had been tossed directly into the water, coating the sea with a thin layer of sludge that never seemed to disappear.

Walking the length of the pier, I made my way directly out to the statue, carefully circling it and checking for anyone lying in wait. Satisfied that I was alone, I unsheathed my sword and lay it against one of the statue's legs, wanting it to be in easy reach in case, or when, the meeting turned violent. Ensuring I was fully prepared, I loaded my crossbow and double checked that all of my throwing daggers were within easy reach.

Only when I was completely satisfied by my preparations did I lean against one of the statue's legs, looking back towards the city and settling in to wait.

As my eyes scanned through the night, waiting for the mysterious woman to appear, I mentally replayed the day's events, trying to make sense of it all. In the span of a single night, the entire social order that governed Eberia's underworld now threatened to come flying apart. If I was lucky, I might have a chance to put an end to whatever was happening and keep things under control.

Or I might only succeed in making it worse.

I banished that train of thought as I noticed movement in the distance. A dark figure walked across the distant harbor, followed by several others close behind. They all paused for a moment at the foot of the pier and looked around, before beginning to walk towards me.

Shit, she brought others, I mentally cursed at myself, having hoped that she would come alone. However, the moment that they crossed the edge of the pier, I felt Molly begin to move behind them as my party sense kept me informed of her direction. *But it's not like I'm alone right now either.*

Pretending like nothing was wrong, I waited patiently for the group to make their way down the pier, carefully watching them as they approached. Playing my role to the fullest, I lifted my crossbow and casually pointed it in the group's direction.

Despite being dressed in heavy leathers with a thick cloak draped over the right side of her body, there was little doubt that the figure in the lead was the mysterious woman that Cayden had mentioned to me. As the distance between us shrank, I felt a strange sense of familiarity wash over me while looking at the woman, even though a hooded mask concealed her face.

I did technically see her before, I told myself, mentally shaking off the feeling of déjà vu as the woman stopped a short distance before me and her followers fanned out beside her. *The game's just blocking my memory of it all.*

Shifting my glance to the woman's followers, I was surprised to see that they were all *Level 4 [Harbor Urchins].* The lowest of the low, harbor urchins lived among the dregs of society, having fallen so far that the only refuge they could find was squatting in ruined or burnt-out hovels. They often lived short and brutal lives, fighting amongst themselves for scraps of food, or dying early from one of the myriad of filth-borne diseases easily picked up when living in the harbor district.

For the woman to have recruited four urchins to serve her told me that she either didn't have any other contacts to fall back on or was reluctant to use them for some reason. But at the same time, the presence of the urchins—and the fact they hadn't torn one another apart so that they didn't have to share whatever she was paying them with—told me that she was more than capable of keeping them in line.

"You're not Cayden," the woman stated with a harsh voice as her followers spread out to either side of her.

"Cayden is dead," I replied in a raspy voice, Molly having told me that I should try to mask my normal pitch. "I'm in charge now."

The woman was silent for a moment as she digested the news. "I wasn't aware Cayden had any adventurers working for him."

"He didn't," I grunted. "It was a hostile takeover."

"I don't like this." The cloaked woman took a step backwards. "I don't know you."

"Imagine how that feels," I replied sarcastically as I lifted up the leather bag and shook it, causing a wet, squishy sound to fill the air. "But we don't need names to conduct business."

"I already paid for that." The woman's voice took on a dangerous tone, her posture going very still. "Hand it over."

"You paid Cayden for it," I countered, hoping that the woman wasn't prone to rash decisions. "I'm going to need more, *especially* after who I found in the basement."

"You realize I could kill you right now?" the woman breathed, anger seeping into her voice.

"And what does that exactly mean to us players?" I asked, spreading my hands out wide and offering her a clear shot of my chest. "As long as I hang on to this little sack when I die, it'll vanish right along with my body and you'll never see it again."

"What do you want?" the woman asked with resignation after a long moment of silence.

"I want to know why the *hell* there was a thief lord in my basement," I demanded, trying to channel the proper tone of an angry gang leader. "And I want to know if I should be stripping every asset I have and heading out to Coldscar to escape the literal shitstorm that is going to break out the minute the rest of the guilds realize what's happened."

"That's none of your business," the woman hissed, taking a step forward.

"It became my business the moment I killed Cayden," I retorted, standing my ground, glancing at the urchins. "Fancy how that works in the criminal world."

"All that you need to know is that he got in the way," the woman ground out. "Really no different than what you are doing right now."

"I'm not the one making this difficult," I grunted while shaking the leather bag. "You should be happy I held up Cayden's end of the deal as it was. I half considered just tossing this into the fire and pulling a fade."

"You really want an answer that bad?" the woman barked, her voice echoing out over the water. "Here's your answer: grab everything of value that you have, *tonight*, and just fucking *run*. Don't stop running until you at least hit Aldford."

"Where the fuck is Aldford?" I replied, too surprised to say anything else.

"Just far enough away that it *might* escape what's coming." The woman sliced a hand through the air and took another step forward. "Now... *Give. Me. The. Bag.*"

I let out a low whistle as I motioned with my crossbow for the woman to stop. "Now that wasn't so hard, was it?" Before the woman could reply, I tossed the bag towards her in a low arc. "But you told me what I needed to know, and the sooner I can get this over with, the better."

Stooping to catch the flying bag with her left hand, the woman set it down on the ground and began untying the knot.

She only has one hand? My eyebrows rose as the woman continued to work with only her left hand, eventually opening the bag and pulling out a pink sheet of bloody flesh. I saw her shift the skin in her hands, attempting to get a better look at the sigil Molly had drawn onto it.

"Wait," the woman demanded, dropping the bloody piece of flesh on top of the bag and reaching for something I couldn't see. "I need to verify this."

"Sure." I tried to sound as casual as I could, wondering just how she was going to manage that. I slowly tightened my grip on my crossbow, keeping it angled towards the mysterious woman.

The woman pulled out a strange-looking crystal that I couldn't quite make out in the dark and waved it over the skin. At first nothing happened that I could detect, but gradually the crystal began to glow with a pale purple light, slowly growing in brightness for each second that passed.

Then suddenly, the sigil on my chest flared with pain, causing me to gasp in surprise.

"What?" the woman grunted with surprise, her eyes looking up at me. "*Cain?*"

"In the flesh," I replied, throwing the cloak off of me with my free hand. "Nice to meet you again."

"I should have known you would continue to interfere," the woman barked in sudden anger.

Continue to interfere? I couldn't help but note her choice of words. *What did I do to interfere in the first place?*

"What did you expect me to do?" I shot back, silently wondering who this woman was. There was something familiar about her voice that I couldn't place. "Lie there in the torture chamber and let them carve a pound of flesh from me?"

"You stole the sigil from me," the woman growled, ignoring my question. "If I can't have it, I will make sure that no one else will!"

"I would like to see you *try*. It didn't work out that well for the Undertakers," I taunted the woman, shifting my glance over to the now nervous-looking harbor urchins flanking her. "And I don't know how much help your minions are going to be, either; they look a little terrified."

"Oh, don't worry about them," she replied before barking an unknown word of power in the air. "I only need their bodies for what comes next!"

With a bloodcurdling shriek of pain, all four harbor urchins clutched at their chests and fell to their knees as the word of power caused something hanging from their necks to burn bright red. The smell of burning flesh and brimstone filled the air as magic flared beneath their skin. Twisting and contorting wildly, the urchins burst into flames, forcing me to shield my eyes from the sudden brightness.

Within seconds the flames died as quickly as they had begun, plunging the night back into darkness, leaving me blinking the after-images out of my vision. Glancing back towards the woman and the urchins, I was shocked to see four monstrous creatures slowly picking themselves up off the ground.

"What the hell?" I gasped, watching a quartet of tags appear in my vision, identifying the transformed urchins as now being a *[Hellborn Brute] – Devil – Level 12.*

Nearly six feet tall, each of the newly transformed hellborn brutes rose unsteadily on cloven goat feet as if they were not yet used to how their bodies moved. Massive muscles rippled as the creatures looked around nervously, their barbed tails whipping through the air. Flexing a set of razor-sharp claws, the devils all brushed off the remnants of the clothes their moral forms once wore, sending ash flying into the wind.

"This time I'm going to cut the sigil from you myself" the woman growled, conjuring a bright purple orb in her hand that forced me to squint my eyes as she barked out an order to her newly spawned devils.

"Capture him!"

SEVEN

WITH A SHOUT, THE WOMAN threw the bright purple orb of energy from point blank range, giving me next to no time to dodge it. Blinding my vision as it flew, I barely managed to shift just far enough so that the overcharged Spirit Bolt smashed into the left side of my chest and shoulder. The impact knocked me backwards into the statue's leg as a freezing cold shot through my body, causing my heart to skip a beat. An alert flashed in the corner of my vision, warning me that the attack had taken nearly a fifth of my health away.

[Unknown Human] hits you with [Spirit Bolt II] for 133 points of damage!

Wincing from the blow, I shifted my aim to the spot where I had last seen the woman standing and pulled my crossbow's trigger, feeling the device kick in my hand as the bolt sped out into the night.

Almost instantly, I was rewarded with a scream of pain and the sound of tearing cloth.

Pushing myself off of the statue, I dropped the spent crossbow to the ground and grabbed for my sword, finding it exactly where I had left it. I had just enough time to get my weapon into a guard position before I was forced to defend myself from a set of razor-sharp claws as an overeager hellborn brute pushed ahead of its mates to attack, momentarily blocking them from reaching me.

Dodging to the side, I barely avoided the creature's claws as they carved deep gouges into the back of the statue's leg, stone shards spraying into the air. I slashed out at the devil as it spun to chase me, drawing a line of blood across its arm and chest. Black ichor burst from the wound and immediately began bubbling as it came in contact with the air.

Howling with rage, the devil pressed its attack, clawing the air wildly as it caused me to backpedal to the edge of the pier. Stopping short of falling into the water, I stood my ground under the creature's rabid assault, earning a pair of long cuts along my hand and forearm.

Damn, this thing is fast! I grimaced as the devil's wounds began to sting. Despite my weapon's longer reach, the hellborn brute's speed advantage was giving it a fighting chance, allowing it to just barely stay ahead of my blade. Yet for all of its ferocity, it had yet to display anything more than sheer animal instinct, intent on overwhelming me as quickly as possible. *Let's see just how smart this devil is.*

Feinting a slip, I tucked one leg under me while pretending to lose my balance, giving the devil an opening it couldn't miss. Without even hesitating, the hellborn brute lunged forward, letting out a glee-filled cackle as it lunged towards me—

Only to meet air as I shifted out of the way, letting it sail right over me and land in the water with a splash.

All muscle and no brains, I thought, allowing myself a small smile as I pushed myself up off the ground and rushed away from the pier's edge.

"Damn you, Cain!" the woman's rage-filled voice reached my ears as I ran, causing me to turn my head towards the noise, where I spotted a familiar, if misshapen face.

Edith.

Bleeding freely from a large wound on her cheek, I felt a jolt of surprise shoot through my body as I realizedthat my blindly aimed crossbow bolt had caught the woman in the face, tearing through her mask and finally revealing her identity. In contrast to the woman I'd once known, Edith's face was now covered in countless scars, the flesh on the right side of her jaw having deformed and melted like a grotesque candle.

"Edith?" I couldn't help but blurt in surprise as she fixed me with a baleful glare. "What the hell happened to you?"

"*You did this to me*!" the dark-skinned woman shouted, as she threw back the cloak that had been concealing the right side of her body. Raising it high into the air, Edith lifted a monstrous claw-tipped arm easily three times the size of the other devils' and launched herself at me with a cry of rage, the other devils following close behind her.

This is bad! Panic began to grip my heart as I desperately angled myself towards the statue, looking to take cover beside it and keep Edith and the other devils from simply swarming over me.

Sweeping my sword in the air as I ran, I caught Edith's massive claws on the edge of the blade, feeling them grate against the metal as they slid off. Attacking with the same frenzied tactics as the other hellborn brutes, Edith slashed out again and again, driving me backwards as I retreated around the front of the statue.

Following close behind their mistress like lemmings, the other devils fought one another for position as they tried to circle around the edge of the platform to get to me, only succeeding in getting in one another's way.

"What happened, Edith?" I demanded as my blade sliced opened a length of her mutated arm, causing black bile to gush from the wound. "What happened in the Arcaneum?"

"Fuck you!" the woman hissed, fury coloring her voice as she continued to press her attack, the injury on her arm doing little to slow her. "You ruined everything!"

Before I could reply, I heard Molly's voice shout out from behind me, "Lazarus, *duck!*"

Reacting at the speed of thought, I pushed away from Edith and rolled backwards as a black missile sailed over my head, slamming right into Edith's body. I heard Edith curse as Molly's spell burst in an inky cloud of darkness, rendering her temporarily blind and deaf.

"Right behind you, Lazarus!" Molly's voice sounded close by as I regained my feet and leaped forward to take advantage of Edith's temporary weakness.

Unable to see my attack coming, Edith was caught completely flatfooted as I sliced open a massive wound leading from her left shoulder to opposite hip. However, instead of the red blood I'd expected to see gush from the wound, more bubbling black bile erupted from the body and began slowly oozing down Edith's chest.

Is she…part devil now? The black blood looked similar to the ichor that had oozed from the hellborn brute when I had sliced it open. *What the hell happened in the Arcaneum that twisted her so badly?*

Shaking off my stray thought, I continued to press my attack, landing another vicious cut across Edith's midsection as she desperately backpedaled trying to escape my reach. But before I could land a finishing blow on the hell-warped woman, I was forced to defend myself against the slashing claws of a hellborn brute that had finally managed to squeeze past his retreating mistress.

Dodging the vicious swipe, I slashed back at the devil, landing a solid hit on the creature's arm at the same moment Molly fell in beside me and slashed open its stomach.

"These things shouldn't exist!" Molly shouted to me as she sliced open another wound in the devil's body. "Not here, not on this plane!"

"I don't know what that means, Molly!" I called back, as a second hellborn brute rushed forward to join its companion. "They're here, they're angry, we need to kill them!"

"They're unbound devils! They shouldn't be able to enter our—" Molly began to explain before letting out a loud yelp as a claw found a way through her guard. "Fuck! I'll tell you later, just hack them to pieces!"

"That I can do!" I growled, calling on the sigil's power once more, reveling in the intoxicating rush of energy that shot through my body. As the crimson haze began to creep across my vision, I heard myself calling out to Molly, "Using the sigil, watch out!"

A heartbeat before the power fully consumed me, it vanished, the burning sigil turning cool against my skin. Bright crimson light flared out behind me, as a flashing alert appeared in the corner of my eye.

The power channeled by your ***Sigil of Rage*** *has been absorbed by a nearby [Chaos Stone]!*

"What the hell was that?" Molly exclaimed, chancing a quick glance behind her.

"Something Edith brought!" I explained as best I could, feeling a strange emptiness where I had once sensed the sigil's power. "It's interfering with the sigil!"

"Shit!" Molly gasped as we were both forced to take a step backwards under the combined attacks by the two devils. "Can you fight?"

"Yeah!" I replied, feeling a little unsettled. Despite using it only twice, the sigil's power had quickly become addictive, and having it so suddenly torn from me left me feeling unbalanced. Glowing bright behind me, the crimson crystal continued to shine, casting the entire battlefield in a bloody haze.

Pushing through the disorientation, I stepped forward against the pressing devils, accepting a wicked slice that ran the length of my arm in exchange for the opportunity to brutally chop my sword into the side of one of the creature's head, cleaving straight into its skull. Thrashing wildly from my blow, I followed up my attack with a heavy kick straight into the devil's stomach, using the motion to wrench my blade free in a spray of gore.

Falling backwards lifelessly, the hellborn brute's body was ruthlessly shoved to the side and onto the black water as the devil behind it slapped it out of its way while rushing to take its place, clawing out at Molly and me in a rabid frenzy, causing the two of us to take a step back from its ferocity.

"Careful!" Molly shouted, parrying a claw that came inches away from stabbing into my unprotected side and forcing it downwards, giving me an opening that I could exploit.

"Thanks!" I barked, taking advantage of Molly's maneuver, slicing a shallow wound down the hellborn brute's shoulder and arm. Pausing for a second as the devil leaped backwards in pain, I glanced at my health and stamina, checking to see just how much I had left.

HP: 526/710
Stamina: 416/710

Satisfied that I was I good shape, I readied myself to spring forward at the hellborn brute and resume my attack, but an alert flashed in the corner of my eye, warning me of a noise behind me, followed by the sound of slushing water. Wheeling around, I saw that the first devil that I had tricked into the water had finally pulled itself out and back onto the pier.

Snorting like a bull, the devil stamped its cloven feet as it put its head down and rushed back into the fray, gradually building momentum with every step it took. Watching the goat-like devil quickly eat up the distance between Molly and myself, I made a split second decision and rushed forward to intercept the creature before it crashed into us from behind. Leading with my shoulder, I feinted to meet the devil's charge in a titanic collision of strength, only to drop down at the last second.

Sneaking under its guard, I slammed my shoulder into the charging devil's hips, its momentum throwing it over my shoulder as it flipped right over me and landed on the ground heavily.

All those years of hockey and football are finally paying off. The stray thought crossed my mind as I twisted towards the stunned devil lying prone on the ground.

Wasting no time on mercy, I stabbed my blade through the fallen creature's heart before pulling it free and slashing through its throat, ensuring that it stayed down for good.

"Lazarus!" Molly's voice was tinged with desperation as she delivered a killing slash to the hellborn brute she was fighting and backpedaled as a recovered Edith and the now sole remaining devil rushed forward to fill its place.

Jumping over the rapidly decaying form of the devil that I had just slain, I rushed to rejoin Molly as she fell in beside me. Familiar with one another's movements, we immediately then launched into a counterattack, stopping Edith's and her minion's advance cold. Swinging my sword through the air with precision, I caught Edith's massive claw on the edge of my blade, halting it long enough for Molly to add yet another vicious cut across the woman's chest.

"Damn it!" Edith roared, frustration taking its toll on the woman. It was clear that she had no practice in fighting as a team with the hellborn brute, assuming it was even capable of such intelligence and teamwork. Shouting something harsh in an unknown language, Edith conjured a glowing Spirit Bolt and tossed it at the ground in front of Molly and me.

Exploding with a burst of energy, the blast forced the two of us to take a step backwards as we instinctively shielded our eyes, momentarily losing sight of Edith and the devil. By the time our eyes readjusted to the sight, Edith had rolled past me, using the distraction to run towards the glowing chaos stone.

Before I could move to follow her, I felt claws dig into my flesh as the devil lunged forwards, grabbing hold of both Molly and me. Grimacing under the devil's brutal grip, I fought to free myself from its hold, driving the claws even deeper into my forearm as I tried to bring my sword to bear with one hand. The light of the stone danced wildly in the night as Edith snatched it up from the ground and clenched it tightly in her left hand.

"It's not how I wanted to do this, but it will have to do!" Bitterness dripped from Edith's voice as she began to conjure a ball of fire in her oversized hand. The fireball rapidly grew in size as the chaos stone dimmed.

"Aaah!" Molly screamed in pain as she thrust her sabre into the devil's unprotected stomach before tearing it out and thrusting it back in. "Kill it! Quick!"

Shit! She's sacrificing the devil just to kill us! With one arm pinned, I quickly reached with my free hand and grabbed a dagger off the bandolier on my chest. Then I followed Molly's example, repeatedly stabbing the devil as I tried to pull myself free.

Working up the creature's chest, I left half a dozen bloody holes before burying the dagger straight up to its hilt in the creature's eye. Combined with Molly's desperate stabbing, it was too much for the creature to withstand and its grip began to weaken. Tearing my arm free of the claws that held me in a spray of blood and pain, I looked back towards Edith, seeing her barely holding onto a beach-ball-sized orb of fire.

Making a split-second decision, I pushed myself away from the falling devil and grabbed Molly as I ran away from Edith, towards the statue of the Stone Sailor. Moving with every ounce of speed I could muster, I ducked in between the statue's legs, desperately seeking cover at the same moment a massive blast of fire exploded behind me.

I felt flames sear into my back a heartbeat before a thunderous concussion knocked me forward, sending me and Molly sprawling to the ground. Wincing in pain, I rolled onto my back to see if I could catch a glimpse of Edith before she followed up with another spell. Looking between the statue's legs, I heard an ominous noise echo through the air as one of the legs cracked, weakened from the explosion, the statue beginning to shift as the stone crumbled.

"Oh, fuck!" I swore, seeing the leg finally give way, causing the statue to break free from its pedestal and it begin its descent towards me. Scrambling on my hands and feet, I pushed myself backward as I tried to escape the Stone Sailor's path, only to spot Molly lying on the ground, still struggling to come to her senses.

She doesn't see it, I realized, a fraction of a second before I threw myself forward, shoving Molly hard enough to send her tumbling away from the statue's path.

Looking back upwards, I had just enough time to make out the statue's face as it fell.

Then everything went black.

Loading, please wait...

EIGHT

PASSING THROUGH THE VEIL OF death, I felt my soul pulled back towards my bind point as I awoke in a plain stone room. A glowing orb set in the wall shone with a vibrant white light, causing me to squint at the sudden brightness. Crossing the entire length of the city in an instant, I found myself deep within the Grim Shadows headquarters, slowly pulling myself back together, my head spinning wildly.

Not my worst death, as these things go, I thought to myself grimly as I slowly moved my arms and legs, no longer feeling the countless injuries from the fight with Edith, though I was sad to note that both my sword and crossbow hadn't respawned with me.

Taking a moment to assess how I felt, I was happy to find that my spirit was fully intact and that my death hadn't afflicted me with death sickness, which would have forced me to return to the harbor to collect a fragment of my soul. *I guess that means Edith technically killed me.*

Striking a balance between encouraging conflicts between players and still having consequences for death, Ascend Online took two different approaches in handling death penalties. In the normal scenario where an adventurer died at the hands of a creature or another non-player character, a fragment of their spirit was left behind at the scene of their death, forcing them to recover their soul fragment, or accept a punishing loss in skills and experience.

In the other scenario, when a player was killed by another player, instead of the normal death sickness, the dying player instead lost a small portion of their renown or infamy, depending on their moral bent. In contrast, the winning player received a slight increase to their renown or infamy, in addition to a fairly substantial reward of experience.

This system ensured that players who repeatedly died against other players wouldn't end up being crippled with impossible experience debts and a loss of their skills, but still carried a reasonably sufficient penalty for dying. From what I've been able to discover so far, high levels of renown or infamy influenced how NPCs reacted to you by either giving you a bonus or a penalty to your reputation, which could lead to rare quests or opportunities that would otherwise be unavailable.

The sound of running feet brought me back into the present as a small, dark-haired boy ran into the room I had just respawned in.

"Lazarus, you're back!" the tiny boy's voice squeaked as he looked around the chamber for anyone else. "Well, I guess if you're in this room, you died, but you're also back. I know how it works for you adventurers. Did dying hurt? What happened? I hope you kicked their butt before they got you."

"Goner." I held up a hand, motioning for the young thief-in-training to slow down, struggling to keep up with his rapid barrage of questions. "Please let my head stop spinning first…"

"No time for that!" the boy exclaimed, stamping his feet while puffing his chest out. "Isabella *finally* gave me a job! She told me that if any of our adventurers popped back into this room, I'm supposed to bring them right to her!"

"That…explains why you're still awake," I said slowly, smiling at Goner's enthusiasm.

At only twelve years old, Goner was the youngest member of the Grim Shadows, an orphan whose parents had once belonged to the guild before tragically being killed on a job gone bad. Since then, he had been adopted by the guild, who made sure that he stayed safe and was taught everything he needed to survive in the world.

"Yep!" Goner urgently motioned me to follow him out of the room. "They even let me have some coffee, too! It tastes the best with a lot of sugar in it. I've already had three cups today! I should get another one, maybe."

"Uh…" I followed the boy as he practically ran out of the room ahead of me. "Maybe you should drink some water instead, Goner!"

"There's water in the coffee, Lazarus!" Goner stopped to look back at me, already halfway down the hall, shaking his head. "I think I'll just stick to coffee for good now, it gives me *so much* energy!"

"*Goner!*" I called after the caffeine-addled boy as he turned away and ran off deeper into the hideout, leaving me behind.

Before I could catch up with the boy, a flashing note appeared in the corner of my vision as Molly finally messaged me, causing me to slow my pace while reading the incoming message.

Molly: Lazarus! You saved me!

Feeling a sense of relief wash through me, I composed a reply back.

Lazarus: I'm glad you made it! Unfortunately, the statue caught me, and I'm back at the guild headquarters. Is Edith still there?

Molly: No, I just made it out of the water, and she's gone. There are burn marks everywhere here. I have no idea how she managed to cast such a powerful spell, but I'm not hanging around in case she returns. I'm going to start making my way out of here and back towards the guild.

Lazarus: Before you go, any chance my crossbow or sword survived the explosion? I didn't respawn with them.

There was a short pause while I assumed Molly looked around the area.

Molly: Found your crossbow and it's in good shape, if a bit singed. Your sword on the other hand, I can't find anywhere. I have no idea if it was thrown into the water or if it's buried under the statue.

Lazarus: Damn. Don't worry about it. I can craft a replacement or go and buy a new one tomorrow. Quick heads-up for when you get here, Isabella will likely want to meet with you. She put Goner on watching the bind point. I'm going to fill her in about what happened to Fairfax.

Molly: Good luck. Maybe we can finally find out what's going on. See you when I get there, hopefully in an hour or so.

Sending a quick goodbye to Molly, I continued down the short hallway and entered the guild's common room, causing more than four dozen heads to turn in my direction the second I turned the corner. Seated around a number of tables and chairs in the room was nearly half of the entire guild. I barely had a chance to take in all of the faces looking at me before a rush of voices shouted out at once.

"Lazarus! You got merc'd?" a voice called out with surprise. "What happened?"

"What did you see out there? Is it true that people are rioting in the streets?" another called out.

"The orcs have come back, haven't they? Are we under siege again?" This time from an older thief.

I raised my hands at the onslaught of questions, taking a step back at the sudden explosion of noise.

"I don't know what's going on," I shouted back to the crowd, realizing that everyone had likely spent the last day in hiding after receiving Isabella's orders to disappear. Being cut off from the rest of the world for a day without any explanation was more than enough time for crazy rumors and imaginations to take hold. "But we're not under attack by orcs, and there's no rioting in the streets!"

Hoping to have pacified the nervous crowd, my response only served to incite more follow-up questions, everyone shouting over one another as they demanded answers that I didn't have.

Or at least none that I wanted to say out loud at the moment. Blurting out Fairfax's death in the middle of a crowd like this would only serve to drive everyone even crazier.

"I need to go see Isabella," I told the group of thieves while pushing my way through the crowd, the noise eventually dying down as I crossed the common room. Spotting Goner waiting impatiently at the far side of the room, I angled myself towards him.

"Hurry up, Lazarus." He beckoned me to follow him and continued moving at his quick pace. "Everyone here has gotten a little stir crazy, as Isabella calls it. Something's worrying her, so she's locked the place down."

"Did she say why?" I asked while following the over-caffeinated boy through our hideout.

"Nah," Goner replied with a shake of his head. "Not to me, at least."

Hmm, while it's not surprising that Goner is out of the loop, it is a little strange that Isabella hasn't told the rest of the guild what is going on, I thought to myself as Goner led me towards Isabella's office on the other end of the headquarters, all the while feeling a sense of dread grow in the pit of my stomach.

"Lead on, little man," I told the boy as my thoughts began to swirl. "I'm right behind you."

SET UNDERNEATH A MASSIVE WAREHOUSE on the northern fringes of the Market District, the entirety of the Grim Shadows' headquarters was underground. Built from the existing ruins left behind by the Nafarr, who once inhabited the city, the guild headquarters was a sprawling network of tunnels and chambers that connected to the underground sewers that ran through the entirety of the city. The setup allowed easy access both into and out of the guild without being seen.

Unfortunately, that also meant that it took a fairly long time to walk from one end of the headquarters to the other, as there was rarely a direct route, forcing us to take a circular one, moving from one chamber to the next. After a few minutes of walking the winding path of tunnels and chambers, we finally arrived in a well-appointed room that had been portioned off from the others. A trio of cutthroats stood watch, guarding a heavy wooden door within the room, each giving Goner and myself a brief appraising look before realizing who we were and waving us through.

"Isabella! Lazarus just came back!" Goner practically shouted as he knocked wildly on the guild lieutenant's door. "Well, he died and came back...but he's here now!"

"*Lazarus?*" I heard Isabella's voice echo from the other side, as a heavy lock along with several bolts were pulled back, causing the door to swing open and revealing an exhausted-looking half-elf.

Dressed in worn brown leathers, Isabella looked like she hadn't slept in days, with heavy lines of stress running down her face. Peering out at me with green eyes, the pale-skinned woman glanced between me and Goner, taking a moment to reply.

"Thank you, Goner." She managed a tight smile as she nodded at the overenthusiastic boy. "I need to speak with Lazarus for a moment; maybe it's time you went to bed?"

"But I'm not tired!" Goner complained, doing his best to stifle an untimely yawn. "I can still help out!"

"I'll need your help in the morning," Isabella replied smoothly, knowing how the game was played. "If you're too tired to help…I'll have to find someone else."

"No! You don't need to do that!" Goner answered, backing away from the door. "I'll go right now!"

Without another word, Goner spun on his heel and ran back the way we had just come, disappearing as he turned around the corner. Saying nothing, Isabella looked back at me and shook her head, causing her blonde shoulder-length hair to sway side to side. Motioning me inside the office, she closed the door behind her, sliding the lock and bolts back into place.

Looking out at Isabella's office and all the papers piled on her desk, I completely understood her paranoia. Her role had her responsible for running the intelligence arm of the guild and keeping tabs on everything that happened in the city. For a guild the size of the Grim Shadows, the information kept in this room was effectively priceless, and any breach of this room could spell disaster.

"Please sit, we can talk safely here," Isabella told me in a steady voice, walking away from the door and taking a seat at her desk. "This room is warded with the strongest protections we know of."

Suddenly feeling nervous about the news I was about to share, I took a seat at a chair set in front of the desk. In my short tenure with the Grim Shadows, I had only met the blonde spymistress a handful of times and had found her to be completely inscrutable. The only person I had ever seen crack her tough exterior was Goner, his child-like innocence somehow slipping through her guard.

"You look like you've had a rough night." Isabella broke the silence as she motioned towards my damaged armor, which was ripped, torn, and covered in blood. "What happened?"

Exhaling deeply, I felt myself at a loss for words. *How do I tell someone their friend is dead?*

"Yeah..." I croaked out after a moment, leaning forward in my chair, feeling a wave of emotions bubble inside me. "Rough is an understatement."

"Is everything okay, Lazarus?" Isabella's voice was tinged with concern.

"No...it's not okay." I felt the words slowly claw their way out of me. "Fairfax is dead."

Isabella froze, watching me with a stunned expression as her mouth worked soundlessly.

"*W-what?*" she finally managed to whisper, the news causing her voice to crack.

"Someone...*something* killed him." I started to explain to Isabella, slowly outlining everything that had happened since I had woken up in the Undertaker torture chamber. I saw her expression harden as I described what I had done to Cayden, then grow cold once I revealed Edith's involvement and how she had summoned devils to aid her.

"Did Fairfax join us on the heist?" I asked once my explanation was finished. "My memory of everything over the last day is still missing, but if my job went bad and he ended up in the same place as me..."

"No, Fairfax...was called to another task that should have taken him far from the Arcaneum or the New District," Isabella replied slowly, looking at the strange coin that I had recovered from the thief lord's body. "He was supposed to be at the palace."

"*The palace?*" I echoed with surprise. "Why the hell would he go there? Hasn't the king sealed the place off to visitors?"

"Fairfax felt he was forced to uphold an old agreement," Isabella replied evasively, anger blooming on her face. "One that I repeatedly told him was no longer valid, but he felt he had to at least *try*, to be sure."

"Hold on." I felt slightly off balance from where the conversation had gone, and I was struggling to catch up. "What sort of agreement could have compelled Fairfax to go to the palace? The whole Royal District is off limits to *everyone* in the underworld, on pain of death or exile!"

"How much do you know about the history of the thieves guilds?" Isabella asked, changing the topic. "Why we came to be in the first place?"

"Not a lot, to be honest," I replied hesitantly, feeling a little guilty that I didn't know more about my organization's history. "Just that the guilds were formed to keep the street gangs in line and to ensure that they didn't cause the guard to go on a purge."

"That is the most commonly held story, and not entirely inaccurate," Isabella said with a nod. "However, the truth is much more complex."

"What do you mean?" I asked.

"The thieves guilds were created by the order of King Cyril," Isabella stated, watching me carefully."What?" I blurted, feeling my heart quiver in my chest. "The king formed the thieves guilds? Why would he have done that?"

"In the early days of Eberia, things were hardly organized," Isabella began, holding up a hand at my question. "Tens of thousands of people had fled across the ocean and landed in the ruins of a city that had been ravaged by time. Resources were scarce, luxuries even more so. It did not take long for the first gangs to form, even if all they stole at first was food, firewood, or a spare blanket to survive the cold.

"Eventually, as Eberia grew and found its feet, so did the gangs, evolving as the kingdom did," she continued. "But it wasn't until the war started when the gangs finally came into their own."

"They formed a black market," I whispered, remembering the stories I had learned about as a child involving Britain during World War II. "The kingdom began rationing food and supplies, didn't it?"

"The kingdom began rationing *everything* as it desperately tried to stockpile," Isabella told me, a sad expression crossing her face. "I didn't taste sugar until I was twelve, and it took until I was nearly twenty before I was able to buy a fresh apple. But yes, the black market allowed the gangs to rise to power, eventually forming themselves into guilds as their influence grew."

I didn't know how to reply to Isabella's statement as she paused for a moment, lost in her memories. Based on her appearance, I had thought her too young to have lived through the entirety of the war, but as I saw her pointed ears, I remembered that she was half elf. Forty years for her kind didn't mean the same as it did to a full-blooded human.

Clearing her throat, Isabella shook her head before looking back at me. "As the war intensified, the demand for supplies only increased. Eventually, the guilds' reach grew powerful enough to extend deep into the military ranks, as corrupt officers skimmed off supplies marked for the frontlines.

"Once this started to affect the war effort, the king took action," Isabella said. "Over time, he collected a loyal cadre of officers and men that were free of the gangs' influence, then conducted a brutal purge of the ranks.

"Everyone caught in the smuggling rings was charged with high treason and summarily executed, which bought the king no favors, considering that the majority of the officers involved belonged to the noble houses." Isabella mimed a cutting motion with her hand as she spoke. "But in order to ensure that the situation never repeated itself, the king didn't just stop with purging the military; he continued his crusade into the heart of the underworld.

"After a sufficiently large example was made of all the criminals in Eberia, King Cyril demanded an audience with the leaders of the five remaining thieves guilds and made them an offer they couldn't refuse: *kneel or die.*"

"He forced them all to swear fealty to him," I gasped as the realization dawned upon me.

"*Precisely*," Isabella stated with a curt nod. "But given the nature of our kind, the king was not satisfied with a simple oath given under duress. He forced each of the leaders to submit to a geas to compel their loyalty."

"Damn," I said slowly. A form of magical compulsion, a geas would make resisting the king's orders all but impossible and would cripple, if not kill, the subject of the spell if they dared break its terms.

"Without his actions, Eberia certainly would have fallen to the orc tribes due to its own greed," Isabella replied. "But as much as the king wanted to stop the flow of smuggled goods and corruption in the ranks, his motivation for bending the guilds to his will was a political one."

"A political one?" I frowned, unsure of what Isabella meant. "It sounds to me like the early guilds were out of control. Stopping them should have been enough."

"In any other kingdom, it might have been, but at the time, the king was desperately seeking allies, willing or not, to counterbalance the nobility, who were becoming more and more fractious," Isabella revealed. "Despite the war raging all around us, the king lived in constant fear of assassination at the hands of a rival faction. Bending the thieves guilds to his will was his only choice.

"And so, over the last thirty years, the guilds have been responsible for keeping the nobility at one another's throats and away from the king's, serving as his eyes and ears in the shadows," Isabella told me. "Any time a new thief lord replaced the old, he was forced to submit to the geas anew, which ensured their guild's obedience. At least until both King Cyril and Prince Rainier died one after another."

"Their deaths broke the geas," I guessed.

"Well..." The spymistress hesitated, her confidence faltering for a moment. "We thought it did. Fairfax told me that when he submitted to the geas, the terms of the binding only included King Cyril and Prince Rainier. Swain had not yet been brought into the fold," Isabella explained. "And ever since Swain has come to power, we have heard nothing from the palace. No demands, no information, and our arranged dead drops have been completely ignored."

"So you think that Swain never had a chance to learn about the thieves guilds," I stated, remembering that both the king and prince had died long before the game had started.

"That was what Fairfax wanted to find out for certain." Isabella nodded. "Not only were the consequences for breaking the geas severe, but the geas on the other thief lords would have compelled them to seek out and kill any of the others who broke it."

"Ruthless, but effective," I noted, feeling a slight twinge of respect for King Cyril. Ruling a kingdom of desperate survivors with clashing ideologies was far from easy, but doing so while managing an all-consuming war was a feat few could match. "But why would he go now? Swain hasn't exactly been present since the Call to Arms ceremony we all had to suffer through."

"That was another part of the reason why Fairfax felt he *had* to go," Isabella told me with a sigh. "You're aware that the king has recently begun courting a commoner and has invited her to live in the palace with him?"

"Yeah, Molly told me." I nodded, remembering her describing the outrage amongst the nobles who couldn't believe that none of their daughters had been able to attract the king's attention.

Though considering what kind of person the king is, they might secretly be rejoicing the fact none of them had to give up a daughter to him.

"Well, two days ago, we discovered that the military attempted to remove the king's paramour and her retinue from the palace, *forcefully.*" Isabella cocked an eyebrow at me as she spoke. "Outraged, the king then ordered the royal guard to intervene, and eventually the military backed down. The moment we found out, I sent out a warning to the guild to lay low until we could learn more about what happened. The last thing we need is to be caught in a feud between the royal house and the military."

"What the hell were they thinking?" I couldn't believe what I was hearing. The military had been the single stabilizing force that had kept Eberia together over the decades, and they were fanatically loyal to the king. To have them interfere meant that they thought there was something seriously wrong. "Who is this woman? Why would the military even care?"

"I'm afraid we've been able to turn up little of Lady Corentine, save that she appeared during the formal gala after the Call to Arms ceremony and caught Swain's attention." Isabella's face shifted into a worried expression as she spoke. "The only thing we've been able to find is her outspoken faith in Nil, the god of vengeance. Supposedly she is an ardent devotee to his cause."

"Nil?" I echoed, trying to recall all of the different gods that I had heard of since I'd started playing Ascend Online. "He's not a popular god, at least not compared to the Dawnfather, or any of the others. Even Azmus has a larger following, and he is rather obscure."

"Unfortunately, due to the old agreements the guilds were forced to abide by, we've never had contacts within the palace, so we have no way of knowing *what* actually happened," Isabella said with frustration.

"But Fairfax feared that something had gone wrong and the king was in danger. He was also worried that *knowing* something was wrong and not doing anything would trigger the geas..."

"And possibly kill him if he did nothing," I finished for Isabella, not envying the situation that Fairfax must have been in.

"Correct." The woman leaned back in her chair, exhaustion visible throughout her body. "How Edith, your heist, or the sigil that you've acquired relate to any of this...I don't know. But based on what you've told me, the geas didn't kill him."

"You think Fairfax stumbled onto something he shouldn't have?" I asked, remembering what Edith had told me before things became violent on the pier. "Edith alluded that something big was happening in Eberia."

"Something big is *always* happening in Eberia," Isabella answered wearily. "The question is *what*."

The two of us sat in silence as we each tried to puzzle out what could have happened to Fairfax, the exhaustion of the night having taken a toll on our bodies.

"Thank you for telling me about Fairfax," Isabella said after a while, looking down at the strange coin that I had found on Fairfax's body. "And for bringing me his coin. It's...more important than you know."

"What are we going to do?" I asked while nodding in appreciation. "As a guild, I mean..."

"I don't know," Isabella replied, standing up. "I'm the senior lieutenant, so I'll likely take over. It's not the first time a thief lord has died; the guild will survive."

"And what about Fairfax?" I asked, following Isabella's lead and standing up.

"Tonight, we'll mourn him," Isabella stated as she began walking towards the door. "Tomorrow, we'll avenge him."

NINE

Sunday, February 24th, 2047 - 11:23 am
The Grim Shadows Guild Hideout

I AWOKE SLOWLY, FEELING MYSELF LYING on my side with something warm pressed against me. Slowly opening my eyes, I saw the familiar black curls and the pale white skin of Molly's back as she lay beside me with my arm draped over her. Lying still, I slowly began to piece together the events of the night before as my brain gradually woke itself up.

After leaving Isabella's office yesterday, we had both returned to the common room to break the news of Fairfax's death to the rest of the guild. Giving them a condensed version of events, one that omitted King Cyril's involvement in the guild's history, we explained that Fairfax had been killed while investigating a rumor and named Edith as the likely suspect.

Taking up the mantle of leadership, Isabella then declared herself as the interim thief lord and seamlessly began Fairfax's wake, asking everyone to put their anger on hold for the night while we remembered our fallen leader.

Being one of the newest members of the organization, I had yet to fully realize how closely knit the guild was and how much everyone would mourn Fairfax's passing. So far, I had seen the underworld as a cruel place, where people only looked out for themselves, uncaring to what happened to those left behind. Watching dozens of people come together in grief for a fallen comrade was more than I had ever expected to find, leaving me feeling emotionally raw and uncomfortable.

I kept trying to remind myself that it was all a game, feeling that I wasn't the first player that had difficulty coming to terms with the realism that Ascend Online portrayed. It seemed like there was something new every day that made me question the new reality I found myself in.

The wake lasted for several hours, giving Molly more than enough time to cross the city and find her way into the hideout. Feeling out of place as everyone began sharing memories of Fairfax, Molly and I did our best to stay out of everyone's way, only to find ourselves actively drawn in and included. Despite only being initiates and members for a short time, everyone made sure to count us as one of the family, an experience the two of us found extremely touching. Up until that point, we had felt like outsiders, not yet having earned a place within the inner heart of the guild.

Molly's stirring beside me had me snap back into the present as I felt her body shift. Slowly turning herself, she rolled around to face me, her blue eyes widening in surprise as they met mine.

"Morning," she whispered, drawing the blanket close over her naked shoulders. "Sleep okay?"

"Mostly," I replied. "Still processing everything that happened last night."

"I know what you mean," Molly replied with a sigh. "I thought this game would be an escape from life, something fun to take our worries away, even with the path we've taken…"

"But yesterday wasn't fun," I said, understanding all too well how Molly was feeling.

"Well…" A devilish smile spread across Molly's face as she touched my chest. "*Some* of it was a lot of fun."

"I'm happy the game didn't seal those memories away." I smiled back, still feeling the large mental gap in my brain.

"Still don't remember anything from the day before?" Molly asked, her expression shifting to one of concern.

"Nothing," I answered with a sigh. "Just completely…*blank*."

"I still find it terrifying that the game is able to do that to us." Molly shuddered, pulling herself close to me. "How did something like that even end up passing the design stage?"

"I don't know." I shrugged as best as I could while lying on my side. "But is it any different than any of the other tricks the game plays on us? Soothing our minds after a battle or coming to terms with dying?

"I got crushed by a statue yesterday, and somehow, I'm okay with it," I continued while tapping my head with a finger. "No mental trauma or anything in here."

"It just doesn't feel ethical," Molly replied. "Soothing bad memories, I understand. But taking other memories away…that seems too much for a game to be able to do. We're just playing this game for entertainment, not to have our personalities altered."

"I'm not happy about it either, but isn't this just the next step past the televisions and video games that society has been playing for the last ten years?" I asked, clasping Molly's hand that was still resting on my chest. "Instead of sitting and watching a show or playing a game, we're *living* it now. Exactly how it would be in a fantasy world."

"I guess it really is." Molly closed her eyes with another sigh, before reopening them and staring back up at me. "What's our plan for the day now? Any tips from your two quests?"

"Not sure," I said, remembering the pair of quest updates that I'd finally gotten around to reading late last night. Double checking to see if I had missed anything, I brought the two descriptions up again to skim over.

▸QUEST UPDATED! THE HEIST!

Going to the meeting in Cayden's stead with Molly, you discovered that the mysterious woman was in fact Edith, your one-time companion. After accusing you of ruining her plans in the Arcaneum and stealing the Sigil of Rage from her, you and Edith fought, eventually resulting in your death. Unfortunately, Edith has since escaped to places unknown.

Meet the mysterious woman: 1/1 (Complete)

Find Edith: 1/1 (Complete)

Find Ransom: 0/1

(Optional) Recover Memory: 0/1

▸QUEST UPDATED! NO HONOR AMONG THIEVES!

Returning back to the Grim Shadows headquarters, you informed Isabella of Fairfax's demise and learned the true history of the Thieves Guilds. Taking the mantle of leadership, Isabella has assumed the role of Thief Lord and has promised vengeance for Fairfax's death.

Inform the Grim Shadows that Thief Lord Fairfax has been killed: 1/1

Wait for instruction from Isabella: 0/1

"Just the same thing as yesterday," I confirmed after dismissing the quest updates. "Wait for Isabella to tell us our next steps."

"It's going to be near impossible to find Edith or Ransom in a city this large," Molly said while giving my chest one last squeeze and turning away as she began to extricate herself from the blankets. "We should probably get ourselves up and see if there is anything we can do to help."

"Yeah..." My reply trailed off as I watched Molly sit on the edge of the bed, admiring her form. "Molly—"

"I know what you're going to ask, Gavin," Molly whispered, using my real name. "My reply hasn't changed—not yet. I still need a bit more time. But for what it's worth, I'm almost there."

"It's okay," I answered, feeling the familiar frustration bubble under the surface. Despite the way our relationship had progressed within the game, I still knew nothing about Molly when it came to the real world. Every time I had asked, she had refused to share even the barest details about her life or even accept a simple email address from me so we could keep in touch offline.

I could understand the precaution of not wanting to give out information to strangers, but given that we had spent nearly every day of the last three weeks together and had some sort of relationship going, it felt strange to not even know her real name. It almost felt to me like Molly was working her way through a previous breakup or some other personal loss. Not that she would tell me what was causing her hesitation, either.

Sensing my frustration, Molly leaned over from the edge of the bed and kissed me. "Your patience means a lot to me. I promise it'll make sense later."

"I can't wait," I replied as she pulled away and began getting dressed. Throwing the blanket to the side, I followed her lead and began looking for my pants. Regardless of what Molly was or wasn't willing to tell me about real life, we were still together in-game.

And right now, that was good enough for me.

CONTRARY TO THE STAGNANT STILLNESS that I had walked into yesterday, the common room was a flurry of activity this morning as Molly and I walked into the room. Guild members moved with purpose as the day crew paused for an early lunch, inhaling quick meals as they caught one another up on what was happening on the streets. There was a sense of palpable excitement in the air, but judging from the tone of the voices I was hearing, there was worry as well.

"What's going on, Bart?" I heard Molly ask an older, grey-haired thief that was nursing a hot drink by himself at a nearby table. "Did something else happen overnight?"

"Ah, Molly, Lazarus." The older man nodded at us in acknowledgement as he set down his cup. "Yeah, whole city is up in arms. Marshal Tarius pulled out this morning with two thirds of the military on the king's orders."

"W-what?" I practically shouted, glancing over at Molly's stunned face.

"Why would he do that?" Molly hissed in disbelief.

"Find the answer to that, and Bella will shower you in coin. She's got everyone combing the streets for news about Fairfax or what the military is up to," Bart told us with a shrug. "Ask me, I think the politicking between us and the Ascendancy is finally breaking down and they sent our troops out to shore up Coldscar."

"Have you heard anything about that?" I looked to Molly as I asked the question, having filled her in about what Isabella told me last night. Despite the military trying to interfere in the king's courtship, I didn't think he would send them away just out of spite.

"No," Molly answered, shaking her head. "But if they're moving the military into position, it's because of a clear and tangible threat. Deploying them outside the city would be just too expensive otherwise."

"Rest of the underworld doesn't know what to make of it either," Bart continued, his gaze landing solely on me. "Also, seems that everyone's a mite grumpy, with Cain rubbing out the Undertakers last night."

"They had it coming," I replied, gritting my teeth as I spoke.

"Don't disagree," Bart grunted. "I figure a dead chap should be able to rest in peace once the life has left his body. Not be all concerned that some skeevy necromancer is going to source their corpse for parts. Problem is, they had a good thing going making unwanted bodies disappear, and you may catch some hate for that."

"They can hate all they want," I told the older thief as I made a mental note to be on my guard while out in the city. "But if they try to do something about it, then I'll be the one with a problem of making bodies disappear."

"Heh, don't I know it!" Bart laughed with a knowing smile before fixing us with an appraising look. "If I had to go into a thrash, I'd make sure that you and Miss Molly would be standing behind me, that's for sure."

"Why, thank you, Bart." Molly couldn't help but laugh. "Hopefully you'll never have to."

"That's the two of us!" the man agreed. "I'm a mite too old to be getting into scraps nowadays, and I'm happy to leave that to you young folk."

"Anytime you need us, just call," I told the man seriously, appreciating his sentiment.

The old rogue nodded as he looked at the two of us silently for a moment. "I may not be a scrapper anymore, but if the two of you are interested in learning a few tricks from an old cat that's survived thirty years on the street, I'm certain there's something I could teach you."

"Th-that would actually be great, Bart." Molly glanced at me in surprise, before looking back at the man. "We would really appreciate it."

"Glad to hear it!" Bart exclaimed while picking up his drink and standing up. "Now if you don't mind excusing me, I need to go find Goner. He's due to be helping me run the drops for the day."

"Not a problem," I replied, holding up a hand. "But before you go, any idea where Isabella is right now?"

"Bella? She's down the hall in the spare room." Bart pointed towards the other side of the common room with his cup. "She said she didn't want people walking across all the tunnels just to find her, so she set up shop close by."

"Thanks, Bart!" Molly gave the man an affectionate pat on the shoulder as he moved off.

"It's not enough to have everything happen with Fairfax and Edith, but now the military is leaving?" I grumbled out loud to Molly as we crossed the room. "What the hell is going on in the city?"

"I think the game's moving to a world event," Molly said with some resignation. "There are tens of thousands of adventurers out in Coldscar that came from Eberia alone, plus however many that came into the area from the Ascendancy."

"What do you think is going on out there?" I asked while waving to a few familiar faces as Molly and I continued to walk. "Do you think we're at war already?"

"There's a whole lot of player-versus-player conflict going on," Molly told me. "I've taken the time to look up some of the feeds over the last couple weeks and I saw several new Eberian guilds fighting amongst themselves, but I also saw quite a few skirmishes with guilds coming out from the Ascendancy as well."

"What were they fighting over?" I shook my head, not quite believing what Molly was telling me. "They have the whole wild to choose from and access to the rest of the continent. Why are they still wasting their time around here?"

"Resources, mostly," Molly replied as we walked out of the common room and into the hallway. "Pretty much everything here in the city that we take for granted, they need to painstakingly craft *and* hope no one destroys it. The major guilds are spending all their time to create a stable powerbase before branching out."

"Sounds chaotic and more than a little frustrating," I said with a scowl. "I'm not much for running around in the wild, fighting and dying in the mud. I spent ten years traveling the world after the global economy fell apart during the nanotech boom. I've had enough of sleeping on the ground and eating bugs to last a lifetime. I'm a city boy through and through now."

"I didn't know you traveled, especially during the collapse," Molly said softly as she looked up at me with an unreadable expression on her face. "You'll have to tell me about it one day."

"I'd be happy to," I replied with a smile as Molly's hand reached out to grab mine.

Finding the spare room that Bart had mentioned, we found Isabella, along with a handful of other guild members steadily streaming into and out of the room. Using the room as a temporary command post, Isabella was directing everyone who had any news about what was happening in the city to drop in and ensure that she or one of her scribes knew about it.

"Lazarus, Molly, to me." Isabella spotted us out of the corner of her eye the moment that we walked into the room and wasted no time in waving the two of us over.

As Molly and I approached, I noticed a familiar person standing by Isabella's side, looking more than a little out of place as he glanced around the room. Tall and lanky, the black-haired man didn't appear to be dressed like a thief, choosing to wear a thick green gambeson with a pair of dark brown leather pants. He fixed both Molly and I with a wide smile as the two of us approached, his green eyes watching us carefully.

"Quinn!" I greeted the adventurer with a handshake. "What brings you down here?"

"Hey, Lazarus," Quinn replied, motioning his head towards Isabella. "Isabella got in touch with me, mentioned that you two had a rough night last night and may need a hand."

"You could say that again," Molly agreed with a sigh.

"Good morning." Isabella nodded to us in greeting, wasting no time in getting the conversation moving. "I called Quinn because I believe he may be useful in making sense of what happened to the two of you yesterday and because he's among the few adventurers that we can trust, given recent events."

"I'm sorry to hear about Fairfax," Quinn said softly, looking between the three of us. "I'm happy to help however I can."

"What's the plan for the day?" I asked, looking towards Isabella after giving the dark-haired man a nod, curious to see just how much she had really told him.

Technically, Quinn wasn't a member of the Grim Shadows, despite having worked with us a handful of times before, which made it all the more interesting that Isabella had invited him into the hideout. It meant that she trusted him quite a bit, and likely that he had finally expressed interest in joining the guild, something that he had been reluctant to do when I had last spoken with him.

"We need more information about what Edith did yesterday with regards to the devils she summoned, and Quinn has finally come to his senses and has taken me up on my offer," Isabella stated while looking at me.

"You're finally going to join us?" Molly asked excitedly.

"Yeah," Quinn stated with a smile. "I'm done lone-wolfing it as a contractor. Too many close calls. A soft, squishy mage like me needs to have people I can count on not abandoning me."

"I have briefed Quinn on the basics of what's happened and he has a contact that may be able to shed some light on what happened, as well as the sigil that you've acquired," Isabella informed us. "I hope you do not mind me sharing that information, but I believe it to be pertinent."

"That's no problem," I said with a shrug, before looking at Quinn. "What sort of contacts?"

"There's an...*eccentric* man I've met while working with the Eberian Mages Guild," Quinn explained. "He may be ancient, but he's also the best source for lore that I've come across. If he can't at least point us in the right direction, I'll be shocked."

"You work for the Mages Guild now?" Molly asked, suddenly excited as she glanced between me and the mage. "You wouldn't happen to have heard anything involving the Arcaneum over the last few days...have you?"

"Well, actually, now that you mention it, yeah." Quinn looked at us suspiciously. "There was some sort of incident that happened in one of the labs a couple nights ago...practically turned the whole room to glass and destroyed half a dozen relics and projects."

"Huh." I looked at Quinn completely deadpan. "That's interesting."

"D-did you guys have something to do with that?" Quinn asked nervously, sensing that something was amiss.

"No," I stated, following my usual instinct to deny everything.

"Maybe," Molly answered a second behind me.

"Molly, *why*?" I glanced over at the petite woman in mock disbelief, only to have Molly shake her head back at me.

"Quinn is on the team now, we should be straight with him."

"What did you do?" Quinn shook his head at us. "There was nothing volatile in that room—"

"Erm." Isabella cleared her throat, clearly tired of being ignored. "I am happy that you're all getting along, but I have *quite* a few things that need to be done today, and I'm not quite finished here yet."

Glancing between the three of us, she continued speaking. "Your orders for the day are to go and collect whatever information you can find about how Edith summoned those devils, and any other information you can find about the sigil if it's relevant. I need to know what scope of threat she and whomever she is working with presents, ideally *before* we meet with the other thief lords tonight."

"You want us to meet with the thief lords?" Molly asked with surprise.

"I do," Isabella stated with a nod. "Your testimony to the council will be invaluable in bringing them up to speed and determining if we need to take any special action to counter whatever threat Edith poses. In addition, while I'm doubtful that anything will come of it, I've also posted a bounty for her to be brought in alive. If nothing else, the added threat should make it more difficult for her to move around the city."

"Assuming the bounty hunters survive bringing her in," I said with a doubtful look on my face, seeing a quest update appear in my vision.

QUEST UPDATED! NO HONOR AMONG THIEVES!

In order to prepare for a meeting with the Thief Lords tonight, Isabella has asked you to speak to Quinn's contact, a man she believes will able to shed some light on both the Sigil of Rage and the devils that you witnessed Edith summon last night.

Wait for instruction from Isabella: 1/1(Complete)

Collect information about the Sigil: 0/1

Collect information about the Devils: 0/1

"In addition," Isabella continued, bringing me back to the present as she gave a dismissive shrug at my earlier statement, "I am promoting both you and Molly to full guild members, effective immediately."

"Y-*you are?*" I stuttered through the question, feeling a spike of shock shoot through me. Molly and I had barely been initiate members of the guild for a week and had been expecting our probation to last several more weeks, if not months, before we were formally accepted into the guild.

"We weren't expecting to become full members for ages," Molly said, her voice filled with the same surprise that I felt. "Thank you."

"Because of you two, we know that Fairfax was killed." Isabella nodded at the both of us in acknowledgement. "Had you two not been involved, we may have never found out, or found out far too late to move against whatever Edith has planned. The guild appreciates your loyalty, and I see no reason to not treat you both as full members."

"We won't let you down," I promised, looking my new thief lord in the eye. "We'll find out what Edith is up to."

"I believe you," Isabella said, offering the two of us a rare smile before it vanished under her stoic expression. "Before you go, you are aware that the military has been ordered out of the city, correct?"

"Bart told us," Molly replied.

"Good," Isabella acknowledged. "If you find *anything* regarding why they left, I want to know it as well. I don't expect it to be related to Fairfax or Edith, but there is only one reason why Marshal Tarius would mobilize several thousand soldiers at a moment's notice."

"*War*," I stated.

"Or the threat of one," Quinn added with a nod.

"Precisely," Isabella said, chopping a hand through the air. "Be on your guard at all times today. There are far too many events brewing in the city that we are blind to. Gather whatever information you can and come back home safely."

Isabella looked at the three of us one last time and gave us a nod. "Good luck."

TEN

LEAVING THE HIDEOUT, THE THREE of us moved through the sprawling Market District as we slowly made our way towards the center of the city. The noonday sun was high in the air as we walked, forcing us to squint from its incessant glare. With Molly and me doing the majority of our work in the night, it was rare that we ever saw the sun, oftentimes getting out of bed as it began to set.

As we crossed the city, I couldn't help but feel naked without the reassuring weight of my greatsword over my shoulder, choosing to leave the guild hideout with only my crossbow, not having been confident that I could craft something worth replacing my old sword in the time we had.

Not planning to run around all day completely unarmed, I decided that I was going to make use of the thirty-five gold pieces weighing my wallet down and pay a visit to the one place in the city where anyone could go to find a reliable weapon at a moment's notice.

The auction house.

A place of absolute wonder, set in the very heart of the Market District, the auction house was the single most important feature of an adventurer's life. It was the place where dreams were made into reality, where hard-earned money was turned into rare and hard-to-find pieces of equipment or crafting materials.

I felt my pulse quicken as we turned onto the central roadway that led towards the auction house, spotting it in the distance. Massive and imposing, the immaculately crafted brown building dominated the center of the square with a steady stream of people constantly milling in and out.

Walking down the road, we saw dozens of other adventurers going about their business, all talking excitedly and making grand gestures as they retold and embellished their latest adventure. The news about the military leaving the city was a hot topic among the adventurers, and many were scrambling to get themselves equipped to follow the departing soldiers, hoping to get in on whatever conflict or event was brewing.

"Everyone seems *really* excited about the military leaving," Quinn commented once the herd of Adventures had begun to thin out around us.

"Yeah, more than I thought they'd be. I don't think there are going to be that many adventurers left in the city by the end of the day today," Molly said, looking at the steady stream of players that were walking out of the auction house. "I'd be surprised if there are more than a thousand left in the city as it is..."

Far too lost in the excitement of approaching the auction house, I barely heard Molly and Quinn talking between one another, already envisioning the weapon I would buy.

I wonder if I have enough gold to buy a relic, or maybe something even better, I thought to myself as I tried to figure out what sort of weapon I should get. *I'll need something that will hopefully last me a few levels, though; something tells me I'm not going to have that much time to take a break over the next few days…*

"Lazarus!" Molly's shout pierced through my train of thought, forcing me back into the present.

"Hey, sorry." I blinked, turning to look towards her, and realized with a start that we had already walked inside the auction house lobby. "I was somewhere else."

"No kidding. I know how you get at the auction house." Molly shook her head with a smile, then thumbed her hand towards Quinn. "I'm going to look at some jewelry and Quinn wants to buy a wand. Meet back here in twenty minutes?"

"Yeah, that's not a problem." I nodded, noticing that Quinn too had been caught up in the auction house's magic and was wandering off ahead of us. "Find me if you need me."

Splitting up from Molly, I entered the main floor of the auction house and into a sprawling room filled with countless stalls. Hundreds of people milled about everywhere as they lined up to talk to the auctioneers that ran the auction house, each of them ready to place their orders.

Finding a middle ground between convenience and realism, the auction house was one of the few places where the game allowed players to search for the items that they were looking for via a search menu displayed in their vision, rather than physically displaying the items on a stall or display like other merchants did within the city.

While slightly unrealistic, it was the best compromise possible, given that the auction house carried thousands, if not tens of thousands of different items. Putting each of them on display would have not only been a colossal task but would also have made it near impossible for adventurers to sift through the items and find exactly what they were looking for.

Pulling up the search menu, I narrowed the options to bring me up a list of different greatswords available for sale, narrowing the search to only include those that gave me a substantial boost to strength. As the results began to filter into my vision, I made my way towards a stall that had a single human adventurer in line, hoping that I'd be able to pick out a sword that I wanted.

The way that the auction house worked in Ascend Online was that once I had found an item or a list of items that I wanted to buy, I would then approach an auctioneer and complete the sale, getting the item instantly. If the auction house was busy, lines would occasionally form before seeing an auctioneer, but given that there were several dozen on duty at any given time, it was rare to wait longer than a few minutes.

Settling in behind the adventurer, I shifted my focus towards the weapons appearing in my vision and set down to making a decision on what I was going to buy.

Bronze Greatsword of Brutality
Slot: Main Hand and Offhand
Item Class: Magical
Item Quality: Exceptional (+20%)
Damage: 22-53 (Slashing)
Strength: +6
Durability: 120/120
Base Material: Bronze
Weight: 2 kg
Class: Any Martial
Level: 10
Seller: Gordian
Buyout Price: 5 gold

Gloomsplitter
Slot: Main Hand and Offhand
Item Class: Relic
Item Quality: Fine (+10%)
Damage: 30-60 (Slashing)
Strength: +8
Durability: 120/120
Base Material: Iron
Weight: 2 kg
Class: Any Martial
Level: 12
Seller: Tyrel
Buyout Price: 30 gold

Claymore of Might
Slot: Main Hand and Offhand
Item Class: Magic
Item Quality: Good (+15%)
Damage: 24-57 (Slashing)
Strength: +6
Durability: 120/120
Base Material: Iron
Weight: 2 kg
Class: Any Martial
Level: 12
Seller: Mufat
Buyout Price: 7 gold

Well, that's a little disappointing, I thought to myself, looking through the list and narrowing it down to the top three items that I felt would be the most useful for me. Objectively, Gloomsplitter was the best greatsword currently available on the market, but at thirty gold pieces, it was grossly overpriced. Had it been listed for anything under fifteen gold, I likely wouldn't have even hesitated and purchased it outright without a second thought.

Removing the overpriced sword from the list, I compared the two remaining weapons and found them to be nearly the same. With only two points of damage separating the swords, I was inclined to choose the well-crafted bronze greatsword over the claymore, if only because it was two gold cheaper and would hurt my wallet less. The extra bit of damage that the claymore had wasn't enough to make up for its increased price.

Maybe it would be better to break into one of the military armories now that they've left the city and see if there's anything worth stealing there, I considered pessimistically, feeling disappointed with the swords available to me. *I really hoped for a better selection, but I guess with all the adventurers gone to Coldscar, the pickings here are slim.*

Driven by the need to have at least a half-decent weapon, I mentally flagged the bronze greatsword while I settled in to wait for the blond-haired adventurer ahead of me to finish. Listening in on his conversation with the auctioneer, it seemed like whatever he was setting up was pretty complicated in nature.

"Sir," the male auctioneer began, clearly overwhelmed at the scope of all the orders the adventurer in front of me was placing. "So if I have it straight for this next buy order, you want to purchase *all* of the copper on the exchange, store it until prices hit at least nine coppers per ingot, then relist it. Then to take all the proceeds from those sales and to buy up all the iron on the exch—"

"Yeah, that sounds about right," the man in front of me interrupted. "I'm sorry for being so rude, but I can see you have all my orders right, and I'm late. Can I sign off on the rest of the listings?"

"Sir, your orders are nothing short of mass market manipulation; you will cause artificial shortages throughout the city!" I heard papers being shuffled ahead of me as the auctioneer rifled through a pile of papers the man had just dropped in front of him.

"Is that *illegal?*" the man asked, his voice taking on an impatient tone.

"Well, no—" the auctioneer grudgingly admitted after a moment.

"Fantastic! Fill the orders *exactly* as I've written them down and list the other item I gave you," the adventurer told the auctioneer forcefully as he began to turn away from him. "I really need to go."

Turning around quickly, the adventurer took a blind step towards me, forcing me to take a step backwards to avoid him running straight into me.

"Whoa, sorry about that, didn't see you there," he said, the man's green eyes darting up to mine as he raised his hands in front of him apologetically. "In a rush. All that took longer than expected."

"No problem." I waved the man away, my eyes noting that the armor he was wearing was better than anything I had ever seen before. "Have a good one."

"You too, man," the strange adventurer called over his shoulder as he ran off across the auction house floor and was met by a waiting group consisting of a dozen other adventurers.

"Must be one of those market players," I said to myself, shaking my head at what I had overheard between him and the auctioneer as I stood up to the counter. "Probably shouldn't buy any crafting materials for the next couple days..."

"One moment, please," the auctioneer told me as he busily scribed the adventurer's orders into a heavy leather book. "These orders are quite complicated and will take a moment."

"Sure." I shrugged at the man at the same moment a soft chime echoed in my ears.

Oh, a new item was just listed! My eyes widened in excitement as I brought up my still open search menu, spotting a brand-new entry in the list and read the item's description.

Dormant Glass-Steel Greatsword
Slot: Main Hand and Offhand
Item Class: Relic
Item Quality: Mythical (+30%)
Damage: 40-70 (Slashing)
Strength: +12
Durability: 200/200
Base Material: Glass-Steel
Weight: 2 kg
Class: Any Martial
Level: 12
Special: Evolving Weapon
Seller: Luke
Buyout Price: 35 gold

Holy shit! This is amazing! I felt my mind go blank as I read over the weapon's stats. *I've never heard of a glass-steel or evolving weapon before. Why would anyone want to sell it?*

Coughing in my excitement, I practically slammed my hands down on the stall in front of me, causing the auctioneer to flinch from the sudden noise and look at me with surprise.

"The *Dormant Glass-Steel Greatsword* that was just listed," I spat, feeling a sense of anxiety shoot through me. If someone stole the item out from under me, I had no idea what I was going to do with myself. "I want to buy it, *right now.*"

"Sir, if you'll let me just finish writing the—" the auctioneer started to say.

"Shut up and take my money!" I barked, practically throwing my money pouch at the auctioneer. "There's *no time!* Someone else might buy it!"

The auctioneer was clearly taken aback at my maniacal expression, his gaze shifting to the heavy pouch of gold that I had slammed onto the table. "Y-y-yes, of c-course."

With a flourish of his hand, my gold pouch vanished from the table and was replaced by an immaculately crafted greatsword. Looking down at the blade, I felt my heart jump as I gently reached down and picked it up in my hands.

At just over four feet in length, the blade of the sword was completely translucent and free from any flaws, appearing as if it were forged entirely from glass. Looking down to the hilt, I saw that it too was made out of glass-steel; however, unlike the rest of the blade, it was dark and opaque.

Grasping the weapon by the hilt with both hands, I hefted it into a ready stance, its perfect balance rendering every other weapon I had ever used inadequate in comparison. After holding the blade for a moment, an alert appeared out of the corner of my vision.

> *You have equipped an* ***Evolving Weapon!***
> *This mystical weapon has the potential to grow with you and increase in power as your skills develop, but before you can fully bond with the weapon, it must be awoken. While this weapon is in its dormant state, it will take 25% of all combat experience you accumulate until it fully bonds with your soul. Please note, any experience received from quests will not be applied to this total. Once the weapon has been awoken, it will become a permanent part of you, and you will be unable to sell or destroy it.*

I need to feed this experience? I cocked my head in confusion, feeling a little overwhelmed as I reread the alert. *Hang on, that's not right…I get an experience penalty while I'm using this.*

Feeling a sense of dread wash over me as I now realized *why* this item was put up for sale rather than being used, I brought up the item's description and searched to see how much experience it would take to awaken the weapon.

Experience needed to Awaken: 0/50,000

"Fuck!" I shouted, startling the auctioneer once again. "This is going to take *forever!*"

"I-is there a problem, sir?" the auctioneer asked hesitantly, his eyes focused on my new sword and the threatening manner I was holding it.

"I...don't know," I replied, pointing the sword towards the ground and mentally trying to figure out just how long it was going to take me to realize the weapon's potential.

Fifty thousand experience points is close to two levels' worth of non-stop grinding since the weapon doesn't take quest experience, but at the same time, it takes a flat twenty-five percent of all combat experience, and I can't adjust it. I paused for a second to do the simple mental calculation. *Which means I have to earn at least two hundred thousand experience points to fully awaken this weapon...and that will likely take me until I'm close to level twenty.*

"A-all sales are final, I'm afraid," the auctioneer said after a moment, sensing my inner turmoil. "If you would like to chase after that gentleman that left, perhaps he will buy it off you and relist it again, unless you wish to relist the item yourself."

"He was the one who sold it?" I asked, looking over my shoulder to see if he was still nearby.

"Yes." The auctioneer nodded, clearly relieved that I wasn't about to take my frustrations out on him. "Mentioned something about finding it in a newly uncovered cache here in the city...but that's really none of my business."

"I..." I trailed off while looking down at the sword.

Sure, it was going to be a pain getting it to awaken, but at the same time, I couldn't help but be curious to see what would happen, and I doubted that I would have the opportunity to find another evolving weapon anytime soon.

"I'll keep it," I said finally, coming to a decision. Even with the experience penalty, the weapon itself was better than anything else I could find on the market at the moment and would remain so for several levels to come.

"Excellent!" The man gave me a half-hearted smile as he moved back towards the heavy leather book he was writing on. "Now if you'll excuse me, I must temporarily crash the city's commodity exchange..."

Almost the second that the auctioneer finished speaking, I began to hear a low grumble start to fill the air as adventurers around me began to murmur and complain. The sound grew to a feverish pitch as more and more adventurers joined in.

I looked back at the auctioneer, who simply sighed and continued to write in his book, occasionally looking at the papers the adventurer before me handed to him.

"Uh, good luck with that," I told the man as I felt both Quinn and Molly start moving towards the lobby as the unrest began to grow. "I think I'm going to get out of here before a riot starts and I need to put this sword to use."

"If that happens," the auctioneer said with another deep sigh, "please use it on me first."

ELEVEN

"WHAT THE HELL HAPPENED IN there?" Molly asked, the three of us having met up in the lobby as we made our way out of the auction house. "Everyone was happy one minute, then chaos the next."

"Someone bought out a huge chunk of the commodities market and relisted it," Quinn said a moment before I could chime in. "I was checking out prices for leather and jute, when nearly all of it was bought up and marked up almost instantly."

"Metals, too," I added, remembering what I heard the adventurer tell the auctioneer. "Must have taken an insane amount of money."

"Not the worst idea, though," Molly said slowly after thinking for a moment. "With the military leaving, and needing resupply on the road, crafted goods and resources are going to be at a premium. Whatever person or guild bought everything out is likely going to clean up."

"That many resources leaving the economy is going to cause problems until it settles down again," I pointed out. "Inflation is going to hit everything for a few days until it's all relisted."

"Might be a good opportunity for the guild to make some money," Molly said thoughtfully. "I'm sure there are a ton of places we can hit for just resources alone and undercut the relister."

"That's actually not a bad idea," I agreed, making a mental note to bring it up with Isabella.

"Well, all that aside, at least we managed to get some shopping done before everything went to hell," Quinn said, holding up a finely polished length of oak with a clear crystal set on top, then motioning to my sword.

"That is a pretty nice sword, Lazarus," Molly noted with the faintest tone of envy tinging her voice.

"It's the best one I've ever wielded," I said with a smile, before going on to explain the awakening process for the sword. "I have a long way to go before I can use it to its full potential, though."

"Damn, that *is* pretty sweet, even with the experience penalty," Quinn said, shaking his head. "I had no idea there was such a thing as evolving items in this game. Maybe once the auction house calms down again, I can take a look if there are any similar ones listed and put in a buy order..."

"That may not be a bad idea," I told the mage in complete agreement. "Just be sure to read the fine print so you know what you're getting into."

"So where are we headed, exactly?" Molly asked, turning her head to look over at Quinn as we started to put some distance between us and the auction house.

"We're off into the Old District," Quinn answered. "Shouldn't take us too long to get there, the streets are emptying out pretty fast."

"Yeah, they are..." I had steadily noticed the amount of people on the streets decreasing as we made our way out of the central Market District and moved northwards. "Not many people go walking about in the Old District, though; it's mostly for nobles or for the merchant families."

"True, but look at those who *have* gone out and tell me something isn't wrong," Molly told me, subtly motioning towards a group of well-dressed people passing by us on the opposite side of the street, escorted by a trio of bodyguards. "Yesterday, they wouldn't have even bothered to take bodyguards with them, but today they have."

"They're nervous," I replied, noticing that two of the bodyguards had chosen to place themselves between us and the group they were escorting. "Really nervous."

"That tells me even they don't know what's going on," Quinn observed. "I'd be willing to bet that even the noble houses don't have any idea where the military was sent to."

"No bet there," I grunted, having come to the same conclusion myself.

Walking for a while, the three of us made our way out of the Market District and found ourselves amongst the largest and oldest houses in Eberia. The clutter and bustle of the Market District slowly faded away into sprawling properties full of lush greenery. Some of the houses were entirely new construction, made out of wood, while others were solid stone, repurposed from the ancient ruins that made up the majority of the city.

"Where does your contact live in here?" I asked, feeling self-conscious that we would be walking into one of the larger houses on the street.

"We're just about here, actually," Quinn said as he motioned to a row of townhouses ahead of us. "William, my contact, has an apartment here...well, actually, *all* the apartments in his building, but he doesn't really use them."

"What does your contact *do* to afford a place here?" Molly asked incredulously as she looked around. "This street puts my home to sha—*erm,* it's really beautiful."

I couldn't help but catch Molly's sudden correction as she turned away from me, making me wonder what exactly she was trying to hide about her life outside the game. *Does she think something will change if I know even the barest details about her life?*

"Based on what I know," Quinn said, completely oblivious to Molly's slipup as we walked up to the building, "he simply outlived everyone, including the landlord, and the city found it easier to simply grant him the property than find someone who wanted to go through the trouble of buying it."

"Really?" Molly asked with disbelief. "No one wanted to buy the place at all?"

"Wait until you see the inside." Quinn gave Molly a thin smile. "You'll understand why."

"*Aw,*" she answered with disappointment. "Is it—"

"I can't even explain it." Quinn shook his head, motioning for the two of us to follow him to the centermost apartment as he unlocked the door and held it open for us. "So I won't even try. Come on."

After exchanging nervous glances, Molly motioned for me to go first, apprehension clear on her face.

"Coming," I said with slight resignation as I stepped through the doorway, my eyes widening in understanding as I saw the inside. "*Oh.*"

ENTERING INTO THE BUILDING, I was forced to turn sideways as Quinn and Molly followed me inside. Books filled the entirety of the house and hallway before me, stacked in countless piles that reached from floor to ceiling. The musky smell of paper mixed in with the faint stench of decaying food met my nostrils the moment that Quinn closed the door behind him, leaving me coughing as I adjusted to the smell.

"W-what the hell, Quinn?" I gagged as the stale air caught me off guard, tickling my throat relentlessly as I spoke.

"Told you," Quinn grunted, motioning me to walk down the hallway. "Keep going. The smell gets better further in. Just be careful and don't knock any of the piles over. I'd rather not be crushed to death by an avalanche of books...*again.*"

"Are you kidding me?" I looked over my shoulder and back towards the mage as I started to sidestep down the book-laden hallway. "That's happened before?"

"First time I was here," Quinn replied with a bit of embarrassment. "This hallway was less organized back then. The piles are much sturdier since I've restacked them, but I don't suggest testing it."

"You did all this, Quinn?" Molly asked from behind the mage. "There has to be thousands of books here!"

"Easily," Quinn agreed. "Probably tens of thousands."

"Quinn." My voice took on a nervous tone as I tried to maneuver my bulk down the hallway without knocking anything over, pressing myself against the one book-free wall. "*What is this place?*"

"This is where all the books that came from Assara ended up," Quinn whispered, referring to the old continent where the original settlers of Eberia had come from. "Once the war started, no one was really that interested in cataloguing old history that didn't matter anymore, nor bothering to learn the dead languages that these books were written in. William is the only thing keeping these books from being tossed into a fire."

"All of this came from Assara?" I repeated, struggling to get a count for just how many books we had walked by, and how many more I could still see down the hall ahead of me. "Where is this *William*, anyway?"

"His office should be coming up behind you," Quinn told me, knocking on the wall I was leaning against. "He usually doesn't leave it."

"Oh," I said, turning my head towards a doorway an arm's length away from me. I had been so focused on not knocking over the wall of books in front of me that I hadn't been paying any attention to where I was going.

Continuing my awkward shuffle a little further, I made it into the doorway, happy to have crossed the book-filled hallway successfully. My tall and bulky stature was great when it came to combat, but unfortunately that also made getting through tight spaces a little trickier. Turning around slowly in the doorway, I looked into the office, finding that it was little different than the hallway leading to it.

Stacks of books were littered everywhere around the room. The majority of them were small, only reaching to waist or shoulder height, conveniently serving as adequate places to put half-eaten plates of food, or empty teacups. Lined up against the far wall were even more books, piled into massive columns that reached up towards the ceiling, the stacking looking very precarious when compared to the work Quinn had done out in the hallway. Set in the very center of the room was a heavy oak desk, completely covered with papers and even more books.

"Oh, hello," a wizened voice called from behind the desk. "Did we have a meeting today? I must have forgotten, my apologies..."

Looking between a gap in the stacks of books set on the desk, I could make out the faintest glimpse of white hair and a single grey eye looking back towards me.

"Uh, I'm here with Quinn," I said nervously, taking a couple hesitant steps into the room as I tried to find a place to stand where I wouldn't knock anything over. Moving behind me, Quinn entered the room and made his way to the desk, stepping around the stacks of books on the ground with practiced ease.

"William," Quinn greeted loudly. "We didn't have an appointment today, but I was passing by and decided to drop in and say hello. I brought some of my friends with me."

"Oh, Quinn, it's you," William replied in recognition as the mage came around the desk. "It is nice of you to drop by. I really don't get that many visitors anymore."

"Because this place is a deathtrap," Molly whispered behind me. "You can still see Quinn's bloodstains in the hall where the books crushed him."

"You can?" I asked, startled that I hadn't noticed anything when walking down the hall. I'd been too focused on not knocking over any of the stacks.

"*Erm*," Quinn cleared his throat loudly, giving Molly and me a pointed look before replying back to the man behind the books. "We're always happy to drop by, William. Do you mind if I move some of these books so you can see your guests?"

"Oh, of course, I'm done with this stack," William told Quinn while pointing to something that we couldn't see. "Just find a place for it...wherever there is space."

"What are you working on?" I asked, making sure to speak up as I watched Quinn shuffle over to the desk and lift a stack of heavy books, revealing an incredibly old-looking man sitting behind the desk.

Weighed down by age, William was the very definition of ancient, his grey eyes slowly glancing between Molly and myself. Wispy white hair barely clung to his liver-spotted head as it cascaded downwards, tucked behind a pair of half-pointed ears, reaching down just past his shoulders. I doubted that the half-elf was ever a large man in his youth, but his advanced years had taken a toll on his body, making it obvious that there was only skin and bones underneath the plain grey robe that he wore.

"Oh, nothing too important," William answered, his weary tone indicating to me that he had long since resigned himself to the fact that few shared his interest. "Just something that keeps an old man's mind sharp and his hands nimble."

"Your work is important, William," Quinn scolded while scowling at the man. "You are cataloging a lost age."

"I am a man who's too stubborn to die and has nothing else to do with his time," William grunted at Quinn, clearly having heard the same words before. "Perhaps one day, if I am fortunate, someone like you will take up my work or make use of it somehow. In the few short weeks that you adventurers have been around, I've had more visitors coming to see me than I've had in the last five years.

"Before Quinn showed up, the last time I had anyone come visit me regularly was a man named Thaddeus, at least before he passed on." William paused for a moment as he searched his memories. "He was always curious to see how I was doing and if I had uncovered any useful tomes that could aid the war effort, or to collect any dangerous ones that needed to be quarantined."

"*Thaddeus Denarius?*" Molly voice echoed with surprise from the far side of the room as she walked up beside me. "The old patriarch of House Denarius?"

"Oh, yes." William waved a bony hand dismissively. "I knew him as a boy, from before the fall. He was one of the few that bothered to remember me."

"What do you mean by dangerous tomes?" I asked, suddenly curious as I picked up a blue-colored book off a nearby stack and ran my hands against the well-worn cover. I looked at the spine to see if I could recognize the title, discovering that the book I held was titled *Fifty Tints of Mana*. "And why would a book need to be quarantined?"

"On occasion," William began to explain, "I come across a book that might be considered *dangerous*, either to the reader themselves or because of what the book contains. Thaddeus was always good in insuring that a dangerous book would be properly cared for or locked away by the Mages Guild."

"Really?" I said with a bit of surprise as I picked up another book from the stack titled *The Ardent Elven Chambermaid* while passing the first book I was holding over to Molly. "I can understand a book being dangerous because of what it contains, such as magical knowledge or even just regular knowledge. But how can a book be *dangerous* to the reader?"

"Some books contain knowledge so perverse or otherworldly that simply *reading* it is enough to damage your mind, regardless if you understand the language or not," William replied. "While others are bespelled with protections to ensure a certain level of...*competence*, before the book can be opened. Should someone unknowingly attempt to read or open such books, their mind could be scarred permanently, if they're not killed outright. But aside from that, some books are simply just *cursed*, either as practical jokes or as defense mechanisms from would-be thieves, much like the book you've just picked up."

"Uh, *what*?" It took me a moment to process what William had just said as I lifted a third book off the stack.

Glancing downward, I didn't even have enough time to read the book's title before it somehow *shifted* in my grasp and bit into my hand, a pair of gleaming white teeth flashing in the light. A spike of pain shot up my arm at the same moment a message appeared in the corner of my vision.

A [Book] bites you for 6 points of damage!

"Ah, what the fuck?" I shouted as I reflexively shook my hand, causing the book to lose its grip and sail through the air. Landing with a dull thump in the middle of the floor, the book began moving on its own as it shot across the room and vanished behind several tall stacks of books. As it ran, I could have sworn I heard the book snicker.

"What the hell was that?" I demanded, casting a glance at William and Quinn, who both appeared to be barely holding back laughter.

"That was a cursed book, if rather harmless," William stated simply, with a smile on his face. "I call him Chomper, and he helps keep the rats in the place at a manageable level."

"Don't feel too bad, Lazarus," Quinn told me with a chuckle. "He does have a knack for appearing in the strangest of places. I think he's gotten me at least three times now."

"Did you ever consider just getting a cat?" Molly's voice had me turning to look towards her, seeing a grin on her face as well. "They're a bit more manageable."

"And put Chomper on the streets?" Quinn countered, completely deadpan as he glanced towards William. "He's too old now. He would never survive. He's an indoor book through and through."

"I literally cannot believe that we are having this conversation right now," I grunted as I put the book I was holding back on the stack and checked my hand where the book had bitten me. "But I think I'll start keeping my hands to myself now."

"It does pay to be mindful of what you touch in a magician's library," William replied sagely.

"Truer words have never been spoken," Molly commented, holding the book I had given her close to her chest. "Speaking of a library, though, Quinn told us all these books came from Assara, but based on what I have heard about the fall, there wasn't that much time to evacuate, nor to bring so much."

"There was not." William's voice took a slightly sad tone as he looked around the room. "All that you see here is a small fraction compared to what I left behind..."

"What do you mean 'left behind'?" I asked, looking to Quinn for explanation.

"William used to be the head librarian of the imperial library in

Meridian before the fall," Quinn helpfully added as he found himself a clear spot to lean against the wall just behind the elderly half-elf. "If William hadn't fought tooth and nail for space on the ships to take *something* with them, all of this would have been lost."

"If I remember my lore right, Meridian was the city where all the settlers of Eberia launched from as they fled Assara," Molly stated, taking a few more tentative steps into the room, watching carefully not to knock any of the book stacks over. "How did you even decide what to take? How *could* you decide what to take?"

"Speed," William replied, his eyes glazing over as he looked back into his memories. "Speed was my only concern.

"When the decision was made to abandon Meridian, I had porters grab everything they could and throw it into crates without even bothering to sort or check anything," the elderly half-elf continued. "I preserved the most important tomes from the archives, but so much was just lost to the shuffle...there is so much that I've catalogued, and yet so much more to go."

"Why are you the only one working on this?" I asked, starting to get a better picture of why Quinn had made such an effort to get to know William. "These books are near priceless; you should have dozens of people helping you catalogue all this."

"Oh, I did once," William answered with a sigh. "Unfortunately, learning about the past isn't that important when there is a war on your doorstep, let alone one that lasts for nearly four decades. By the time my few assistants grew old and retired, Eberia had forgotten what it meant to be a scholar, and I found replacements far too much trouble than they were worth. Well, at least until Quinn showed up on my doorstep."

"I'm always happy to help," Quinn acknowledged with a smile. "We were actually hoping to pick your brain while we're here about a few things that we've come across."

"Oh?" the old man said, looking between the three of us with sudden curiosity. "You adventurers tend to lead interesting lives; I hope that I am up to the task."

"I'm sure you are," Quinn said warmly while motioning for Molly or me to start.

Casting a quick glance at me, Molly nodded to herself as she took another step forward into the room before speaking.

"Yesterday, a woman managed to somehow summon four devils into this plane of existence. These devils weren't summoned as magical entities like a warlock would create, but she somehow physically manifested them by using an actual person as a host," Molly explained. "Based on what I have learned about the other planes...what she did should not be possible."

"She summoned devils physically into our world?" William echoed, a concerned expression coming over his face. "You're right, that *should* not be possible...short of the hosts inviting the devils to take possession of their mortal bodies, but they would have known that would make their lives forfeit."

"I don't think it was a willing possession," I added, remembering the burning talismans that I had seen the urchins wearing. "Those who transformed all wore strange necklaces that began to glow after the woman shouted a trigger word. They had no idea it was coming."

"Hm, a forced possession, then. Most unusual..." The old librarian looked down at the desk as he tapped his finger idly. "I am far from an expert in these matters, but a forced possession might be possible if an object holding the devil's spirit was touching flesh. Especially if the wearer was not expecting to resist the devil's assault."

"How easy is it to get a devil's spirit?" I asked. "I can't imagine that's something you'd be able to find at the market."

"Unless things have changed drastically since the last time I left the house, no. I agree it wouldn't be." William nodded at me with a curious expression. "The spirits would have had to have been bound to the talismans by a ritual, a feat that would take a rather in-depth knowledge of demonology and fairly powerful magic to execute."

"I don't think Edith would have been able to manage that," I stated. "I'm pretty sure she took the disciple base class."

"But Ransom, on the other hand, is a warlock," Molly countered as she glanced at me grimly, then back over to William. "Do you have any idea how much time it would take to create such a talisman?"

"I have no way of knowing for certain." The old man shrugged. "A few hours, maybe? That would also be in addition to whatever materials were needed to create such a talisman in the first place. Simple rocks or jewelry wouldn't suffice; it would have to be something that the devils would have an affinity with."

"Which really puts us back to square one." I sighed loudly. "We strongly suspected that someone powerful was backing her. This just more or less confirms it."

"What exactly is going on?" William asked, glancing suspiciously between Molly and me, then turning to look at Quinn. "This *Edith*, she is an adventurer?"

"She is," Quinn replied with a nod. "She is an independent thief that contracted to the Thieves Guilds in Eberia, but it appears she's gotten herself mixed up in powers we don't quite understand."

"And your two friends here have been sent by the guilds to find her," William stated flatly, turning his gaze towards Molly and me. "Which of the guilds do you two represent?"

Silence gripped the room as the three of us stared at the ancient half-elf in surprise, none of us knowing what to say.

"H-How did you even—" I started to say before William let out a loud bark of laughter.

"You young folk are all alike! Thinking that just because I am old that I'm also blind!" He stared at me intently as he thrust a finger out at me. "I am one hundred and fifty-three years old and I have likely lived at least twice as long as all three of you put together! Do you honestly think that you are the first thieves to have stepped into this place? I had you both figured out the moment that you walked into the room."

"We can leave if this is a problem," Molly said in a small voice, clearly caught off guard by the man.

"Goodness, no!" William snorted. "I'm not in the habit of turning away guests seeking knowledge. Well, truthfully, I'm not in the habit of *guests* at all...but back to my previous question, which guild do you two represent?"

"The Grim Shadows," I admitted, glancing over at Quinn who was staring at William in surprise.

"Now was that difficult?" William shook his head at us, causing his wispy hair to fly side to side. "Now tell me what *really* happened to get you all involved in this. What else did she do to get the guild so interested?"

"We think she may have had a hand in killing our thief lord, Fairfax Grimm, two nights ago," I told William, feeling the familiar pang of sadness well in my chest.

"Well—"William's eyes widened at that admission and he inclined his head to the both of us, "—my apologies for your loss."

"Thank you," I acknowledged, feeling the sudden tension in the room begin to dissipate. "It's a bit of a long story how everything happened."

"Do I look like I have many places to be?" William asked, motioning to the room around him. "Tell me what happened."

"Well," I started to explain, after seeing both Molly and Quinn nod at me in acceptance, "I guess it all started when I woke up strapped to a cold table with a strange sigil tattooed on—"

"What did you say?" William interrupted, his voice completely flat as he slowly stood up from his chair and grabbed a wand off the desk, pointing it directly at me.

"A sigil. I woke up with a sigil tattooed onto my chest," I repeated looking at the intense expression on the half-elf's face.

Glancing at Quinn behind him, William pushed himself off of the desk with one hand and slowly began to move around the table, his face completely blank.

"Show it to me. Now."

TWELVE

"W-WHAT?" I TOOK A STEP backward as the half-elf advanced towards me with a glowing wand in his hand, pointing it directly at me.

"*Take. Your. Shirt. Off,*" William demanded, waving the wand in the air threateningly. "Show me the sigil."

"Uh..." I felt my back hit the wall as I ran out of space, the elderly half-elf crossing the room faster than I would have thought possible for someone his age. "Quinn?"

"William, what is this about?" Quinn had a confused expression on his face as he put a hand on the man's shoulder. "Why does Lazarus need to take his shirt off?"

"Let go of me!" William barked, throwing the mage's hand off his shoulder with surprising strength. "I need to see if his will is still his own! Show me the sigil, or *get out!*"

"Lazarus..." Molly whispered in a worried tone as she too backed away from the advancing librarian.

"Okay, okay!" I raised a hand in front of me to get the man to stop his advance while the other went to a buckle to undo a strap. "I'll show it to you! Just give me a moment!"

"Quickly now," William ordered, keeping his wand pointed directly at me.

"I didn't plan to put a show on today," I quipped nervously as I continued to loosen a number of straps on my armor and slowly pulled it over my head. Holding my tunic in one hand, I turned sideways slightly as I pulled up my shirt, giving William a perfect view of the Sigil of Rage.

"How long have you had this sigil?" William asked me as his cold hand touched the side of my chest and stretched the sigil. "How many times have you used it?"

"Uh, roughly a day, maybe slightly longer," I told the man, feeling more than a little awkward as he invaded my personal space. "I've used it twice, well, three times...but it didn't work the third time."

"It didn't work?" William looked up at me, alarm visible on his face. "What do you mean *didn't work?*"

"It was while we were fighting Edith after she had summoned the devils," I told him, effectively skipping over half the night's events. "It's a long story, but she knew about the sigil and wanted to have it cut from my chest. She had some sort of stone with her that somehow kept the sigil from working."

"A chaos stone," William stated. "It absorbed the energy of the sigil."

"Yeah." I nodded, remembering the message that had come up when the strange stone that Edith had had begun to glow purple. "It blocked the sigil from working for a while, but it feels fine to me now; I could probably activate it if I needed to. What does a chaos stone do?"

"It traps primal energy, which you unknowingly fed it full of when you activated your sigil within its range," William said, taking a step back from me, trembling with anger. "You are fine. There are no compulsion elements written into the sigil; it is a plainly written Sigil of Rage."

"Compulsion elements?" A look a panic crossed Molly's face as she watched William nervously. "Are you all right? Do you know what these sigils are?"

"Oh, I know them all right," William's face turned red as he began to yell, anger clearly visible on his face. "I grew up seeing these sigils all my life back in the Ascendant Empire. I had hoped, *prayed*, that they had died with Assara, but it seems to me I was wrong!"

"You saw these before?" I asked, looking at the librarian intently. "What are they, exactly?"

"Hubris!" William spat as he began to gasp for air, his recent exertions having taken their toll on him. "They were once considered to be gifts from the gods themselves, but the Ascendant Emperor perverted them over the course of millennia. He twisted them in his vain pursuit to become a god and killed a civilization! They should have been left behind. *I made sure they were left behind!*"

"William, slow down!" Quinn shouted as the elderly librarian's gasps for air became more and more desperate. "You're going to give yourself a heart attack!"

"I-I..." the elderly man wheezed as Quinn slowly led him back towards the desk and sat him down into his chair.

"Take deep breaths," Quinn ordered, giving the two of us a worried look as William began to violently cough.

The three of us watched on in panic as the librarian's coughing slowly evened out and he began to regain control of his breathing.

"I'm okay," William said after a few minutes, color having returned back to his face. "I was just surprised, that's all."

"Are you sure you're okay?" Molly asked, having made her way to Quinn's side, watching the elderly man carefully. "We can take you somewhere if you're not."

"I'm fine," William repeated, waving a hand weakly through the air. "It's just been a while since I've gotten that worked up."

The three of us traded glances as both Molly and Quinn stood up, looking towards me as I readjusted my armor.

"Can you tell us what these sigils are?" I asked the recovering man as I walked across the room towards him. "I have no idea how I even got it, let alone why Edith wants it so badly. I just woke up with the last day completely missing from my memory."

"You wouldn't remember getting it," William replied after taking a deep breath, his gasping and wheezing having finally stabilized. "The power of the sigils does not play well with mortal minds, and memory loss was—*is*—a common side effect."

Looking up at Molly and me, William took a second, even deeper breath before motioning for us to continue speaking. "Tell me everything that happened yesterday, everything that you remember, at least. Then I'll tell you what I know about the sigils."

"Well," I started slowly, taking a moment to collect my thoughts. "The last thing that I remember before the memory loss was getting ready for a heist..."

I then went on to explain everything that had happened over the last day, from waking up in the Undertaker torture chamber, to killing Cayden and being crushed by the falling statue.

"Then as soon as I resurrected, I felt the sigil's presence as if nothing had ever happened," I finished, watching the amazed expression on William's face.

"I have only known your kind for a few scant weeks, and yet

your adventures already astound me. To be so cavalier about death..." William shook his head in amazement at the three of us. "Without knowing what Edith has stolen from the Arcaneum, I cannot even begin to fathom what her end goals could be. But if she has discovered a way to physically manifest devils into this world in addition to finding a chaos stone, then whatever she is planning certainly does not bode well for the city."

"What exactly is a chaos stone?" Molly asked, clearly intrigued by what William was saying. "Or primal energy, for that matter. You don't mean æther, do you?"

"No." William shook his head patiently. "Æther and primal energy are two completely different forms of energy, and the chaos stone only carries an affinity for primal energy."

The man paused for a moment as he collected his words. "If I would liken the two of them to common terms more easily understood, primal energy is the raw essence of creation itself. It is what the gods used to create reality, the very ground that we stand on.

"Æther, on the other hand, is the natural coalescence of magic, and it is what the gods used to create life," William continued, his explanation completely capturing our attention.

"I think I understand," Molly said slowly. "Without primal energy, life wouldn't exist. Without æther, life wouldn't have *anywhere* to exist."

"In essence, you are correct." William nodded, before holding up a hand in warning. "However, it is much more complicated than that in practice."

"How does this relate to the sigils?" I asked, feeling slightly lost. "The sigils somehow channel primal energy?"

"That depends on the sigil," William said. "The sigil you have on your chest, the Sigil of Rage, is one tied to the primal energy source. There are others that are tied into the ætheric source, and a rare few that are tied into both."

"Just how many sigils are there?" Molly asked.

"That answer is only known by the gods," William replied. "In my time before the fall, I have seen Sigils of Alacrity, Power, Fortitude, and Intellect, in addition to the one Lazarus has, with multiple variations of each. It is my theory that the sigils were created by the gods to empower their servants as they went about the task of creating reality. As the eons wore on, ambitious mortals such as the Ascendant Emperor discovered the sigils too, turning them to serve his own purposes.

"That is why I had to be sure how the sigil had been written onto your chest." William focused his grey eyes on me as he spoke. "In the Ascendant Empire, the emperor had sole control over the distribution of the sigils and purposefully restricted them for himself, his inner circle, and his elite guard, the Sigilbound. But being the paranoid man that he was, all the sigils that he inscribed carried a component that compelled a near-permanent, undying loyalty to him, allowing him to commit a millennia's worth of atrocities without fear. For the briefest of moments, I was terrified to think that somehow the knowledge of that compulsion had somehow survived the fall."

"I understand," I told William. Living under an immortal tyrant for the majority of one's life definitely left a mark, and seeing the symbols of his oppression would understandably stir up memories rather forgotten. "How were the sigils granted? With my memories gone, I have no idea how I even got the sigil in the Arcaneum. We were supposed to be looking for a single artifact."

"Truthfully, I do not know," William told me. "My position as a head librarian gave me an insight to a great amount of lore that was otherwise restricted from the common populace of the empire. But as for how the emperor granted the sigils…that was a closely guarded secret."

"Well," Molly said with a sigh as she turned to look towards me. "All that does is just raise more questions than answers."

"Going back to the chaos stone that Edith has?" I said, steering the conversation back on track. "What were they used for?"

"That depends," William said thoughtfully. "The stones were originally designed to keep renegade Sigilbound in check; it would temporarily deprive them of the sigil's power, allowing them to be caught or killed. A side effect of the stone negating the sigil's power was that it would be filled with the sigil's energy instead, allowing the wielder to tap into that energy to fuel their own spells without drawing on their natural reserves."

"That explains how she managed to cast such a powerful spell," Molly commented, looking over at me. "But how did she end up so... *deformed?*"

"She alluded to something happening back in the Arcaneum and blamed me for it," I said with a sigh, glancing in Molly's direction as I placed my hand on my chest directly over where the sigil was, sensing the well of energy hiding behind it.

"Yeah, but *what?*" Molly asked with frustration. "Something to do with the artifact she wanted us to help steal?"

"I don't know," I whispered, feeling the sickening sensation that we might have hit a dead end. William had clearly done his best to answer our questions, and had raised several more in the process. But we still had no clear idea of what Edith was up to, or what our next steps would be.

How much of what Edith is doing is related to what happened in the Arcaneum? I wondered, trying to piece together everything that had happened. *Did she have all of this planned before seeking Molly and me out? Or is she just scrambling after everything came apart?*

"I appreciate your help on this, William," I said, looking towards both Molly and Quinn to see if they had any other questions for the man. Without any leads to follow, I figured that we might as well head back to the guild and fill Isabella in on what we had learned so far.

Nodding slowly at me, William let out a small smile. "It is nothing. And I apologize for reacting so harshly earlier. A lifetime of fear and hate is hard to overcome, especially for a man as old as me."

"I appreciate your help, William," I replied with a smile.

"Are you sure you're going to be okay?" Molly asked with a worried expression on her face, looking at the much-recovered half-elf. "We can stay a bit longer if you're not feeling well."

"I don't mind staying," Quinn said. "It really isn't any problem."

"No, no, I am fine," William replied earnestly. "If nothing else, this was a sign that I should move around more often, instead of spending my days sitting. I may be old and have death looming over me, but I do not wish to make it any easier on him than I must."

"Be that as it may, I think it's time you looked at getting someone to help around here," Quinn said seriously.

"Hey," I interjected before William could reply, an idea coming to mind. "Would you be interested in teaching? There is a boy in the guild that needs a more rounded education than the guild can provide, and he would be able to help you get around. Plus, with all the training he's had so far, he should be able to avoid Chomper or any falling stacks of books easily enough."

"You mean Goner?" Quinn looked at me with surprise before nodding quickly. "That would be a great idea! He can help you around here on a regular basis."

"I haven't taught since I was in my early seventies," William hedged as he looked at all of our faces, seeing our excited expressions. "But perhaps I could teach the boy something useful. At any rate, another pair of hands to move some of these stacks around and clean up would be most helpful."

"I'll ask him and see if he's interested," I told William, feeling happy that Goner would be somewhere safer than the heart of a thieves den. I had a feeling that William's apartment was a much more appropriate place for a growing boy than an underground lair filled with cutthroats and murderers.

"Of course." William nodded, sensing that our visit was coming to a close. "But before you go, I have an odd question for all of you, if I may."

"Sure," Molly replied the quickest, having warmed up to the elderly man during our short visit.

"How many times have you all died?"

Each of our eyebrows shot up at the odd request, and we looked at one another in surprise. It certainly was an unexpected question, but I couldn't see any harm in replying.

"Six," I replied, filtering through the number of reckless or poor choices that I had made over the last two weeks.

"Two," Molly added, giving me an odd look at my rather high number.

"Once," Quinn replied, coloring as Molly and I looked at him in disbelief.

"Your only death..." I said slowly as a grin crossed my face.

"...was being crushed by a pile of books?" Molly couldn't help but laugh as she finished my sentence.

"Yeah, well," Quinn said with a shrug. "I consider that a *good* thing. I don't know about you, but I prefer not to die, on general principle."

Looking at us with a sense of bewilderment, William's mouth fell open, completely at a loss for words.

"I am an old man, reaching the end of my natural life, and I find myself thinking of death often, worrying about what I will find on the other side," William managed after a moment. "Yet you all stand here before me, having passed through that veil, multiple times in some cases, and still remain in good spirits. It warms me in knowing that there is something more waiting for me one day. I look forward to seeing you all again soon." William waved his hands as if he were shooing us away. "Go find this woman wreaking havoc in the city, and perhaps then we will be able to talk at length."

"Thank you for everything, William," Quinn said as we all began to shuffle out of the room.

"No, thank *you*, Quinn," William said as he watched us leave. "Good luck in your hunt. I sense that you will need it."

THIRTEEN

"HE REMINDS ME OF MY grandfather." Quinn was the first to speak once we left William's apartment and out into the fresh air again, walking back towards the Market District on our way to the guild headquarters. "It's a little hard to constantly remind myself while I'm there that he's not really real."

"I know exactly what you mean, Quinn," I said. "This game has only been out for a short time and I'm already feeling the lines between this world and reality blurring. I can't imagine how we'll feel in a few months or a year."

"I don't think any of us expected to ever find a game this *real*," Molly whispered quietly. "Did you watch his expressions when he spoke about the Ascendant Empire, or when he saw Lazarus's sigil?

His emotions were real, raw, as if he actually lived them."

"Maybe he did," Quinn offered. "CTI hasn't released anything about how they developed this game; we don't even have the faintest glimpse of what sort of technology they used to create these NPCs. They're a scary level of *real.*"

"I don't know about that, Quinn. William said he was a hundred and fifty-three years old!" Molly exclaimed, waving her hands around to the street around us. "But we know that this game has only been on the market for barely two weeks!"

"Time is relative to a computer program," Quinn said with a shrug. "If there weren't any players plugged into the game, what's not to say that CTI just sped up the rate of time when compared to reality? You know, like one second in the real world is equal to a day inside the game. If these NPCs are as real as we think we are, they could have let the world's history write itself."

"Now *that* is a scary idea," I stated as I mulled over Quinn's theory.

"Why?" Quinn asked, a quizzical expression on his face. "It's not *impossible*, given what we've seen."

"That's exactly why it's scary," I told the mage. "It means CTI isn't actually interacting with this world, but is letting it evolve on its own instead."

"So it's just like real life, then," Quinn replied, clearly not sharing the same worry as me. "Just better."

Is it, though? I couldn't help but shake a chill that crept down my spine as we walked in silence for a few blocks and made our way back into the Market District. If all of the NPCs in this world had evolved according to their experiences, how were they any different than people in the real world? Was there a difference because they were just digital constructs, and we were actually flesh and bone? Or was there someone looking down at us from above that regarded us the same way we did at our creations?

The thoughts swirled around in my mind as we retraced our steps through the Old District, passing through the lavishly appointed street quietly and crossing back over into the Market District. Taking a moment to glance around my surroundings, I noticed yet another flashing quest update, in the corner of my vision. With nothing better to do as we walked across the city, I brought up the update and skimmed through it as it appeared in my vision.

> **QUEST UPDATED! NO HONOR AMONG THIEVES!**
> *Your meeting with Quinn's contact, William, turned out to be a bit unusual, but you managed to uncover a wealth of lore regarding both the sigil on your chest and the devils that Edith summoned. Return to Isabella to tell her what you've discovered.*
> *Collect information about the Sigil: 1/1 (Complete)*
> *Collect information about the Devils: 1/1 (Complete)*
> *Return to Isabella and inform her of your discovery: 0/1*

I hope this quest doesn't end up taking me all over the city and wasting all our time traveling, I thought to myself with a sigh as I dismissed the update from my vision. I had noticed that city-based quests tended to force the adventurer to range from one end of the city to the other on a fairly regular basis, giving frequent and small updates each and every time a quest goal was achieved. *Likely a balance decision, since we don't have as far to travel as adventurers who choose to make their life out in the wild. That, and traveling is relatively 'safer' in the city.*

Well, most of the time.

Continuing our trek back towards the guild headquarters, I noticed few adventurers or citizens on the streets, allowing us to make great time as we crossed the length of the city. It seemed that the news of the military leaving had finally caught up to the remaining adventurers in the city. The short time that we had spent visiting with William had been more than enough for the adventurers to ready themselves and rush after the departing soldiers and for the civilians to take shelter back in their homes.

Hopefully we'll find out why they were sent out, I thought to myself as we turned off of one of the main roads and onto a side street. *Then we can figure out if the kingdom is about to be plunged into war once again, or if all of this is just a huge waste of time and stress.*

I felt a sudden wave of nervousness wash over me at the thought of open warfare. I had no frame of reference to even picture how a conflict between two nations would play out in Ascend Online, vaguely imagining thousands of troops charging into one another and hacking each other to pieces. I had trouble envisioning myself in such a conflict and felt my anxiety increase.

Taking a deep breath, I banished the spiraling thoughts and focused on the moment, scanning the area habitually for threats, just like Fairfax had taught me a few days ago. Looking to my side, I noticed that both Molly and Quinn were also lost in their thoughts as we walked, their eyes staring blankly ahead of us, staring at a pair of adventurers in the distance. A quick glance behind me showed an empty street behind us, but despite looking around the area, my body felt tense, as if there was something it was trying to warn me about.

Why are my nerves so shot? I asked myself as we continued to walk down the side street, trying to distract my overactive mind by forcing it to study my surroundings. *There's nothing here, it's just a normal side street, everything is nice and quiet…*

"It's quiet," I whispered, realizing what was missing and why my body was on edge.

"What?" Molly replied, startled out of her train of thought. "Sorry, just thinking about the day."

"No, not us, the street," I said as I subtly glanced behind us again, spotting three adventurers as they came walking around the corner. Turning my head the other way, I saw that the two adventurers ahead of us had since turned around and were making their way directly towards us, effectively boxing us in. "Heads up, I think we've attracted hunters."

Both Molly's and Quinn's eyes widened as they shook off their mental cobwebs.

"Plan?" Quinn whispered through his teeth. "Attack first?"

"Follow my lead," I hissed back, seeing a familiar flash of red armor and a golden shield between the cloak of one of the adventurers ahead of us. There was only one bounty hunter I knew that wore armor like that. "I think I know one of these guys."

I saw Quinn flinch out of the corner of my eye at my statement, turning to look at me with surprise. Knowing a bounty hunter often meant that one of you had died the last time you met, which understandably led to hard feelings between the two parties the next time they crossed paths.

Of course, this time was no exception.

"*Sawyer*!" I shouted from across the street, visibly startling the pair of adventurers walking towards us. "What are the odds that I'd meet you again here?"

"Better than you'd think, Lazarus," a male voice called back after a moment to recover from the surprise. "This city isn't that big for people like us."

"I don't know, man," I replied, spreading my hands out wide, indicating the city around us. "Seems like *plenty* of other people are finding other places to be today."

"Yeah, well..." The red-armored Eberian man came to a stop a short distance away from us, fixing his dark eyes on me. "Not many other people are responsible for taking out the *entire* Undertaker gang in a single night. Something like that catches a lot of heat from those invested in their services."

"The Undertakers are *gone*?" I asked mockingly. "*Damn*, you'd think that if a single person were capable of taking out an *entire* gang in a single night, others would know well enough to just leave them the fuck alone."

"You know, I thought the same thing," Sawyer admitted, putting his hands on his hips as he threw back his cloak, revealing a heavily muscled body underneath his blood-red armor. "But it's strange how a pile of gold coins can change someone's mind."

"*Shit,*" I gasped sarcastically, glancing between Quinn and Molly, seeing my girlfriend roll her eyes at my attempt at theatre. "They're offering gold for this guy? How much? If the price is right, we wouldn't mind getting in on it and splitting the bounty. Besides, if I remember the last time we met, you had a rough time doing everything by yourself."

"This guy is a hunter's wet dream, Lazarus." Sawyer took my jab in stride without flinching. "Request is a little different on this one, though—they're offering eighty gold pieces to take the target off the board for two days. Doesn't even need to get violent, just a snatch and grab."

Despite the by-play that Sawyer and I were exchanging, I couldn't help but raise my eyebrows in surprise.

"Eighty gold just to put him on the sidelines for a few days?" I exclaimed incredulously. "Who the hell is the client? If they're tossing that amount of money around like idiots, might be a better idea to roll them for everything they have."

"Oh, you know how clients are, Lazarus." Sawyer shook his head sadly, causing his thick black hair to sway side to side. "They like to keep things close to their chest, their identity especially. If a target ever found out who the client was, *well*, I'd imagine they'd do something rash."

"Of course," I acknowledged while nodding my head in disappointment.

"But with that being said, I'm still interested in offering you half,"

Sawyer offered, a slight flash of nervousness passing over his companion's face beside him.

"*Half*?" Molly finally spoke up, causing Sawyer's gaze to shift over to her. "And what exactly would we be doing for that half?"

"Relaxing, sleeping, whatever you want really, so long as it's in a secure place I can verify," Sawyer stated before shifting his glance over to me. "Seems like a pretty good opportunity to make some serious cash without having to work too hard."

"It almost sounds too good to be true," I replied, letting a scowl cross my face. "And two days is a really long commitment. With the military gone now, I was planning on doing a bit of shopping and maybe poking my head into places normally a little too risky."

"Aw, come on, man." A worried expression crossed Sawyer's face. "I'm a big enough man to say that I really don't think I'd be able to pull it off without your help. I'd still have to try, you see, but that just introduces too much risk I'd rather not have to deal with."

"I appreciate your candor, Sawyer, I really do." I nodded at the man, knowing how much it must have pained him to admit what he'd just said. "But we kinda have a timed quest on the go, and I have a sneaking suspicion that it won't be around in two days."

Sawyer's face fell as understanding crept across his face. "Aw, fuck, you and the client are competing over something, aren't you?"

"*Competing* implies that there are rules," I replied as I lifted my hands in the air and mimed hitting someone. "This is more of a bare-fisted back-alley brawl, where the winner takes all."

"*Perfect*," Sawyer spat, anger crossing his face. "I really hate getting involved in personal problems."

"You don't have to, Sawyer," I told the man slowly. "Just walk away, pretend you never saw us, and once this all settles down, I'll buy you a brew and tell you the entire shitstorm that caused all this."

"I really want to do that, Lazarus, I really do," Sawyer replied with resignation. "But at the same time, eighty gold will go a long way to getting me to where I want to be, and I really can't pass that chance up."

"That's a real shame," I told the man, subtly tensing my muscles for what was about to happen. "You sure I can't convince you otherwise?"

"Sorry, Lazarus, but—" Sawyer's reply was cut off as I leaped towards him.

Crossing the distance in a heartbeat, I drew my new sword in one smooth motion and sent it chopping downward in a sweeping arc, hoping to catch both Sawyer and his companion.

Reacting on pure instinct, Sawyer barely managed to leap backward as he evaded my attack, his eyes shooting wide open as my glass-steel blade swept through the air. Cleaving through the space just vacated by the red-armored man, my blade continued downward towards the other adventurer, who had been caught completely flatfooted, biting deep into the side of the man's knee.

And slicing straight through it.

Barely feeling any resistance as my new sword sliced through flesh and bone, I was just as surprised as the adventurer when he toppled to the ground, his severed leg flopping sickeningly to the side.

"*What the hell, Lazarus?*" Sawyer shouted as he drew his sword from his waist and pulled his golden shield from behind his cloak in one smooth motion, a second before the fallen adventurer screamed in pain.

"Sorry, man," I grunted, sidestepping the growing puddle of blood gushing from the screaming man and rushing Sawyer. "New sword, still getting used to it. Apparently, it's *super sharp*."

"Where did you even *get* that?" Sawyer visibly winced as my blade slammed into his and bit deep into the metal as he parried my attack.

"Bought it on the auction house for a small fortune today," I told the man as a thundering crack of magic echoed behind me, signaling that Molly and Quinn had entered battle with the rest of Sawyer's entourage.

Shaking his head at me with a frustrated growl, Sawyer braced his shield against his shoulder as he lunged towards me, attempting to get inside my reach where it would be more difficult for me to bring my sword to bear. "Damn it, Lazarus! You're making this more difficult than it needs to be!"

"How is that my problem?" I called back, moving to meet the bounty hunter's assault as I crashed into his shield with my shoulder and stopped his charge before he could build momentum.

Like two dance partners familiar with one another's habits, I knew with firsthand experience what kind of warrior Sawyer was, having killed him and been killed by him at least twice in the past. So I wasn't surprised that the moment that my shoulder connected with his shield, he pulled back and sent a vicious knee towards my groin.

Shifting to take the blow on an armored part of my leg, I swept my other foot forward, looking to sweep Sawyer off his feet. Unfortunately, as much as I knew his tricks, Sawyer knew mine, and he easily hopped over my ankle-high kick, a grin crossing his face as he did so.

"We've done this too many times for the same moves to work, Lazarus!" Sawyer shouted as he continued his attack, using both his sword and shield to drive me backwards towards his fallen comrade. "We're just wasting our time here! Come on, put up your fancy sharp sword and take a couple days off!"

"You're free to stop at any time!" I called back as I hammered a powerful blow into Sawyer's shield, causing an ominous cracking sound to fill the air. "The stakes are too damn high on this to bail on out."

"Come on, man!" Sawyer's face winced at the sound of the shield cracking and he withdrew a step as he quickly scanned it for damage. "I just got this thing! Don't fucking break it!"

"I'm being serious, Sawyer!" I yelled back at the man as I seized the opportunity to check behind me, seeing that the wounded adventurer had yet to overcome the shock of losing a limb and was busy trying to stanch his bleeding stump. "The client that hired you, her name was Edith, wasn't it?"

"I was being serious too, Lazarus!" Sawyer spat back at me, as he finished inspecting his shield and rushed forward once more. "I can't tell you anything about the client! The system doesn't work that way!"

"What if I told you that the guild just put a bounty on her head?" I barked as Sawyer and I collided into one another again, grinding our blades together as we exchanged blows. "We're offering a hundred gold for her capture!"

Before Sawyer could reply, a sudden flash of magic flashed behind me, causing a look of panic to appear in his eyes as he looked past me.

"Lazarus, look out!" Molly's desperate cry echoed out, as I felt a sudden wave of heat descend upon me.

Reacting instinctively, I threw myself to the side while shoving Sawyer away from me as I tried to evade whatever was happening behind me. Staggering from my push, Sawyer's sword flailed through the air, slicing a thin line across my forearm as I fell to the ground, dropping my sword in the process.

With a heavy thump, I fell on top of the legless adventurer, the same instant a ball of fire flew past me and slammed directly into the bounty hunter. Catching the fireball on his shield, Sawyer avoided the worst of the blast as it exploded and threw him backwards down the street.

Closing my eyes, I felt the flames wash over me, singing my face and eyebrows. A helpful message appeared in the corner of my vision, alerting me of what had happened.

An [Unknown Player]'s [Fireball] hits you for 73 points of damage!

Blinking the message away, I felt the adventurer under me thrash as he twisted his body, followed by a stabbing pain in my ribs. Scrambling in distress, I felt a second thrust pierce into my side before I was able to bring my hands to bear and grab hold of the adventurer's hand, which held a bloody shortsword. Slapping the blade away, I knocked it out of the adventurer's grip, causing it to skitter across the ground at the same instant a fist appeared out of nowhere and caught me in the jaw.

As I staggered from the unexpected blow, the adventurer landed a second hit as he struck me in the face again, his free hand grabbing me by the throat. Feeling his hand tighten around my neck, I hit the man back, slamming my fist heavily into the side of his head as I fought to dislodge his arm, but to no avail.

Shit, this guy found his stones. I thought as the adventurer stubbornly maintained his grip, not even flinching as I pummeled his face. Reaching out with my free hand, I groped around blindly, desperately looking for the shortsword that I had just knocked out of the adventurer's hand.

After a few seconds of panicked searching, I felt my hand come down on something hard and reflexively grabbed hold of it, raising it over my head. Looking past me and at what I had in my hand, I saw the adventurer's hate-filled expression shift to one of revulsion and panic, his hand squeezing my throat even harder.

Unable to see whatever I had grabbed, I swung it downwards at the adventurer's head, seeing a booted leg smash into the man's face.

I just grabbed his leg, a distant part of my brain acknowledged as I desperately swung my improvised weapon at the adventurer's head again and again, watching blood spray through the air with every hit. After my fifth swing, I heard a wicked crack fill the air and felt the adventurer's hands go limp, his arms falling from around my neck as his spirit fled his broken body.

Gasping for air, I sucked in a deep breath as I looked towards my impromptu weapon, seeing that my powerful blows had broken the foot's ankle and it was now lolling awkwardly to one side. Feeling my stomach roil at the sight of the leg and the adventurer's face, I instinctively threw the leg away from me, pushing myself off of the body.

"Lazarus," I heard Sawyer call my name, his voice filled with both disgust and awe. "What the fuck, man?"

Staggering to my feet, I glanced upwards and spotted a badly singed Sawyer staring at me in horror.

"Sorry, Sawyer," I told the man, stooping to pick up my fallen sword, already trying to forget what I had just done. "What Edith and I have going on is personal, I can't afford for *anyone* to get in my way. I'd really rather not do what I just did ever again, but if you force me to...*I will.*"

Sawyer's eyes shifted from me to the adventurer I had just killed, then finally behind me, his expression falling as he absorbed what he saw.

"The risk I took was calculated," the dark-haired man sighed as he threw his weapon on the ground in front of him and held his hands above his waist. "But man...am I bad at math. Even with you all outnumbered, we never had a chance, did we?"

Trusting that Sawyer wouldn't do anything, I turned around to look how Molly and Quinn had fared with the other three bounty hunters that Sawyer had brought with him. My eyebrows rose in surprise as I saw the street behind me completely covered in burns and magical scars, making it readily evident that Molly and Quinn had just finished a close-range duel with a trio of magic users.

Despite being singed, burnt, and covered in blood, my two companions turned towards me, seeing the disarmed Sawyer holding his hands up high, and slowly began to move towards us.

"That went well," Quinn greeted me once he came into range, moving with a slight limp. I saw him take a look at the bloody adventurer on the ground, then give me a slight nod of approval. "Seems like everything is in order here."

"That was pointless, Sawyer," Molly scolded the red-armored man, scowling as she spoke. "I'm not one to turn down a bit of experience or a fight, but we didn't have time for this."

Sighing loudly, Sawyer nodded apologetically. "I can see that now, but I wouldn't have been able to live with myself if I hadn't tried, though. Eighty gold is…a hell of a lot of money."

"It is," I agreed, knowing Sawyer's motivation all too well. "And any other day, I might have taken you up on your offer…"

"But not today," Sawyer stated, a frustrated expression passing over his face. "Can you even tell me what the hell is going on? What the hell did this *Edith*, do that has you all so worked up?"

"She or someone she's working for killed Fairfax Grimm," I whispered, seeing understanding dawn across Sawyer's face.

"Oh," he said, looking towards the body of the adventurer that I had just killed as it dissipated into nothingness. "*Fuck*."

"Do you understand now?" I asked Sawyer softly as I too watched the game world clean up after itself.

"Yeah." The man ran a hand through his singed hair. "Is what she's doing related to the military leaving the city?"

"I don't know," I told the man honestly. "That's part of what we're trying to piece together. There's a hell of a lot of things going on that we haven't been able to figure out."

Sawyer was quiet for a while as he absorbed my statement, still staring at the spot his comrade had just vanished from. "I like our rivalry, Lazarus. It's fun. It keeps me on my toes and has me learning new things. But what happened here, this wasn't fun, not today…" He trailed off shaking his head. "This is really important to you, isn't it?"

"It is," I stated simply, watching the bounty hunter carefully.

"Okay." Sawyer fixed me with an intense stare. "If it's not too late, what can I do to help?"

"Y-You want to help?" Sawyer's reply had caught me completely off guard.

"I do now," Sawyer told me, an understanding look crossing his face. "I know what it means to want revenge on someone."
"Well, for one thing, you can keep fucking hunters like yourself off our tail," Molly told Sawyer bluntly as she mimed a cutting motion with her sabre. "We have enough shit on our plate to deal with and don't need people making our lives any harder."

"I know what you're getting at," Sawyer replied with a wince. "But this is a business, and hunters aren't exactly known for *listening* to one another; they go where the money is."

"Then spread the word of Edith's bounty," I grunted. "I wasn't lying to you when I told you the guild put a hundred-gold reward on her. For that amount of cash, you should be willing to get nearly every hunter left in the city looking for her."

"The cut will suck," Sawyer began, before seeing all of our unhappy expressions and adjusting his response. "But I'm pretty sure we can drown her in numbers, if nothing else. I can't cancel the bounty on you, though; that's not how the system works."

"That's fine," I replied with a shrug. "The more people that are busy specifically looking for her, the fewer people will be out looking for us."

"And if we do find her?" Sawyer asked. "You want us to kill her?"

"Captured," Molly answered, glancing between Quinn and me. "In fact, send us a private message if you find her, and we'll come running."

"That may be a bad idea with the bounty still on Lazarus," Sawyer warned. "Being greedy as hell is a prerequisite to be a hunter, and seeing two huge bounties side by side could cause everything to go to shit."

"We'll cross that bridge if we get there," I said, holding up a hand, indicating that I still had more to say. "One thing you should know about Edith, though, she's been...*twisted* by magic and doesn't entirely look all that normal anymore."

"Of course she wouldn't be," Sawyer deadpanned, looking at me with an unreadable expression. "Why would anything be simple?"

"Don't underestimate her," I told the man.

"I'll see what I can do," Sawyer said confidently, before a worried expression crossed his face as he looked at my sword. "So what happens now? You going to give me a free ride across the city? Or do I get to walk away from this in one piece?"

"You may be a persistent pain in my ass, Sawyer," I said, letting a small smile creep across my face as I lowered my sword and stepped to the side, giving the man plenty of room to pass. "But I think we're done fighting each other, at least for the next little while."

"Until this is all sorted out," Sawyer stated, returning my smile.

"Until this is all sorted out," I acknowledged.

FOURTEEN

"ARE YOU SURE IT WAS a good idea to tell Sawyer about Fairfax?" Molly asked nearly a half hour later, once we were off the street and descending down into the guild headquarters. "Isabella hasn't decided to make that public yet."

"Sawyer might be a greedy hunter," I replied with a confident nod, "but over the last couple weeks, we've developed an understanding between one another, and I felt it was something I could trust him with."

"How do you even know Sawyer that well?" Quinn questioned. "I've run across hunters a handful of times, and they're only interested in the bounty. Not whatever you two have going on."

"I first met him during Fairfax's initiation trials," I told the mage. "Fairfax had me doing a quick break-and-enter into a merchant's office, and I had the bad luck to crawl out of a window the same moment that Sawyer was watching.

"We had a running fight halfway through the city," I continued, remembering the chase. "Ended up with me taking a dive off of a building to get away."

"Hang on, that was the ledger mission." Molly looked at me with a curious expression. "Wasn't that also the day when you crushed that produce vendor's stall and came back all covered in...*juices*?"

"Uh, yeah." I coughed with embarrassment, remembering both Fairfax's and Molly's reaction when I had returned from the mission. "It was the softest thing I could find to land on."

Molly couldn't help but giggle as she shook her head. "You never said anything about being chased by a bounty hunter!"

"I figured Fairfax would have excused clumsiness more than he would have getting a hunter's attention," I answered with a sigh.

"He didn't." Molly laughed again.

"No." I shook my head, remembering the grueling training regimen that he had assigned to me afterwards to *cure* me of my made-up clumsiness. "But it sure did help me with my fear of heights."

"We really need to sit down one day and trade stories." Quinn let out a soft laugh beside me as we continued our descent into the guild's lower levels. "I thought I had an interesting run with the odd burgle here or there, but it seems to me I might be the most boring one here."

"Lazarus likes to live life on the edge," Molly said somewhat mockingly. "Or maybe he doesn't, seeing how he's died *six* times already."

"That's nearly a death every three days since the game came out," Quinn observed, doing the mental math.

"They weren't all my fault," I replied defensively, motioning a hand towards Molly. "And I did save you from the statue, after all."

"That's right," Molly admitted, conceding the point. "Thanks again for that, by the way."

Chatting amongst ourselves as we finished the trek, we found our way into the guild common room, finding it nearly deserted as we entered the room with only Bart and Goner sitting at a table together.

"Lazarus, Molly!" Goner's voice called from the other side of the room as he waved towards us. "You're back! How did everything go?"

"Not as good as we would have liked, but not as bad as it could have been," I answered with a sigh, seeing Bart's weathered eye look us over, noting the singed and ragged parts of our armor.

"Looks like you three had trouble," Bart said slowly. "That or you decided to take a tumble in a fireplace with razors in your hands."

"Ha!" Quinn snorted. "Had a problem with hunters on our way back."

Bart's eyes rose in surprise. "Hunters? Do tell."

"You were right earlier today about someone being angry about last night, though we are pretty sure Edith was behind it. She's put a fat enough bounty on my head that Sawyer caught wind of it and he tried to collect," I told the old thief. "Things got a bit rough, but they didn't put up much of a fight. I think I may have convinced Sawyer to leave us alone for a time, too."

"I warned ya," Bart replied as he shook his head. "Heard enough complaints today while we were walking our route about the city being turned upside down. Surprised none of the gangs took a swing at you out of spite."

"Me too," Molly agreed. "The streets felt wrong today, especially the few nobles and merchants we saw walking around. They all had guards with them and looked like they were ready to bolt if the wind changed."

"About sums up what we saw too," Bart agreed, looking over to the young thief listening to us intently. "What do you think, boy?"

"Everyone is scared, and fewer people are buying or selling at the markets," Goner replied while trying to look at all of us at once. "A bunch of the drops we were supposed to pick up were empty today, too, at least half of them."

"Everyone who was out buying today was looking for food," Bart told us while nodding at the young thief-in-training. "Prices have already gone up at least by half compared to yesterday."

"People always buy and store food when they think something is going to go wrong," Quinn said. "It's no different if there's a snowstorm or a hurricane warning."

"Wish I could say that all of this would pass as quickly as a bad storm," Bart stated with a sigh. "I have a feeling we've only begun to see what is in store for us."

"You think there's going to be a war?" Goner asked, nervousness clearly evident in his voice.

"I don't know, Goner," Bart replied as he looked at the boy. "But the military doesn't leave the city just to stretch its legs."

"I know," the boy said. "I used to watch the soldiers when we were still fighting the orcs. Every day, I'd see them going towards *The Bulwark*, and every day, I'd see the hurt ones coming back. Ma and Da just told me that's the way things were, that the war had gone on for longer than they were alive and they were sad about that. But when the war ended, everyone was so happy. If it starts again…"

The older thief was silent for a moment as thoughts raced around in his mind. "I should see if we can get you somewhere safer than in the den here, Goner."

"Wait, what? I don't want to leave here!" Goner practically shouted as panic crossed his face. "This is my *home*!"

"You deserve a safer home than this, Goner," Bart said, looking towards us for support. "At least until you're older and can protect yourself."

"I'm *Eberian*," the boy hissed. "I was born knowing how to protect myself! The guild took me in when Ma and Da didn't come back; it's only fair I find a way to help it back! I'm not going to abandon it, not when you're all finally giving me jobs to do!"

"You're right, Goner," I cut in, happy that this opportunity had arisen. "But there is more than one way to help, and what the guild needs the most isn't a boy who knows how to swing a sword or pick someone's pocket."

"What do you mean?" Goner looked at me suspiciously. "That's what the guild does; we steal what we want, and we fight if we need to."

"There is a lot more to the guild than that," Molly added, seeing Bart's slow nod of approval. "Can you read? Can you write? If you want to really help the guild, you need to know how to do that."

"I can read!" Goner exclaimed defensively before he started to deflate. "Not very well, though…"

"And that's okay," Molly told the boy soothingly. "You have plenty of time to learn."

"But I don't want to leave here to do that!" Goner whined, his voice taking on a desperate tone. "This is the only family I have left!"

"Leaving here won't change anything, Goner," I said, remembering Fairfax's wake last night. "You're one of us, no matter where you go, but if you want to find out the best way to help the guild, you're going to have to go out and learn."

"Oh yeah?" Goner looked up at me from the table. "Where am I going to do that? That takes money, and I don't have any."

"Well," I started with a smile. "Quinn happens to know a man that needs help managing his library and has offered to teach you a few things if you're willing to help him out."
"Lazarus is right," Quinn confirmed, nodding at the young boy. "William may be old, but he's also a mage. He might be able to teach you a few things."

"You mean I can learn *magic*?" Goner asked, jumping to the one thing all young children fantasized about.

"You *might* be able to," Quinn replied. "That depends if you have the gift, and if you work hard enough."

"It would really help the guild out a lot, Goner," Bart added, his eyes twinkling as he looked at us. "We need to have guild members that can read and write, but if you can learn how to do magic...now, that would be *something*."

"Well, that may not be so bad, then," Goner admitted. "I can learn what I need to learn, then I can come back and be helpful!"

"You would have to study very hard," Quinn warned, waving a finger at the boy. "William is really old and doesn't have a lot of time; you'd have to make sure to pay attention to what he says."

"I can do that!" Goner stated enthusiastically. "I won't let the guild down!"

"We will have to check with Isabella before any of this can happen." I looked towards Bart, who winced before nodding in agreement.

"I'm sure Bella would have no problem in letting Goner go study with the man," the older thief began somberly. "But there's been some more bad news coming down since you lot left. Perhaps it'd be best to ask her in a day or two when she's got her head on straight."

"What happened?" Molly asked, the three of us freezing at Bart's grave tone.

"You'd be best to get it from her, to be honest," he replied, motioning towards the far side of the common room where Isabella had set up her office this morning. "I don't know if it's free to be spread just yet, though if she doesn't soon, word's likely to get out on its own anyway."

"Shit," I heard Quinn curse. "What else could go wrong?"

Bart looked at us with a sad expression. "What couldn't?"

TAKING A MOMENT TO COLLECT ourselves after the older thief's warning, the three of us hesitantly made our way across the common room and towards Isabella's temporary office. Finding the door closed as we approached, I knocked on the door while exchanging worried glances with Molly and Quinn.

"Isabella, it's us," I called through the door. "We're back from seeing Quinn's contact."

There was a moment of silence before Isabella replied, "Enter."

Pushing open the door, the three of us walked into the office and closed the door behind us, spotting Isabella sitting alone at a paper-covered desk on the far side of the room, her hair disheveled and eyes red.

"Isabella, are you okay?" Molly was the first to ask, as she saw the stress on our thief lord's face.

"No," she replied quietly, looking up at us in shock. "No, I am not."

"What happened?" I asked, seeing her glazed-over eyes as they stared blankly towards us.

Staring blankly, it took a few moments for my voice to reach through her stupor and her eyes finally focused.

"Crawridge's heir was just killed by Amberwain's heir in the New District a couple of hours ago," Isabella whispered, her eyes shifting across each of us as she spoke. "Wynbrandt's heir was apparently there as well and was seriously injured; she's not expected to live out the day. There are over two dozen dead in total, when you include retainers, guards, and other bystanders. The three houses are furious at one another, and from the little that I've heard so far, they're on the verge of breaking out into open warfare."

The three of us just stared at Isabella blankly as we absorbed her statement, our mouths having fallen open as we stared on in disbelief, trying to understand how three of the five major noble houses had gotten themselves in a brawl.

"But that's not all," Isabella continued as she shook her head. "According to the witness, it seems that there were devils involved."

"Devils?" I asked, feeling the bottom of my stomach fall out as I heard the word from Isabella. "*How?*"

"Exactly how you told me it happened to you," Isabella explained. "A pair of retainers, possibly three if the rumors are true, *transformed* and burst into flames without warning...twisting them into unholy creatures."

"How did all three houses even get involved?" Molly asked, processing everything Isabella had told us much faster than Quinn and I. "Amberwain hates both Wynbrandt and Crawridge; they wouldn't want to be in the same *district* as them, let alone close enough to fight."

"From what I've been able to discover so far, they were each invited to an early-morning soirée at a new banquet hall," Isabella told us as she clasped her hands together to keep them from trembling. "How they arranged the timing of it all to keep them from seeing one another, I do not know, but everything happened once they were all led into the dining hall..."

"That's when the retainers transformed..." Quinn guessed. "They all must have thought it was treachery from the other side."

"Edith did this," Molly stated bitterly, her voice turning to anger. "She organized this and trapped all of them there."

"Yeah," I agreed, echoing Molly's tone. "But *why*? What would she gain from killing off the two heirs and effectively framing another?"

"Inciting conflict?" Quinn offered. "Seem obvious to me."

"But to what end?" I questioned. "I can't even imagine what she or anyone else would stand to gain from this."

"Has the king done or said anything?" Molly asked Isabella, watching the woman shake her head.

"If he has, it hasn't reached my ears yet, though at this point, the attack isn't common knowledge on the street yet, either," the woman told us as she cast her eyes downward. "Though I expect him to do exactly what he's done since the Call to Arms ceremony. *Nothing.*"

"The king is useless," I said out of reflex as a thought occurred to me. "Wait, why were only three of the houses involved?"

"What do you mean?" Isabella asked as she looked up at me. "This disaster was bad enough; we're lucky enough *only* three were involved."

"No, not that, I think Lazarus is onto something," Quinn interjected. "Both House Phineas and Denarius weren't involved in this. Though in the case of House Denarius, I can understand; they're pretty insular as a whole."

"Phineas definitely isn't, though," Molly said. "They're renowned for being socialites. Why were they excluded?"

"You have a point," Isabella admitted. "We'll have to investigate both houses and determine why neither was present."

Letting out a deep sigh as she composed herself, Isabella looked up at the three us with a hopeful look in her eye. "With all we have going on, *please* tell me that you've learned something useful from Quinn's contact."

"We've learned quite a bit from William," I started while collecting my thoughts. "Though I'm not sure how much of it is *useful.* He wasn't able to shed much light on how Edith was controlling or summoning the devils with the strange talismans that I saw before," I explained. "Save that it would be a reasonably time-consuming process to create them and would involve a great deal of knowledge and access to rare crafting materials."

"Which pretty much confirms what we thought before," Molly added. "Edith isn't working alone and has to have a fair bit of financial backing."

"Given the size of the bounty that was placed on Lazarus's head, I think that's pretty evident, too," Quinn chimed in, seeing a surprised look cross Isabella's face as he spoke.

"You ran into hunters?" Her eyes dropped down to our armor for the first time, seeing the scratches and burns from the battle.

"We ran into Sawyer and his crew looking to collect," I replied as I waved my hand dismissively at Isabella's concern. "But after taking the time to listen to me, Sawyer decided that his energies would be better spent looking for Edith instead of me. If he finds her, he's promised to send word."

"And you trust this hunter to fulfill this promise?" Isabella looked at me with disbelief.

"I trust him to try," I stated, meeting Isabella's eye as I spoke. "We've agreed on a temporary truce until she's caught."

"I don't share your optimism," Isabella told me as she shook her head. "But we have so few options available to us that I'm willing to grasp at straws if it allows us even a moment to catch our breath. It was the whole reason why I posted the bounty on Edith in the first place. What of the sigil?" Isabella prompted. "Is this something that we need to be concerned about as well?"

"That…I don't know either," I admitted as I began to explain everything that had happened with William once he had seen the sigil. "Without knowing how exactly I got the sigil in the first place, William wasn't able to tell me much else, other than it being a clean sigil, without any controlling influences from the Ascendant Empire that he saw before the fall."

"I have far too much on my mind to even *consider* what I would do if your will was not your own, so I will count it as a blessing that it is not the case," Isabella breathed softly as she shook her head at my explanation.

"Unfortunately, past that, William wasn't able to add in anything more concrete without knowing exactly what sort of artifact was stolen from the Arcaneum," Quinn told Isabella. "We can only guess at what Edith has planned at this point."

"Which makes it all the more important that we find her before she can put her plan into motion," Isabella replied with a curt nod at the mage as she unclasped her hands and pushed herself up from her seat. "I will take pains to explicitly stress that point at the meeting with the thief lords tonight. If the four other guilds can combine with our resources and the hunters, I am confident we can drive her out of hiding. Short of leaving the city, no one can hide from the Eberian underworld forever."

"We can't forget about Ransom, either," Molly added, remembering the other party member that had joined us on our heist. "He's been missing this entire time, but given the fact that he's a warlock and that there are devils involved…we should probably be looking for him, too."

"A good idea," Isabella agreed with a nod as she walked around her desk and stopped before us, looking at each of us in the eye in turn. "I've long prided myself on knowing everything that happens in Eberia, keeping tabs on what each faction is doing and how the guild could best exploit it. The last two days have humbled me in a way that I have never been before.

"First with Fairfax's death…" Isabella swallowed hard as she spoke, pausing for a moment before continuing. "Then again with the military suddenly leaving, and now with the slaughter of the noble heirs. It has become readily apparent that I need more help in order to manage all of the guild's affairs, and I want to extend my thanks for the work each of you has done so far," Isabella continued. "Things are changing faster than I could have ever imagined since you adventurers have joined us, and I for one am glad to have you three on my side."

"We'll catch Edith," I said, glancing over at Quinn and Molly, who nodded in agreement. "And we'll find out who killed Fairfax, too."

"This is our family," Molly added softly, capturing exactly how I had come to feel in the last day. "There's nothing we wouldn't do for our family."

"It warms my heart to hear that," Isabella replied sincerely. "The meeting with the thief lords is a few hours away, so we still have time before we must depart. Take some time to rest and clean up. If the meeting goes as well as I hope it will, then this will likely be our last chance to rest for a while. Because once we find out what really happened to Fairfax, *there will be hell to pay.*"

FIFTEEN

"NOW THIS IS MORE LIKE what I thought being a criminal would be like," Quinn said with an eager smile, his voice echoing all around us as we walked. "Skulking around the sewers and going to a secret meeting underground."

"Speak for yourself," Molly replied with a strangled cough. "This place smells *awful.* I can't wait to get out of here."

"The smell will only get worse the deeper we get," Isabella commented. "We have a quite a bit further to go until we reach the meeting place, but in the meantime, keep your voices down. Echoes carry far here, and I rather not attract any caimans by being careless."

"Wait, there's caimans down here?" I saw Quinn's smile fade off his face as he spoke.

"And more." Isabella gave Quinn a grim smile as she looked over her shoulder towards him, then motioned to the river of fetid water that filled the massive channel in the center of the sewer. "They enjoy hiding in the water and prey on other creatures in the sewer."

"Ah," Quinn replied nervously, his head swiveling to follow Isabella's hand. "Okay, I can't wait to get out of here either now."

Chuckling softly to myself at Quinn's sudden change of heart, I decided to listen to Isabella's advice and scanned the slow-moving river of dirty water as it slowly filtered itself through the ancient sewer. In contrast to the rest of the Nafarrian ruins in the city, the sewers that survived them were in near perfect condition, having been protected from the centuries of exposure that the surface ruins of the city had been forced to endure.

Set with a walkway on both sides of the channel, the four of us easily traveled through the sewers, happy that we did not have to wade through the endless filth that flowed out of the city. Isabella hadn't mentioned to us how far we needed to travel to the meeting place where the thief lords traditionally held their meetings, only that it would take us nearly an hour to wind our way through the convoluted tunnels of the sewer system and take us into the deepest levels that normally went untraveled.

Keeping an eye on the waters as we walked, I found my mind wandering from the boredom of watching the relatively placid waters and replaying the events of the last few hours.

After being dismissed by Isabella, the three of us had enjoyed the opportunity to catch our breaths and clean ourselves up after our short but violent excursion out into the city. However, as we rested, more word had gradually filtered in about the attack on the noble heirs, none of it filling us with any cheer. True to the news that Isabella had received earlier, the one wounded heir belonging to House Wynbrandt had ended up succumbing to her wounds quicker than anticipated, leaving the house pointing angry fingers at both Crawridge and Amberwain, condemning both houses for being caught in the middle of their feud. The last that we had heard before setting out to the meeting was that each of the houses had mobilized their house guards and were taking aggressive precautions to fortify their residences should events spiral out into open conflict.

To make matters worse, there had been no word from the palace since the attack occurred, despite watchers for the guild spotting at least three messengers, one from each of the affected noble houses, going to notify the king. I had no idea what he found to be more important than running his kingdom, but it seemed that the king had no interest in the conflict that was brewing between all the nobles.

The city might just collapse into civil war, I thought to myself grimly as I continued to scan the waters below us, keeping a wary eye out for any of the caimans that Isabella had mentioned. *And with nearly everyone in the city having military training of some sort, any civil war is bound to get bloody fast.*

"The Nafarr must have been really advanced," I heard Molly whisper, bringing me back to the present as Isabella led us down a passage that began to gradually slope downward. "This whole sewer looks like it could have supported hundreds of thousands of inhabitants easily."

"They certainly built this to last," Quinn agreed, his eyes darting around as he admired the construction. "I would have never known something like this was under the city. Have you two been down here before?"

"Not this deep," I answered softly, scanning ahead to see if I could figure out where Isabella was taking us.

"Same," Molly replied as she let out a small cough, the stench of the sewers still affecting her.

Moving without any hesitation, Isabella gradually began to pick up her pace as we entered the deepest levels of the sewer. Looking at her posture and how quickly her eyes scanned the area, I sensed that the urgency was due to the creatures that she had referred to earlier. Given the way that our day had played out so far, the last thing we needed was to be ambushed at this point in time.

Though a fight might help Isabella relax, I said to myself, unable to help but notice how high-strung Isabella was at the moment. Multiple crises had been dropped into her lap within the span of two days, and NPC or not, that was bound to put someone on edge. I hoped that after meeting the other thief lords, we would get a chance to catch our breaths and start to restore some semblance of balance within the city.

For the next twenty minutes, Isabella's pace continued to increase as she led us into the deepest parts of Eberia's sewer system until we were nearly jogging, speed becoming more important than stealth the further we went. We wound through countless tunnels, eventually leaving me feeling completely lost as any sense of direction I had vanished. Staring directly at the back of Isabella's head, I began to resign myself to the fact that it would be easier to die and respawn back at the guild headquarters than it would be to find my own way out of the sewer. Judging from the lost expressions that I saw on both Molly's and Quinn's faces, I didn't think that they felt any different.

"We're here," Isabella whispered finally as we turned into an abrupt dead end, causing all of us to stare at her numbly.

"They're going to meet us here?" I asked, looking around the small platform we were standing on. "There's barely enough room for the four of us on here, let alone the other thief lords and their retainers!"

"Not *here.*" Isabella shook her head at me with an ominous smile as she reached into her pocket and pulled something out. "This is just the entrance—*our entrance.*"

"Our entrance?" Molly echoed as she tried to look around me.

"This is the Grim Shadows' entrance into the Council of Thieves," Isabella explained as she held up a familiar coin. "Each of the guilds have their own entrance to the council, and each entrance will only open to a specific key."

"That's the coin I found on Fairfax!" I hissed in surprise, seeing my old mentor's face still emblazoned on the side of it.

"It is." Isabella nodded at me with a smile. "It is the most important thing that the guild possesses, and without it, we would be barred from entering the council or having a say in how the other guilds conduct business in Eberia."

I looked at Isabella with a stupefied expression on my face. Had I not gone back to search Fairfax's body in the Undertaker chamber, the guild would have been rendered completely impotent, losing its place in the city's criminal hierarchy until it was found.

If it was found.

"How does it work?" I asked, looking towards the featureless wall behind Isabella and wondering where the entrance was. "I don't see anything on this wall."

"This isn't a wall," Isabella replied, her smile widening as she turned around and held the coin up in the air. "At least not one made of brick and mortar."

Before any of us could ask Isabella what she meant, the coin pulsed with a gentle flash of white light, causing the entire sewer wall in front of us to dissolve as if it were never there, revealing an ominous tunnel leading to the dark.

"*Oh*," I gasped, my brain completely caught by surprise, hearing both Molly and Quinn have similar reactions.

"It is partly an illusion combined in with a host of other magics I do not understand," Isabella explained as she motioned for us to follow her. "Regardless, it will reseal itself within a few moments. Come quickly."

"How did you even create something like this?" Quinn asked, completely dumbfounded as the four of us hurried down the tunnel.

"The king made it for us," Isabella whispered. "As part of his deal long ago."

"Hold on," Quinn gasped, not knowing the true story of the guild's origin. "*The king?*"

"I'll tell you later, Quinn," I whispered to the man as I spotted the mouth of the tunnel in the distance. "It's a long story."

"No fucking shit!" Quinn muttered under his breath.

Walking down the tunnel in silence, the four of us entered into a massive, five-spoked chamber that I could only describe as the Nafarrian equivalent of a sewer hub. Reaching nearly forty feet into the air, the huge room made me realize just how deep we had traveled underground.

"Damn, everyone is waiting," Isabella said as she pointed to a large circular platform ahead of us, suspended a few feet over a massive basin. Looking in the distance, I could see several figures waiting, each of them standing far apart from one another. "We're the last ones to arrive; we'd best hurry."

Moving with purpose, Isabella led the way, stepping out onto a metal walkway that bridged the gap between the tunnel and the central platform. Following close behind, I couldn't help but look down as we walked, feeling uncomfortable as I gazed into the black, foul-smelling water that filled the basin a few short feet below us. As we crossed the walkway, I noticed occasional ladders built into the side it, reaching down into the water.

Maybe to help people get out of the water? I mused as my eye followed the ladders downward, spotting something ripple beneath the surface. Eyes widening, I blinked them furiously as I tried to make sense of what I had seen. No sooner had I reopened them than did I see a tentacle poke free of the water and immediately vanish.

"Isabella, there's something in the water," I whispered, suddenly feeling exposed as I saw another tentacle appear a short distance away.

"I know," the woman whispered back to me with a raised eyebrow. "Where did you think all the garbage in the city went? It's constantly being eaten by a colony of otyugh."

"*Oty-what?*" I heard Quinn gasp behind me the same moment I felt Molly grab my back.

"Are they dangerous to us?" I hissed, vaguely remembering the three-legged and three-tentacled creatures from other games I had played.

Isabella cocked her head at me as if I were stupid. "Of course they are, but only if you fall into the water."

"Right," I said slowly as Isabella turned around and continued walking towards the platform, causing us to follow closely while keeping an eye on the water below us.

Glancing ahead as we approached the center of the hub, I saw four figures standing on the edge of the platform, each of them watching us silently as we approached.

The thief lords are all here. I felt my heart beat in excitement as we began to ascend up the platform, allowing me to spot several pairs of retainers, waiting an arm's length behind each thief lord. *And they all brought people too. But is it because they don't trust one another, or is it because the sewers are that dangerous?*

"It's about time you all showed up," a harsh voice called out towards the four of us as we all stopped at the very edge of the platform. "Being late to your own meeting is bad enough, but—*wait.*" The voice paused for a moment. "Where is Fairfax? Why isn't he with you?"

Looking towards the voice that had just spoken, I saw a tall, wiry Eberian man completely covered in dark leather armor, watching the four of us intently as his bright blue eyes searched for our old thief lord.

"That is why I called this meeting, Dorian," Isabella replied. "Fairfax is dead. Murdered, we believe. I've come to claim his spot on the council and inform everyone of what we've learned surrounding his death. We believe that it is linked to all the chaos consuming the city."

There was a moment of silence as Isabella's words were processed, followed by murmurs throughout the assembled thief lords and retainers.

"Two nights ago, after we received word of the incident between the Royal Guard and the military, Fairfax departed to the palace, fearing that the geas was still in effect," Isabella wasted no time in continuing, the whispering voices ceasing the moment that Isabella mentioned the old king's binding. "The following morning, his body was discovered by one of my guild members, cut, burned, and beaten."

"It has long been determined that the geas is no longer in effect," Dorian answered Isabella derisively. "If it were, *all* of us here would have felt its consequences, yet none of us have."

"Or have none of us felt its consequences because Fairfax went in our stead?" a feminine voice asked, as an orange-robed thief lord slowly walked towards the center of the platform.

"We have been ignored for over a *year*," Dorian exclaimed tiredly, clearly having had this argument before. "We have felt nothing from the geas in all that time because it is *gone*."

"Regardless, the death of one of our own is most serious, especially so if it wasn't compelled by the geas that has hung over us," the orange-robed woman stated aloud, before directing a question towards Isabella. "Do you have proof of Fairfax's death, beyond the key that allowed you here?"

Feeling a sense of unease shoot through me as I glanced at the thief lord's face, I found myself gazing directly into a featureless jade mask that had been polished completely smooth. Stopping directly in the center of the platform, I was close enough to see our reflections in the thief lord's mask as she regarded us impassively.

This must be Smiling Jade, I told myself, remembering the little that I had heard about the enigmatic leader of the Faceless Ones, a guild of thieves who all wore masks to hide their identity, even amongst themselves.

"I do," Isabella stated confidently, as she inclined her head towards me. "This is the guild member who found Fairfax's body; he was the one responsible for recovering Fairfax's key. Without him, we would have never known of Fairfax's death."

"Indeed?" The masked thief lord's voice sounded curious as I somehow felt her gaze shift onto me. "We have heard your name before, adventurer. However, formalities must be observed. Introduce yourself to the council."

They know me? I thought to myself, suddenly feeling nervous. I glanced at Isabella, who nodded at me curtly and motioned for me to answer the question.

"My name is Lazarus Cain," I replied as I took a step forward towards Smiling Jade.

"The council recognizes you, Lazarus." Smiling Jade nodded to me as she swept her hand to indicate the other thief lords circling the platform. "I presume you are aware of the other lords who share this council with me?"

"Only by reputation," I answered, looking towards the two other thief lords who had yet to say anything since our arrival.

"But of course." Smiling Jade inclined her head in understanding. "You are new to the underworld, fresh as a babe torn from the womb. Perhaps introductions are in order before you are put to the question."

I felt my stomach churn at the thief lord's choice of words, but I slowly nodded in agreement, feeling it was wiser to remain silent for the time being.

"You have already been introduced to Dorian, the leader of the Damned, his warm greetings notwithstanding." Smiling Jade shifted her body towards the dark-haired Eberian that had greeted Isabella earlier, only to have the man scowl at me as his name was mentioned.

"Next we have Stroud." Smiling Jade then motioned towards a hulking mountain of a man who inclined his head towards me at the sound of his name. "The leader of the Dead Eyes."

Taller than even I was, it was clear that Stroud shared the same half-giant ancestry as I did, though with a human half instead of my elven. Clad in a mix of chainmail and leather, the thief lord's face was the only bit of flesh that was visible on the massive man's body, and even then it was covered by a thick brown beard. Holding a massive two-handed axe on his shoulder, the thief lord regarded me with a blank expression, his eyes completely devoid of emotion.

"And then there is Kiera," the orange-robed thief lord finished, sweeping her hand to indicate a Tul'Shar bearing a fur pattern resembling a tiger. "The leader of the Crimson Rats."

"It is always exciting to have fresh meat in our circle," Kiera purred as she appraised me, her yellow eyes causing a chill to descend down my spine. "Perhaps this one may yet survive long enough to be entertaining."

In great contrast to Stroud, the feline thief lord hardly wore any armor at all, choosing to wear a scandalous array of leather straps across her body that just barely managed to cover everything important—leaving plenty of skin, or in her case, fur, exposed for all to see. Hanging from her waist, I saw a pair of scabbarded shortswords shifting from side to side as she swung her hips.

"And I am Smiling Jade." The masked thief lord stopped moving, and I felt her focus her faceless gaze onto me once again. "I represent the Faceless Ones."

"It is an honor to meet you all," I said nervously, not knowing anything better to say.

"Is it?" Smiling Jade asked, sounding amused. "*Curious.* Not many think so."

Staring at the strange thief lord, completely at a loss for words, I ground my teeth together, deciding that remaining quiet until I was asked a question was the best idea.

"He remains silent," Smiling Jade noted with amusement. "Perhaps he will survive in our world after all."

"*Enough*, Jade," Stroud's deep voice grumbled. "One of our own lies dead, and the city above us is in chaos. We do not have time for your games."

"Pity." The woman turned her body towards the massive warrior. "Since you are so eager, I will allow you to begin with the questioning."

"If I must," the large man grunted as Smiling Jade whirled around and began to glide back towards her spot, where I was shocked to discover that three identically dressed retainers waited, each appearing exactly like Smiling Jade.

Clearing his throat to get my attention, Stroud's commanding voice filled the air. "Describe to us how you came across Fairfax's body. I am curious to hear *why* you were near the palace in the first place. Since such a transgression would normally be punishable by death, or in your kind's case, exile."

"I didn't find Fairfax's body in the palace," I answered as I shook my head at the thief lord. "We weren't anywhere near it, in fact."

Raising a single eyebrow in curiosity, the thief lord looked at me thoughtfully. "Oh? Where, then?"

"In an Undertaker torture chamber," I stated, meeting Stroud's eye as I spoke. "Someone was trying to get rid of Fairfax's body, and it was only dumb luck that I was there before they managed to dispose of it."

"An Undertaker torture chamber?" Stroud repeated, his nose and beard twitching at the mention of the street gang's name. "What were you doing there?"

"I...was a prisoner," I admitted after a moment, feeling embarrassed at the admission under the large thief lord's glare.

"Why—"

"Let the man tell his story, Stroud," I heard Kiera's voice hiss from behind me, already tired of the other thief lord's interruptions. "My fur is becoming damper every moment we spend here; let us finish this quickly so we can be gone. Ask your questions afterward."

"Very well," Stroud replied with a frustrated sigh before nodding at me to continue.

Speaking carefully, I retold the story of waking up in the torture chamber with the Sigil of Rage emblazoned on my chest, and how my memories had been blocked from the heist at the Arcaneum. The moment that I had mentioned the Mages Guild building, I heard a sudden intake of breath from everyone in the room, but no one interrupted my explanation as I outlined what had happened in the torture chamber and my decision to confront Cayden.

"Then Cayden told me he was supposed to meet—"

"So, *you* were the one responsible for destroying my gang and setting my building on fire?" Dorian's rage-filled voice cut through the air, causing me to turn around towards him, seeing the dark-haired man completely consumed by rage as he slowly stalked towards me. "Do you have *any* idea how much trouble you have caused by doing that?"

"*Dorian, what is the meaning of this?*" Kiera snarled viciously as she rushed in front of the thief lord and cut him off before he could reach me. "Your street gang was responsible for aiding someone who *killed* one of our peers. Lazarus was well within his rights to do what he did; I would *expect* my guild to do the same for me."

"Are you actually buying any of the filth that he is spewing, Kiera?" Dorian spat, as he looked over the Tul'Shar's shoulder towards me. "He claims that his memories have been stolen from him 'somehow' during a heist into the Arcaneum, which we all know is nigh impregnable, and that afterwards he just happened to wake up halfway across the city, in the chambers of one of the most profitable street gangs in Eberia, which he then promptly destroyed, *just because* Fairfax's body was conveniently there, also somehow appearing halfway across the city from the palace where he was rumored to be visiting.

"This story is full of too many holes to hold water," Dorian declared, shifting his glance towards the blonde-haired spymistress. "This is merely an elaborate concoction *with* Fairfax just to destroy one of my most profitable assets and weaken my guild."

"*Are you serious?*" I couldn't help but hiss as I stared at Dorian over Kiera's smaller form. "I *saw* Fairfax's body with my own eyes. I took his key off his body."

"Yet no one else did, and you conveniently don't have a body to show us, either! With the geas gone, all Fairfax would need to do is *give* you his key to be allowed into here!" Dorian growled at me. "Oh, and this *mysterious woman* that supposedly delivered both you and Fairfax to Cayden, who is she? Where is she? I find it remarkably convenient that there is someone nameless to blame in all of this."

"I never said that I didn't know who the woman was," I replied, feeling my hackles rise as I took a step forward, refusing to be intimidated by the belligerent thief lord. "You interrupted me before I could finish my story! Cayden set up a meeting with her at Stone Sailor's Pier, a meeting I attended in his stead! I in fact *know* very well who she is!"

"Do you now?" Dorian answered mockingly. "And how are we to know that this isn't yet another fabrication in your carefully crafted web of lies?"

"This is ridiculous!" Isabella shouted from the far end of the platform. "Everything Lazarus has said is true, stop trying to turn this onto yourself, Dorian!"

"Isabella is correct, Dorian, you overstep yourself!" Smiling Jade's voice rang out from behind me, her earlier playful tone gone. "I have heard nothing unbelievable in Lazarus's tale, and it brings me to wonder why you seek to censure him so."

"His actions have directly cost me hundreds of gold pieces a month in income during a time that the city is in unrest!" Dorian snarled. "It will take me time and money I do not have to rebuild a similar organization! I have a *right* to be angry!"

"You do have a right to be angry," Stroud commented behind me. "However, it seems to me it should be directed solely towards Cayden."

"It's hard to be angry at a dead man!" Dorian barked as he began to turn around and stalk back towards his side of the platform. "I have had enough of this. As it is, I already have far too much to do with too little time, let alone spend it here while my holdings are being razed to the ground."

"Dorian!" Isabella's voice shouted through the air. "Where do you think you're going?"

"I am leaving," the thief lord called over his shoulder. "I am tired of talking to those who will not listen to me, and I no longer wish to be here."

"We are in the middle of a question, Dorian!" Smiling Jade exclaimed. "Just because you do not like the answers you are hearing does not mean you are free to leave!"

"Watch me!" Dorian shouted.

"Who was this woman you met, Lazarus?" Kiera asked, turning her head as she looked over her shoulder towards me, trying to get the meeting back on track. "Was she an adventurer like yourself?"

"Yes," I stated with a nod while staring directly at Dorian's back. "Her name is Edith, and she confessed to me that she witnessed Fairfax's death when I confronted her yesterday. Furthermore, I saw her summon the same kind of devils that were rumored to be involved in the slaughter of three noble houses' heirs this afternoon."

Dorian stopped walking, and I heard him whisper a faint curse.

"Her name is...*Edith?*" Kiera's yellow eyes widened as her head snapped back towards Dorian, a low growl emanating from her throat. "Dorian, the new adventurer you presented to us last week shared the same, did she not?"

Several heartbeats passed as Dorian did not reply.

"I remember that name as well." Smiling Jade's voice grew louder as she glided across the platform towards us. "*Curious*. Perhaps your sudden haste to leave is because you are aware of what she has done? Perhaps she has done it on your order? This is *most* serious, Dorian."

"I tried to save all of you," Dorian said aloud with his back still turned towards us as he began shaking his head, his voice growing angry. "I tried to make sure that no one died needlessly."

Spinning around with an angry expression on his face, Dorian's eyes landed on me.

"But you just had to meddle in things you didn't understand! You have no idea what I'm trying to prevent!"

Shouting the same word of power I heard Edith shout the day before, Dorian quickly conjured a ball of fire in his hand and, before I could react, threw it directly at me.

SIXTEEN

COVERING MY FACE AS THE fireball detonated just in front of me, I felt a wash of searing heat singe my body, followed by the twin shouts of surprise from Kiera and Smiling Jade as they were caught in the blast.

"*Dorian!*" I heard Smiling Jade shout a heartbeat before the dark-haired thief lord followed up his surprise attack with a wave of pure force that knocked Kiera and me completely off our feet and sent us flying backwards across the platform.

Taking the brunt of the blast, Kiera yelped in panic as the force sent her bouncing across the platform and over the edge, straight into the fetid black water below. Rolling in a heap, I bounced across the platform twice, before crashing into Stroud's legs as he began to rush forward.

"Ugh, *get out of my way!*" Stroud grunted as he stumbled over my body.

"I *tried* to save you all!" Dorian repeated with a shout as he threw another fireball at Smiling Jade, only to have the enigmatic thief lord catch the spell on a force shield and effortlessly toss it to the side. "You have me left with no other choice!"

"What is this all about, Dorian?" Smiling Jade yelled as a spell sent half a dozen purple bolts of energy streaming at the man. "You are committing *treason* against the underworld! Stop now and you may yet save your life!"

"You don't understand! My life is forfeit if I *don't* do this!" I heard Dorian scream as I began to push myself up off the ground and saw Dorian's retainers rushing to attack Smiling Jade.

What the hell is happening? The thought thundered through my head as I pushed myself upward, trying to shake off the stunning effects of Dorian's attack that had scrambled my brain. *He already knew what Edith was up to! He wanted to get out of here before I said her name!*

"What have you done, Dorian?" Stroud's voice rang out in front of me, the massive warrior long having sidestepped my prone form as he ran towards the renegade thief lord. "Did you arrange to have Fairfax killed?"

Any reply Dorian had was cut off by a quick array of magical blasts that slammed into Smiling Jade's force shield, sending rapid thunderclaps echoing through the massive chamber in a bright flash of light. No sooner had the magic cleared than there were four identical copies of Smiling Jade throwing magic directly back at Dorian as the thief lord's retainers joined the battle.

This is chaos! My ears could barely hear anything as the battle began, Dorian desperately trying to hold off the four spellcasters at once while Stroud rushed towards him.

Moving to protect their thief lord, two of Dorian's retainers split up to block Stroud while two others rushed to threaten the cluster of Smiling Jades in melee range. Feeling that Stroud would be able to take care of the two thugs targeting him, I rushed towards the other pair, looking to intercept them before they could reach the quartet of casters.

Drawing my sword as I ran, I recklessly charged in front of the assembled Faceless Ones, trusting them to watch their aim as I slammed into one of Dorian's thugs with my shoulder, sending the surprised man staggering off balance. Giving the man no chance to recover, I swept my translucent blade in a vicious downward arc, catching the man high on the collarbone and cleaving deep into his body.

Ruthlessly wrenching my sword free, I then landed a powerful kick into the mortally wounded man's stomach, the impact completely carrying him off the edge of the platform and into the water below. Watching the second thug spin in surprise at my sudden dispatch of his comrade, I pressed my attack, forcing the man backwards towards the edge of the platform as he desperately tried to play for space.

Outclassing the thug in both skill and strength, I easily kept up with the man, parrying a poorly timed slash and then smashing the hilt of my weapon into his face. Stunned from my blow, the man reeled backwards, allowing me to once again land a heavy kick that sent him falling off the edge and into the basin.

Following the man's fall, I couldn't help but notice that the once placid water was now a near maelstrom of rage. Countless tentacles thrashed beneath the water's surface, marking the spot where the man had just fallen in. Flailing desperately, I saw the man surface for the briefest of moments before a tentacle wrapped around his neck and pulled him back underwater.

What a way to go. I swallowed hard as I moved to turn away from the edge, still hearing the thunderous crash of magic all around me.

But before I could move further than a stride away from the edge, a column of water shot up from below, followed by a massive tentacle, easily ten times larger than the one that I had just seen pull the man under.

"Oh shit!" I gasped as the grey appendage began its ascent towards the platform, exactly where I was standing.

Dodging to the side, I barely avoided being crushed as the tentacle slammed into the platform, causing it to crack ominously as whatever creature the limb belonged to begin to pull itself up and out of the water. The thunderous cacophony of magic ceased as the platform shifted, forcing everyone off balance.

Water steamed from the tentacle beside me as a wave of heat emanated from it, filling the air with the smell of burning sewage. Staggering from the powerful stench, I backed away from the edge as a second tentacle rose into the air and smashed into the far side of the platform.

"*Dorian!* What the hell did you do?" I shouted, dread filling my stomach as the platform shifted once more.

"What I had to!" the thief lord shouted, uncertainty filling his voice as we all watched the creature pull itself free of the water.

Continuing my awkward stumble away from the edge of the shifting platform, the sound of rushing water filled the chamber as something gigantic strained to pull itself out of the basin. Steam began to fill the air as more and more of the creature's body emerged from the depths, completely obscuring the far edge of the platform.

With a heavy thump, a thick, clawed leg crashed into the platform, at the same moment a bloodcurdling cry exploded into the chamber, sending a primal fear coursing through my body as I scrambled to get even further away from the ledge.

This is why I stayed in the cities! I cast about in panic as Stroud ran past me, towards the middle of the platform. *I didn't want to have to deal with huge monsters like this!*

Two more legs slammed into the platform as the creature finished dragging itself out of the water and onto our small patch of dryness. A second roar tore through the chamber as the two tentacles that had lifted the creature let go of their hold and whipped themselves angrily through the air. With the thrashing limbs moving the air, the steam quickly began to clear, revealing a twisted-looking otyugh of gargantuan proportions.

Standing nearly fifteen feet tall, the aberrant creature was covered in a layer of stone-like crimson flesh with a giant tooth-filled maw accounting for the majority of its twisted and deformed body. Three tentacles sprouted from its sides, two of them ending in a wicked array of barbs at the tip, and the third possessing a set of burning red eyes. Whatever transformation Dorian's magic had attempted on the creature, it had only been a partial success, serving only to mutate and enlarge an already dangerous beast, leaving all of us staring at the creature in disbelief, a small tag helpfully appearing in my vision, highlighting the monster.

[Hellborn Gnasher - Rare Boss – Level 13]

Oh fuck. I felt my eyes widen at the gnasher's level and rank, having never even seen a rare creature before, let alone a rare boss creature. *How are we going to kill something this big?*

Everyone stood deathly still as the twisted creature's tentacled eye slowly swept through the air, glancing around its new environment, until it spotted all of us standing on the platform surrounding it. Bellowing with rage, the gnasher's maw flared red with magic and it began spitting out burning globs of fire all around the platform.

Of course, it can breathe fire now! Pandemonium erupted as everyone broke out into shouting, while simultaneously moving as they all tried to avoid the burning spit flying through the air. Forced to dodge in between two well-aimed globs, I felt my face burn as the gnasher's spit splashed when it hit the ground and filled the air with a spray of fire.

"Ah!" I yelped as the burning spittle caused my eyes to burn, reflexively closing them while I stumbled along the length of the platform and away from the acrid glob of fire.

"What the hell is this?" I heard Stroud's voice shout out as I rubbed the spray of spit from my eyes. "These beasts shouldn't breathe fire!"

"It's being possessed by a devil!" Molly's voice replied through the cacophony of sounds echoing through the air.

Opening my tear-filled eyes, I found myself in the clear on the far end of the platform, spotting Dorian and a single remaining retainer edging their way towards the walkway that they had arrived from.

"This is all your fault!" Dorian shouted at me, having seen my mad escape from the creature's attack, and began to conjure a ball of fire in his hands. "Do you have any idea what you've done?"

"My fault? You had Fairfax killed!" I yelled back at Dorian as I rushed towards him and his retainer, my free hand reaching for the bandolier on my chest, pulling free a throwing knife. Not wanting to let the thief lord complete his spell while I dealt with his minion, I timed my step and threw the knife towards Dorian's head while triggering my Deadly Throw ability.

"Ah!" Dorian screamed in pain as the small knife slammed into his cheek and pierced deep into his mouth, causing his fireball to fizzle in a flash of light.

With Dorian temporarily neutralized, I charged into his last retainer, driving the thug backwards as he caught my vicious overhanded blow on his sword. Shoving against the man, I trapped his weapon against his chest and drove my knee deep into his side, only to have the man viciously headbutt me in the face as he absorbed my blow.

Shit, this guy isn't your run-of-the-mill thug! I cursed to myself as I tried to banish the all-too-familiar feeling of a broken nose and inhaled a sewer-tainted breath of air through my mouth. Not wanting to lose my temporary advantage with Dorian being out of the fight, I pushed through the pain, working to overwhelm the skilled thug with my strength, pummeling him with relentless and punishing attacks.

Forcing the man to retreat, I managed to push him close enough to see Dorian pull my throwing knife free from his cheek and spit out a mouthful of blood.

"Surrender or die, Dorian!" I called out to the man, feeling my own blood from my shattered nose begin to drip down my throat. "There is no third option here!"

"Oh, how I beg to differ, adventurer!" Dorian slurred through his broken mouth, before shouting something incomprehensible in the air. "It just so happens that *your* only option is to die!"

Almost instantly after Dorian finished speaking, I heard Quinn's distant voice shout out, "Lazarus, look out behind you!"

But it was too late.

Smashing into me from behind, the gnasher's tentacle swept straight through where I was standing, sending both me and the thug I had been fighting cartwheeling into the air.

And into the water below.

Hitting the water with a thunderous splash, I felt a throbbing sensation in my back as I reeled from the brutal blow that the gnasher had landed. Floating completely insensate for a moment I distantly noted an alert appear in my combat log telling me exactly what had happened.

A [Hellborn Gnasher] hits you with [Tentacle] for 204 points of damage!

Nearly a third of my health, a part of me noted as I slowly became aware of a persistent stinging sensation on my face as dirty sewer water leeched into my eyes, nose, and burns. Moving slowly, I tested my range of motion, happy to find that the gnasher's attack hadn't crippled me, or that my flight through the air hadn't caused me to lose my sword.

Hang on, this basin is full of otyugh. I suddenly realized as I felt something brush against my chest, forcing me into a panic as my brain envisioned myself being drowned and devoured alive. Swinging my sword in front of me, I felt the blade weakly slice through something, prompting me to start kicking my legs furiously as I propelled myself upwards towards the surface.

Breaking through the surface of the disgusting water with a desperate gasp for air, I found myself retching from the stench as I forced myself to open my eyes to see where I was. The burning sensation intensified as the filthy water pooled in my eyes, I shook my head to clear them as I swiveled about and tried to find a way out of the basin before any other otyugh discovered me.

Spotting one of the walkways nearby, I began to paddle my way over, seeing several flares of fire burst from above as Molly, Quinn, and the rest of the thief lords fought for their lives against the massive gnasher that Dorian had summoned.

That just fits you perfectly, doesn't it, Gavin? I berated myself as I swam towards a walkway. *Everyone is fighting and you're too busy taking a swim.*

Continuing to retch and berate myself as I swam, the ladder quickly grew closer, and I began to allow myself the faintest hopes that I would be able to make it out of the basin without attracting any attention to myself.

Unfortunately, I was wrong.

Feeling a tentacle wrap around my ankle, I found myself yanked sharply under the dark waters, my eyes searing as the water invaded my vision. To my surprise, however, I was somehow able to see through the murk, spotting a second tentacle reaching outward and wrapping itself around my crossbow, which hung from a belt around my waist.

Making a split-second decision, I swung my trusty blade through the strap tying the crossbow to me, causing my weapon to speed away from me as the dimwitted creature pulled its tentacle back towards its mouth, thinking that it had secured a tasty morsel. Pulling even harder, the second tentacle gripping me by the ankle gradually dragged me further from the surface of the water, seeking to drown me in the filth-filled basin.

Fighting the near unbearable pain of leaving my eyes open, I saw the otyugh swimming through the gloom as it struggled to pull me downward with only a single tentacle, the second busily throwing my stolen crossbow into its open maw. Kicking as hard as I could, I worked to loosen the creature's grip while swinging downward with my sword. Used to fighting aboveground, the blade moved at a snail's pace as my arm guided it through the water and slowly sliced through the tentacle holding me, sending the hungry otyugh retreating into the murk in pain.

Almost instantly, my downward descent stopped, and I thrashed my way upward back to the surface, breaking through an arm's reach away from a ladder.

Reaching upwards, I grabbed hold of the ladder and dragged myself out of the water, gasping wildly as my heart hammered in my chest. Sucking in a deep breath, I forced myself onto my feet and began moving towards the platform. As I ran across the walkway and back towards the fight, my eye caught movement from a distant walkway as Dorian fled, running at a full sprint down his entrance's walkway.

He's escaping! My heart jumped into my mouth as I tried to find a way that I could catch up to the renegade thief lord, realizing that there was nothing I could do. *By the time I reach the center platform and run down the walkway, he'll be gone and the wall will be sealed behind him.*

Gritting my teeth as I ran, I pushed Dorian's escape to the back of my mind as I redoubled my efforts to reach the center platform and get back into the fight that I had effectively abandoned in favor of catching Dorian.

Rushing up the ramp of the platform, I arrived just in time to see Stroud land a powerful blow across the creature's maw with his massive axe and carve a row of teeth from its jaw. Several magic missiles crossed through the air a heartbeat later as Quinn and three remaining Smiling Jades continuously threw magic at the possessed creature, scoring its rocky hide with dozens of magical burns and pockmarks.

Littering the ground were over half a dozen bodies of the retainers that the thief lords had brought with them, some of them crushed, having fallen prey to the thrashing tentacles, while others appeared to have been burned alive, unable to dodge the creature's burning spit in time.

Charging forward, I continued my scan across the battlefield, searching for both Molly and Isabella, fearing that they were among the dead on the platform or had also been knocked into the water below.

"Lazarus!" Molly's voice called out, causing my head to swivel in its direction, spotting her kneeling over Isabella's fallen body as she turned to look towards the gnasher's tentacle that was lifting itself high into the air, readying itself to crush the pair. "I can't move her! Not in time!"

"Stay there! I'm coming!" I shouted back at Molly, seeing her eyes widen in surprise as I angled my charge towards her.

This is going to be close, I told myself as I dug my feet into the ground and sprinted across the platform, seeing the gnasher's tentacle begin its downward descent towards Isabella and Molly. Pumping my feet wildly as I ran, a desperate plan slowly came together, one that I had no idea whether it would work and which stood a good chance at getting not only myself killed, but both Molly and my new thief lord. *I'm going to need the sigil's help for this and pray that it is enough.*

Triggering the sigil for the first time in what felt like ages, the crimson haze immediately consumed me as fire shot through my veins.

Feeling the power of the sigil in my step, I tightened my grip on my sword as I ran, lifting it up over my head as the gnasher's tentacle continued to fall.

As I rushed to my fallen thief lord's aid, I spotted a massive wound crossing Isabella's chest; Molly was desperately trying to heal the gushing wound while Isabella's eyes stared blankly into the air. With a single glance, I knew that Isabella only had seconds remaining before death took her, unless Molly managed to stem the flow of blood gushing from her chest.

I've already lost one thief lord this week. I felt the sigil pulse in sympathy as it sent yet another wave of energy through my body. *I am not going to lose another one!*

With a scream of pure rage, I rushed past Molly and ground to a halt, staring up at the massive barbed tentacle descending towards me. Bracing my feet for the impact to come, I hefted my blade above my head as I continued to roar in defiance, praying that my reckless idea didn't end up killing all three of us.

I heard Molly scream as the gnasher's tentacle came down on the edge of my blade, the impact driving me down to my knees. I felt bones crack in my hands from the blow, causing my grip on my sword to falter momentarily. Yelling through the pain, I fought to maintain my grip on the blade as I felt it bite through the gnasher's stone-like hide, forcing hot ichor to spew from the wound.

Pushing back against the tentacle's incredible strength, I slowly forced myself back onto my feet, feeling my weapon slice even deeper as the tentacle began to thrash in pain. Sawing my sword through the tentacle's flesh, I cut upwards with every single ounce of strength in my body, feeling the translucent blade carve through the creature's limb and burst free from the other side.

With a primal roar of pain and fear, the gnasher pulled back the now bleeding stump of its tentacle as the severed half landed heavily by my side. Swinging the gushing limb around wildly, foul ichor rained from the air as the creature whipped its sight-seeing tentacle towards me, its burning eyes staring at me with rage.

Growling furiously, the creature's body began to glow once more, signaling yet another round of burning spit as it looked to seek vengeance for its severed limb.

"Lazarus, I need more time!" Molly shouted out behind me, her familiar voice easily piercing through the veil of rage that hung over me. "You need to distract it!"

"Got it!" I grunted as I forced my battered body to move away from Molly and Isabella, feeling spikes of pain shoot through my hips and knees with every step I took.

Hobbling along the platform, I drew the gnasher's attention away from Molly as she continued healing Isabella. Watching the creature's body carefully, I saw the flare of magic in the creature's mouth brighten a second before it launched the burning spit out of its maw. Having seen the ability before, I had a better idea of what to expect when the creature launched three burning gobs of fire at me and managed to evade them as I rushed towards its main body.

"Its body is too tough!" I heard Quinn yell as I ran past him and the three identical copies of Smiling Jade. "Focus around its mouth where the armor is weaker!"

With no time to acknowledge the mage, I continued my charge towards the bulk of the gnasher, wary of its one remaining tentacle that it kept positioned high in the air. Shifting my glance downward, I saw a burnt-looking Stroud flanking the side of the creature swing his axe once more at the gnasher's maw, only to have it impact stony red flesh as the creature shifted, causing his weapon to rebound harmlessly.

"Damn it!" Stroud shouted, seeing my approach out of the corner of his eye as he wound up for another strike. "Watch for the tentacle above!"

Stroud's warning came in the nick of time as my temporary glance downward was enough to miss the limb's sudden descent as it swung towards me, seeking to crush me from above. Making an instantaneous decision to roll forward, I barely managed to tumble under the tentacle's heavy attack as its impact caused the entire platform to rock.

Feeling bones protest as I forced my broken body back up to my feet, I found myself staring upwards at the massive bulk of the gnasher as foot-long teeth protruded from the possessed abomination's maw. Following Quinn's advice, I swung my blade in a powerful cleave, the wickedly sharp weapon easily slicing through the thinner armor surrounding the creature's mouth and several teeth in the process. Howling in pain, the creature rocked backwards as it reflexively forced its body upwards away from my attack, giving me a perfect view of the three stubby limbs that it balanced on.

"Its legs!" I shouted out loud as an idea came to mind, hoping that Stroud would be able to hear me and understand what I meant.

Rushing forward before the gnasher recovered from my earlier attack, I ducked under the gargantuan creature's bulk and thrust my blade deep into what I could only assume was the otyugh equivalent of an ankle. Feeling bone crack as I brutally drove my sword straight through the gnasher's leg, the limb gave way, sending its massive body crashing to the ground.

Not wanting to risk trapping my sword, I pulled my weapon free and played for space as the gnasher's body rolled forward, then to one side as Stroud's axe found another one of the creature's legs. Backing away from the creature, I winced as a howl of pain erupted from the massive maw before me, the point-blank cry loud enough to leave my eardrums ringing.

Thrashing wildly as panic began to set in for the creature, the gnasher's sightseeing tentacle whipped downwards as it desperately scanned around its fallen bulk for either me or Stroud. Finding me first, the gnasher's red eyes flailed through the air as the body opened its massive maw with a roar, revealing countless rows of wicked teeth. Gagging from the stench of raw sewage that emanated from the gnasher's mouth, I couldn't help but notice rotting and decaying clumps of flesh and garbage caught in between the creature's teeth, along with fresher body parts whose clothing reminded me of the other thief lords' retainers.

Within seconds of the mouth opening, a cascade of magic flew through the air, hammering the tender and vulnerable flesh within the creature's maw, causing the gnasher to shut its mouth with a snap.

The mouth is its weak spot! I realized, mentally kicking myself as a sudden and crushing fatigue fell upon me and caused me to stumble as I backed away from the fallen creature. An urgently flashing alert appeared in the corner of my crimson-hazed vision.

You are low on health!
HP: 193/710

Damn it! The sigil is killing me! I realized as I dismissed the ability, feeling the intoxicating rush of power fade away from me. *How long have I had it activated?*

With the veil of rage dissipating from me, I felt all my wounds intensify, causing me to groan in pain. Feeling incredibly hot, I realized that moisture was steaming off my body as it desperately tried to cool itself, the prolonged use of the sigil having caused my temperature to skyrocket. Panting with deep breaths, I forced my legs to keep moving as I put distance between me and the fallen gnasher as it writhed in pain from the combined assault of the mages.

"Wait for it to open its mouth again!" I heard Quinn's voice shout from behind me. "That last attack really hurt it—*shit, look out!*"

Whipping a tentacle faster than it ever had before, the gnasher swept its appendage in an arc high over my head and directly towards the assembled mages. Caught flatfooted by the sudden attack, the barbed end of the tentacle slammed into one of the three remaining Smiling Jades, impaling the mage onto its spikes before yanking backwards and lifting the screaming mage into the air.

"No!" The two remaining copies of the thief lord shouted simultaneously as they threw a wave of magic at the fleeing tentacle. A handful of the attacks splashed across the gnasher's relatively unarmored appendage, scarring it wickedly as it lifted the flailing mage towards its body, the spines holding its victim firmly in place.

"It's going to eat her!" Quinn shouted behind me as the gnasher brought the tentacle in front of its toothy maw. "Focus on its mouth when it opens! It's only weak from the inside!"

It's only weak from the inside, Quinn's voice echoed in my head as I watched the gnasher's mouth begin to open, revealing soft pink flesh inside the creature's body. *Barely anything that we're doing right now is hurting it, and despite losing a tentacle and two legs, it's still full of fight. We need to—I need to—try something different.*

Swallowing hard, I stopped backpedaling away from the creature as I summoned my courage for what I was about to attempt, hoping that I would be able to survive long enough to do some damage. Putting one foot in front of me, I pushed off of the ground as I launched myself forward towards the gnasher, watching the creature's mouth stretch wide open, completely filling my vision with wicked teeth.

Magic flew over my head as I charged towards the creature's open mouth, the bolts of magic singing deep wounds into the creature's sensitive flesh. Finding a burst of speed I hadn't known I had left, I closed the final few feet towards the creature as its tentacle brought the impaled mage into its mouth and viciously began to shake her loose.

Reaching the edge of the gnasher's open maw, I leaped straight into the tooth-filled cavity. Timing my jump carefully, I landed on what used to be a torso of one of Stroud's retainers, the remnants of the thug's body having been caught between the creature's teeth. Pushing off before I lost my momentum, my legs carried me deeper into the creature's mouth as I leaped to another severed appendage and one step closer to the black pit that was the gnasher's throat.

I never thought I'd be force-feeding myself to a creature, I thought to myself grimly as I readied myself for one final jump that would send me plummeting down the gnasher's gullet. Just before I leaped, a raspy, gurgling cry echoed from above me as the Smiling Jade caught on the gnasher's tentacle finally tore free of the thrashing appendage and landed limply on the edge of the creature's throat.

Flailing weakly, the wounded mage desperately scrambled to find something to hold on to in an attempt to stop her slide backwards into the creature's stomach, her now unmasked face spotting me rushing up the creature's mouth.

"*Help*," the young elven woman gasped, her eyes widening in terror as she slid over the edge of the gnasher's throat and vanished.

Hardening my heart at what I had just witnessed, I didn't hesitate in jumping after the falling woman, despite knowing full well that there was nothing I could do to save her. I had only one shot to try and kill the gnasher from within, and based on how much health I had remaining, I couldn't risk taking a detour.

No matter how much it pained me.

Sailing over the edge of the gnasher's throat, a wave of rot swept over me as I plunged down the creature's gullet, emanating from the stomach below. Gripping my sword tightly in my hands, I thrust the razor-sharp glass-steel blade into the gnasher's throat, using it as a brake to control my fall.

The dormant relic easily sliced through the gnasher's soft innards, rending a massive line down its throat and causing a thick, goopy ichor to burst from the wound. Pushing my legs against the sides of the throat, I stopped my descent as the gnasher began to thrash in pain.

Feeling my balance shift as muscles around me began to contract in an attempt to dislodge me, I thrust my sword deeper into the slimy wall, earning a savage roar as the beast howled in pain.

Pushing myself forward, I thrust my body into the wound I had opened and clawed forward as I looked to escape the gnasher's digestive tract. Hot black ichor continued to gush all around me as I blindly cut through layers of flesh and muscle, forcing me to hold my breath, lest I breathe in the rancid substance.

With a final slice, I felt my blade carve through the last layer of flesh and I found myself falling downwards as I slid into a cavity deep inside the gnasher. Scrambling to shift my body around, a thunderous pounding sound filled my ears as the creature's heart echoed all around me. Getting my feet under me, I planted a hand against a squishy organ I couldn't identify to help find my balance, only to find myself tumbling once more as the gnasher rolled in pain.

Stop moving, you fucker! I cursed mentally as the little my enhanced eyesight could see inside the total darkness of the creature's body spun wildly as I lost my balance and landed on my back. Thrusting my sword into the flesh around me to serve as an anchor point, I scrambled onto my knees and I searched around for the creature's heart. *I can hear it, but where is it?*

Casting about wildly, I gripped my sword as hard as I could, the gnasher continuing to thrash in desperation. Focusing on the near deafening sound of the creature's heart, I fought my way through the creature's body and towards the noise, using my sword as a cane to keep my balance. Staggering through the gloom, a wave of dizziness passed over me as my lungs slowly began to burn from a lack of air. An alert popped up in the corner of my vision, warning me that my air was quickly running out.

It has to be in here. The hazy thought floated through my oxygen starved brain as my hand landed on a thick cage of flesh that pulsed with a rapid beat, the vibrations traveling straight up my arm.

Moving mechanically, I swung my sword in a shallow arc, barely having any space to wield my blade as I carved a slice into the protective covering of flesh around the heart. Parting a layer of flesh with every swing I took, I worked the glass-steel blade as I forced it deeper and began to saw. Cutting through the final layer of membrane, I was rewarded with a gush of fluid as I breached the creature's pericardium and rent it apart as I savagely twisted my blade.

Ripping free a dangling chunk of flesh with my hand, I spotted the gnasher's gargantuan heart, rapidly thundering before me as existential panic gripped the gnasher's mind. Wasting no time, I lifted my weapon up high, looking to finally put an end to the monstrosity that Dorian had twisted with his foul magic. But as I thrust forward, the gnasher thrashed one last time, sending me staggering off balance. Reflexively letting go of my sword as I lost my footing, I panicked and fell forward, catching myself on a throbbing mountain of flesh as I grabbed on to the creature's very heart.

Fuck! I cursed to myself as I struggled to maintain my grip on the panicked heart, watching my sword tumble out of reach. Digging my fingers deep into the tough muscle of the heart, I felt my vision begin to dim as my lungs reached their final limits. *No...I'm so close, I can't fail now. I won't fail now!*

Feeling a sudden burst of adrenaline course through my body, I fought against my dimming vision and tightened my grip on the gnasher's heart. *If I can't cut this thing apart with my sword...I'll just have to tear it apart with my bare hands!*

Heaving against gnasher's heart, I pulled myself closer to the beating muscle and reached out for one of the massive arteries that ran from the creature's heart. Closing my hand on the massive vein, I felt a torrent of blood pulse under my hand before I clenched the artery tight and sharply twisted. Not designed to withstand being crushed and pulled, I easily tore through the rubbery artery in a torrential spray of blood and gore.

With blood spurting wildly all around me, I closed my eyes tightly as I shook the chunk of flesh from my hand and blindly reached out for a second artery. Grasping another vein, I repeated the process, sending yet another downpour of blood down onto me. Feeling the heart tear free of its position as I tore through the second vein, I gripped the now weakly beating muscle with both my hands.

Sensing my temporary burst of strength begin to wane as I used up the final bit of my reserves, I dug my feet into the gnasher's side and embraced the creature's heart before twisting sharply to one side. I felt the one remaining artery stretch, the vein stubbornly refusing to let go as I pulled downwards. Inch by inch, it stretched, until it finally gave up with a sudden snap, sending a gush of blood over my body as I tore the hellborn gnasher's heart completely free of its body.

Splashing into the pool of blood that was rapidly filling the inner cavity of the gnasher, I felt my mind give up its tenuous hold on consciousness as I faded away into blackness, barely registering the notices that danced across my vision.

You have slain a [Hellborn Gnasher]!

You have gained Experience!

Congratulations! You have reached Level 13!

SEVENTEEN

I AWOKE ON MY BACK TO a gentle shaking motion after what seemed like hours later, the raw smell of the sewer filtering into my lungs slowly telling my brain that I was still inside the massive sewer hub, having somehow survived the gnasher's death. Opening my eyes slowly, I found myself staring up into Molly's concerned face as she knelt over me.

"Hey," I said weakly. "Did we win?"

"*Gavin,*" Molly breathed, using my real name as she broke into a wide smile as I opened my eyes, shaking her head incredulously. "What did you do? We all saw you dive right into the gnasher's mouth."

"Nothing we were doing was hurting it," I replied slowly as I motioned Molly to help me sit up. "Not until Quinn pointed out that its mouth was its only weak spot. I figured I could do more damage from the inside. Thankfully I gained a level when I killed it and I healed…"

"I thought—*we all* thought that you died!" Molly scolded me with a harsh expression on her face as she helped pull me up, but after a moment of staring into my eyes, she relented. "But I don't have any better ideas on what we could have done. We were slowly being picked off one by one…"

Molly paused as she nodded her head towards the rest of the platform around me, giving me a chance to witness the damage that the gnasher had caused.

The once-immaculate metal platform was now badly deformed, the creature's tentacles having left massive dents in it from its repeated impacts, as well as countless scars from its burning spit. Blinking through my tired eyes, I couldn't help but make out the remains of the other thief lords' retainers, some having been crushed to a pulp, others partially consumed by fire.

"We don't think Kiera made it," Molly continued, my eyes landing on the two remaining Smiling Jades standing at the far edge of the platform with a pair of surviving Crimson Rats as they looked out into the basin below us. "She never came up from the water after falling in."

"The basin is full of otyugh," I said, remembering my harrowing experience when I had fallen in. "I barely made it out myself. If she fell in first and attracted the majority of them…"

I felt a shiver cross my spine as I remembered the otyugh that had pulled me under after I had fallen into the water. If I had had to deal with more than one, I had no idea what I would have done.

Probably drowned, I told myself morbidly.

"Did you hear everything that Dorian said?" Molly whispered to me in disbelief. "He *knew* he was in trouble the moment we stepped in here."

"Yet he had enough time to prepare for…*whatever* he did to the gnasher, even if the transformation didn't completely affect it," I replied as Stroud, Isabella, and Quinn walked back up the far end of the platform, their eyes focusing on Molly and me.

With a sense of relief, I spotted Isabella and felt the tension fade from my muscles, happy to see that she had survived the battle. Judging by the amount of exposed skin I saw across her chest as she walked towards us, I guessed that she had been caught by a glancing blow from the gnasher's tentacles.

"I think the gnasher was a contingency, something he didn't plan on using," Molly told me as she followed my glance and saw the group walking towards us. "Any sign?"

Shaking his head, the half-giant warrior growled out a single word in frustration. "No."

Standing up with Molly's help, I got my feet under me as everyone approached and noticed Stroud's eyes shifting over to me.

"Well done with the beast," Stroud stated with a tinge of respect in his voice as he inclined his head towards me in a nod.

"I did the best I could," I replied, trying not to think about the bodies that were littered around the platform and how big of a loss it was for all of the remaining thieves guilds to lose their most experienced members, or in the Crimson Rats' case, their thief lord. "I just wish I did it sooner."

"Hindsight is a burden the survivor must always bear," Stroud told me philosophically. "Do not let it consume you."

"I'll try," I told the man, remembering the panicked expression the unmasked Smiling Jade had given me before falling down the gnasher's throat. Swallowing hard, I exhaled sharply, hoping that the game would work its eerie magic and gradually smooth out the memories of what I had just experienced.

"I lost him in all the fighting," Isabella began, looking towards me, "but what happened to Dorian? I saw you fighting with him briefly, before that…creature rose from the basin."

"He escaped," I answered with another sigh as both of the Smiling Jades and the two surviving Crimson Rat retainers walked over towards us. "I saw him run down the walkway after I got knocked off the platform."

"He will have to be brought to account," Stroud stated as he looked over towards the two Faceless Ones. "Are either of you the *true* Smiling Jade, or do we now have three vacancies among the council?"

"I am still alive," Smiling Jade replied as the other copy of herself bowed slightly and took a step backwards.

Taking a look at the enigmatic thief lord dressed in the hooded orange robe and jade mask, I had no way of knowing if this truly was the same woman that had spoken to me earlier, but at this point I found myself too tired to care.

"Good, then on to business," Stroud grunted, clearly sharing the same opinion as me as he then looked over towards Isabella. "First things first. Given the light of Dorian's betrayal and his murder of Kiera, I have no reason to not to recognize you as the thief lord of the Grim Shadows."

"I concur," Smiling Jade replied.

"Thank you." Isabella nodded curtly as Stroud continued talking.

"Second," Stroud stated, turning towards the two Crimson Rats that were standing nearby. "Your thief lord has been killed and the key to the Council of Thieves lost with her body. In normal circumstances, this would result in the loss of your guild's membership in the council; however, these are not normal times.

"Your guild will retain its full membership, and instead this place will no longer be used," Stroud continued. "Given the magnitude of Dorian's betrayal, this place is no longer safe, and it would be a foolish to continue meeting here."

"Instead, the Crimson Rats will elect another leader and make them known to us," Smiling Jade added, seamlessly picking up where Stroud had left off. "And they will be recognized as a thief lord."

"T-thank you," one of the still shocked Crimson Rats stuttered, not yet having fully recovered from everything that had just happened. "We'll make sure the entire guild knows what Dorian did here today."

"We'll make sure the entire underworld knows what Dorian did here today," Isabella corrected bitterly as she glanced over to the two other thief lords. "He murdered Kiera, and his *adventurer*—whom I was not told about, by the way—is implicated in the death of two noble heirs, in addition to Fairfax's death. War is the *only* appropriate response we have to his actions."

"I agree," Stroud said as he looked over to Smiling Jade with an unreadable expression on his face. "The Damned will need to be purged, root and branch, if we are to have a chance at escaping notice from the nobility. If they hear even the slightest rumor that one of the thieves guilds orchestrated the death of their heirs, their wrath will be turned upon all of us."

"Do either of you have any idea why I wasn't *told* that another adventurer had been brought into the council?" Isabella asked Smiling Jade and Stroud pointedly, venom dripping from her voice. "Fairfax said *nothing*. Had I known who Edith was from the beginning, we could have avoided all of this!"

"Fairfax was excluded from the meeting where she and the other adventurer were introduced." Smiling Jade shifted her faceless gaze towards Stroud, who nodded at her once before turning his attention back towards Isabella. "Not all of us were happy with Fairfax's decision to bring adventurers into one of the thieves guilds so quickly. We feared that it would disrupt the relative balance between the guilds and allow the Grim Shadows to become ascendant, leaving the rest of us behind."

"Edith and the other adventurer, Ransom, were meant to be a

hidden counterbalance to you two, in case you needed to be contained," Stroud explained bluntly as he motioned between Molly and me. "Adventurers are already known to be extremely power hungry and greedy when confined by the law. We were concerned how two adventurers without that restraint would behave."

There was a moment of deathly silence as the four of us stared incredulously at Stroud and Smiling Jade, our mouths hanging open at what we had just heard.

"*You did what?*" Isabella started to grind out between clenched teeth before I interrupted her.

"You fucking idiots brought Ransom into this, too?" I shouted at the two thief lords as a spike of rage pulsed from the sigil on my chest and sent my heart racing.

"Lazarus!" Isabella barked as her head snapped towards me. "This is not—"

"His anger is justified, Isabella," Stroud replied contritely as he nodded towards me in apology. "We were fools to trust what Dorian presented us, but let us not pretend that you would have not acted in your own best interests should the tables have been turned."

"We *told* you we recruited two adventurers," Isabela spoke in clipped tones as anger simmered in her voice. "We even told you we were entertaining recruiting a third after Lazarus and Molly proved to be such useful assets. Fairfax and I were completely open about our decision making. You not only betrayed our trust, but you got Fairfax *killed!*"

"We understand the scope of our failure and recognize that we are indirectly responsible for both Fairfax's and Kiera's death," Smiling Jade acknowledged with a tinge of regret in her voice. "However, this isn't a time for recrimination; we must move quickly to counteract whatever plan Dorian has in place. Once we have dealt with him, we can discuss whatever...*reparations* are appropriate for our lapse in judgement."

"*That's it?*" I asked, not quite believing what I was hearing and feeling another spike of anger shoot through me. "You just say that it's your fault and offer us a pile of cash to smooth over hurt feelings? And you call us adventurers fucking greedy!"

"*Lazarus*, that's enough!" Isabella spat as the two other thief lords flinched at my anger. "Come with me. Molly and Quinn as well."

Grabbing me by the forearm, Isabella had no illusions of her ability to force me anywhere I didn't want to go, but when she looked up into my eyes, I saw a spark of anger that made me pause and let her pull me away. Leading the three of us a short distance away from the other two thief lords, Isabella didn't waste any time berating me in hushed tones.

"Your behavior right now is *unacceptable*, Lazarus, regardless of how you may feel at the moment!"

"This is bullshit, Isabella," I hissed back, looking her straight in the eye. "They fucking lied to us. Worse, they went behind our back and *caused* all of this!"

"You don't think I know that?" Isabella growled at the two of us. "This is how the underworld *works*, or did you think you were signing up for a world filled with saints and paladins? No, this is a world of thieves, cutthroats, and murderers," Isabella continued while thrusting out a finger towards me. "I know they fucked up, they know they fucked up, and they're going to pay us a giant fucking pile of gold to make us forget about it. Then we're going to do exactly that: *move on and forget about it*."

"So that's it, then, we just forget about Fairfax?" I retorted bitterly. "Maybe we can cast a golden statue out of the money that they give us and tell it we're sorry?"

"Lazarus!" I heard Quinn gasp.

"You fucking bastard!" Isabella hissed back as she stepped closer to me and stared straight up into my eyes. "You've been a member of the underworld for barely twenty days. I've been a member of this guild for *twenty-five* years! I came up through the ranks with Fairfax, and I've shared more with him than you could ever know. This is simply the way things are, so either you're going to have to accept that, or you're going to have to get the hell out of the underworld entirely."

"You never told us anything about how they resented us or were afraid of us," Molly finally spoke up in a small voice, something I knew she did to hide the anger that she was feeling. "Why didn't you tell us?"

"Because you didn't need to know, and we didn't want it in the back of your minds when we put you through the trials," Isabella explained as she took a step back from me, blinking heavily. "Fairfax didn't want to put any unnecessary pressure on you two and to let you two know that you were the first two adventurers accepted into one of the thieves guilds.

"There was a reason why Quinn was kept as a contractor until recently," Isabella continued, motioning to the quiet mage. "Why *all* of the other adventurers in the underworld were kept as contractors. You two were our test cases."

"That ended up saving the day," I stated, looking down towards the scar in Isabella's armor from the gnasher's attack that had nearly killed her.

Following my glance, Isabella raised a hand to touch the exposed skin that her armor no longer covered and nodded at me curtly. "You three did save the day, along with me and the other thief lords. I saw you step before the creature's tentacle to give Molly the time she needed to save me. Then saw you leap straight down the creature's throat to find a way to kill it, something that none of us in our wildest dreams would have even dared to attempt.

"*Those* are the reasons why Fairfax and I wanted to recruit adventurers we could trust." Isabella looked between the three of us. "Times are changing, and we don't want to be caught unprepared, like the rest of the Thief lords were today. I daresay by the end of the week there will hardly be a contractor left in the Eberia. They will all be offered positions within the other thieves guilds."

"Is this how things really work between the thief lords, Isabella?" Quinn asked, chancing a glance over at me as he spoke. "I never knew him, but Lazarus is right. A pile of gold for one of our own seems… hollow."

"As much as it pains me to admit it, what is happening here is no longer about Fairfax. It is now about the survival of the guild and the stability of Eberia." Isabella swallowed hard as if it pained her to speak the words aloud. "If we cannot put an end to Dorian before the nobles catch wind that the underworld was involved in the deaths of their heirs, we will face a purge that will make King Cyril's look tame in comparison."

"What's our next step, then?" Molly asked after a moment, realizing that I wasn't going to speak.

"I will fill in the thief lords of what you've told me about Edith." Isabella motioned towards the two thief lords standing nearby, giving us some semblance of privacy. "Then we will return to the guild…and prepare for war."

"The sooner I can hit something again, the better," I muttered under my breath as I took a step forward to return to the two other thief lords, only to have Isabella raise a hand to stop me.

"I think you've said enough to the two of them for now, Lazarus," Isabella told me as she indicated for all three of us to stay here. "I can handle this by myself."

Walking away from the three of us, Isabella rejoined the waiting thief lords and moved the conversation that the three of them were having to the far end of the platform.

"Well, you really went off on her, Lazarus," Quinn grunted while pushing me in the shoulder. "Can't say I blame you, but are you okay?"

"Not particularly," I sighed as I rubbed my face. "I'm not use to this level of—"

"Pragmatism? Backstabbing?" Quinn supplied helpfully. "Betrayal? Greed?"

"Sure." I waved a dismissive hand in the air. "Any of that works."

"Money makes the world go around," Molly stated softly as if she had something else on her mind, her eyes glazing over. "No different in this game than the real world."

"I guess not," I said as I looked around the platform and found myself staring at a large grey sack lying on the ground in the exact same spot I remembered the gnasher being in. Perking up slightly, I pointed towards the bag. "Speaking of money, I think the gnasher dropped loot."

Eyes widening, my words were enough to break through whatever was on Molly's mind and cause her to follow my finger.

"Loot?" she asked excitedly as her eyes focused on the bag. "I'd completely forgotten!"

"Speaking of forgotten," I began, remembering that I had hit level thirteen after killing the gnasher, "I gained a level!"

"Ah! I forgot to mention I did too!" Molly told me excitedly, her eyes widening as she saw something on her character sheet. "Neat! I learned a new spell! It's a damage shield!"

"That'll definitely be handy with the way our day's been," I replied with a smile, seeing Molly nod at me enthusiastically.

"We'll have to try it out," Molly said as she inclined her head towards the loot bag. "I don't know what I like more, new abilities or new items."

"Abilities, definitely, for me, though I can't remember the last time I saw a loot sack," Quinn commented thoughtfully as the three of us moved towards the bag. "I think I killed a snake outside the city on launch day and it dropped a fang for me. Then I decided to go back into the city and find a different way to level."

"Yeah." I nodded at Quinn in agreement as I assigned my five newly gained attribute points into constitution, immediately feeling my health and stamina improve. Taking a moment to check my character sheet, I scanned it to see what had changed with the new level.

LAZARUS CAIN – LEVEL 13 BRUISER

Half-Giant/Half-Elf Male

Statistics:

HP: 800/800

Stamina: 800/800

Mana: 255/255

Experience to next level: 1232/27000

Attributes:

Strength: 79 (89)

Agility: 65 (70)

Constitution: 49 (54)

Intelligence: 10

Willpower: 10

Abilities:

***Sneak Attack II** (Passive) – Attacks made before the target is aware of you automatically deal weapon damage +35.*

***Bleeding Attack I** (Passive) – Enemies who take sneak attack damage will continue to bleed for 5 seconds, taking 40% of the sneak attack damage dealt.*

***Power Attack II** (Active: 50 Stamina) – You slash viciously at the target, putting extra strength behind the blow. Deal weapon damage +25.*

***Ambush I** (Active: 60 Stamina) – You ambush your target, striking them in vulnerable location. Deals weapon damage+125. This ability can only be used on a target unaware of you.*

***Kick** (Active: 20 Stamina) – You kick your enemy for 10-20 points of damage and knock them back 1-2 yards. Depending on your Strength/Agility score, you may also knock down the target.*

***Shoulder Tackle** (Active: 40 Stamina) – Stun enemy for 1-2 seconds with chance to knock enemy down based on Strength and/or Agility attribute.*

***Deadly Throw I** (Active: 30 Stamina) – Throw a weapon with extra strength behind it. Deals weapon damage +15. This ability has a chance to interrupt spellcasting if thrown at the target's head, force them to drop their weapon if thrown at target's hands, or slow their movement if thrown at target's legs.*

Skills:

Weapons:

***Unarmed Combat** – Level 12 – 21% (Increases knowledge of Hand-to-Hand fighting and improves related Abilities.)*

***Swords** – Level 12 – 89% (Increases knowledge of Sword fighting and improves related Abilities.)*

***Daggers** – Level 11 – 43% (Increases knowledge of Dagger fighting and improves related Abilities.)*

***Crossbows** – Level 12 – 22% (Increases knowledge of Crossbows and improves related Abilities.)*

***Throwing** – Level 10 – 10% (Increases knowledge of Throwing Weapons and improves related Abilities.)*

Other:

***Stealth** – Level 12 – 84% (Decreases chance of being detected while attempting to stay hidden. Improves related Abilities.)*

***Lockpicking** – Level 12 – 89% (Increases knowledge of lock mechanics, allowing you to pick harder locks.)*

***Wordplay** – Level 12 – 84% (Increases chance to persuade others, resolve differences, and/or get information.)*

***Perception** - Level 13 - 3% (You are skilled in spotting hidden creatures and places. Depending on your skill level, hidden* *creatures and places will be highlighted in red.)*

Tradeskills:

Blacksmithing – Level 11 – 12%

Cooking – Level 10 – 34%

Alchemy – Level 12 – 11%

Leatherworking – Level 12 – 17%

Racial Ability:

***Titan's Might** (Giant) (Passive) – Your giant ancestry has given you the ability to wield large weapons in with exceptional strength. All damage dealt by two-handed weapons is increased by 3%.*

***Keen Sight** (Elf) (Passive) – Your elven ancestry has given you exceptional eyesight, granting you the ability to see twice as far as normal in all lighting conditions. This ability also grants you Darkvision.*

***Darkvision** (Elf) (Passive) – While in total darkness, your vision will have near daylight clarity up to 100 feet.*

Traits:

***Sigil of Rage** – A magical sigil written in the Primal Tongue has been carved deep into your flesh, causing it to pulse with an unfathomable torrent of energy. When activated, Primal Rage suffuses your body granting you +10 to Strength and Agility. While this ability is active, you are consumed by pure rage as your body is burned from within, dealing 10 points of damage per second. This ability scales per level.*

Evolving Weapon:

Dormant Glass-Steel Greatsword

Total Experience Gained: 1699/50000

"You don't see that many loot bags in the city." I said while dismissing the sheet from my vision, silently noting just how far my relic was from awakening, and motioned towards the bag. "You just pretty much take what you see."

"Open it, Lazarus," Molly told me. "You killed it, it's only fair."

Seeing Quinn give me a thumbs-up in approval, I reached down to pick up the bag and saw a handful of items appear in my vision.

[Citrine] x3
[Tiger's Eye] x2
[Garnet] x2
[Sapphire]
[Ring of the Mind]
[Necklace of Intellect]
[Ruined Relic Cuirass]
[Armguards of Arcane Potency]
[Ornate Hardened Steel Lockbox]

"Wow." I sharply inhaled as the item list appeared in front of me. "Maybe we're missing out on something, not fighting these sorts of creatures on a regular basis!"

"I think there's a pretty big difference fighting a *rare boss* and regular run-of-the-mill creatures," Quinn said dubiously as he indicated for me to hurry up. "Come on, slowpoke, what's in the bag?"

"Gems, jewelry, and a strange lockbox," I told the pair as I pulled out the assorted items and handed them over to both Molly and Quinn, taking a moment to call up the items' stats as I held them. "Along with a cuirass of some sort, and a pair of armguards."

Ring of the Mind
Slot: Ring
Item Class: Magical
Item Quality: Average (+0%)
Intelligence: +1 Will: +2
Durability: 0/0
Weight: 0 kg

Necklace of Intellect

Slot: Neck

Item Class: Magical

Item Quality: Average (+0%)

Intelligence: +3

Durability: 0/0

Weight: 0 kg

Ruined Relic Cuirass

Slot: Chest

Item Class: Relic

Item Quality: Mastercraft (+20%)

Armor: 0

Strength: +3 Agility: +3

Durability: 0/0

Weight: 5.5 kg

Note: A skilled smith might be able to re-forge this item.

Armguards of Arcane Potency

Slot: Arm

Item Class: Relic

Item Quality: Good (+15%)

Armor: 40

Spell Penetration: +10% Mana Regeneration: +10%

Durability: 80/80

Weight: 0.5 kg

Ornate Hardened Steel Lockbox

Special: This item appears to be locked by a complex mechanism.

This looks really intricate. And ancient, even, I thought to myself as I examined the etchings on the well-crafted lockbox, passing the jewelry and armguards to Molly and Quinn. Feeling like a solid brick of metal in my hands, I found the rectangular lockbox to be surprisingly heavy as I inspected it, the box making no sound at all when I shook it. *Huh,*

I wonder if there's anything inside here. Guess I'll have to see if I can pick it open once things settle down.

"This is awesome!" Quinn exclaimed, catching my attention as he examined the armguards excitedly. "I could definitely use this!"

"Seems like it's better suited for you than me," Molly replied while trying the ring on her hand. "This ring is a pretty good boost for me."

"Do you want the necklace, too?" Quinn asked, wasting no time in pulling his new armbands over his forearms.

"I just bought one with similar stats," Molly answered, shaking her head. "Take it if you need it; Lazarus and I can split the gems between the two of us to even it out."

"Sure, that works for me!" Quinn didn't even hesitate in accepting Molly's offer.

"Is the armor any good?" I saw Molly shift her attention towards me as Quinn began fumbling with the necklace. "Looks a bit worn out."

"Yeah…" I said slowly, having since put the lockbox into my inventory and picked up the metallic cuirass in my hands, slowly realizing that it was just an empty shell of the armor that it once was. "It's a relic, but looks like it's seen better days. I guess spending…well, however long it spent down here in the Gnasher's stomach, all of the leather and other bits have been eaten away."

"You should be able to repair it with the Re-Forge crafting trait," Quinn spoke up helpfully as he appraised the armor. "I've seen a few similar pieces of armor and other items recovered from the caches still hidden around the city. Based on the style, my guess is that this piece is Nafarrian in origin."

"Re-Forge?" I echoed as I raised an eyebrow at the mage. "I don't have that trait."

"Really?" Quinn looked at me with surprise. "I thought you crafted?"

"Only leatherworking and blacksmithing, and even then, I really haven't had the time or money to get any rare materials," I replied with a shrug. "I mostly just use it to repair my armor."

"Hrm," Quinn grunted while nodding his head towards the armor that I was wearing. "Well, I learned the trait from one of the instructors at the Mages Guild and it only took about an hour. I don't know how much time we'll have once we get back, but given the state of your gear, I think you're due for an upgrade and some repairs. I can see if I can teach it to you once we get back to the hideout."

"Uh, sure," I told Quinn as I glanced down towards my armor and found it completely covered in filth, with multiple tears along the seams that held it together. "I'd really appreciate that. The last day has been pretty rough on my gear; hell, it's been rough on everyone."

"Something tells me that it's going to get a hell of a lot worse before it starts getting better," Molly said, cocking her head to one side as Isabella broke away from the other thief lords and started making her way towards us with a grim expression on her face.

"*Yeah*," Quinn agreed morbidly as he blew out a loud sigh. "I think you're right."

EIGHTEEN

"AND SO, BASED ON HIS actions and the evidence that we have accumulated against him, the other thief lords and I have decided it is in the best interest of the Underworld to declare war against Thief Lord Dorian and his guild, the Damned," Isabella's voice rang loudly in the air as she addressed nearly the entirety of the guild, who had packed themselves into the common room, listening in rapt attention as she spoke while standing on a table. "But this will not be a war of conquest, one for territory or for material gain; instead, this will be a brutal and savage *purge* as we cut out this rot from the underworld."

Isabella paused for a moment as she waited for her words to sink in for the assembled guild members.

"With the city in near chaos and the nobility at one another's throats, we cannot afford to do anything other than make Dorian and his followers a bloody example and pray that they are satisfied with his head." Isabella made a slicing motion across her neck as she spoke. "Because if they are not, they will be out for ours shortly after, and we will face a purge the likes of which we have not seen since the days of King Cyril.

"But be assured that this is not a burden that the Grim Shadows will bear alone! Each of the other three guilds stands firmly with us, and they have promised their full support in the war ahead," Isabella soothed as she began to wrap up her speech. "I am confident that the Grim Shadows will persevere through this conflict and emerge stronger from the other side. We may all be a band of cutthroats, but each of us loves Eberia in our own way, and today she needs our help. I am counting on all of you to help me put an end to this war as soon as possible, so we can return to the things we do best and put all of this bloodshed behind us.

"Thank you all for listening," Isabella finished as she made to leap down from the table. "Some of you have received your assignments already; for those who have not, I will be by shortly with your team and targets."

"Good speech," I told Isabella as she walked around the table and towards the spot where Quinn and I had been standing.

"Hopefully it's enough," Isabella said as her eyes watched me carefully.

We had barely exchanged a dozen words since our return from the sewers, both of us clearly carrying baggage from our earlier argument. I was still angry about how the other thief lords had blatantly lied to us and frustrated by how quickly Isabella had accepted their bribe to let the issue drop.

How are we supposed to fight a war with allies that could be working against us behind our backs? I felt the familiar question cross my thoughts once more, still being unable to come up with a good answer.

All this time, I'd thought I had a good understanding of how the underworld worked, but I was beginning to realize just how naïve I'd been. The thief lords operated on a level of misdirection and subtlety that far outclassed anything I had ever experienced before. Would I have been able to do the same thing Isabella had done with the other thief lords had it been Molly or even Quinn in Fairfax's place? Better yet, would I have been able to live with myself if I did?

"I can see the fire in everyone's eyes," I replied after a moment, trying my best not to show the turmoil I was experiencing within. "They'll do their part, and I'm sure that by the end of the night, Dorian will regret ever being born in Eberia."

"We can only hope," Isabella agreed as she turned towards the rest of the room, watching the guild members begin sorting themselves out as they formed into their assigned teams or sat nervously at the tables, waiting to find out what would be needed from them. "I'm praying that the price we pay to put an end to him won't be too high."

Higher than we've already paid? I thought to myself as I bit down on my tongue, not wanting to start another argument with Isabella.

"Here comes Bart." Quinn pointed into the milling mass of people as the older thief gently navigated his way towards us. "Ah, he found Goner."

"Oh, good," Isabella replied as she turned to look out into the crowd as Goner and Bart came into view. "I'll feel better when we have him somewhere safer, in case things go wrong tonight."

"Isabella!" the small boy cried out as he sprang forward to hug Isabella around the waist. "Bart's told me what happened and what you're going to have to do tonight."

"Then you understand why we're sending you and Bart to be with Quinn's friend for the next little while, right?" Isabella asked as she looked down at Goner with a gleam in her eye. "We need to make sure that you're safe."

"I understand," Goner said as he pulled away from Isabella and rubbed his face on his sleeve. "I promise I'll be good while I'm there."

"I know you will be, Goner," Isabella told the boy softly before nodding her head towards the older thief. "Be sure to listen to Bart if anything happens when you're out today; there's a reason why he's survived this long."

"I will," Goner acknowledged. "I'll do my best to learn everything while I'm staying with William and pick up all the magic he knows. Once I come back, I'll be ready to help and do anything, you'll see."

"I believe you, Goner," Isabella said with a laugh as she tousled the boy's hair and turned her gaze towards Bart. "You're going straight to Quinn's friend's place?"

"Yeah," Bart answered while waving a hand at the mass behind him. "We have a group heading through the Old District anyway; the two of us are going to move with them and make sure we're covered the whole way."

"Good," Isabella said, then turned her glance towards Quinn. "You're sure William won't mind both Bart and Goner arriving out of the blue, will he?"

"Should be fine," Quinn replied confidently. "I gave Bart a note explaining everything to William and that I would check up on them as soon as I had a chance."

"We'll manage, Bella," the grey-haired thief groused. "If we're in dire straits, I'll just jimmy one of the locks in the apartments next door to William's place and hold out for the night. According to Quinn, they're all empty anyway."

"All right." Isabella stated with a nod then motioned towards the room. "You two be safe out there tonight. I need to start making my rounds and getting everyone else moving."

"Take care of yourself, girl," Bart said in a fatherly manner before moving to embrace Isabella. "Do what you need to do to protect our home, but don't lose yourself in the process."

"I'll try," Isabella promised in a small voice as she locked eyes with Quinn and me. "I have Lazarus, Quinn, and Molly to lean on."

"Then I know you'll be fine," the elderly thief replied with a smile as he pulled away from Isabella and gave both Quinn and me a departing wave. "We'll see you when this is all over."

"Bye, Isabella!" Goner sniffed, giving all of us a wave as Bart turned to leave. "Bye, Lazarus and Quinn! Say bye to Molly for me!"

"Bye, Goner," I called after the boy, feeling a lump rise in my throat as I tried to imagine what the boy must be feeling, silently hoping that he made it to William's place safely.

"He'll be safe with William," Quinn said as he glanced between both Isabella and me, seeing that we shared a similar expression.

"Yeah," I exhaled with a sigh as I watched Isabella turn around to look at us.

"You two should double check on Molly and see if she's put together a plan of attack for you three," Isabela suggested, her eyes dropping downwards to the clothes that we were wearing. "And see if you can finish patching your armor."

She looked at us meaningfully. "I have a feeling that we're going to need every edge we can get tonight."

"UGH! THIS THING IS FUCKING useless!" Molly's voice shouted from behind the door at the same instant Quinn and I entered the guild's secure information room, having crossed the length of the guild's headquarters.

Stepping through the door ahead of me, Quinn flinched as something struck him in the face, causing him to throw his hands up in front of him in reflex. “Hey, *ow!* What the hell was that for?”

“Ah! Quinn! I’m so sorry!” I heard Molly’s chair scrape against the floor as she rushed across the room towards Quinn, who was now clutching his face. “I was just frustrated and…”

“You throw a mean book,” Quinn grumbled nasally as he stooped down to pick up a small book lying on the ground.

“Hey, that’s Cayden’s book,” I said, noticing the familiar cover as the two of us moved further into the room and closed the door behind us. “Why did you throw it across the room?”

“Because I can’t figure out if it’s useful or not!”

Molly hissed in frustration as she motioned for the three of us to sit down in front of the paper-laden desk I remembered from my visit with Isabella.

“Having had a chance to look at Cayden’s ledger in more detail, I am thoroughly creeped out just *holding* the stupid thing. He’s shipped countless body parts, blood, organs, bones, you name it, all across the city for years and years on end. Whatever you did to him was too kind, Lazarus.” Molly fixed me with a haunted look. “I know this is all just a game, but Cayden was *evil,* horrifically so. Given just how real this world is, I can barely wrap my head around what I’ve read in his book. Part of me just wants to curl up in a corner and cry, while the other part of me is just so angry I’m afraid I’m going to hurt myself.”

“Shit,” Quinn cursed as he looked down at the book, then tossed it onto my lap. “I think you should hold on to this, Lazarus, at least until you burn it.”

“Gee, thanks,” I said grimly as I looked back up at Molly. “Is there anything useful at all in it? When I paged through, I saw it mentioned a few safe houses and dead drops.”

“It did,” Molly acknowledged with a nod, and pointed to a large map of the city that had been tacked onto a corkboard behind us. “I marked those safe houses on the map…along with every other safe house that the guild knows about belonging to any of the gangs affiliated with the Damned. I was looking to see if there was any pattern that I could spot from the deliveries to see if there was any one place we could prioritize over the other, but I haven't been able to figure anything out."

"Who has been ordering all this...*stuff* from Cayden?" Quinn asked, a distasteful expression crossing his face. "I know necromancy isn't illegal in Eberia, but it's not something that is exactly flaunted, either."

"To be honest, Cayden has been supplying nearly everyone in Eberia with *something*," Molly answered with a disgusted look on her face. "Our guild mostly used him for corpse disposal, but we've been known to place the odd order for something more *exotic*. The same goes for nearly every other thieves guild. I found a few notes in the ledger that I *think* track back to each of the noble houses, too, and that includes the Mages Guild, since they're practically run by House Denarius."

"I figured that the Mages Guild would have ties," Quinn commented with a shrug. "I've seen firsthand what some of the labs look like in the Arcaneum; it doesn't surprise me in the slightest."

"So what does this all mean for *our* next steps?" I asked, motioning towards the map on the wall. "Isabella is letting us pick and choose our own plan of attack once the war kicks off, though I'm sure she's expecting us to be in the thick of it."

"That's what I figured too, and I have a few places in mind where we can start," Molly said as she stood up from her seat behind the desk and waved us over to the map posted on the wall. "Though I have no real idea of what we're going to find there."

Pointing to a red tack on the map deep within the New District with several other blue and black tacks clustering around it, Molly began to explain her labeling system as she laid out her plan.

"This red tack is the banquet hall where the noble heirs were killed earlier today, and the blue tacks represent gangs affiliated with the Damned." Molly pointed to each of the tacks in turn as she spoke. "And the black ones are hideouts or safe houses that directly belong to the Damned. As you can see, Dorian and his group have a pretty dense following throughout the entire district."

"No kidding," I muttered in surprise as I looked over the map, counting well over three dozen blue tacks and nearly just as many black ones. "How the hell does he have so many followers? I had no idea that the Damned had this many members or gangs under their control!"

"They don't," Molly corrected with a shake of her head. "It only looks that way because they've chosen to have a distributed organizational structure across the entire district, rather than a handful of larger bases. All of these hideouts or bases likely only have a few members in each place, which is why I think we should start closest to the hall where the attacks took place."

"The number of them will make it a hell of a lot harder to dig them out, since these are only the places we know about," Quinn noted as he drew an imaginary circle around the red tack and counted the tacks within. "Just around the banquet hall there's what…four, five, six different hideouts within two blocks of the place? Even if we have all four guilds working on this, it's going to be nearly impossible to be sure we've cleared out all of them."

"I don't disagree," Molly said with a nod. "Which is why I think we're going to have to prioritize the guild bases over the gang bases. If we can remove Dorian from the picture, then the rest of the gangs will get back in line, and if they don't, we can always pay them a follow-up visit."

"That's probably our best option," I agreed while looking over the map and trying to picture the street-level view of where all the hideouts and bases would be. "Because they're spread so far apart, any warning Dorian has sent out is going to take a long time to make it to each and every place. There's a good chance we'll be able to catch the majority of them with their guard down."

"That would certainly help," Quinn agreed as he pointed at a few different spots on the map. "If we can get a few people in position at a bunch of these streets here, we can possibly intercept any runners going out to warn Dorian or any of the other hideouts. Make it easier for us to hide what we're doing."

"Oh, that's a good idea!" Molly exclaimed. "I'll make sure to mention that to Isabella and see if we can get the other guilds to lend some manpower to help handle it."

"Have you heard anything from Sawyer, by chance, and his search for Edith? He hasn't messaged me at all," I asked while mulling over Molly's tacks on the map.

"Actually, I have," Molly answered with another sigh. "And it's not good news."

"Why would it be?" Quinn mumbled as he looked up to the sky. "We're already playing Ascend Online on *hard mode*; God forbid things get even the slightest bit easier."

"What's happened now?" I asked Molly hesitantly.

"Things are getting worse within the city—*much* worse, actually. Amberwain and Crawridge have *escalated* matters between one another and are now enjoying a standoff in the middle of the street in the Old District," Molly began to explain. "I don't know who started it, but one of the houses thought it'd be a good idea to pay a visit to the other house with a small army of armed guards, which forced the other house to reply in kind. Thankfully, the military caught wind of what was going on and managed to head both of them off with whatever soldiers they have left, but they're all basically sitting in the street and shouting insults at one another now."

"You have to be fucking kidding me," I growled as I rubbed my head in disbelief.

"I wish I were," Molly said sympathetically. "What's left of the military is just *barely* keeping the two of them apart, but if either house decided to make a serious push for it, they'd overrun them easily. Sawyer's also told me that the two houses have started putting bounties on certain members of the rival houses, and have pulled nearly every single hunter in the city to stand by and watch things go to hell. Last I heard from him is that the Amberwain heir's bounty was well over three hundred gold pieces—*dead*, mind you. They're not interested in a live body."

"So Sawyer's pretty much just looking for Edith on his own, then," I guessed, seeing the frustrated expression on Molly's face as she spoke.

"He and two others have managed to stick around so far," Molly told me. "He wasn't optimistic that they would hang around much longer, though."

"Did you mention anything to him about what happened down in the sewers?" Quinn asked while pointing at the map. "Or anything about the coming war?"

"No." Molly shook her head, the motion sending her long hair cascading from side to side. "He's not an idiot, though, and knows that there's something big going on."

"We should probably fill him in about the bare bones of what's happening and how to get in touch with us," I said slowly as I stared at the map Molly had put together. "Once we start our attacks, things are going to start getting rough, and if we're in combat, we'll likely get locked out of messaging."

"Isn't that something we should run by Isabella?" Quinn asked, turning his head to look at Molly. "I get the impression she doesn't trust hunters and wouldn't want any word of our plans getting out."

"Yeah, well, I don't see a ton of people lining up to help us," I answered as I shot a glance towards Molly. "You're organizing all of this, Molly. What do you think?"

"I think Sawyer should be in the loop, if only a little bit," Molly replied after a short pause to gather her thoughts. "But we should also let Isabella know; the last thing we need right now is to start doing things behind her back. You weren't exactly easy on her back at the sewer hub, and I can tell there's still tension between the two of you."

"I was angry—no, I'm *still* angry," I corrected myself as I spoke. "She barely even batted an eye when Stroud and Smiling Jade admitted to working behind her back with Edith and Ransom, just because of *us*. She should have stood her ground and told both of the thief lords to go straight to hell."

"Did you ever stop to think that's what she had *you* do?" Molly looked at me with a raised eyebrow. "As a thief lord, she needs to work with both Stroud and Smiling Jade in a professional capacity and act in the best interest of our guild, even if she wanted to claw both of their eyes out."

"What do you mean?" I cocked my head at my girlfriend, having not quite expected the response I'd just received.

"You called Stroud, the *thief lord* of the most vicious guild in Eberia, a 'fucking idiot' to his face and had him effectively apologize in front of everyone," Molly told me, holding a single finger up high. "Then a few seconds later, when the two of them offered to pay for Fairfax's death and you exploded at them, *they flinched*. Isabella couldn't have done that, not if she wanted to maintain any sort of relationship with them long term."

"What?" I looked at Molly in confusion. "Why does any of that matter? It didn't change anything."

"Oh boy," Molly muttered under her breath as she shook her head at me. "Thankfully, you're handsome..."

"Ha!" Quinn snorted in amusement at Molly's comment.

"You really think causing two thief lords to flinch in *fear* didn't change anything?" Molly asked me rhetorically. "If anything, it made them *increase* whatever they planned to give us, just to make sure Isabella wouldn't feel slighted and to reassure themselves that she could still control you."

"Why the hell would they be afraid of me?" I questioned as I glared daggers at Quinn. "They didn't even know me before today. Only by reputation, if anything."

"You leaped straight into the gnasher's mouth and killed it from the inside, Lazarus," Molly shot back at me. "Sure, if it hadn't worked out, you would have respawned and it would have been fine, but if any of them had tried it and failed, that would have been it, they'd have been dead forever. You showed them the very thing that they fear about adventurers."

"Our immortality," I stated, realizing what Molly was getting at. "We don't care if we live or die, because we know that we'll always have another chance."

"Exactly," Molly acknowledged. "They're afraid that if we really wanted to, we would keep coming after them, no matter how many times they killed us. We would only need to get lucky once and they'd be gone forever."

"I never thought about it from their perspective," I said thoughtfully as I realized that Molly was completely right. "From their point of view, adventurers must be…terrifying."

There was a moment of silence as both Molly and Quinn looked at me expectantly.

"I think I owe Isabella an apology," I admitted, feeling a weight shift on my heart.

"I wouldn't consider her *entirely* blameless in this," Molly allowed. "But given what we're about to head into, it'd be best if you cleared the air between you two."

"You're right. Best if I get this over with right now while there's still time," I said with a sigh, turning my head towards Quinn. "Meet you over at the crafting area?"

"Sure thing," Quinn replied. "I'll prep your gear and we'll see if we can get your new cuirass fixed up in time."

"Thanks, Quinn," I said to the mage before giving Molly a quick peck on the cheek as I made my way out of the room. "I won't be long."

NINETEEN

LEAVING MOLLY AND QUINN BEHIND, I retraced my steps back towards the common room, feeling the weight of everything I had said to Isabella earlier in the day fall upon my shoulders. Intellectually, I could understand why we had been kept in the dark with regards to the political workings between the guilds, and I could even understand why the other thief lords had decided to keep both Edith and Ransom a secret.

What I was having trouble processing, however, was the chilling disregard that the other thief lords had displayed when their involvement had been found out, seeking to simply pay us off as an apology.

Technically, they admitted their involvement, though, I thought to myself, remembering Stroud's explanation of events back at the sewer hub. *They hid the whole thing for as long as it served them, but the moment it was in their favor to tell the truth, they did.*

My mental train of thought paused for a moment as I walked past a group of fully kitted-out thieves that were making their way towards one of the entrances back up to the surface, the five of them chatting confidently amongst themselves as they outlined a plan of attack on whatever target Isabella had assigned to them.

Taking in the sight for a moment, I felt my brain lurch forward as a subconscious revelation finally bubbled its way to the surface.

Damn it, I'm such an idiot! I've been thinking of them like they're normal people! I kicked myself as I tore my eyes from the departing thieves and glanced around me as if seeing the guild's headquarters for the first time.

Here I was in a deep underground hideout that had been purposefully designed not to be found by what passed as the law in Ascend Online, living a life as a criminal, completely surrounded by ruthless cutthroats, smugglers, and pickpockets. There really weren't any truly *good* people around me. The reason why I was having such a struggle in coming to terms with how I was feeling was because I had been trying to apply a real-life view of morality onto them.

Everyone here was guilty of at least something that would have had them ending up in prison had they done it in reality. Hell, in contrast, some of the things that I had done since I had started playing Ascend Online had a good chance of landing me in Eberia's prison if I were ever caught. Up until this moment, I had considered my choice to be a criminal player as an academic point, something that simply affiliated me with one faction within the city rather than the other.

I couldn't have been more wrong.

Everyone that belongs to a thieves guild is a hardened criminal, having survived long enough to make it up from a gang, I realized as I thought through the typical recruitment process that the thieves guilds employed. *And anyone who has managed to rise high enough to become a thief lord would naturally be the most ruthless and pragmatic of them all.*

I shook my head as I tried to switch my mental gears on how I had been looking at the underworld and what it truly meant to be a criminal player in Ascend Online. I'd thought I'd known what sort of tough moral choices I would be facing and had managed to come to terms with them, but the more I thought about it, the more I realized just how limited my experiences had been.

So far, all I had done in this game that had actually tested my morality had consisted of breaking into a few dozen buildings, then raiding the place, or roughing up a few unruly gangs that had stepped out of line. Thinking about it even further, I realized that everything I had done up until this point had been carefully orchestrated by Fairfax as he put Molly and me through the trials. I almost had a feeling that we had been soft-pedaled through the hard choices that the game would demand of us if we decided to stay on the criminal path. Just to make sure we weren't overwhelmed and rejected it out of reflex.

It worked reasonably well...at least until Fairfax died and I confronted Cayden. I closed my eyes as I recalled the dwarf's death. It had taken him some time to die after I had shot him in the throat, and the memory of him slowly gurgling to death wasn't one I was about to forget anytime soon.

Had I not killed him, Cayden would have been a permanent threat and would have never forgiven me for killing his entire gang, I mentally justified to myself. *He would have bided his time until he had an opportunity to strike back at me, and I would have likely found myself back in his torture chamber again.*

I slowly worked through my revelation as I continued my walk through the length of the guild headquarters, causing the chambers and people moving through them to blur around me. Eager to get my mind off of my spiraling thoughts, I brought up my quest journal and skimmed over my two active quests, realizing that both of them had updated without my notice.

▹QUEST UPDATED! NO HONOR AMONG THIEVES!
Betrayal! Your meeting with the Council of Thieves has implicated Thief Lord Dorian in Fairfax's death. However, when confronted with the accusation, Dorian attempted to kill you and all of the other Thief Lords. Through sacrifice and blood, you managed to survive his treacherous attack, all of the remaining Thief Lords agreeing on one course of action: War.
Tell Isabella your plan of attack: 0/1 (Timed: 87 minutes remaining)
Find Dorian: 0/1
Discover what Dorian has planned: 0/1

▹QUEST UPDATED! THE HEIST!
During your meeting with the Council of Thieves, you have learned that both Edith and Ransom were recruited by Thief Lord Dorian into his guild, the Damned, and was indirectly responsible for hiring you to infiltrate the Arcaneum. Given the scope of Dorian's betrayal in [No Honor Among Thieves], the Thief Lords of Eberia have tasked you in recovering the Artifact that you stole as well as finding both Edith and Ransom.
Find Edith (again): 0/1
Find Ransom: 0/1
Recover the Stolen Artifact: 0/1
(Optional) Recover Memory: 0/1

Going to have to move fast, I told myself, just realizing now that there was a time limit associated with the quest as I turned the final corner that led back towards the common room. *I still need to meet up with Quinn to see if I can re-forge that chestpiece before we all need to head out.*

Silently rehearsing what I was going to say to Isabella, I walked into the common room, surprised to see that in just the short few minutes that I'd been gone, it had managed to nearly empty itself.

Isabella doesn't waste time, I noted with silent appreciation as I walked into the room and spotted her standing by a larger group of thieves.

"Elmar, as requested, you and your group will be assigned to the adventurers," I heard Isabella tell a heavily muscled half-orc that was standing in front of her before she spotted me out of the corner of her eye. "I expect that—*eh,* Lazarus, you're back? Is something wrong?"

"No." I waved off her look of concern. "I actually just wanted a moment to talk with you before we all left."

Pursing her lips, Isabella stared at me for a moment before nodding once.

"All right," she stated, before motioning towards the half-orc she had been talking to earlier. "But before that, I would like to introduce you to Elmar, one of our best bruisers, and the rest of your team."

"Team?" I echoed with a slightly confused expression as I extended my hand to the half-orc, counting the group gathered around us. "I didn't think we had enough bodies for us to have our own team, let alone a *dozen!*"

"We all volunteered," Elmar replied in Isabella's stead as he grasped my hand and gripped it tightly. "Adventurers always seem to end up where the fighting is the thickest, and after what that *bastard* Dorian did to Fairfax, we all want our pound of flesh, either from him or from his followers. You're our best ticket to getting that."

"We won't turn away help," I told the half-orc with a small grin as I looked towards the group of assembled thieves, seeing all of their eager expressions. "But at the same time, we're planning on jumping right down the dragon's throat. Molly's picked out six of the Damned's largest hideouts closest to the hall that the noble heirs were killed at today, and we're looking to hit each of them back to back. Are you all ready for that kind of heat?"

"Sounds like a fucking party for the ages," Elmar said with a fang-filled grin, despite his eyes taking on a faraway look as he understood my meaning. If we were focusing on hitting the hardest and most heavily defended hideouts that the Damned had, casualties were going to be inevitable. Turning his head towards the group, Elmar quickly barked, "What do you all think? Can we keep up with Lazarus and his crew?"

A disembodied chorus of cheers and profanity echoed from the group of cutthroats gathered around us as they all expressed their excitement.

"We're ready for anything you got, adventurer!" a voice called out.

"You're going to have to worry about keeping up with *us*, scrub!" a second voice shouted.

"Just fucking watch us!" a third chimed in, even louder than the others.

"I think you have your answer there," Elmar told me with a raised eyebrow. "The Damned won't know what hit them."

"Damn right." I nodded in approval towards Elmar and the rest of the thieves while silently hoping that the majority of them would survive the night.

"We're counting on you to make a big impact tonight," Isabella said, addressing all of us as she spoke. "You're going to be one of the largest groups on the streets tonight and the only one with adventurers—on our side, at least."

I saw a wave of nervousness cross Isabella's face at her last statement.

"As I've told the other groups before you, our primary goal for this war is the complete and utter purge of Dorian and his guild," Isabella continued, giving each of us a hard look as she spoke. "But in order to do that effectively, we need to make sure that nothing escapes our notice, and that requires information. If, during your assaults, you come across *anything* that may help expose other cells belonging to the Damned or anything that pertains to the dark magic that Dorian has been using, collect it and bring it to me or one of the other thief lords as quickly as possible.

"It may be the difference between interrupting whatever Dorian has planned, or having Eberia descend into civil war," Isabella finished morbidly.

There was a short pause after Isabella finished speaking, everyone quietly mulling over just how close the city was to descending into anarchy. Looking at the faces of everyone gathered around us, I could tell that they knew all too well what a civil war would do to Eberia as it tore itself apart from within.

"Finish getting ready and make sure that your gear is in order," Isabella ordered while looking at Elmar, breaking the awkward silence that hung over us. "I'll speak to Lazarus privately in the side room."

"Yes, ma'am," Elmar replied somewhat somberly as he gave me a nod. "We should be ready within the hour, Lazarus. Just let me know when you're ready to move out."

"I will," I acknowledged as I turned to follow Isabella, who led the way to the same spare room where she had set up a temporary office what seemed like a lifetime ago.

Closing the door behind me as the two of us entered the room, I didn't waste any time in broaching the subject that I had come back this way for.

"Isabella, I came here to apologize about how I behaved around the other thief lords," I said, watching the blonde-haired woman's expression go flat as she turned around to face me. "I was angry about their betrayal and how they simply tried to buy us off. I-I'm not used to that way of thinking, and while it's not the best excuse, I was caught off guard and reacted poorly."

Staring at me intently, Isabella said nothing as her green eyes bored into mine. Silence filled the air as I waited for her to say something, if only to berate me, then throw me out of the room.

"Fairfax and I...were lovers," Isabella finally whispered, her throat visibly twitching with emotion as she spoke. "And have been for nearly twenty years."

Eyes widening, I felt my jaw drop slightly as Isabella continued speaking.

"You said only a fraction of what I wanted to say to them," Isabella ground out slowly as she struggled to get her grief under control. "I wanted to *kill* them where they stood."

Isabella coughed as she cleared her throat and looked at me with misty eyes.

"I knew we *could* have killed them where they stood and blamed it all on Dorian, but—"

"That would have likely cost us Eberia," I finished in sudden understanding.

"It would have," Isabella agreed as she crossed her arms over her chest protectively. "And Fairfax would have never forgiven me for that. He loved both Eberia and the guild far too much to see it go to ruin, even with the stranglehold that the king had on him for the majority of his life."

"I wish I'd had a chance to get to know him better," I said with a deep sigh, unsure of how to process what I was feeling. Here I was, living in a virtual reality completely divorced from real life, yet I found myself mourning a digital entity, one that I had barely known for three weeks.

"Fairfax and I weren't fools," Isabella continued in a husky tone as she looked towards the ground. "We knew that our relationship would likely end with the other's violent death. Very few have ever had the luxury to die of old age in the underworld. Yet for all that rationalization, we never anticipated a betrayal of this magnitude."

"Did you really have that many problems bringing Molly and me into the underworld?" I asked, remembering what Stroud and Smiling Jade had said. "It seems to me that all of this started because of us."

"The other thief lords were highly resistant to the idea," Isabella admitted. "More so than either Fairfax or I ever realized, in hindsight. They all wanted to take a wait-and-see approach, and to allow the majority of adventurers to disperse away from Eberia before beginning any recruitment.

"We, on the other hand, didn't want to recruit the dregs that stayed behind," Isabella said while motioning to me. "We wanted to lay claim to the best candidates as early as possible, before they left the city and sought their fortune out in the wild."

"I was close to leaving," I admitted as I thought back to launch day. "Had I not seen Molly lift a key from a blacksmith in the marketplace and decided to follow her, I would have likely left with the rest of the adventurers to Coldscar."

"And we would have missed out on the chance to recruit you." Isabella nodded in understanding. "Given the asset that both you and Molly have been to the guild since joining, I daresay that Fairfax and I had the right approach. But more importantly, if it weren't for you, Lazarus, it is likely that we would have never found out what happened to Fairfax." Isabella looked at me intently as she spoke. "I would have simply assumed he was delayed in meeting with the king and turned my attention towards the conflict brewing between the nobles. All the while, Dorian and the other thief lords would have continued to work behind our backs."

"Do you think that the others had any idea of what Dorian has been planning? With Edith murdering the noble heirs and whatever he had us steal from the Arcaneum..." I asked, suddenly feeling uncomfortable on how much had hinged on my coincidental discovery of Fairfax's body.

"No," Isabella replied after a moment of thought. "They fully admitted that they knew about Edith and Ransom and that their role was to masquerade as independent contractors within the underworld. But when I asked them about both the Arcaneum and the summoned devils, they were surprised beyond measure. The more I think about what you and Molly have told me, the more I'm inclined to believe that Dorian orchestrated the heist to frame both you and Molly," Isabella told me in her normal tone, the raw emotion in her voice having faded away. "But something went wrong and Edith was forced to improvise."

"You think it relates to the sigil?" I asked, feeling the ever-present energy of the strange rune pulse on my chest. "Edith…was twisted by something the last time I had fought her; it was almost if she had been partially transformed. She also accused me of ruining whatever she had planned."

"I truly do not know," Isabella said with a resigned shrug. "But unless we stop whatever Dorian has planned tonight and present his head to the nobles, I don't think it will matter. So much has happened in the last two days that I had never dreamed was possible, and yet my stomach is in knots, fearing that it is likely going to get much worse before it will get better."

"We'll see it through to the end," I told Isabella confidently, despite sharing the same twisting sensation in my stomach. "We've managed to get this far, and we have Dorian on the run. It's only a matter of time before he makes a mistake, and then we'll tear him to pieces."

"I hope so," Isabella replied with a thin smile that didn't reach her eyes. "It may be dramatic for me to say, but I believe that the fate of Eberia depends on our actions tonight. Should we fail…all might be lost."

"Then we better not fail."

TWENTY

WE WERE ALL HUDDLED ON either side of Quinn, pressed hard against the wall as the mage slowly conjured a burning orb of fire in his hands. Standing half a step behind him, I momentarily tore my eyes off the growing fireball and glanced behind me, checking on the remaining members of our team that filled the long hallway. Scanning their faces, I saw that they were all intently focused on the heavy wooden door ahead of us, bloodied weapons held high in their hands. Feeling Molly's hand touch the small of my back as a shimmering shield enveloped me, I turned back towards the door and gripped my sword tight.

"Five, four, three," Quinn counted down in hushed tones as he strained to contain his spell. "Two, one! Breach!"

Quinn called out as the fireball sped from his hands and smashed into the heavy door before us, sending it crashing inwards with explosive force.

"Go, go, go!" I shouted, leaping into the room behind the exploding door, not even bothering to wait for the flames to clear. I felt the power of the sigil consume me as I sprinted through the shattered doorframe, my vision clouding over into a now-familiar crimson haze.

It had been three hours since we'd left the guild headquarters, three hours that the entire underworld had been at war.

And it was even more vicious and brutal than I ever thought it would be.

Rushing through the billowing smoke of Quinn's fireball, I found myself bursting into a large room filled with overturned tables and piled chairs, serving as makeshift defenses to slow down our assault. With everyone flinching from the sudden explosion, I managed to clear nearly half the distance to the barricade before the panic-stricken defenders recovered and fired a volley of crossbow bolts in my direction.

The majority of the bolts directed at me were aimed out of reflex and flew wide as I sprinted across the room. However, a handful of the more experienced defenders took a moment to check their aim before firing, their bolts crashing into the magical shield that Molly had cast upon me. Pulsing with a dull flash of light, the shield managed to deflect two crossbow bolts into the ground before shattering, leaving a third bolt to slam straight into my chest.

Feeling like I had been struck by a hammer, I couldn't help but grunt as the bolt rebounded off of the heavy chestplate that was my newly reforged armor, leaving me slightly winded but otherwise unharmed. Continuing my charge forward, I heard the room break out into shouts as the deafening echo of Quinn's spell began to fade from the air. With my full momentum behind me, a powerful leap easily sent me over the barricade and crashing into the cowering group of defenders hiding behind it.

Kicking one of the defenders hard in the chest as I landed, I sent him sprawling backwards, feeling ribs crack and snap under my heavy boot. Giving no time for the other defenders to recover, I swept my blade around myself in a wide cleave, barely feeling its razor edge slice through the two defenders standing on either side of me, causing both of them to fall to the ground, each clutching a massive wound across their body.

Whirling to my left where the defenders were thickest, I rushed down the enemy line, barely noting the fleeting tags that appeared in my vision as I picked out my next target.

[Guild Cutthroat] – The Damned – Level 8

The sigil's rage flowing through me felt muted and distant as I dispassionately carved my way through another thief, splitting the terrified man's chest open with a near effortless swing of my sword, then kicking the falling body away from me.

I had long lost count of how many people we had killed since the war began, focusing instead on the task at hand while reminding myself that this was just all a game. Whatever soothing magic that the game system played on my psyche was all that was keeping me standing, constantly blurring the nonstop combat over the last three hours into a distant memory.

I thought I had understood what Isabella had meant when she'd said that this war wasn't one of conquest and that it would it be a vicious, bloody fight through the city.

I was wrong.

This was a war of vengeance, a savage example of what the consequences were for betraying the underworld. There were no warnings, ultimatums, or threats given to the Damned. There was simply a sudden rush of violence as hard men and women broke into the Damned's hideouts with murder on their minds.

By the time the morning sun rises, the Damned will no longer exist as a guild, I told myself through gritted teeth as I mechanically smashed the hilt of my sword into a cutthroat's face to knock him backwards, then drew my glass-steel blade across his body. *Even if we don't end up finding Dorian and Edith.*

"Clear!" Elmar's voice rang out behind me, bringing me back into the present and piercing through the crimson veil that hung over me.

It's clear already? The thought pierced the crimson veil that hung over me as several other voices began calling out the same. I turned to cast a glance around the room, startled to find that the barricades I had leaped over had been completely shattered by magic. A handful of bodies littered the ground in front of the barricade, some singed with arcane fire while others were filled like pincushions with crossbow bolts. I felt my heart flip in my chest when I noticed that two of the fallen belonged to Elmar's group of thieves.

I didn't even hear any of the magic behind me. My eyes drank in the sight as I slowly processed what I was seeing.

"Clear," I called out belatedly as I dismissed the sigil's power from my body and shifted my glance back to the path of carnage that I had wrought through the defenders' ranks. Eight bodies, all belonging to the Damned, littered the ground behind me as I realized that I had taken just under half of the defenders singlehandedly, sweeping through them with little more effort than a scythe did to wheat.

But what scared me most of all was that I barely even remembered doing so, the combat already appearing as brief, passing flashes in my memory.

"What a waste," I spat bitterly, feeling the acrid smell of copper in my throat as I slowly became aware of my body, the lingering effects of the sigil finally fading away.

Reaching up to my chest, I felt a dull aching pain in the exact spot where the crossbow bolt had struck me.

Damn, that was lucky. I ran my fingers along the newly reforged armor and found a small scar in the metal, centered right over my heart. Swallowing hard, I couldn't help but glance once again at the fallen bodies, unconsciously bringing up the item's stats in my vision as I made a mental note to thank Quinn again for his help.

Grim Shadow Bruiser's Cuirass
Slot: Chest
Item Class: Relic
Item Quality: Mastercraft (+20%)
Armor: 110
Armor Type: Light
Strength: +3 Agility: +3
Durability: 179/180
Weight: 5.5 kg
Grim Shadow Bruiser Armor Set: 1/7

That could have been me, I thought to myself as a wave of guilt then forced me to tear my eyes away from the sight and look around the hideout that we had just stormed.

It was the fifth hideout on Molly's list belonging to the Damned that we had attacked, and the second one with a significant amount of opposition. The element of surprise had lasted long enough for the three of us, aided by Elmar and his crew, to easily raid and destroy the first three hideouts without any serious casualties. But by the time we had reached the fourth, word had begun to get out about the war consuming the district and we had begun running into prepared defenses.

And had begun losing people.

Judging from the bodies lying on the ground before me, our casualty count had now risen to four. A third of all the team that had been assigned to us, that *volunteered* to come with us.

"Lazarus!" Molly's voice echoed from the far end of the rectangularly shaped room, which I realized was much larger than I had thought, now that I had a chance to look around and collect my bearings. "We have a prisoner."

"A prisoner?" I called back with surprise as I started walking towards her voice, passing by a pair of guildmembers that had begun the grisly task of checking and moving the dead. "I thought we weren't taking prisoners."

"We still might not be," Molly called back to me as I finally spotted both her, Quinn, and Elmar standing on the far side of the room in front of two massive tables with a man kneeling before them. "It depends on how cooperative he is."

As I approached the trio, my eyes were drawn to three intact skeletons that lay on the two tables behind them, one of them being notably smaller than the other. Shifting my glance towards the man in front of her, I noted that he was much better dressed than any of the other thugs that we had just sliced our way through, and his demeanor was far too haughty for one caught in the middle of an underworld war.

Clutching at a wound in his arm, the silver-haired man had been clearly burnt and beaten during our attack as he stared up defiantly at Molly, the sleeve of his finely crafted grey robes slowly turning dark while a small puddle of blood dripped down on the floor from his hand. Holding her sabre to the man's throat casually, Molly nodded her head towards me as I came into range.

Looking up at me with pale blue eyes, I saw the faintest flash of fear cross the man's eyes before it was replaced by a scowl.

"You have all made a *dreadful* mistake tonight," the man hissed as he slowly shifted his glance away from me and back towards Molly, mindful of the sabre sitting on his neck. "The Damned will have your heads for this."

"I doubt it," Elmar stated bluntly while shaking his head at the man as if he were a small child. "Seeing how the Damned is set to be purged tonight."

"You are insane!" the man exclaimed in disbelief. "You can't *purge* a guild the size of the Damned!"

"You can when all four of the other guilds are helping you," Quinn replied to the silver-haired man.

"They would never do such a thing," the man snorted in derision, despite a sudden twinge of nervousness in his voice. "It would cause chaos!"

"Have you even *looked* out into the city today?" I asked rhetorically, cutting into the conversation while casting a glance towards my girlfriend. "Why are you keeping this guy alive, Molly? He's an idiot."

"He is," Molly agreed while motioning her head towards something on the table with the three skeletons on it. "But we found *those* things here."

Glancing towards the table, I saw a number of various tools and implements scattered amongst the bones of the three skeletons, their purpose not easily recognizable to me. Judging from the fine powder that covered nearly everything on the table, along with the surrounding floor, I guessed that they had something to do with either cutting or working bone.

Continuing my scan, I found my eyes landing on three spherically shaped pieces of bone that lay separate from the other tools. Each of the pieces appeared to be engraved with a variety of runic marks, half of which had been inlaid with gold and the other half with silver. Joined to the bone with a golden clasp was a dull gray length of leather that looked like it had been braided together from several smaller pieces.

Feeling my skin begin to crawl the longer I looked at the grisly craftsmanship, I called up the item's tag, already suspecting what was lying before me.

[Hellborn Soul Shard]

Shifting my glance back towards the one smaller skeleton, I noticed that it was missing several of the bones that belonged to its leg.

"So, you were the one who made those." The words hissed out of my mouth as I looked down towards the kneeling man. "What are they, exactly?"

"Like I would divulge guild secrets to you!" the man countered without even bothering to look in my direction.

"You wouldn't be divulging much," Molly said as she pressed her sabre into the man's throat, drawing a thin line of blood and causing the man to gasp. "We already know that they are used as vessels to store the spirits of devils called from another plane and that they can be given to unwitting people, then forcefully possessed by a command word."

The man's eyes widened slightly at Molly's information, but to his credit, he maintained a silent and defiant glare as he looked up at her.

"I would take this opportunity while we're still asking politely and at least tell us *something*," Quinn told the man. "We're not exactly in a patient mood, and you're not really giving us a reason to keep you alive."

"Then stop wasting your time," the man goaded in a shaky voice as he leaned forward into Molly's sword. "Let us be done with it, then; death would be a small price to pay compared to what the Damned would do to me if they even *suspected* me of speaking secrets."

"We can protect you from that," Molly offered, easing her weapon from the man's throat. "But only if you tell us *everything* about these soul shards and what Dorian has planned for them."

"You are wasting your breath, girl," the man growled. "Assuming I even know anything, I wouldn't betray my guild so easily."

"That...is a shame," Molly replied sadly as her eyes flicked over to me meaningfully while removing the sabre from the man's throat. "Because we're really not in a position to take no for an answer."

Staring up at Molly for a moment, the man processed her words, his face turning pale as he caught her hidden meaning. "Do your—*oof!*"

His reply was cut off as my boot smashed into his kidneys and sent him sprawling to the side, cracking the side of his head off of the heavy table before crashing into the ground. Not letting up for a second, I stepped closer to the man, using the momentum to send an even more powerful kick into his body, the meaty thump of my foot connecting with his body echoing through the air.

Concussed from the impact of hitting his head, the man threw up almost immediately as he fell to the ground before contorting wildly in pain from my thunderous kicks with a desperate moan. Taking a step back from the dazed and wounded man, I noticed that the fall had caused his already weeping arm to begin gushing with blood as it began to pool on the ground.

Motioning to Molly, I took a second step backwards as she knelt down towards the fallen man, touching him gently with a glowing hand.

"This will happen as many times as it needs to." The man flinched in surprise as she whispered to him before standing back up and giving me a nod.

Bending down, I grabbed the man by the ankle and effortlessly dragged him across the ground and away from the table, turning him over onto his back in the process. Looking up at me with a freshly healed face, the man's defiant expression had been replaced with one of pure terror as Molly's words sank into his mind.

Pulling back a fist while wrapping my other hand around the man's throat, I added my own words for the man to ponder.

"You should have talked while you had the chance."

"NOW, THAT YOU'RE FEELING MORE cooperative, Hedon, I'm going to ask you again," Molly said to the dazed man sitting on the floor as she held one of the soul shards in front of his face with a pair of pliers. "What is this?"

"It's a type of soul shard," Hedon replied numbly, his eyes straining to focus on the bone talisman that Molly was holding. "One attuned to a specific plane."

"And which one is that, exactly?" Molly asked.

"I do not know," the man replied before blinking twice, then suddenly lifting his hands towards Elmar and me in a panic. "I *honestly* do not know! The instructions I were given did not say, *I swear it*!"

"Instructions?" I queried while looking down at the uninjured, yet still blood-covered man.

"On how to craft the soul shard," Hedon explained. "Thief Lord Dorian presented the blueprints to me and the other bonecarvers. We were not permitted to ask questions, only to follow our orders."

"There are other...*bonecarvers*?" Quinn jumped in with a note of worry in his voice. "How many of you are there?"

"Nine, that I know of," Hedon replied with a shrug. "Possibly more if they trained their own apprentices or if the guild recruited others."

"And you were all tasked with creating these soul shards?" Molly glanced at Quinn, catching on to his train of thought.

"As far as I know," Hedon answered slowly as he inclined his head towards the skeletons on the table. "The materials needed to create them aren't the easiest to come by, but Dorian was...adamant that we not slow our pace."

Following the man's glimpse towards the table, something finally clicked and caused my eyes to widen in surprise.

"You're HP," I stated as I recited one of the entries in Cayden's ledger. "Three intact skeletons, two human, one elf. Dry and clean."

"Damn," Molly cursed in surprise as her head swiveled towards the table and landed on the skeletons. "You're right, Lazarus."

"H-How do you know that?" Hedon's eyes widened as he cowered away from me.

"I killed Cayden," I answered bluntly while motioning towards the table. "Where is the rest of the order?"

"Y-You did *what*?" Hedon stuttered, his eyes widening in fear.

"You heard me," I growled at the cowering bonecarver. "Where is the rest of the order? The gold, the crystals, the skin?"

"Gone, used up," the man answered. "The crystals were taken to another location. I don't know where, but the rest of it..."

Hedon waved at the necklace that Molly still held before him.

"How many of these have you created?" Quinn asked slowly before correcting himself. "*No*, how many of these do you think have been created between you and all of the bonecarvers?"

"That's hard to say," Hedon hedged. "I don't know how fast the others may have been working, or if they ran short of materials..."

"Take a guess, then!" I barked harshly, a sudden pit of dread filling my stomach.

"Ah!" Hedon flinched as he reflexively covered his face. "I don't know! At least a hundred, probably closer to two hundred by now!"

Feeling the world lurch out from under me as I processed the implications of what Hedon had just said, I slowly looked towards Molly and Quinn, seeing pure shock written across both of their faces.

Making eye contact with me, Molly was the first to recover from the man's words, her simple statement managing to capture exactly what each of us were thinking at the moment.

"Oh, fuck."

TWENTY-ONE

TWENTY MINUTES LATER, WE WERE all sprinting through the moonlit streets of Eberia as if Hell itself were chasing us, which given Hedon's gut-wrenching revelation, we fully expected to become reality. Even in our wildest estimates, we'd never imagined that Dorian would have been insane enough or even able to produce so many soul shards in such a short timeframe.

The only silver lining that we were all desperately clinging to was that the soul shards had yet to be filled with a devil's spirit, a process that, despite repeated questioning, Hedon had been unable to shed any light on.

What the hell could Dorian be planning with so many soul shards? I fervently thought to myself as we continued to race through the city, desperate to reach the command post that the thief lords had established in the district and inform them of our discovery. *He can't possibly believe that he'd be able to control that many devils all at once!*

My mind drifted back to the battle in the sewer hub just after Dorian had shown his true colors and attacked us. *He said something about wanting to save everyone, but that his life was on the line too. Does that mean that someone else is controlling him?*

How do the nobles factor into this too? What would Dorian gain by having them at one another's throats? I started to feel overwhelmed as I tried to unravel everything that had happened over the last day. *Even with everything that we've discovered so far, we're still five steps behind.*

Shouts ahead of us echoed through the air as we approached a hidden checkpoint, followed by a group of rough-looking men and women running out of the shadows ahead of us.

"Hold up!" a deep, raspy voice called out of the shadows. "Identify yourself!"

"Grim Shadows!" I barked. "We need to see the thief lords!"

"For what—" a second voice started to challenge, before being overruled by the first voice.

"Shut up! These are the adventurers we were told about! Let them through!"

Reflexively scanning the area as we closed the distance, I counted six cutthroats that were manning the checkpoint, along with two others hiding on the nearby rooftops. One of the larger cutthroats waved at us as we slowed down, his voice revealing that he was the one who had called out the challenge.

"Any heat on your tail we need to know about?" The experienced thief didn't waste any time as he waved the rest of the guards away, picking up his pace to match ours as we jogged through the checkpoint.

"No, nothing we saw, at least." I shook my head as I thumbed a hand behind me towards Elmar, who was carrying a bound and gagged

Hedon over his shoulder. "We found some really hot intel that the thief lords need to know about."

"Shit," the man cursed. "How hot are we talking about here?"

"You could say Hell is *literally* about to break loose," Quinn panted from somewhere behind me, completely winded from the long run.

"Fuck, man, that's no joke tonight," he cursed a second time before pointing straight ahead of us at a well-lit tavern. "The command post is in there. I'm going to put everyone on high alert right now just in case."

"Probably a good idea," I heard Molly comment behind me as the veteran thief peeled away from us and began calling out orders to nearby guards that I couldn't see.

Keeping a brisk pace, we closed the remaining distance between us and the tavern, only to have a loud, angry voice greet our ears as I pushed the door open.

"I don't *fucking* care what sort of shit you're sorting out between yourselves! I don't want to know about it! I just want you to fucking finish it as quickly as goddamn possible!"

"I assure you that is exactly what we are doing, *Captain Fontaine*," I heard Isabella's voice reply curtly as I stepped inside and spotted a tall, grey-haired man dressed in bright chainmail standing a short distance away from the four thief lords, who all stood shoulder to shoulder, including a new thief lord that I did not recognize.

Whipping his head around towards me as the door creaked, the man's piercing green eyes locked on to me, before shifting behind me as the others passed through the door. Taking a halting step forward, I glanced down at the heraldry on the man's armor, my brain skipping a beat as I recognized that it belonged to the city guard.

Did Isabella really say "Captain Fontaine"? I felt my breath catch slightly as I looked back up towards the man's now scowling face.

"I should have known you had a group of fucking adventurers involved in all of this." Captain Fontaine shifted his head back towards the four thief lords. "Anything that goes wrong in the city these days is because of a fucking, gods-cursed adventurer, and I'll bet this time is no—"

"Are you done here, *Edward*?" Stroud interrupted in a loud and commanding voice. "You've delivered your threats and we've listened to them out of respect to our *arrangement*."

"Oh, I'm fucking done here all right!" Captain Fontaine growled before spitting on the ground in front of the thief lords and holding up his finger. "*Pray* that this works for you all, because if it *doesn't*…I am going to come back with every single guard under my command and tear this district apart until I get each and every one of your heads to lay at Crawridge's and Wynbrandt's feet."

"Overly dramatic," Smiling Jade replied coolly. "But your point has been made, captain, twice now."

Grunting in anger, Captain Fontaine glared at the thief lords for a moment longer before tearing his gaze away and moving to leave the tavern. Pressing myself against the wall as the man made to move past me and out the door, I couldn't help but flinch out of reflex when he stopped in front of me.

"I'll tell you the same thing I told them," he growled as he reached out for the door handle. "Fix. This. Shit. *Now.* Cause if you don't, I am going to make it my life's mission to see you lot thrown into the Tower of Atonement for an indefinite sentence, even if I have to drag my own ass in with you."

Wrenching the door open before I could even think of a reply, the captain of the Eberian Guard stepped through and slammed it behind him with such force that I could hear the frame crack from the impact.

Stunned from the scene that we had just walked in on, I couldn't help but glance towards Molly and Quinn, seeing the same expression of surprise on their faces that I knew was on mine.

"What the fuck was that?" Quinn gasped. "That was Captain

Fontaine, he's the—"

"Leader of the Eberian Guard, yes," the new thief lord that I didn't recognize finished wearily as she beckoned us forward. "And *that* was politics."

"Politics?" I asked in disbelief as I looked at the dark-furred Tul'Shar. Dressed in much more sensible clothes when compared to her predecessor, the Tul'Shar wore a finely crafted suit of dark leather armor that matched almost perfectly with her fur, complete with a long, thin blade hanging from her waist. "Sounded like he was ready to tear this place down on your heads."

"Men like Edward feel the need to shout to make their point," Stroud commented dismissively. "They believe that their noise and bluster hide the fact that they are afraid. It does not."

"What's going on, Lazarus? We didn't expect you back so soon," Isabella remarked as we made our way into the tavern with a worried note in her voice, her eyes shifting to the bound and gagged Hedon as Elmar pulled him off his shoulder and set him on the ground.

"Uh," I stalled for a moment, torn between wanting to press harder on why the captain of the city fuard was on a first-name basis with the thief lords, but also remembering the reason why we had rushed so quickly across the city.

"We have a *serious* problem," I began as I forced my curiosity down, waving at Hedon's bound and gagged form. "We were wrong in thinking how many of those talismans Edith and Dorian may have had available to them.

"According to *him,* they're actually called hellborn soul shards, and Dorian has conscripted a team of Bonecarvers to craft them en masse," I continued explaining as Molly strode towards the thief lords with a heavy leather bag in hand. "Based on what he's made alone, he thinks that Dorian may have at least a hundred, if not closer to two hundred soul shards at his disposal."

There was a deathly silence as all of the thief lords stiffened at the news, the features of those with visible faces widening in shock.

"T-This...was not anticipated," Smiling Jade replied haltingly as Molly approached and showed her the contents of the bag. Hesitantly, the thief lord reached inside and pulled one of the soul shards free, letting it dangle in the air from its leather cord. "How could Dorian have hidden all this from us?"

"Hm," the new Crimson Rat thief lord growled under her breath softly, glancing at the hanging soul shard briefly before turning her bright red eyes towards us. "None of the parties that have checked in have reported finding any of these...*soul shards*. If so many have been made, why haven't we found any thus far?"

"I don't know," I said honestly, pointing once more towards the terrified bonecarver lying on the ground, his eyes staring intently at the four thief lords before him. "Hedon here told us that his instructions were to leave the soul shards at specific drop points in the city, where they would be picked up later by another cell and delivered to their final destination. Based on what we've been able to learn, it would likely take a ritual of some sort to bind a devil's spirit to the soul shard, which would take time to set up."

"Which could also be anywhere in the city," the woman added with a scowl as her predatory eyes glanced down towards Hedon, easily spotting the dried blood that covered his face and body. "Are you certain he is not holding anything back?"

"As certain as I can be given the time we had," I replied as I looked down towards Hedon and seeing him squirm under the implied threat. "Based on what he's told us, we thought it would be best to let you know as soon as possible."

"If what he's saying is true," Isabella said with a sigh as she rubbed her head, trying to stave off an impending headache, "it was good you did."

"We will know for certain before the night is out, one way or the other." The Tul'Shar's eyes focused on the bound mage as she spoke, then flicked towards Elmar and the remaining thieves. "With your permission, Isabella, perhaps Elmar can begin a second round of… *questioning* to be sure that there is nothing else being withheld from us?"

"I believe that might be appropriate," Isabella replied, heedless of Hedon's panicked shouts through his gag as he lay on the floor. "Elmar, if you'd please? There is a room in the back that you can use. The rest of you can join the guards outside for the time being."

"Of course," Elmar affirmed as he bent down to lift Hedon off the ground again and threw the now thrashing bonecarver over his shoulder, giving us all a wave as he walked towards a closed door on the far end of the room. "In case you all get sent out again without me, thanks for the great night, everyone."

"Bye, Elmar," I called after the bruiser at the same time that the rest of the thieves that had joined us for the night filtered out of the tavern.

"Now that we can speak a bit more freely," Smiling Jade commented. "Was there anything else that you found?"

"We found supporting evidence at the scene that implicated the Undertakers," Molly answered with a nod. "There were materials needed to create the soul shards at the hideout that corresponded directly to a ledger that Lazarus recovered from Cayden."

"Then there is no doubt that he was involved from the very beginning?" Stroud asked.

"As a supplier, most definitely." Molly nodded as she shook the bag containing the soul shards. "Now that I have a better idea of what it takes to create the soul shards, I'm all but certain that Cayden has supplied the bulk of the materials that were needed to create them."

"Given the Undertakers' affiliation with the Damned, that is unsurprising," Smiling Jade noted as she continued to inspect the soul shard dangling from her hand. "However, there is a rather substantial amount of gold and silver required in this piece, enough that it should have affected market prices and drawn our notice."

"Not if Dorian melted down coins," Quinn said, causing all of us to turn in this direction and for him to take a step backwards at the sudden attention. "Ah, I mean, he'd have gold and silver coins on hand, right? If he smelted them down, he wouldn't have had to buy enough raw gold and silver to attract attention."

"That would be almost prohibitively expensive," Smiling Jade replied slowly as she cocked her head over to one side. "But it would work..."

"It doesn't explain why Dorian would choose to burn a sizable portion of his treasury to create what I understand is a single-use item without expecting something even greater in return, though," the dark-furred thief lord pointed out as Smiling Jade dropped the soul shard back into the bag Molly was holding.

"Whatever he has planned, Dorian has proven to be no fool, and I am certain he has an end goal in mind," Stroud said with a rare note of frustration seeping into his voice. "Even with the short amount of time available to him since his betrayal, he's managed to mobilize his guild faster than we had thought was possible."

"What do you mean?" Quinn asked, walking forward to stand beside me. "Is the war not going well?"

"It...*goes*," Isabella replied, mirroring Stroud's tone. "The Damned have proven to be harder to find than we anticipated, and many of the hideouts we've managed to raid so far have been empty or abandoned, some seemingly long before today, others just bare minutes before our raiders arrived."

"Abandoned hideouts?" I echoed in confusion. "We didn't find any abandoned hideouts in the northern half of the district. Granted, we only managed to hit five of the six on our list before coming here, and each of them were packed with the Damned."

"*Really?*" the still nameless Tul'Shar replied thoughtfully as she turned around and practically ran towards a large table set up behind the thief lords. "That is extremely interesting."

"What are you looking for, Sable?" Isabella asked as we all rushed forward towards the table and spotted a familiar-looking map of the New District that had been laden down with countless markers.

"I didn't think anything of it before, but look at how many abandoned hideouts have been discovered in the southern and southwestern portions of the district," Sable said excitedly, waving a fur-covered hand over a multitude of grey-colored markers. "Nearly two thirds of them are in the southern half of the district and were abandoned before our attacks even started, compared to barely a quarter the further north in the district we look. All of this despite our raids starting at roughly the same time.

"Even if we account for those that may have been abandoned naturally since we've discovered them, there are a disproportionate number of abandoned hideouts to the south," the thief lord continued.

"You think that the hideouts in the southern half of the district must have gotten Dorian's warning first and had a longer chance to flee," I said, realizing what the feline thief lord was getting at.

"I do," Sable answered with a nod. "We have had to re-task several teams that have come up emptyhanded after visiting their prearranged locations in the south, and we sent them north without much of a second thought. I didn't think anything of it at the time, but you're the only team we've sent that far into the northern reaches of the district that has returned to us so far."

"Hm." I paused for a moment, looking at the map as my eyes absorbed the countless markers that had been stuck onto it. "Looking at this, I'm inclined to believe that Dorian's gathering his forces somewhere in the southern reaches of the district."

"Why would he do that, though?" Stroud asked while motioning towards the map. "The southern portion of the New District borders the ocean and can easily be cut off from the rest of the city if we seize these two streets leading back into the Market District. All Dorian has done is trap himself with nowhere else to go."

"Maybe he doesn't need to go anywhere." I walked around the table until I stood beside the giant warrior and looked at the streets that Stroud had just indicated. "The same streets that we'd use to cut him off from the city, he can also use to cut us off from the southern part of the district. I think he's just stalling for time."

"What do you mean?" Sable queried as she slid down the table towards me and Stroud. "Why would time be important to him?"

"We caught him unprepared earlier," I remembered as a few pieces began to fall into place. "Whatever he was planning wasn't ready yet, and he's been forced to accelerate his plans."

"Lazarus is right," Molly whispered as her eyes met mine, the same realization crossing her face. "We got so caught up in the war that we forgot about the one most important thing that Dorian has."

"The artifact Edith stole," Isabella hissed as she looked down at the map, the other thief lords following suit. "But there's a problem with that. If he's blocked off the southern—"

"Hey!" a loud voice shouted from just outside the tavern, causing all of us to turn towards the door as the sound of several crossbows firing filled the air.

"Stop him!" a second voice yelled a moment before something heavy hit the tavern door and tore it completely free from its hinges, sending it crashing to the floor with a thunderous bang.

"Shit, wait! Stop shooting!" a raspy voice managed to wheeze from its position directly on top of the broken door a heartbeat before three large shadows landed on top of it. "*Oof!* Let me go! I have information! I found her! I found Edith!"

Wrestling the intruder up off the ground, two of the shadows lifted a blood-covered man off the door, leaving me staring directly into a familiar face.

"*Sawyer?*" I heard myself shout as he was hefted upwards and muscled towards the now gaping doorway. "Wait! Let him stay! It's Sawyer!"

"Lazarus, *this* is the hunter you spoke about?!" Isabella asked in a commanding voice, the tone stopping the two men in their tracks.

"Yes!" I exclaimed as I shot a glance towards her, then back towards the dark-haired man. "What the hell, Sawyer? Why were they shooting at you?"

"They wouldn't let me pass," Sawyer said slowly as he panted from his earlier exertions, still being restrained by the two guards' grip, giving me, Quinn, and Molly enough time to note that his blood-red armor had been seriously scarred and damaged since the last time we'd seen him. "Told me this wasn't a place for bounty hunters."

"In normal circumstances, they would be right," Stroud stated rather brusquely.

"Is there *anything* about today that's normal?" Molly shot a dirty look towards Stroud as she moved forward to check Sawyer. "Are you hurt?"

"Nah, these scrubs couldn't hit the broad side of a barn." Sawyer shook his head as his breathing returned to a more normal rate. "But as for the armor, Edith roughed me up before she took off, but it took me a while to get here and I'm fine now."

"You found her?" Isabella asked at the mention of Edith's name, looking over Sawyer, unable to not notice the dried blood streaked across his face. Motioning for the two guards to let him go, she glanced at the other thief lords briefly before pressing on. "What happened?"

"We were outclassed," Sawyer sighed defeatedly as he rubbed his wrists while carefully watching the two thugs exit the tavern and take up position just outside the now broken door. "Not just me and my team, but an entire group of thugs that managed to get the drop on her."

"What do you mean?" Sable asked with concern, jumping into the conversation at the mention of a group of thieves being involved.

"We didn't see the beginning of the fight," Sawyer began to explain. "We were still, uh...*tracking* Edith when a fight drew our attention."

"Wait, tracking?" Quinn questioned. "What do you mean?"

"Uh, it's something that bounty hunters can do," Sawyer said as his eyes flicked to the mage before shifting back to me. "To help us find our targets instead of wandering around aimlessly all the time."

"I didn't realize you could do that," Quinn said uneasily. "But that explains how you found us earlier in the day."

"Yeah, well, we don't talk about it that much. For *obvious* reasons," Sawyer replied, clearly unwilling to divulge any more secrets than he had to. "Anyway, we were about a block away from her when one of your groups—" Sawyer waved at the thief lords, "—beat us to the punch and broke into the safe house she was hiding in...not that the surprise did them any good, from what I was able to piece together after the fact.

"I know you said Edith had *changed*, Lazarus," Sawyer continued, looking at me with a bewildered expression. "But I really wasn't prepared for what you meant by that."

Thinking back to the moment when I had first seen Edith at the pier, I couldn't help but nod grimly in understanding. "Yeah, I know exactly what you mean."

"By the time we realized that it was Edith causing the commotion and managed to make our way closer, there was nothing we could do to help the thieves." A haunted look crossed the warrior's face as he recalled the scene. "We intercepted her just as she finished off the last thief, and despite the injuries she had from the fight before, she still managed to put down both of the other hunters I had with me without too much trouble—not that they were exceptionally skilled to begin with."

"Shit, man," I cursed.

"After that—" Sawyer motioned to his armor as he spoke, "—the two of us proceeded to have a vicious duel in the middle of the street, and while I was able to keep pace with her, nothing I did could put her down. The longer the fight went on, though, the more frustrated she got, and eventually she landed a solid enough hit that threw me through a storefront window."

Sawyer let out a sigh and splayed his hands out in a gesture of helplessness. "By the time I managed to get my shit together and crawled out of the mess, she was gone."

"She just ran away?" Isabella said in disbelief.

"Like a lightning bolt," Sawyer replied. "We didn't exactly exchange that many words during our little brawl, but she seemed to be in a damned hurry; I think the thieves knocking on her door must have really surprised her."

"Why didn't you just keep tracking her?" I asked. "You did it when you found her the first time; can't you do it again?"

"No," Sawyer replied with a pained expression on his face as he was forced to disclose more of his faction's secrets. "My tracking ability only works for a short period of time every day. It eventually resets itself, but I've used all of it up looking for Edith. That's part of the reason why I tried so hard to keep the other bounty hunters with me, so we could split the use of our ability."

"I don't suppose we can count on them for help, can we?" I asked, already knowing what Sawyer would tell me.

"They dropped group as soon as they died," Sawyer answered bitterly. "It was hard enough keeping them interested this long, with the nobles getting ready to brawl in the middle of the street."

"Fantastic," I grunted as I rubbed my forehead in frustration.

"I don't think Edith knew Dorian had been discovered," Molly said softly as she brought a hand to her face in thought.

"Doesn't sound like it," Quinn agreed. "Which way did she run?"

"Which way?" Sawyer looked confused as he looked at the mage. "What do you mean?"

"North, south, east, west." I waved my hands around as I rattled off the compass directions, understanding what Quinn was getting at. "Do you have any idea which street you were on?"

"Oh." Sawyer blinked twice as he considered my question. "She ran south. I was able to make out that much, at least. As for the street, I don't know what its name is offhand..."

"We have a map. You can show us." I waved the bounty hunter over towards the table, only to find myself staring at both Stroud and Smiling Jade, who had moved to interpose themselves in front of the table.

"That will not be possible," Smiling Jade stated in a firm tone. "There is a substantial amount of information on this table that would best not be disclosed to a...*hunter*. It could prove to be problematic in the future."

"You have to be fucking kidding me," I hissed as I shifted my glance from Smiling Jade's faceless mask over to Stroud's unreadable expression. "We don't have time for this! If you haven't noticed, Sawyer is actually trying to help us!"

"*Today*," Stroud explained as he watched me unflinchingly. "Tomorrow he may not be."

"Eberia may not be here—" I felt my temper begin to flare at the two thief lords' comments, before Sawyer interrupted me from behind.

"They're right, Lazarus," Sawyer said wearily. "I know what sort of reputation my job brings in certain circles and why hunters have always been kept at arm's length."

"This isn't the time for this sort of petty shit!"

"It isn't," Sawyer agreed, directing his voice towards the thief lords. "But this isn't productive either. All I can tell you for certain is that I was in the northwestern part of the district about two streets west of the main thoroughfare, which I remembered crossing on my way here."

Saying nothing, I saw Sable turn to look over the table as Stroud and Smiling Jade stood in front of us stoically. After a few moments of scanning, the dark-furred Tul'Shar let out a low growl.

"It was one of your crew assigned to that area, Stroud." Sable's voice was tinged with anger. "The streets also give Edith a clear route towards the south, and while we have a handful of checkpoints along the way, I'm not confident that they would slow her down."

"I see," Stroud commented tonelessly, his only reaction to the news being to momentarily close his eyes for a few seconds and reopen them.

"If Edith was that far north into the district, then she wouldn't have had time to be warned by Dorian, assuming he even knew where she was," Molly stated as she moved to stand beside Sawyer and me. "I'm tempted to believe that he had no idea where she was hiding out, either, or else she wouldn't have been caught by surprise."

"Was there anything of interest in the safe house?" I turned to look at Sawyer while doing my best to push down the anger I was feeling.

"It was pretty plain and hidden away, just a small apartment above a few shops," Sawyer said. "I tossed the place after Edith got away, but there wasn't anything inside it other than some food and a bed."

There was a short pause as we all digested that information, giving Sawyer a chance to look around at all of our expressions in confusion.

"What's going on?" he asked. "Why does it matter which way she ran or where in the district this happened?"

"Dorian beat us to the punch and managed to put out a warning to the rest of his guild," Quinn explained while looking directly at Stroud and Smiling Jade, watching to see if they would interject. "Based on the number of empty hideouts we've had reported to us, we think he's gathering his forces somewhere in the southern end of the district, since they got the warning to abandon ship and others further north into the district didn't."

"And that's where we may have a problem," Isabella said in a tone that none of us had ever heard before. "That entire southern half of this district is owned by House Phineas; in fact, their familial estate overlooks the ocean. If Dorian is gathering his forces there..."

"*What?*" I managed to gasp, feeling my blood go cold as I turned my head to look towards Isabella, then towards the rest of the thief lords, all of whom already had made the connection.

"Phineas and Denarius are the only two houses that haven't been drawn into the standoff between the other three," Molly spoke, instantly realizing the implications. "That means either House Phineas is involved..."

"Or more likely, it is Dorian's next target," Isabella finished grimly. "And I cannot stress just how *disastrous* it would be for us if Dorian openly attacks a noble house."

"We need to check it out," I stated, a sudden feeling of dread passing through me as I remembered what Edith had told me what seemed like a lifetime ago on the pier. "I—"

"Whoa!" a shout of surprise echoed from just outside the still broken tavern door as a crimson light flashed through the tavern's windows.

"What the hell was that?" Quinn exclaimed, the first to react to the light as we all turned around to face the entrance.

No sooner did we all turn around than did the familiar face of the veteran thief rush through the open door, a look of confusion and worry on his face.

"There's something weird going on with Eris," he said, clearly not knowing how to explain it any better. "It's...*smoldering* in the sky."

Moving without a word, I took a single step forward, which caused everyone to follow me as we all rushed outside and into the crimson glow that now bathed the night. Running away from the building, I craned my head upwards as I searched the sky for the larger of the twin moons, my vision finally landing on the bright crimson orb that peeked from a gap in the cloud-covered sky. Glowing with a red aura, a vibrant corona billowed out around Eris's edges, making it appear as if the night itself were on fire, casting its eerie light through the heavy clouds. A soft chime rang in my ears as a bright and urgent text appeared in my vision.

> ***A World Event has begun!***
> *Strife and Discord has consumed the city of Eberia, causing Eris to burn in the sky as a Lord reaches for power beyond his station. In his quest, he seeks to bring down one of the founding pillars of the nation, his hand forced by distant whispers in his ear. Unless the Lord is brought to heel, a new power will rise in Eberia with the morning sun, and woe to all who dare to oppose it.*

"It wasn't like that when I got here!" Sawyer exclaimed as we all huddled into a mass and stared up at the moon.

"This is wrong," Smiling Jade whispered as she looked up into the sky. "This is very wrong."

"Is Dorian doing this?" Molly asked aloud as she looked towards me. "*Can* he do this?"

"I don't know," I replied slowly as I gazed up at the burning moon. "But something tells me we've just run out of time."

TWENTY-TWO

FINDING MYSELF RUSHING THROUGH THE streets for a second time in the last hour, I did everything I could not to gaze upwards as Eris slid behind the thick summer clouds and its crimson light faded from the sky, temporarily plunging the night back into darkness. Turning my head slightly as I ran, I saw Molly, Quinn, and Sawyer easily keeping pace with me as we moved through the streets, each of their faces nervously scanning ahead of us.

Things had moved almost blindingly fast after witnessing Eris's transformation. The thief lords immediately dispatched each and every spare guard at the command post to comb through the district and locate all the teams they could find.

And to send them towards House Phineas.

Having already seen Dorian's hand in arranging the murder of the noble heirs, none of the thief lords doubted his resolve should he have decided to move against House Phineas and were terrified of the fallout if he had. It was already a longshot that Dorian's head would be enough to satisfy Crawridge's and Wynbrandt's desire for vengeance, and adding in a third angry noble house into the equation was the last thing that any of the thief lords wanted.

While the rest of the thief lords reorganized the guilds, Isabella had chosen to send the four of us ahead to scout out House Phineas's estates, which made up the entire southern portion of the New District and presented us with a rather unique problem.

It was completely walled off from the rest of the district by a fifteen-foot tall stone wall.

A byproduct from the early years of the war, when an unruly populace was just as viable a threat to the nobility as the orc tribes that besieged the nation, the wall was once intended as a safety barrier to the house by providing a line defense should the commoners within the city break out into riots.

Now, in more recent years, with the war slowly becoming a fading memory, the weathered wall now served more as a symbolic barrier rather than a defensive one, reminding everyone of the separation between the common folk and those from the higher class, only admitting those with express permission into the world past it.

Fortunately for us, however, thieves didn't tend to care much for walls or for obtaining permission.

"Turn here," Molly whispered just loud enough for all of us to hear as we ran, indicating a back-alley street that led behind a row of apartments.

Trusting Molly's sense of direction, I didn't hesitate as the four of us turned down the alley, the sound of dried leaves crunching softly under our feet while we ran.

"Why here?" Sawyer asked softly, curiosity tinging his voice, despite moving to follow her without any hesitation. "This is a dead end."

"Main street has a direct sight to the gate leading in," she answered in between breaths before motioning for all of us to slow down once we had made it halfway down the alley and were far enough away from the street. "We'll get spotted if there's anyone watching."

"Ah," Sawyer grunted in understanding. "What's the plan, then?"

"We go up," Molly stated as she pointed up towards the apartments surrounding us. "The wall is tall enough, but it was built before these buildings were. We won't find a better vantage point anywhere else."

"Oh," Sawyer replied, as he followed Molly's finger upwards. "Is this a bad time to mention that I'm not that great with heights or climbing?"

"I'm going to second that, actually," Quinn added, waving a hand over his thinner body. "One of the side effects of being a mage is next to no upper body strength."

"No time like the present to get over it," I grunted as I began to walk towards the building while looking up at its side for handholds.

"Actually, no," Molly whispered. "If you can't climb quickly and quietly, stay down here. The last thing we need is an inept climber causing noise and waking anyone inside these houses."

"I'll stay, then," Sawyer said with a shake of his head.

"Yeah, me too," Quinn chimed in.

"Go wait at the alley entrance, then, and send the thief lords our way when they arrive," Molly ordered as she motioned for me to start climbing. "Lazarus and I will go up together."

Wasting no time as Sawyer and Quinn retreated back down the alley, I focused my attention on the building, quickly pulling myself up to the flat rooftop.

Guess those two days of nonstop climbing Fairfax subjected us to the other week have really been burned into my memory, I thought to myself, feeling a distant pang of sadness wash over my heart before fading as my deceased mentor came to mind. Rubbing my face as I waited for Molly to catch up to me, I let out a soft sigh before moving away from the edge and scanned the rooftop, in case any guards had been posted up here. *Hard to believe so much has happened in the last two days.*

Finding the roof empty, I let myself relax slightly, hearing Molly's feet brush the hard title behind me as she pulled herself onto the roof a moment before her hand landed on my shoulder and gave me a squeeze.

Moving with a practiced ease, the two of us crouched low while crossing the rooftop, barely making a sound as we made our way towards the far edge of the building that overlooked the main street that led into the House Phineas Estate, blocked by a large, ornate gate that controlled access into the gated community of nobles.

Squinting at a sudden brightness, the first thing that we spotted was that the neighborhood behind the wall was illuminated by several mage lamps, large glass orbs that had been enchanted to cast a brilliant, pale light in every direction. Scanning the horizon first, I counted several tall buildings that reached even higher into the sky than the one we stood on. Given the late hour, I wasn't surprised to find all the windows dark, yet there was something that I couldn't quite put my finger on that had me feeling unsettled.

Maybe these buildings are all housing for servants and extended family who wouldn't have a place within the main house? I thought to myself as my eyes passed from building to building, silently wishing I could see the Phineas mansion from our perch but found it to be blocked from the building ahead of us.

"The trees are bare," Molly whispered softly. "All of them. Look at all the leaves on the ground."

"Hm?" I let a faint grunt pass through my lips as I scanned the area and found that all the trees planted along the inside of the wall and along the street below us were completely barren of any foliage.

"That's weird, it's early summer..."

Frowning, I shifted my glance from the bare branches of the trees and inspected the wall itself, the light from the mage lamps and my racial vision more than enough to cut through the gloom. Withered grey vines covered the entirety of the wall that divided the two communities, and after a moment of careful watching, I noticed countless leaves blowing in the wind as they tumbled across the street below us.

"Vines on the wall are dead," I told Molly softly. "I remember there being leaves back in the alley, too."

"It all looks...fresh," she replied as her eyes absorbed the sight. "Like all the trees and plants here dropped their leaves at once."

I couldn't help but glance over at Molly in worry, having come to the same conclusion myself. Meeting my eye for a few seconds, Molly shook her head at me silently before glancing further down the rooftop.

"Let's move further down," Molly whispered as she lowered herself from her crouching stance into a prone position. "We should be able to get a better angle to see what's behind the wall."

"All right," I hissed back as quietly as I could manage while laying myself flat on the rooftop.

Moving slowly, the two of us then crawled the length of the apartment rooftops, paying a careful mind to the light that was being cast by the mage lamps below. The last thing we needed was for someone to catch sight of us and raise the alarm.

Waiting for Molly to crawl ahead of me, I paused to look over the edge of the building and spotted the familiar shapes of guards standing along the wall overlooking the wooden gate, their metallic helmets glinting in the night as they slowly shuffled from side to side. Counting, I made four guards standing on the wall, a number I considered to be rather small given everything that had happened in the city today.

Shouldn't they be on a higher alert? I thought suspiciously. *They have to have heard about what happened to the other noble heirs and be even the slightest bit concerned. Four guards hardly seem like they're taking the threat seriously.*

Pulling my eyes away from the gate, I noted that Molly had crept far enough ahead of me to resume my progress and slowly began pushing myself against the rooftop, taking extra care not to make any noise. Keeping an eye on Molly as I crept forward, I couldn't help but feel a spike of fear shoot through my heart when she suddenly flinched in surprise, pressing herself flat against the rooftop a short distance from the edge of the building that overlooked the wall.

Freezing instantly, adrenaline surged through my body as I waited for a shout of surprise or alarm to fill the air, possibly then followed by a volley of magic or arrows as the guards began to rain death upon us. Keeping as still as possible, I fought through the impending sense of doom and focused my attention on Molly's prone figure before me, watching for any sort of signal of what to do next. Waiting on pins and needles with nothing but silence greeting my ears for over a minute, I almost breathed an audible sigh of relief when Molly's right foot pointed itself towards the inside of the rooftop, before beckoning me forward.

What did she see? I asked myself as I slowly crawled sideways, away from the edge of the rooftop that overlooked the main street below, before starting to move forward again. Shuffling with the utmost care, I patiently worked my way up to Molly's side, mindful of the fact that she hadn't moved a hair since signaling me. Reaching her side, I carefully peered over the edge of the building and towards my left, the extreme angle working in our favor as we practically overlooked the stone wall.

Giving me a picture-perfect view of what had to be nearly a hundred cutthroats and thieves working feverishly as they built barricades in the middle of the street.

My blood turned to ice as I absorbed the sight below us, the realization that we were too late causing my heart to momentarily skip a beat. Taking in the full sight before me, I spotted signs of recent combat, my eyes flitting from magic-scarred cobblestones, to a handful of broken windows, to a shattered wagon that was on its side with half a dozen crates spilled all over the ground.

To a pile of bodies, stacked on top of one another haphazardly in the middle of the street.

We're too late, I realized as my roaming gaze finally returned to the small army of thieves that were urgently fortifying the place. *The Damned have completely overrun the estate, and judging from the preparations, they knew that it was only a matter of time before we found them.*

Moving slowly, Molly gradually turned her head to look towards me, her eyes completely wide with panic, echoing the same emotion that I felt running through me. We stared at one another in complete disbelief for what seemed like an eternity before she silently moved her hand to tap her ear, then pointed towards the gate.

We can't hear them, I clued in, realizing that all I could hear at the moment was the distant ocean and the faint whisper of the wind that sent all the loose leaves rustling. Glancing back at the thieves, I focused my attention on their actions, silently thankful that we weren't so far away that we wouldn't be able to make out detail.

Watching carefully, I could see several of the thugs talking amongst one another as they dragged tables, chairs, and shattered furniture across the ground, one of them pausing in his work to wave his hands towards the sky. No doubt referring to the strange moon still concealed by the clouds above.

Seeing a movement catch my eye, I then noticed another pair of thugs emerge from one of the buildings, dragging a hooded person into view. Crossing the length of the inner plaza, the two thugs carried the thrashing hostage towards a large group of similarly masked prisoners sitting on the ground, before unceremoniously shoving them forward into the mass and causing the figure to fall to the ground.

But despite all the action and motion that was happening below us, no sounds greeted our ears.

Did they enchant the wall to block sounds? I asked myself, silently wondering if the nobility would have been vain enough to do that, then immediately realizing how naïve that thought was. *Of course they would; rich neighborhoods do the same thing in reality, if with sound barriers and not magic.*

Looking back towards Molly, I saw her expectant eyes on me and nodded back in agreement. Motioning with her free hand that faced me, she pointed back towards the way that we came and slowly began crawling away from the edge.

Following her lead, I glanced one more time at the army of thieves below us, a sinking suspicion in my stomach. *If they really wanted to get away, they could have easily left the city by now and hid out in the wild for a few days, then filtered back in piecemeal. Why are they digging in to meet us head on? They have to know that they can't stand up to all four guilds. Even if they're hiding behind these walls.*

As I lay watching the thieves working below, a cool breeze picked up in the air at the same moment that the clouds high above parted, revealing the crimson moon's burning gaze. No sooner did Eris appear in the sky than did a single tendril of crimson light reach up from behind the buildings before me to touch the fiery orb, strengthening in intensity the higher it went.

He—I had barely begun forming the thought when a wave of indescribable *wrongness* swept over me and caused my body to shudder in shock. For the faintest of moments, it felt like all warmth had left me and that something vile had brushed my very soul, somehow leaving me feeling dirtier than I had after swimming in the massive waste-filled basin back at the sewer hub.

What was that? I shouted internally as I recovered from the strange event, seeing all of the Damned below me stagger under the same influence that had affected me. Some shuddered visibly as they then turned to look towards the burning moon, while others shrugged it off and continued working.

The artifact has to be causing this, I thought to myself, looking at the beam of light that reached towards Eris. *The moment that the moon appeared, that light shot up from where the Phineas mansion is...which means Dorian and Edith won't be that far away from it.*

If we want to stop them, we're going to have to fight our way through all of them down there. I cast one final look down towards the army of thieves fortifying the inner compound below us as I pushed myself away from the edge.

Moving with urgency, I crawled backwards until I could stand up without alerting anyone to my presence. Turning around, I looked across the roof for Molly, spotting her far ahead of me as she greeted Smiling Jade and Isabella, who had just arrived on the scene. Closing the distance quickly now that I was on my feet, I made my way over towards them, catching the last bits of the conversation as Molly filled the two thief lords in on what we had seen.

"—then some sort of...*energy* hit all of us as soon as Eris appeared in the sky. I'm not sure if you felt it on the way here," Molly whispered softly, turning her head towards me as I arrived.

"We did," Isabella replied, her face looking pale as she glanced towards Smiling Jade, the masked thief lord taking a few steps away from us. "I've never felt anything like it before."

"I have once, during the early days of the war," Smiling Jade said in a small voice as she looked up towards the sky, then looked back towards us. "It belongs to a branch of dark magic that was discarded after we realized its side effects."

"It kills plant life," I said, realization dawning upon me as I waved at the barren trees on the street below.

"Among other things," Smiling Jade whispered, shaking her head in disbelief. "What have you done, Dorian? You are working magics that you cannot even begin to understand."

"Do you know what he's doing?" I asked, sensing that the magically gifted thief lord had a better understanding of how magic worked in the world.

"He's using a ritual to draw power from Eris," Smiling Jade explained. "And storing that energy in something, likely in preparation to activate the artifact."

"Is that what that strange feeling was?" Molly queried, her voice barely loud enough to hear. "The ritual?"

"Yes," Smiling Jade stated simply, refusing to elaborate further as she turned her gaze back up towards the sky. "It is imperative that we stop it as soon as possible. If this street has already been blighted, then there is no telling how far it may yet reach as the ritual progresses."

"Wait, it can keep spreading?" Molly asked in an alarmed voice. "What if it gets to the farmland?"

"Then all the crops will wither and Eberia will slowly begin to starve," Smiling Jade stated as she tore herself away from the burning moon and fully turned around to face us. "And we will be forced to abandon the city."

The three of us stared at Smiling Jade in shock, her faceless mask reflecting each of our expressions.

"Fuck that!" I said as my shock slowly kindled into anger. "We aren't going to let Dorian go through with whatever he has planned, and we're far from beaten."

Everyone's glance shifted to focus on me as I continued speaking. "We caught Dorian with his pants down once already, and from the looks of what's going on down there, his followers are scrambling to fortify the place. If we hit them hard, they'll shatter. They don't have the numbers to stand up to all four guilds."

"Lazarus is right," Molly added with a nod, motioning towards the distant walls where the Damned were busily digging in. "They're all off balance and on unfamiliar ground. We still have a chance to end this before it's too late."

"It may already be too late," Isabella replied sadly as she shook her head. "Dorian's attacked *another* house, maybe even destroyed it completely. Even if we somehow manage to stop him…we'll never escape the wrath of the other houses."

"We can deal with that problem when we get to it," I told Isabella. "Unless we stop him here and now, we're going to have much bigger problems than worrying about the nobles' vengeance."

Blowing out a deep sigh, Isabella looked up at me and nodded. "You're right, Lazarus, right now we need to worry about ensuring that Eberia lives to see the morning. Everything else that comes after that…we can deal with as it comes."

"Good," I said with a strained smile. "We need to attack them as soon as possible. Where are Stroud and Sable?"

"Collecting whomever they can find and sending them this way," Isabella answered. "They were only a few minutes behind us, they should be here soon enough."

"What are we going to do about the gate?" Molly asked as she waved a hand in the direction of the Phineas Estate. "We're not going to get anywhere unless we can open it or knock it down, and I don't think we're going to get the time to assemble siege gear."

"The other mages and I will take care of the gate," Smiling Jade said confidently. "It will not be a challenge."

"You really think you can knock it down so easily?" I looked at the brightly dressed thief lord with surprise.

"Child, I fought in the war for thirty years." Smiling Jade made a clucking sound underneath her mask as she chided me. "I have shattered defenses far greater than a flimsy wooden gate made to deter a horde of angry civilians. It will not be a problem."

"Uh..." I felt a little embarrassment pass through me at the mage's chastisement. "Okay, then."

Pausing for a moment to collect my thoughts, I glanced up towards Eris, just in time to see it vanish behind the heavy clouds once more, the crimson gloom filling the night fading along with the strange beam of light.

"Looks like we caught a break and the weather is buying us some time," I said, breathing a sigh of relief. "Let's get back down to the others and plan our attack. It's time we finished this."

TWENTY-THREE

STEPPING OUT INTO THE MIDDLE of the street, I felt my heart flutter in my chest as the sounds of countless feet shook the ground behind me. Gripping my sword tightly, I tried to steady my nerves by focusing on the distant gate ahead of me, seeing the shiny reflections of the helmeted guards that stood watch. By the time enough people had arrived, we had run out of time to plan any sort of detailed strategy, at least beyond getting everyone to move in the same direction. Not that a few minutes or even an hour more would have helped in getting rough cutthroats and thieves to behave like common soldiers.

No, this wasn't going to be a battle that would be won by a cunning strategy or careful planning. This was going to be a battle of sheer brute force and violence, one without mercy or quarter. A battle that we all knew we had to win at any cost.

Leading the vanguard of our army of thieves was Smiling Jade, flanked by her equally attired double, Quinn, and four other mages whose names I had promptly forgotten after being introduced. In each of their hands, except for Smiling Jade, they all held a roiling ball of fire as they carefully poured mana into their spells, holding them at the ready for the thief lord's command.

Contrary to the rest of the casters, Smiling Jade channeled her mana into a swirling orb of wind that struggled to escape from her grasp with every step that she took. Maintaining the spell with no visible effort, the thief lord stoically led us down the street as we slowly inched towards the gate with no pretense of stealth.

I saw the guards behind the gate visibly panic at our approach, three of the shiny helmets vanishing from behind the wall as they rushed to alert their comrades.

For the little good it would do them.

"On my mark," Smiling Jade announced in a commanding voice as she stopped her advance halfway to the gate and looked down the line of mages. "Get ready!"

Pausing for a heartbeat to ensure that everyone was ready, the thief lord then released the maelstrom of wind that she now held and sent it screaming towards the Phineas gate with blinding speed. Before I could even make sense of what was happening, the gate vanished in an explosion of dust as the orb unleashed its pent-up magic in a screaming howl of wind.

"Fire!" Smiling Jade shouted over the noise, her voice now carrying a tone of fatigue that hadn't been present a moment earlier.

Wasting no time in obeying the order, Quinn and the other five mages let go of their spells, sending the six overcharged fireballs screaming towards the temporarily obscured gate where they detonated simultaneously in a fiery inferno.

Wincing from the blast, I covered my face with my arm, spotting Sawyer and Molly doing the same beside me as chips of wood flew through the air and pelted all of us. Billowing smoke and dust rose from the gate as burning pieces of wood flew through the air, before crashing into the ground. Within seconds, the cloud began to thin, revealing the shattered remains of the Phineas gate that had been flung inwards and partially torn off its hinges.

Staring in disbelief from within the Phineas compound, I saw the stunned faces of countless Damned guild members look out towards us from behind their half-finished barricades while others slowly picked themselves up off the ground, shaken by the blast. Feeling a flare of rage pulse from the sigil on my chest, I felt adrenaline shoot through my body as I took the first step forward, my voice breaking the deathly silence.

"FOR FAIRFAX!" I screamed, taking my second step towards the gate, finding myself at the head of the army as it began to surge forward.

"FOR KIERA!" a second cry rang out into the night as we all gained speed, our feet thundering across the cobblestone like a vengeful avalanche.

"FOR EBERIA!" The deafening shout tore itself from the throats of over a hundred thieves as we closed the final distance between us and the terrified defenders who scrambled to meet our assault.

Refusing to slow down even one iota, I put on a burst of speed, feeling Sawyer, Molly, and Quinn barely keeping pace behind me as I charged through the shattered Phineas gate and bore down on a cluster of thieves caught out in the open, away from any of the barricades. Seeing our rapid approach, the thieves scrambled in panic, some seeing no escape and standing firm and raising their weapons, while others broke ranks in sheer desperation as they tried to run for cover behind one of the distant barricades.

Focusing on those before me, I timed a sweeping stroke of my blade in front of me a moment before impact, knocking a trio of weapons out of the way before smashing into the wall of bodies.

And running straight over them.

Speed and momentum carried me through the mass of now panicking thieves as I used my size and weight to bull my way through them, knocking several of them to the ground. I felt bones crunch under my boots as I ruthlessly stomped on the fallen bodies, swinging my sword in a deadly arc before me in a spray of blood and gore. Passing through the group of thieves like a deadly scythe, the four of us burst free from the other side at the same moment I heard a thundering crunch as the four combined thieves guilds trailing us crashed into the enemy.

The battle for Eberia had begun.

Intent on causing as much mayhem as possible, the four of us pressed into the mass of bodies that surged forward to meet us, vengeance burning in our hearts. With Sawyer guarding my flank, I swung my glass-steel blade in wide arcs through the air, using its long reach to carve us a pocket of safety amid the chaos of battle.

Standing in a zone of relative safety between Sawyer and me, Molly worked her blade with blinding speed, alternating between aiding us with timely parries and striking out at any enemies that dared to enter range. Blood dripped from her heavy sabre as she screamed wordlessly into the cacophony of battle, her free hand spraying an arc of ink-colored magic towards the enemies pressing down on us.

"Keep hitting them!" Sawyer shouted, his golden shield already covered in blood as he rushed forward to take advantage of the temporarily blinded thugs affected by Molly's spell.

Moving with blazing speed, Sawyer landed three vicious stabs into the chests of the afflicted cutthroats, which had them staggering backwards into the press of bodies, clutching their wounds as they fell to the ground.

Not to be outdone, Quinn wielded his wand to deadly effect, sending a steady stream of bright red energy into the ranks of thieves ahead of us, their bodies packed far too tightly for all to avoid its burning wrath. Conjuring balls of fire with his free hand, the air echoed with the constant thunder of exploding magic as he ravaged the leading ranks of the defenders.

With the opening assault spent, the battle then blurred into an orgy of bloodshed and death as the two forces began to relentlessly grind away at one another. Despite the haste that they were constructed with, the poorly crafted barricades were enough to prevent us from simply overwhelming the Damned, forcing us into narrow funnels where our numbers were less effective as they desperately fought to hold us at bay.

Mages did their best to aim their spells at the barricades blocking our way, but with the thick press of bodies obscuring them and the inability to attack from higher ground, the mages were relegated to a secondary role. Yet this did not render them completely ineffective, as they lobbed their deadly spells in high arcs, causing them to sail into the air before crashing downwards, landing in the rear ranks of the defenders and wreaking havoc.

Fighting through a chokepoint with Sawyer by my side, the two of us ground forward like two unrelenting juggernauts, working together in near perfect sync as we gradually forced a line of cutthroats to give way under our attacks. Blood seeped from ripped leather and scarred metal that was once unbroken armor, the two of us bearing countless wounds as the price of our progress. It was only because of the timely ministrations of Molly, who followed behind us, that we still stood, her magic sealing our wounds or providing a protective shell of magic when we were hard pressed.

Slashing through an exposed guard, the tip of my blade caught my opponent just below the shoulder, its razor-sharp edge easily parting armor and flesh as it bit deep. Pulling my sword free, the arm fell to the ground still clutching its weapon as I quite literally disarmed the thief. Howling beyond pain, the man had enough time to glance down at his fallen arm before Sawyer's blade found its way into his throat and ended his suffering for good.

"Fuck!" Sawyer exclaimed in grim amusement as he seamlessly pulled his blade free and blocked a second cutthroat's attack. "I need to get me a fancy knife like that!"

"Well, it was pretty expensive," I replied while swinging the weapon in a low sweep, catching the man attacking Sawyer in the leg and severing it in a similar fashion as the arm before it. "It cost me an arm and a leg!"

"*Oh, God,*" Sawyer groaned theatrically, delivering a killing thrust to the falling man's chest, allowing us to push forward a few steps as others behind the two fallen cutthroats hesitated in moving forward to meet us. "Your battle puns need work!"

"Look, they're breaking!" Quinn called out as he took advantage of the momentary gap ahead of us and threw a fireball directly into a thief's face from pointblank range, sending the man falling to the ground, screaming in pain.

True to Quinn's word, I looked up over the crowd of terrified thieves backing away from us and saw that the pulse of the battle had begun to shift. The relentless push that had characterized the first few minutes of the battle had been replaced by a growing sense of fear as the mounting losses that the Damned were suffering began to take its toll.

Bellowing loudly, I spotted a massive half-giant standing head and shoulders above the crowd before us, shoving his way forward as he rallied the panicking cutthroats around him, going as far as to cut a retreating thief down with a single swing of his jagged axe in an attempt to restore order. Stunned by the brutal maneuver, the majority of the panicked thieves ground to a halt, the half-giant gesturing in our direction as he continued to shout. Staring at the man for a heartbeat, I saw a tag appear in the corner of my eye.

[Guild Crusher] – The Damned – Level 13

“Shit,” I cursed while taking the opportunity to catch my breath. “That didn’t last long.”

“Looks like a tank,” Sawyer replied calmly as the line in front of us slowly regrouped, the armored half-giant taking the center position. “This guy is going to be a pain to wear down.”

Catching sight of the massive half-giant, I silently echoed Sawyer’s sentiment, seeing the heavily armored thug for the first time as he stepped out of the crowd. Outfitted with a thick breastplate protecting his chest and chainmail running down both his arms and legs, the crusher’s armor was an order of magnitude better than anything we had seen in the battle so far.

But as if the armor weren’t enough, the half-giant had a jagged slab of metal strapped to his forearm that, judging from the countless scars upon it, served as a shield in addition to being a deadly weapon in its own right. Pointing a wicked-looking axe at the two of us, the half-giant screamed a wordless challenge as he beat his shield against his chest, before slamming it into the ground hard enough to smash the cobblestones underneath.

“This is going to suck,” I grumbled as I watched the crusher’s weapon intently, shifting my sword into a guard position. “You ready, Sawyer?”

“Right behind you, man,” Sawyer agreed with a curt nod, his attention focused on the growing wall of thieves that began to rally behind the half-giant.

“Wait!” Molly shouted while grabbing me by the shoulder. “Quinn, shield!”

Before I could turn my head to glance towards her, several thunderous explosions rumbled through the air, causing us to stagger as a wave of force threatened to sweep us off our feet. Falling from the sky above, a ball of fire landed directly between us and the Damned's reformed line of battle, exploding with burning heat.

Rushing towards us with blinding speed, I had enough time to see a wall of fire fill my vision before instinct forced me to cover my face in an attempt to protect my eyes. Cowering from the blast, I braced myself for the inevitable searing pain to wash over my body, praying that there weren't any other attacks following it.

But it never came.

"*Shit*, that was close!" Quinn gasped from just beside my ear.

Looking up from behind my arm, I saw a gleaming distortion just inches away from my face as the last vestiges of fire swept up and over the hastily cast Force Shield that Quinn had managed to place before us.

"You're a lifesaver, Quinn!" I praised the mage, seeing that he had thrust his hands between Sawyer and me before conjuring the shield. Looking through the mild distortion of the shield, I saw that the both the crusher and the thieves standing before us hadn't been lucky enough to have a mage to blunt the fireball's rage.

Nearly half a dozen thugs lay on the ground thrashing wildly in pain as they tried to slap out burning bits of armor, and in some cases, burning flesh. Kneeling on the ground, having taken cover behind his heavy shield, the crusher appeared to be slightly stunned as he slowly staggered to his feet, looking somewhat singed.

"Where the hell did that come from?" Sawyer shouted as he started glancing around. "Was that us or them?"

"*Them!* From up high!" Molly exclaimed from behind me. "They had mages hidden away in the apartments above us!"

Whipping my head upwards, I looked up in time to see another wave of fireballs fly from several shattered windows on the second and third stories of the building overlooking the battleground. The fireballs sailed through the air before venting their fury amid the crowd of tightly packed attackers.

Presented with a target their spells could now reach directly, the surviving mages of the thieves guilds' army retaliated within seconds, a torrent of spells rising up in response to the Damned's mages' surprise attack.

Several figures caught standing in front of the windows vanished with pained screams under the onslaught of spells as they practically tore the face off of the building, sending burning debris and glass raining down on us below. Ice, fire, and lightning ravaged the side of the wooden structure as mages refused to let up and relentlessly poured magic into each and every window above us.

"Retreat!" an unfamiliar voice boomed over the crash of battle in pain, clearly aided by magic. "Retreat!"

Almost instantly, the momentum of the battle shifted from a slow and drawn-out grind to a full-on retreat as the Damned suddenly disengaged from the raging battle around us and turned to flee down the streets deeper into the Phineas Estate.

"Retreat?" Sawyer questioned while looking around for the source of the voice. "They just rocked us with that attack and still have fortifications we haven't even reached!"

"Their morale is breaking!" Quinn stated from behind us as he dismissed his shield.

"Not for all of them," I replied, motioning towards the burnt crusher, who looked livid at the early call for retreat, but nevertheless began to turn to follow the rest of his fleeing comrades. "Let's—"

Cutting me off, the voice boomed through the air once more, hissing a now familiar word of power that I had heard far too many times in the last day, the same word that both Edith and Dorian had shouted to trigger the possession spell built into the hellborn soul shards.

The echoing voice didn't even have time to fade from the air before the crusher unleashed a bloodcurdling scream as he fell to the ground. He desperately clawed at something under his armor but refused to drop his jagged axe. Before any of us could react, the half-giant burst into a small pillar of flame as a gout of fire erupted from underneath his armor and consumed his body, forcing us to shield our eyes from the glare.

"They're panicking!" Quinn shouted, recovering the fastest from the scene unfolding before us. "They screwed up the timing for their next trap! They're summoning the devils now!"

"Damn it!" I cursed while gritting my teeth together as more screams began to echo across the battlefield. I had known going into the battle that there was a good chance that Dorian had managed fill at least some of the soul shards that he had crafted, but I'd been hopeful that we would only have to worry about a handful of devils as the attack unfolded.

A quick glance around the battlefield told me I was wrong.

Scattered among the crowd of fleeing thieves, I counted over three dozen similar bursts of fire as bound devils were released from their bone prisons and rapidly possessed their new bodies, violently remaking them in their own image. The smell of burning flesh and brimstone filled the air, layering itself over the acrid stench of spilled blood as the howling screams of pain belonging to their hosts died out with a sickening finality.

With the last soul-wrenching wail fading from the air, the battlefield fell nearly silent, save for the distant rumble of the fleeing thieves as they desperately sought to put distance between themselves and the hell that they had purposefully unleashed. Recoiling from the flaming pyres, I saw the thieves guilds' army pull back from the transforming devils, shocked by their sudden appearance deep within their ranks.

"*Lazarus.*" I felt Sawyer's elbow poke me roughly in my side, bringing me back into the present as I twisted my head towards him and saw his pale face staring straight ahead. "Look."

Following his gaze, I turned my head towards where I had seen the crusher fall and felt my breath catch in my throat. Looking nothing like its original form, the heavily armored half-giant was now a grotesque mound of purple-colored flesh and blackened metal.

Glancing around wildly with a single crimson eye, a low moan escaped from the devil's tooth-filled maw as it lifted its now corpulent body off the ground, standing unsteadily on short, stubby legs. The once finely crafted armor that had covered the half-giant was now rent apart and partially melted into the creature's flesh from its blistering transformation, with thick rolls of fat spilling out amid the gaps of broken chainmail. Fused to each arm were the twisted remains of the crusher's jagged shield and axe, the metal having become one with the devil's flesh.

"I've had just about enough of this," I replied, feeling a spark of anger kindle inside me as I looked at the devil, taking a deep breath as my thoughts began to rage.

The last day had driven me past limits that I hadn't known I had, while forcing me to make choices that I never would have believed that I was capable of making. This had gone beyond just being a game I was playing for entertainment.

No, right now I was fighting to protect my home. A home that someone was doing their damned best to destroy.

I bared my teeth as the sigil pulsed violently across my chest, the raging energy behind it begging to be released, to bring vengeance against those who dared to stand before me. It was all I could do it keep the searing rage at bay as I stared at the devil intently, causing a blinking tag to appear in my vision.

[Hellborn Devourer] – Boss – Level 13

I heard a growl escape my throat as the intensity of the sigil increased, my hands causing my sword to tremble as I struggled to hold the growing rage in check.

The devil's eye widened as it heard my subtle challenge, the blood-red orb shifting towards me with curiosity, its mouth opening slowly as a slender black tongue reached out to lick its lips. Thick black drool, oozed from its maw as the tongue then vanished back inside the creature's mouth, the motion causing the slime to spill over its chin and land on its chest. The devil smacked its lips disgustingly as it sucked in a deep breath; a feral hunger crossing its twisted face, its eye narrowing at me.

Replying in a growl that quickly grew into an earthshattering roar, it launched itself forward at us, its cry shattering the unearthly silence that had filled the air, all of the other devils responding in kind as the battle began anew.

"Raaaaah!" A primal howl erupted from my throat as the raging energy behind the sigil threatened to overwhelm me, crimson streaks appearing in my vision as I barely kept the rage at bay. Unable to stay standing for any longer, I leaped forward to meet the obese devil's charge, leaving a surprised Sawyer scrambling to follow me half a step behind.

Feeling the ground shake underneath my feet as the devourer lumbered forward with heavy steps, a freezing cold surged through my veins as I closed with the corpulent creature, my vision sharpening beyond anything that I had ever experienced before. The devourer's motion slowed as I thundered towards it, its massive bulk jiggling with each step it took as it swiftly raised its jagged axe. Swinging it forward, the devil aimed the half-melted weapon directly at my head in an attempt to decapitate me with one massive blow. Shifting my sword to intercept the blow, I channeled all my might and momentum into my counterattack as the devil and I collided in a titanic display of strength, our weapons crashing together with a bone-shattering crunch.

Even through the rage that consumed my body, I felt both of my arms go numb from the impact as the devourer's momentum stopped my assault cold, the creature's flabby arm bending under the exchange. Sliding my blade downwards, I carved a furrow into the devourer's axe as I instinctively ducked under its follow-up attack, the jagged shield attached to its other arm passing straight through the spot where my head had just been in a savage hook.

Rolling to the side as the numbness in my arms gave way to a distant pain, I forced myself to maintain a firm grip on my weapon while tumbling out of the creature's reach, allowing Sawyer following behind me the opportunity to strike.

Shit, it's strong. I mentally winced as I forced myself back up to my feet, checking to make sure I hadn't broken the bones in my forearms. It wasn't often that I was physically out-muscled, and even rarer since I had awoken with the Sigil of Rage tattooed onto my chest, but the blow that I had just exchanged with the devourer had been a close thing. Had I been even slightly weaker, my reckless attack would have backfired.

With likely fatal consequences.

Bounding up onto my feet on the devourer's side, I rose in time to see Sawyer land a vicious stab into the devil's arm, the speedy warrior pulling his blood-covered blade free. The devil barked in pain as it swung its shield back towards Sawyer in an attempt to get it back into position before the warrior could attack again.

"Flank it from the rear!" Sawyer shouted as he danced backwards from the devourer, forcing the creature to choose between chasing him or exposing its guard and turning to face me. "It doesn't look like it can turn fast! Try to keep it off balance!"

"Right!" I called back as I began sidestepping to flank the fat devil, feeling somewhat surprised that I could hear and understand Sawyer, despite the sigil being active and its energy coursing through my body.

It feels different this time, I mused to myself as I sliced through a roll of exposed fat on the devourer's side, causing a black ichor to pour forth. *The energy feels...cold, and I can actually think!*

I didn't have time to continue pondering over the different energy I felt coming from the sigil as the devourer howled in pain from my blow and swung his axe in a wild cleave in my direction faster than I'd thought his bulk would allow. Throwing my sword upwards in a desperate parry, I felt the hilt rattle in my hands once more as I deflected the blackened axe away from my body and upwards into the air.

Arriving seconds after the parry, Quinn joined the fight with a cluster of azure-colored missiles slamming into the side of the devil's face, his wand's crimson beam of light following a heartbeat behind. The twin waves of magic split flesh everywhere they touched, leaving savage burns and weeping wounds all across the devourer's face.

"Watch the crossfire!" Quinn shouted over the growing cacophony of battle as the roars and cries of the other devils grew in intensity around us.

"Heads up!" Molly added immediately after Quinn's warning as an inky orb of darkness sailed through the air and splashed across the devourer's face. "I'm moving in to flank too!"

Recognizing the black orb as it temporarily rendered the devourer blind and deaf, I wasted no time in taking advantage of the gap in its defense, thrusting my sword deep into the devil's side, sawing the blade viciously as I ran to get in position behind the creature. Flashing in the corner of my eye, I saw a combat notification blink once as it notified me of a critical hit.

You critically [Sneak Attack II] a [Hellborn Devourer] in a vulnerable location for 267 points of damage!

Tearing my blade free, a torrent of black blood gushed from the wound as the devourer bellowed in pain, several other messages appearing in my vision behind the previous alert.

Your [Bleeding Attack I] hits a [Hellborn Devourer] for 22 points of damage!
Your [Bleeding Attack I] hits a [Hellborn Devourer] for 22 points of damage!

Yes! Finally that ability comes into use! I felt a feral grin cross my face as I continued to run behind the Devourer, lifting my sword for another attack.

Only to run into something hard and unyielding as it hit me directly in the face and knocked me right off my feet.

"Whaaa?" I moaned softly while reeling from the stunning blow, my head throbbing viciously as my eyes began to water from a broken nose. Blinking furiously, I found myself lying on my back just behind the devourer, thankfully still holding my sword, who had its attention focused towards Sawyer. Looking up at the devil's back, I saw a second crimson eye staring down at me, set directly in the back of the creature's head, along with a single arm coming out of the center of its mass.

"You have to be kidding me," I wheezed, spitting out a mouthful of blood as I saw the claw-tipped hand reaching out for me.

"Lazarus! Are you okay?" Sawyer voice called out, followed by the sounds of clashing metal. "What happened?"

"There's a third arm that's coming out of its back!" I called out as I rolled away from the devourer, eager to put some distance between me and the devil before I tried to stand up. I already felt lucky enough that the arm that had hit me was unarmed. Had it been holding a weapon of any kind, I was fairly confident that I would have found myself respawning alone back at the guild headquarters.

"Wha—*urk!*" Sawyer's reply choked off as I saw the devourer lurch forward out of the corner of my eye.

"Sawyer!" I heard Molly's voice shout in panic as I tried to get my feet back under me and push me back into a standing position.

Forcing myself upwards, I looked up in time to see that the devourer had somehow managed to trap Sawyer's weapon and shield with its own and had wrapped its tongue around the red-armored warrior's throat. Straining with all his might, Sawyer fought to keep his distance from the strangling devil as its tongue slowly retracted, gradually pulling him closer and closer towards its open maw.

"Hold on!" I exclaimed while sprinting towards the devourer, seeing Sawyer's face begin to turn purple. I knew it was only a matter of time before he ran out of air and passed out, which would have him ending up in the devourer's mouth in short order.

Charging at the devil from its flank, I lifted my glass-steel blade up high above my head as I ran, desperately trying to come up with a plan. With his strength flagging from the loss of air, Sawyer had slowly been pulled far too close to the devourer's mouth for me to risk trying to sever the creature's tongue. A slipup on my part or a feint on the devourer's could have my sword crashing down into the top of Sawyer's head, killing him just as easily as the devil's teeth would.

The best thing I could do at this point was to make holding on to Sawyer a costlier proposition than letting him go and dealing with me.

Shouting loudly in the hopes of attracting the devourer's attention, I leaped forward and chopped down with my blade, targeting the arm that carried the partially melted shield. Slamming into the limb with my full momentum behind it, my sword bit through the fused links of chainmail that had imbedded themselves into the devil's flesh, cutting deeply in a spray of black blood. Roaring in pain, the devourer's bulbous eye shot towards me as I began to work my weapon deeper into the wound, slicing it back and forth.

Feeling the edge of the sword grate against bone, I was rewarded with a panicked flinch of the arm, the devil pulling its shield away from Sawyer in an attempt to dislodge me. Twisting my blade as the arm shifted, I jerked it upwards violently, causing a chunk of fatty flesh to tear free, along with another spurt of hot ichor.

"Lazarus, *move!*" Quinn's shouted from behind me. "Incoming!"

Taking the mage's warning to heart, I spun to the side reflexively, a crackling fireball passing straight through the spot that I had just been standing in and slamming into the devil's side. Feeling the heat of the spell vanish as quickly as it arrived, I completed my spin, using the momentum of the maneuver to slash a shallow wound along the exposed fatty rolls protruding from the devourer's side.

"Pull harder!" Molly yelled amid the chaos of battle, her voice coming from the far side of the devourer, who roared in pain from something she did.

Checking my swing from the wild slash, I looked up in time to see the devourer's protruding stomach roil, then heave itself inward, as a disturbing retching sound filled the air. Belching violently, a torrent of vile-smelling black fluid shot out of the devourer's open mouth, hitting Sawyer from pointblank range, completely covering the red-armored man from head to toe.

Seconds after the expelling the slimy vomit, I saw the devourer's tongue pull itself free from around Sawyer's neck and vanish back into its mouth, causing the now drenched warrior to stagger backwards as the resistance holding him at bay vanished. Blinded from the slime, Sawyer was then caught completely flatfooted when the devourer's shield swung out and caught him straight in the chest, sending the man sprawling to the ground with the sound of cracking bones.

"Sawyer!" I shouted out of reflex as I saw the bounty hunter begin to convulse after hitting the ground, followed by the sound of heaving as the stench of the devourer's vomit overwhelmed his stomach. Catching a whiff of the black slime as the wind shifted, I couldn't blame him for being sick, feeling a wave of nausea rise up from my own stomach in sympathy.

Shuffling to face me, the devourer belched loudly, black vomit completely covering the front of its chest as it lifted its axe and began staggering towards me, its footsteps causing the ground to shake. Glancing at a motion out of the corner of my eye, I saw Molly dart past the turning devil and rush towards Sawyer's aid.

"I got him!" Molly called to me as she dropped her bloodied sabre to the ground, not hesitating in the slightest to lay her hands on the broken warrior to heal him. "Keep the big guy busy!"

"Got it!" I grunted, my eyes shifting back towards the devourer while tightening my grip on my sword.

Meeting the advancing devil, I leaped forward once again, swinging my sword in a punishing downward blow as I purposefully targeted the creature's weakened shield arm. Slow to realize what I was doing, the devourer didn't hesitate in raising the weakened appendage to block my attack, only to have it buckle under the violent impact.

With the sickening sound of tearing flesh, the shield twisted violently from its fused position on the devourer's forearm as the wound I had inflicted earlier split open even wider, causing the fatty tissue to tear itself from the bone underneath. Howling in pain, the devourer froze, its large crimson eye darting downwards to inspect the twisted limb in disbelief.

Not giving it a chance to recover, I sidestepped to the creature's flank, rushing to get out of range of its axe and to get a better angle for my follow-up attack. Lifting my sword upwards once more, I saw the devourer's ruined shield-arm, split flesh giving way to gleaming bone.

There it is! I bared my teeth in a savage grin as I brought the glass-steel blade down onto the devourer's arm, feeling its razor-sharp edge bite deep into the exposed bone.

And carve straight through it.

"*Raaaaah!*" The devourer screamed in an unholy rage as it began to flail wildly in pain, its shield-arm swinging limply through the air, the motion causing the last shreds of muscle and fat to tear away from the rest of its body before landing sickeningly on the ground.

No sooner did the arm fall than did another cluster of missiles and fireballs arrive on the scene, hammering the stunned devil rapidly along its face and neck as Quinn unleashed his full arsenal of spells, pouring all of his mana into the creature without a thought for preservation. With the devil's blood gushing from its severed limb, the devourer continued to roar in pain, its sinister eye focusing intently on me as it shifted its massive bulk.

Taking a step back from the creature while Quinn rained destruction upon it, I couldn't help but notice the countless wounds that covered its body and an ever-so-slight fatigue to the devil's motions that hadn't been present a moment earlier. Slowly but surely, we were wearing the creature down, and it was only a matter of time before one of us landed a killing blow.

We're running out of time, though. I grimaced as the night began to turn crimson once more, the clouds hiding the burning moon above us beginning to thin. *We need to finish this fast, before the moon comes out again.*

Checking out of the corner of my eye, I saw that Molly had managed to roll Sawyer over onto his side and that the red-armored warrior was slowly pushing himself up onto his feet, his violent coughing slowly fading as the devourer's vomit began to dry and lose its potent stench.

Just a few more seconds, I thought to myself as I reflexively checked my remaining health, having forgotten about the freezing energy of the Sigil gripping my body. The last thing I needed was to have a repeat of my earlier fight and realize that the sigil had burned away the majority of my health.

HP: 501/800

Relieved to see that I was still in reasonably good health, I focused my attention back towards the Devourer, who had since managed to overcome the shock of losing one of its arms. Growling angrily, the devil's maw opened as it bared its long, serrated teeth at me.

"Watch for its tongue!" Sawyer's coughing voice rang out from behind me, a heartbeat before the devourer's tongue shot forward, like some grotesque parody of a frog.

"Ah!" I flinched in surprise, Sawyer's warning giving me just enough time to raise one hand in front of my face before the tongue hit me.

Wrapping itself around my arm, I felt tiny barbs pierce through my armor and dig into my flesh underneath as the devil yanked its tongue backwards and pulled me off balance. Staggering forward, I had enough presence of mind to drive my sword down into the ground, the strange translucent metal biting through the gap in the cobblestone and anchoring me in place.

Wincing in pain as the tongue threatened to tear the flesh straight off my bones, I did the only thing that I could do. I reached down with my trapped hand and grabbed hold of the Devourer's tongue.

Then began to pull.

The Devourer's eye widened in surprise as it realized that I was both heavier and stronger than Sawyer, its head jerking forward under my surprising strength, forcing it to brace its stubby feet on the ground.

"Oh, you done fucked up now!" I yelled at the devil as I fought through the searing pain of the tongue's barbs in my palm. Inhaling deeply, I strained with all of my might while pulling the devourer's tongue taut, in a deadly game of tug-of-war.

"We're coming, Lazarus!" Molly shouted as another inky orb flew through the air and splashed across the Devourer's face, causing the creature's crimson eye to turn black.

The sound of running feet greeted my ears as Molly then rushed back into combat, passing directly under the devourer's tongue that stretched out before me. Her heavy sabre flashed briefly in the night as she slashed through the barbed tentacle, severing it an arm's length away from me. Hot on her heels was Sawyer, the crusty remains of the devourer's bile flaking off his armor as he charged directly at the devil, eager to exact vengeance for its earlier attack.

Catching myself as the tongue's resistance vanished, I pulled my sword free from the ground, the devourer's tongue uncoiling itself from my hand as its strength faded and fell to the ground with a wet-sounding thump. Pushing myself forward to rejoin combat, I looked up in time to see Sawyer leap onto the devourer's protruding stomach and sink his blade deep into its throat, driving his weapon straight up to its hilt.

Not to be outdone, Molly angled her charge and moved to attack the devil's flank, dragging her curved sabre along the devourer's unarmored flesh, slicing a deep wound that immediately erupted with blood.

"Lazarus!" Sawyer called for my attention as he pushed himself off of the devourer's chest and dropped back onto the ground, catching a wild blow from the still blind devil's axe on his golden shield. Shifting his shield, Sawyer absorbed the attack, then quickly hooked the edge of the axe on the shield's lip before the devourer could pull it back, effectively trapping it. Pushing back on the limb, Sawyer then forced the arm out of position, completely exposing the devourer's stomach and began stabbing repeatedly with his weapon. "Stab it deep! I can't hold this forever!"

Not wasting the breath to answer Sawyer, I rushed forward, bracing my sword's hilt against my hip as I ran. Thundering towards the devourer, I saw its clouded eye regain its crimson color as Molly's spell wore off once again. With the tip of my bloody sword barely a foot away from his body, I saw it widen in panic as it spotted me attacking from point blank range.

My sword vanished into the devourer's stomach with the disturbing sound of slurping flesh, the blade penetrating deep into the devil's gut. Gasping from the impact, the devourer's gurgling breath rushed out in an instant, a low moan of pain escaping its ruined throat. Switching my grip on the hilt for leverage, I stepped to the side and sharply yanked on my blade backwards, using the length of the weapon to rend and tear the delicate organs buried inside the devourer's body.

Slicing viciously through the devil's innards, blood poured from the massive wound as I completed my brutal evisceration, the vile fluid washing over both mine and Sawyer's feet. The latest wound far too much for the devourer to withstand, the devil sagged forward, as life began to fade from its twisted form and fell to the ground.

Dancing back from the falling devil to avoid being crushed, Sawyer and I exchanged relieved glances, a heartbeat before Molly's shout caused the two of us to flinch.

"Don't just stand there! Finish it!"

Leaping between the devil and I, Molly chopped down with her heavy sabre held in both hands, catching the dying devourer at the base of the neck. Biting through bone and flesh, Molly's blade flashed again and again, her third blow in as many seconds finally severing the devil's head, sending it rolling to the ground by our feet. Only then did I see a pair of notifications appear in my vision.

Molly has slain a [Hellborn Devourer]!
You have gained Group Experience!

Looking up at Molly in surprise, I saw her cock an eyebrow towards both Sawyer and I, then slowly shake her head.

"Come on, guys," she admonished, breathing heavily, as a slow smile spread across her face. "You know the rule. The fight's not over until you get experience for it."

TWENTY-FOUR

"SO MANY DEAD," SABLE EXCLAIMED wearily as she joined the circle that the four of us and the other thief lords had formed a short distance away from where the Devourer had fallen, a bag of still untouched loot marking the spot where the creature had been before fading away. "At last count, we've lost nearly half of what we arrived with, including those who have taken serious wounds and can no longer fight. But to counteract that, we've gained a little more than a dozen in additional reinforcements as they've made their way across the district."

"It's better than we could have expected, all things considered," I replied with a sigh, seeing all of the other thief lords wince before nodding grimly. "They could have had more soul shards ready to use in their trap."

"That is true," Stroud agreed in a raspy voice, the partially healed burns across his face indicating that he had been in close proximity to one of the fireballs that the enemy mages had unleashed during the battle. "A handful more devils would have caused our forces to break the moment they appeared. As it was, it was a close enough thing to keep their morale from faltering."

"They certainly sprang their trap at an opportune time," Molly commented with a grimace.

"Be that as it may, we can reminisce about the battle later, *if* there is a later," Isabella cut in, before turning her head to address Sable. "How quickly can we get everyone moving again? Every second that we spend standing here blights another inch of the city."

"They're ready to move now," Sable replied with a grimace crossing her face. "The healers should have finished healing everyone who is able to be healed by now, and I've already told those who have lost limbs to stay behind at the entrance here and send any late arrivals forward."

"Good," Isabella stated, just as Eris momentarily poked free from the clouds above before vanishing again.

Reflexively, we all glanced upwards towards the hidden moon, feeling a sense of impending doom looming over us as we watched the shifting clouds. In the distance, a clear patch of nighttime sky was slowly drifting towards us, Eris's crimson light brightly illuminating its edge.

"We're running out of cloud cover," Smiling Jade said tonelessly as she looked away and back towards us. A hairline crack ran down the left side of her mask, along with a small chip missing, something having hit her hard during the battle. "We must go, *now*."

"I agree," Isabella grunted as she moved to step out of the circle. "Gather your forces, we're moving out in two minutes."

Echoing their assent, the other thief lords all stepped out of the circle as they moved towards the various groups of thieves, who had all instinctively huddled together based on their guild affiliation. Hanging back for a moment, Isabella glanced towards the distant group of Grim Shadows members, before turning her head back towards us.

"If there's anything else that you need to sort out before we get going, do it now," Isabella whispered. "I don't think we're going to have another chance to take a break until we take down Dorian, *assuming* that's where everything ends tonight."

"We'll be ready," I replied to Isabella, seeing Molly nod out of the corner of my eye as well.

"Good." She breathed a low sigh of a relief before completing her turn and starting to walk towards the waiting guild members. "I knew I could count on you all."

"Hang on," Sawyer asked in a hushed voice after Isabella and the other thief lords were firmly out of earshot. "What did she mean by 'assuming that's where everything ends tonight'? That sounded strange to my ears."

"She's worried that once Dorian is out of the way, the other thief lords may betray us," Molly explained to Sawyer as she motioned for us to walk towards the still waiting bag of loot. "There have been... *trust issues* lately."

"Are you fucking kidding me?" Sawyer hissed under his breath in disbelief. "After all this, we still need to worry about betrayal? I thought trust among the hunters was bad, but this is completely on another level!"

"Welcome to the underworld, the society where paranoia is a survival trait and alliances last for as long as they're convenient," Quinn told Sawyer with a fatalistic shrug as the four of us gathered around the bag of loot. "That's simply the way life is here."

"So I see," Sawyer replied with an uncomfortable expression on his face. "Should I be expecting the same thing once this is all over?"

Sawyer's question caused both Molly and Quinn to slowly turn their heads towards me, their expression going completely blank.

"You're a good person, Sawyer," I stated simply before bending down and opening the loot bag that the Devourer had dropped. "And you've helped us quite a bit today...despite what happened earlier in the day."

"Uh, thanks?" the red-armored warrior replied, sounding confused. "But I'm not sure that answered my question."

"Didn't it?" I asked, looking up to meet the man's eyes.

Sawyer paused for a moment as he replayed my reply in his head, understanding slowly crossing his face. "Oh...*thanks.*"

"Don't mention it," I replied, a thin smile crossing my face before it faded. "Seriously, *don't.* It might get us killed and ruin our reputation."

"Sure..." Sawyer said uneasily as he glanced between the three of us, seeing the serious expressions on each of our faces. "What do you say about taking a look inside that bag? Before everyone starts moving and rushes us?"

"That sounds like a great idea," I replied, reaching into the bag, watching their descriptions appear as I pulled them out and handed them to the rest of the party.

Helltouched Soul Shard Fragment

Quantity: 2

Item Class: Magical

Item Quality: Fine (+10%)

Strength: +1 Agility: +1 Constitution: +1 Intelligence: +1

Willpower +1

Durability: 0/0

Weight: 0 kg

Helltouched Iron Axe

Slot: Main Hand or Offhand

Item Class: Relic

Item Quality: Good (+15%)
Damage: 30-45 (Slashing)
Strength: +6
Durability: 140/140
Base Material: Iron
Weight: 1.5 kg
Class: Any Martial
Level: 13
Special: Helltouched

Vial of Devil Blood
Quantity: 5
Item Class: Magical
Item Quality: Average (+0%)
Durability: 0/0
Weight: 0.5 kg

Helltouched Slag
Quantity: 15
Item Class: Magical
Item Quality: Average (+0%)
Durability: 0/0
Weight: 15 kg

"A lot of crafting components this time around," I commented as I finished handing out the items to the rest of the party, pausing to take a closer look at the *[Vial of Devil Blood]* and *[Helltouched Slag]*. With nothing special on their item descriptions, I didn't have any other idea what they could be used for.

"The axe is actually pretty decent," Sawyer commented hopefully as he inspected the very same weapon that the devourer had wielded in the battle a few minutes earlier. "It may look a little melted, but the balance is surprisingly good, and it's still sharp. Not sure what the 'Helltouched' special does, though."

"Feel free to take it," I told the warrior with a shrug. "I don't think any of us are trained in axes anyway."

"Just swords and daggers for me," Molly affirmed as she held up what appeared to be a broken fragment of a soul shard. "Given what I've seen these things do, I'm a little hesitant about having one of these on me, but it does give a pretty wide boost to everything."

"I know what you mean," Quinn said, inspecting a similar fragment. "Looks like a crafting component to me, though; maybe it can be added onto something else."

"If that's the case, you better hold on to it," Molly replied while holding out her fragment. "You and Lazarus are the only crafters I know."

"Fair enough," Quinn said as he took the soul shard fragment and put it into a pocket along with the one he was holding. "We'll have to take some time after all this calms down to do some experimenting."

"I won't say no to taking a break." I nodded at Quinn in agreement while adding the *[Devil Blood]* and *[Helltouched Slag]* into my inventory, feeling the strange blackened lumps of iron as being slightly hot to the touch. "Gods know we could use it."

"Amen," added Sawyer as he tested the grip of his new axe.

"Looks like everyone's almost ready to move," Quinn said half-heartedly as he turned away from us and began walking towards the rapidly assembling guilds. "We better catch up."

"Go on ahead," I told the departing mage, seeing Sawyer turn to follow, the warrior taking slow practice swings as he walked. "Just grabbing the rest of the loot."

Checking to make sure that I hadn't forgotten anything inside it, I let go of the now empty loot bag, and it vanished the moment that it touched the ground. Standing from my kneeling position, I felt my sore muscles protest from the movement. It had been a long and brutal day so far with no sign of it ending anytime soon, and the stress and fatigue was starting to take its toll on me. I had no idea how the rest of the night—or week, for that matter—was going to play out, but I was silently considering taking the first opportunity I had to log off for at least a day and do nothing but sleep.

Sighing softly, I decided to take advantage of the current lull in the action to look over my character sheet, something I had barely even scanned after turning level thirteen.

LAZARUS CAIN – LEVEL 13 BRUISER

Half-Giant/Half-Elf Male

Statistics:

HP: 800/800

Stamina: 800/800

Mana: 275/275

Experience to next level: 6136/27000

Attributes:

Strength: 79 (92)

Agility: 65 (73)

Constitution: 49 (54)

Intelligence: 10

Willpower: 10

Abilities:

***Sneak Attack II** (Passive) – Attacks made before the target is aware of you automatically deal weapon damage +35.*

***Bleeding Attack I** (Passive) – Enemies who take sneak attack damage will continue to bleed for 5 seconds, taking 40% of the sneak attack damage dealt.*

***Power Attack II** (Active: 50 Stamina) – You slash viciously at the target, putting extra strength behind the blow. Deal weapon damage +25.*

***Ambush I** (Active: 60 Stamina) – You ambush your target,* *striking them in a vulnerable location. Deals weapon damage+125. This ability can only be used on a target unaware of you.*

***Kick** (Active: 20) – You kick your enemy for 10-20 points of damage and knock them back 1-2 yards. Depending on your Strength/Agility score, you may also knock down the target.*

***Shoulder Tackle** (Active: 40 Stamina) – Stun enemy for 1-2 seconds with chance to knock enemy down based on Strength and/or Agility attribute.*

***Deadly Throw I** (Active: 30 Stamina) – Throw a weapon with extra strength behind it. Deals weapon damage+15. This ability has a chance to interrupt spellcasting if thrown at the target's head, force them to drop their weapon if thrown at target's hands, or slow their movement if thrown at target's legs.*

Skills:

Weapons:

***Unarmed Combat** – Level 12 – 51% (Increases knowledge of Hand-to-Hand fighting and improves related Abilities.)*

***Swords** – Level 13 – 2% (Increases knowledge of Sword fighting and improves related Abilities.)*

***Daggers** – Level 11 – 47% (Increases knowledge of Dagger fighting and improves related Abilities.)*

***Crossbows** – Level 12 – 22% (Increases knowledge of Crossbows and improves related Abilities.)*

***Throwing** – Level 10 – 36% (Increases knowledge of Throwing Weapons and improves related Abilities.)*

Other:

***Stealth** – Level 12 – 93% (Decreases chance of being detected while attempting to stay hidden. Improves related Abilities.)*

***Lockpicking** – Level 12 – 89% (Increases knowledge of lock mechanics, allowing you to pick harder locks.)*

***Wordplay** – Level 12 – 89% (Increases chance to persuade* *others, resolve differences, and/or get information.)*

Perception *- Level 13 - 8% (You are skilled in spotting hidden creatures and places. Depending on your skill level, hidden creatures and places will be highlighted in red.)*

Tradeskills:

Blacksmithing *– Level 11 – 12%*

Cooking *– Level 10 – 34%*

Alchemy *– Level 12 – 11%*

Leatherworking *– Level 12 – 17%*

Racial Ability:

Titan's Might *(Giant) (Passive) – Your giant ancestry has given you the ability to wield large weapons in with exceptional strength. All damage dealt by two-handed weapons is increased by 3%.*

Keen Sight *(Elf) (Passive) – Your elven ancestry has given you exceptional eyesight, granting you the ability to see twice as far as normal in all lighting conditions. This ability also grants you Darkvision.*

Darkvision *(Elf) (Passive) – While in total darkness, your vision will have near daylight clarity up to 100 feet.*

Traits:

Sigil of Rage *– A magical sigil written in the Primal Tongue has been carved deep into your flesh, causing it to pulse with an unfathomable torrent of energy. When activated, Primal Rage suffuses your body granting you +10 to Strength and Agility. While this ability is active, you are consumed by burning pain and your body is burned from within, dealing 10 points of damage per second. This ability scales per level.*

Evolving Weapon:

Dormant Glass-Steel Greatsword

Total Experience Gained: 2925/50000

Oh, I gained a level in Swords and Perception! I realized after looking at my character sheet. *That last battle was pretty intense, I completely missed seeing the notification for the Swords skill increase, and I can't even remember when Perception would have leveled.*

"Damn, I'm starting to miss things," I muttered while rubbing my face and reevaluating just how exhausted I really was. *Was it earlier today that we saw William? That seems like it was ages ago.*

"You doing okay?" Molly asked as she stepped close to me, concern written all over her face.

"Feeling worn out," I replied as she leaned into me. "Just looked at my character sheet for the first time today; it almost felt like I was looking at someone else's."

"I know what you mean," Molly said with a sigh. "It feels like it's been go-go-go ever since the heist."

"The heist." I shook my head as I probed the black spot in my memory. "You know, I'd just forgotten that I had forgotten about it?"

"With everything that's happened over the last day, I can believe that," Molly replied sympathetically. "But does it really matter anymore? If we put an end to Dorian and Edith…then missing a day may not matter much at this point."

"I think you're right," I said with a shrug. "But at the same time, I also want to know what happened, if only to understand how I got the Sigil of Rage."

"I guess it's *my* turn to forget about things now." Molly placed her hand on my chest right where the sigil was. "I hadn't thought twice about it since we left William's place. Has it been bothering you at all?"

"Not really, though it felt a little different when I used it this fight," I said, thinking back to the battle with the devourer.

"Oh?" Molly looked up at me with a curious expression. "Different how?"

"Well, for one, it activated itself this time, right when the devourer appeared," I explained, remembering how the sigil's energy had changed. "And the energy behind it was...*cold* this time. Normally it's hot, like my blood is on fire."

Molly's eyes widened as she listened to me speak. "It activated it by itself? I thought you were completely in control of it."

"So did I," I replied with a shrug. "I'll have to ask William about it...assuming we survive all of this."

"It'll be our first stop once this is all over," Molly told me, the tone of her voice telling me that I didn't have a choice in the matter. "We'll make sure that there is nothing wrong and figure out what we can do to make sure that you're truly in control."

"No argument from me," I replied with a smile as I looked into Molly's eyes.

For a moment, the world stopped as we stared at one another, the two of us barely having had the chance to catch our breaths since the morning, let alone find a quiet minute together. Placing a hand on the side of my face, Molly pulled me closer, giving me a soft kiss before pulling away.

Molly looked like she was about to say something but was interrupted by a sudden part in the clouds above us, Eris's crimson light shining down from above. The two of us couldn't help but look up at the burning moon, the moment vanishing as a crushing sense of urgency reasserted itself, punctuated by the slow rumble of shuffling feet as the remaining thieves began to move.

"Once more into the breach," Molly said with a sigh as she pulled away from me and turned to look towards the departing thieves. "We better catch up."

"Yeah," I replied, my eyes fixed on Eris high above as it vanished behind the final block of clouds, the large gap Isabella had mentioned earlier just minutes away. "Let's keep moving and hope we're not too late."

TWENTY-FIVE

RUSHING DOWN THE ABANDONED STREETS, we were forced to pick our way through the wreckage of the battle, stepping over broken bodies and shattered barricades. Traveling in a pocket of relative safety a short distance behind the frontline, the four of us hustled alongside the thief lords silently as we made our way towards the Phineas mansion. It didn't take long for us to pass through the small neighborhood, our eyes picking out the telltale signs of the battle that had preceded us when the Damned had first attacked the Phineas Estate.

Several windows among the buildings flanking the street were broken, along with countless shattered doors that had obviously been beaten down. There was no sign where any of the inhabitants had gone, or that they had even survived the renegade thieves guild's attack in the first place. As it was, the pitiful few hostages that we had seen before the attack had taken place had accounted for a substantial portion of the devils that the Damned had summoned, the guild choosing to sacrifice as many as possible outside their membership before turning to their own.

"Gods, what happened here?" a voice rang out ahead of us, with others of similar sentiment filtering back towards us as we rounded the final bend that led out of the cloistered neighborhood, the tall buildings giving way to a scene out of nightmare.

"Oh, damn," I breathed, looking ahead at what once was the verdant grounds that surrounded the Phineas mansion, staring in shock at the desolate wasteland before me.

Gnarled and twisted trees reached up into the clouded sky, their bare branches barely moving in the gentle ocean breeze. Mounds of withered leaves piled themselves amongst the skeletal remains of countless hedges that flanked the brightly illuminated road before us, dozens of mage lamps casting their pale light into the night. Abandoned tables and chairs were visible through the gloom, indicating areas where people once sat and enjoyed the immaculate garden that used to encompass the estate.

"Everything is dead," Molly whispered in horror, her voice breaking slightly as she refused to look away. "The grass has turned grey and died. The trees look like they have been petrified. There are leaves everywhere..."

She turned her head towards Smiling Jade, who was gazing forward stoically, completely silent. "Is this what will happen to Eberia?"

"Yes," Smiling Jade replied simply. "If not worse."

It was at that moment that Eris poked free of the clouds above for the very last time, the final clouds of the nighttime sky finally passing over the city as they continued on their journey over the ocean. The crimson light of the burning moon made it appear as if the Phineas grounds had been showered in blood, easily drowning out the mage lamps that lit the path before us.

We barely had a moment to take in the new sight before a flash of crimson in the distance caught our attention and a pillar of light rose up into the air, reaching out for the moon above. No sooner did the light touch Eris than did we feel something pulse far ahead of us, a heartbeat before a familiar wave of *wrongness* swept into us, causing a handful of screams and moans to erupt from the thieves around us, the strange energy causing many to fall to their knees.

"*Shit*," I cursed, feeling my head spin from the magic as a wave of nausea threatened to overwhelm me. "That was even worse than the last time."

"Yeah," Molly agreed as she leaned into me, her hands visibly shaking.

"Much worse," Sawyer panted as he kneeled down to the ground, his balance swaying precariously.

"Look at the house," Quinn cut in with a strained voice, pointing straight ahead at a crimson glow in the distance that was rapidly growing in intensity. "It's burning with magic. I shouldn't be able to see it from this far away...but even from here, it's painful to even look at."

"You can see magic?" I asked Quinn, realizing how little I knew about mages as I followed his hand and spotted the Phineas mansion for the first time.

"It's an ability spellcasters can get," Quinn explained, shielding his eyes for a moment as the intensity of the glow increased. "Normally, it has a limited range, but the house is bleeding so much magic into the air..."

"What does that mean, exactly?" Sawyer asked as he forced himself back up onto his feet with a grunt. "Explain it to me like the idiot warrior I am."

"It means Dorian's ritual is gaining strength," Smiling Jade interjected, the orange-robed thief lord standing completely still as she stared ahead. "And that we are running out of time."

"Then let's get moving," I said while staring at the mansion in the distance, seeing vague shapes silhouetted in the glow. "On second thought, I think I see movement up ahead."

There was a short pause as everyone squinted in the direction of the house, trying to pick out signs of movement.

"Me too," Molly said, using her hand to block the moon's light from her eyes. "It must be the rest of the Damned."

"I agree," Stroud declared in his typical toneless voice. "With the garden ravaged by Dorian's magic, there is no other place for them to hide. They would all have to rally in front of the house to repel a frontal assault."

"And are we going to give them a frontal assault to repel?" Sawyer asked hesitantly. "Is that even a good idea?"

"I don't see any other choice," Stroud replied. "We do not have the option for subterfuge, and time is of the essence. The only option I see is to hit them with all our might in hopes of shattering them."

"But it will still take time to fight through them all and break into the mansion," Sable countered, doubt filling her voice.

"I am open to better strategies," the large man grunted, looking down at the black-furred Tul'Shar with a hint of frustration seeping into his voice.

"What if we tried both a frontal attack *and* a bit of subterfuge?" I asked, causing everyone to look in my direction as I waved a hand at Stroud. "You said it yourself, sneaking past them isn't really an option; there isn't anywhere to take cover and they would spot us easily. *But* if all of you were to assault them head on…"

"They would be distracted and unable to intercept the four of you as you infiltrated the house," Stroud replied as he considered the idea.

"Assuming you were even spotted in the chaos."

"Exactly." Molly nodded, catching on to my plan. "Once we get into the house, we can try to find a way to delay or disrupt the ritual until you all make it inside."

"What if there are more of the Damned inside the building?" Sable queried, silently accepting the prospect that we wouldn't find any survivors. "We have no way of knowing how many could be lying in wait; you could all be walking yourselves into a trap."

"It would make little sense for them to split their forces at this point," Sawyer answered with a shrug. "And if they do for some reason, then we'll deal with it ourselves. We are more than capable to do so."

"That is true," Sable admitted with a nod. "Very well, I am in favor."

"It gives us more options than we had before and will allow us for a less risky assault on our part," Stroud said in agreement, looking towards Smiling Jade and Isabella. "I am in favor as well."

"As am I," Smiling Jade stated.

"Then we should stop wasting our time standing here," Isabella finished, her expression one of pride as she smiled at us.

"Indeed," Stroud said as he waved a hand forward, motioning for the other thief lords to follow him to the front line. "Come, it's about time we led this army from the front, to show the Damned that the other Eberian thieves guilds stand united before them and that utter destruction awaits them."

"A bit melodramatic, but...*apt*," Smiling Jade replied with amusement, turning her head towards us and giving us a nod before moving to follow Stroud. "Good luck, adventurers. I have an idea that may aid you in getting to the house. You will know it when you see it."

"See you all soon." Sable gave us a brief wave before vanishing into the crowd.

We were left with Isabella as the three other thief lords made their way to the front. The blonde-haired spymistress gave us each a nod.

"It goes without saying that I wish the four of you luck. But there is one thing I wanted to impress on you all.

"If you have the opportunity to kill Dorian, *take it,*" she told us forcefully. "Do not hesitate, do not attempt to take him alive, and do not stop until you are *sure* he is dead, preferably with his head or heart in your hand.

"Based on what we've seen today, he has singlehandedly massacred an entire noble house, arranged the deaths of two noble heirs, and has unleashed magic that is in danger of blighting the entire city," Isabella continued, her head indicating the ravaged gardens and buildings behind us. "A purge at this point is inevitable, but being able to present proof of his death *may* deflect the worse of it from us, or at least cause them to stop once they've taken their pound of flesh."

"We understand, Isabella," Molly replied, her face serious. "We'll do whatever we have to do."

"Good." Isabella nodded as she made to follow the other thief lords. "We'll do our best to fight through the Damned as fast as possible and come help you, but there is a chance we might not arrive in time...or at all."

"Hopefully it won't come to that," I told Isabella, silently wondering what we would do if all of the thief lords were killed tonight. "But we'll do our best."

"Then it should be enough." Isabella gave us one last crooked smile before she stepped forward and vanished between the press of bodies.

Within seconds of her disappearing, the thieves ahead of us began to surge forward, their earlier fears and hesitation banished by their leaders taking point and striding forward with confidence. Shuffling awkwardly to the side through the press of bodies, the four of us slowly extricated ourselves from the crowd, watching all of them move quickly down the road before us.

Following at a distance, the four of us kept pace with the guilds, waiting for our moment to step off the road and sprint through the desolate grounds in an attempt to get to the house unnoticed.

"This is a good spot," I whispered to the party behind me as we came to a gap in the carefully manicured garden that flanked the road. "We should have a clear path running through here and around to the side of the house."

"Sounds good to me," Quinn replied, speaking softly. "Just lead the way and we'll follow."

"Be sure to stay low and move fast," I ordered needlessly, feeling slightly skittish as I waited for the thief lords to begin their attack. We only had one shot at making this work, and the price for failure in this case was higher than I cared to think about.

Calm down, I told myself, letting out a sigh before a loud shout caused me to look towards the house.

"Here we go!" I heard Sawyer exclaim as several thunderclaps of magic filled the air, followed by a bright, almost blinding light that flared into existence at the head of the army we had just left before narrowing itself into a cone, pointing directly at the Damned. "Shit, that's bright!"

"That has to be Smiling Jade's signal!" I exclaimed, motioning for everyone to follow me off the road as I launched myself into a sprint. "That light will ruin everyone's night vision and blind anyone looking this way!"

Rushing through the gardens, I couldn't help but marvel at Smiling Jade's maneuver; the crafty thief lord had blinded everyone with her spell, effectively drowning them in an ocean of light. Any movement or sign of our passage would be nearly impossible to spot from those caught in its effect.

Now it's up to you to make the most of it and get to the house in one piece! I told myself while leading the party through the dead garden, feeling the dead grass turn to dust under my feet. Whatever Dorian's magic had done to kill the plants surrounding the estate, it had also made them extremely brittle and weak to the touch. *Is this what will happen to all of Eberia's food and crops? They'll just waste away to nothing the moment someone touches them?*

Gritting my teeth at the thought of abandoning the city, I spurred myself onwards and picked up my pace as I ran, my goal being to run past the house and out of sight from the Damned arrayed out front before circling back and finding an entrance. With how big the house was, I had no doubt that we would the able to find a side entrance without any problem.

Continuing our sprint across the grounds at a blinding pace, we crossed the length of the gardens, trailing a stream of dust as we ran. Surprised at how easily the foliage was crumbling to our touch, I swiped out at the twisted remains of what was once a massive hedge, only to have it burst into dust as my hand passed through it, the same way the grass did under my feet.

If everything gives way so easily, we might as well take a more direct route, I thought to myself, angling my approach to take us straight towards the house and plowing through a row of desiccated shrubbery.

My direct approach brought us closer to the house, the four of us shielding our eyes as we briefly passed through the blinding light that Smiling Jade had cast.

"Slow down!" Molly hissed from behind me as I felt the ground under me change, her magical vision recovering the fastest out of the three of us. "We're coming up on a patio!"

Blinking furiously to restore my night vision, I slowed down as my eyes rapidly readjusted themselves to the nighttime gloom, causing the blurry shapes before me to resolve themselves as tables and chairs that had been carelessly knocked over and strewn about. Reacting instinctively, the four of us spread out as we came to a stop, scanning the area for threats.

Glancing behind us, I reflexively checked to see if we had been spotted during our run across the Phineas grounds, feeling a sense of relief wash through me when I saw the brightly lit but empty grounds behind us.

No one saw us. I breathed out a sigh in silent relief.

"*Oh, shit,*" I heard Molly curse, followed by the sound of her sword pulling free from her sheath.

"What did you find?" I asked while spinning towards the sound of her voice and reaching for my sword that I had slung over one shoulder during our sprint.

"Bodies," Molly stated while trying to suppress a gag.

Gritting my teeth as I completed my turn, I spotted Molly standing at the edge of a nearly overflowing pool, staring at several shapes floating in the water. Walking over to her side, I couldn't help but curse in sympathy.

"They just killed them," I grunted as I looked down at five ravaged bodies that gently bobbed in the pool's crimson water, each of them bearing a combination of jagged wounds and wicked burns. "They weren't even a threat."

"Why would they bother killing everyone?" Molly asked aloud. "Even if they wanted to kill the nobles…that's fine. But the servants too?"

"That is a good question," I replied, shaking my head as I continued to scan the area, noticing that there were several other bloodstains and claw marks around the patio. "Judging from the amount of spilled blood everywhere, it was probably chaos."

"Explains how Dorian managed to invade the place so easily," Quinn said thoughtfully. "If they brought a handful of devils with them as shock troops, it would have sent everyone into a panic."

"Hey, I'm not so great at this sneaking thing," Sawyer cut in softly. "But we probably shouldn't be talking this much, right?"

"You're right," Molly stated, tearing her eyes away from the pool. "Let's keep moving."

Passing by the bloody pool, the four of us continued to explore the patio as it flanked the side of the mansion, searching for an entrance inside. Signs of battle were evident everywhere as we wove our way through countless shattered tables and chairs before finally spotting a side door that had been completely ripped off its hinges leading into the house.

At least we don't have to start fumbling with picking locks or needing to break a window to get inside, I thought to myself quietly as the four of us entered the house, keeping our ears open for any noise.

Gliding through what once used to be an immaculately decorated waiting room that had the misfortune of being on the receiving end of a thieves guild's wrath, we followed a trail of destruction and carnage as we made our way deeper into the Phineas mansion. Several times we were forced to step over bodies of fallen nobles or servants, some having clearly being torn to shreds by rampaging devils, while others had been clearly stabbed or beaten to death by the invading cutthroats.

"You hear that?" Quinn's voice was barely audible as he tapped me on the shoulder, then pointed to his ears. "Something's humming."

Cocking my head to the side, I picked up on the noise that Quinn had mentioned. It was as if there were a distant vibration somewhere in the house.

"Magic?" I asked Quinn, keeping my voice as low as possible while Molly and Sawyer watched us silently.

"Think so," he whispered back with a shrug.

With no better lead at the moment, we resumed our exploration of the seemingly abandoned mansion, trying to find the source of the eerie hum. Thankfully, the noise grew in intensity the further that we traveled into the mansion, gradually increasing until it became an audible drone. I had no idea where we were in relation to the rest of the mansion, but given the sprawling size of the manor, I had to assume that we were nearing its center.

And we *still* hadn't seen anyone, either belonging to the Damned or the Phineas nobles that lived here.

"—obeyed all of your orders and I am on the verge of success!" We all flinched as a familiar voice boomed from the hallway ahead of us, the angry words causing us to stop in our tracks. "I *demand* that you send some sort of help; the other guilds are in danger of breaking through what remains of my followers!"

We all stared at one another in shock, immediately recognizing who the voice belonged to.

"*Dorian*," Molly hissed through her teeth as she urgently motioned for me to continue moving forward.

Not needing to be prompted a second time, I practically sprinted down the hallway, choosing to sacrifice a bit of stealth in favor of speed. All the while, a single question kept repeating itself in my head.

Who is Dorian talking to?

"Your success or failure at this point no longer concerns me," a man's voice replied. "While your service has been impressive thus far, I see no reason for me to intervene. As it is, I have already loaned Edith into your service, and you have damaged her."

"Are you *insane?*" Dorian shouted, his voice burning with rage. "After all I have done and risked for you, you will not raise a single hand in assistance?"

"You speak of your actions like you had a choice in the matter," the mysterious voice rebuffed. "With the geas I hold over you *and* your guild, you are all nothing more than glorified puppets under my control. Your only choice was to do my bidding or die like the other thief lord did."

"I am starting to wish I had!" Dorian barked, the humming noise intensifying in tone until it nearly drowned out all hearing.

He was the one that killed Fairfax? The twin revelations of Dorian and the rest of the Damned being subject to a geas, in addition to the news about Fairfax's death, caused all of us to stop dead in our tracks and glance back at one another, exchanging looks of pure shock. *Could that be the king? Did he somehow renew the geas and only have it affect Dorian?*

Feeling the shock wash over me, I forced myself to focus on the task at hand as I motioned for everyone to keep moving, seeing a three-way intersection at the end of the hall before us. Rushing forward, I crossed the length of the hallway and glanced around the corner, reflexively squinting my eyes at bright crimson light that poured through shattered floor-to-ceiling windows, leading to what appeared to be outside.

Crouching down low, I picked a direction at random and took cover against the opposite wall before me, careful not to step on the broken glass that littered the ground, the rest of the party following closely behind. Using the angle to my advantage, I peered through the open gap, seeing that it led to an interior courtyard set in the very center of the Phineas mansion, providing a soothing and relaxing view outside.

Or at least they did once.

Now, the interior of the courtyard could only be described as a blighted hellscape, the lush greenery that once filled the interior garden now a pale grey as it slowly crumbled to dust. Leaning forward, I carefully poked my head out around the window's edge. Blinking repeatedly as my eyes adjusted to the light, I noticed that the heart of the courtyard had been completely cleared and that someone had thrust a dozen large crystals into the ground, each of them burning with intense crimson energy.

Movement caught my eye, and I saw the familiar form of Dorian come into view as he frantically adjusted the positioning of a crystal on the opposite end of the courtyard so that it aligned perfectly with the center, the near deafening hum vanishing the moment that he finished his adjustment.

"We are ready!" Dorian barked at someone I couldn't see. "Bring him to the center and hold him in place. *Be careful not to disrupt the crystals*! The rest of you get into your positions!"

Shifting my glance inwards, I felt my heart leap as I spotted Edith come into view, dragging a blue-robed half-orc into the center of the courtyard, with four large devils following in her wake, recognizing them as the same kind that Molly and I had fought on the pier. Keeping a vicious grip on the struggling man with her powerful twisted arm, she easily forced the half-orc into the circle without disrupting the placement of any of the crystals and kicked out his feet from under him, sending him to the ground.

That's Ransom! I realized with a start, recognizing the bright blue robes that he wore as Edith leaped on top of him, driving a knee into his back and pinning him in place. *I guess he wasn't working with Edith after all! That or he got cold feet.*

Desperately trying to pull himself free of the stronger woman, the half-orc warlock thrashed wildly, his antics annoying Edith enough for her to hit him viciously in the back of the head and shove his face down into the dirt. Glancing towards the devils, I saw them move to surround the inner circle of crystals, one of them stepping right behind Edith, its large body effectively blocking her and Ransom from view. Focusing on the devils for a heartbeat, I saw four identical tags appear in my vision.

[Hellborn Brute] – Level 12

Well, it could be worse. They could all be higher levels, I thought to myself, letting out a slow sigh as I motioned for the others behind me to get ready, my eyes searching for the other man I'd heard Dorian talking to in the courtyard. *Where is he? Did he somehow leave?*

Worried that I had missed something, I scanned the inner courtyard a second time, my heart racing in panic, fearing that I had lost an opportunity to identify Fairfax's killer. Squinting through the bright crimson light, I saw Dorian turn his head and scowl as an ethereal silhouette of a masked man dressed in robes stepped out from behind a glowing cluster of crystals, the mysterious voice filling the air once more.

"I am impressed, Dorian; you may actually yet succeed. After your latest failure, I did not have high hopes," the apparition said approvingly as he walked towards Dorian, his voice then turning to one of command. "Do you understand the full scope of your orders?"

"Yes," Dorian acknowledged through gritted teeth.

"Yes, *Master*," the ghost corrected brusquely as he raised a hand in Dorian's direction, causing the thief lord to wince in pain. "Regardless of the latitude I have given you, do not forget that you are my *servant* and that you *will* address me appropriately at all times."

"I, uh, yes, *Master*," Dorian ground out. "I m-meant no disrespect."

"Of course you did," the man countered as he lowered his hand. "But that is understandable. I have placed you in a difficult situation and you are under a great deal of stress. Fortunately for you, however, I have reconsidered your request to lend assistance."

Damn, time to move! I mentally cursed while taking a step away from the window and gripping my sword tightly, the rest of the party doing the same as they looked at me for the sign to move. Given what we had heard so far, I had hoped we would have had a chance to learn the identity of Dorian's master and set this whole chain of events in motion, but it looked like our time had just run out.

"You have?" I heard Dorian reply, his voice hopeful as I hefted my sword in one hand and began counting down with my fingers so the rest of the party could see.

"Indeed," the man replied, his voice sounding amused. "I am afraid it is only limited to information, however. Nevertheless, I believe it will be most enlightening."

I paused with a single finger in the air, curious to hear that the man would say.

"Information?" Dorian asked, poorly concealing the disappointment in his tone. "What is it?"

"There are four adventurers behind that wall there getting ready to burst in here and kill you."

There was a moment of silence as we all absorbed the mysterious man's statement, the context of the words taking a few seconds to sink in.

"Oh, fuck," I gasped, realizing that the man was referring to *us*. "Go, go, go!"

Wasting no time, I leaped forward, rushing through the broken window and into the blighted courtyard, hearing similar curses behind me as the rest of the party scrambled to follow. Dust billowed all around me as I plowed through the remains of a half-dissolved fern, my long strides eating up the distance between me, Dorian, and the ethereal man.

"*WHAT?*" Dorian's shout was punctuated by the vicious snarls of the four devils as my sudden appearance caused them to spin from their positions surrounding Edith at the heart of the ritual circle.

"I hope that was of *some* help," the mysterious man said with a mocking laugh as he began to fade out of existence. "Good luck, Dorian. Maybe I will see you again if you survive."

"Damn it! Keep them away from the crystals!" Dorian barked. "Edith, trigger the artifact now!"

"Lazarus! Keep Dorian busy!" Molly's shouted from behind me as a loud clap of magic filled the air, followed by several roars as the hellborn brutes joined the fight. "We'll try and disrupt the ritual!"

"You're too late to disrupt anything!" Dorian shouted as he conjured a ball of fire in his hand and threw it in my direction. "All that you've done is get people killed needlessly!"

"*Needlessly?*" I screamed back at the warlock, not believing what I was hearing as I somersaulted under the fireball and rolled back onto my feet, finding myself just a few feet away from the man. "You massacred an entire noble house!"

"I didn't have a choice!" Dorian snarled as he drew a sword from his waist and braced to meet my charge. "Your meddling forced my hand and threw everything I had worked towards into jeopardy! If it weren't for you, they would still be alive!"

"Bullshit!" I howled at the thief lord as I finally closed with him and swung my sword in a wide, sweeping arc. "There is always a choice!"

"Death was the only other choice!" Dorian replied as he nimbly dodged under my wild attack and stepped within my reach, his sword moving with blinding speed, cutting a line across my bicep.

"Gah," I grunted in surprise, reflexively shifting my body to catch the thief lord's follow-up strike on the edge of my chestpiece, keeping him from burying the tip of his blade in my shoulder.

Not giving the agile man a chance to launch a third attack, I kicked out with my leg as he attempted to dance out of reach, feeling the tip of my boot connect with the thief lord's hip and sending him staggering backwards. "Then you should have died!"

"That is easy for you to say!" Dorian shouted derisively as the two of us sized one another up, looking for weaknesses in one another's stance. "*Your kind is immortal!* Death means nothing for you!"

"Maybe it doesn't," I admitted to the thief lord. "But even if I weren't immortal, there are some lines that aren't worth crossing."

Giving me a look that amounted to pure hate, our conversation died away as Dorian leaped at me with a renewed ferocity, causing our battle to blur into mad flashes of desperate parries and vicious blows as I tried to keep the thief lord occupied, while Molly and the others fought their way through the quartet of devils that defended the ritual circle.

As the two of us brawled, it was all I could do to keep from tapping into the burning rage of the sigil that relentlessly pulsed across my chest, fearing that either Edith or Dorian would have the chaos stone that I had seen earlier. The last thing that this battle needed was another supercharged spell like the one Edith had cast back on the pier yesterday.

The world regained clarity as my fist slammed into the side of Dorian's face, feeling his jaw break under the strike, but the attack had left me far enough out of position for the thief lord to slap a conjured glob of green fire onto the arm that held my sword.

Recoiling in pain as the flames burned through the thin armor protecting my forearm, I reflexively went to slap it out with my free hand, causing the strange goop to splash everywhere from the impact and spreading the burning substance across my body, rapid alerts appearing in my vision.

Dorian's [Fel Ooze] burns you for 16 points of fire damage!
Dorian's [Fel Ooze] burns you for 11 points of fire damage!
Dorian's [Fel Ooze] burns you for 18 points of fire damage!

Writhing in pain, I urgently tried to scrape the burning ooze off my armor as it began to catch on the thinner material, only serving to badly sear the palm of my hand as I flung chunks of it away from me. Staggering away from me in a daze, Dorian took advantage of my momentary distraction to collect his bearings and recover from the latest injury that I had given him.

Getting the worst of the fel ooze off of me, I took a moment to take stock of my injuries, feeling a growing fatigue in my body as the battle wore on. Like two boxers in the final rounds of a championship match, both Dorian and I stood bruised and beaten, countless injuries having piled on top of one another, but neither of us willing to be the first to fall.

A bright flash of crimson light from the ritual circle caused the both of us to flinch, Ransom's screaming voice filling the air. Taking my eyes off Dorian for a split second, I saw Edith slowly backing away from the inner circle of crystals, a thin pillar of light having pinned Ransom in place. Fighting at the very edge of the ritual circle was Molly and the rest of the party, the four hellborn brutes having barely managed to keep them at bay. But despite the hellborn brutes' efforts, I saw that the party had managed to knock two of the twelve crystals out of place, seemingly to no effect of the overall ritual.

"Finally!" Dorian exclaimed, his words slurring around his shattered jaw as I saw him turn to sprint towards the ritual circle, leaving me scrambling to catch up.

Turning to follow the speedy thief lord, I saw a second flare of magic catch my eye, followed by a deafening thunderclap as Quinn threw a fireball directly into a badly wounded devil's face, sending it falling to the ground. Immediately, the three remaining hellborn brutes were forced to step back as Molly and Sawyer both pressed their attacks, driving them deeper into the ritual circle.

"Stop him!" Dorian's commanding voice rang out ahead of me, causing the closest devil in the melee to look up from his bout and spring forward to intercept me, completely ignoring a long, gaping slash that Molly's blade inflicted as he shoved past her.

"Lazarus, heads up!" Molly warned as she shot a glance over her shoulder to see where the devil had gone.

With only seconds to react before the devil hit me, I barely had enough time to brace myself for the impact as the charging hellborn brute slammed into me and tackled me to the ground. Feeling the wind rush out from my lungs as I slid through the ritual circle, the creature straddled me and began raining heavy blows down on my head.

Letting go of my sword, I threw up both my arms in front of my face as I desperately tried to buy myself a chance to recover from the devil's attack, my head spinning violently from the repeated impacts. Cocking back an arm in a wild swing, I punched the side of the hellborn brute's face, stunning it momentarily, giving me the chance to grab its other arm and hold it in place while my vision cleared.

Within seconds, my world realigned itself and I found myself gazing up at the vicious-looking devil on top of me, the horned creature baring its wicked teeth as it howled at me with rage. Feeling a surge of strength erupt from the arm I had gripped, I fought to keep it at bay as I instinctively punched out at the creature's face once more. Teeth flew in the air as my brutal blow caught the devil square in the mouth, a second flattening its grotesque nose, a third blinding an eye.

Pushing through my relentless onslaught, the devil thrust its head downwards, the edge of its horned crown smashing into my face as it returned the favor and crushed my nose in retaliation. Stunned from the all-too-familiar feeling of yet another broken nose, my grip slackened long enough for the devil to pull itself closer, its remaining teeth biting deep into the meat of my neck.

"Ah!" I screamed in pain as I reflexively grabbed at the hellborn brute's head, trying to find leverage to get the devil off me. Feeling my hand wrap itself around one of the thick horns that protruded from the devil's head, I heaved against it, feeling flesh tear from my neck as I slowly forced the devil away from me.

Eyes widening against my superior strength, the devil growled in defiance as it forced itself against me, giving me a perfect view of its now bloody maw. Yanking hard on the horn, I twisted the devil's head to one side to keep it off balance, hearing the bony spur crack from the motion. A desperate idea came to mind, causing me to pull on the horn even harder, the cracking sound intensifying as it shifted in my hand ominously before finally snapping free.

Howling in pain, I didn't give the devil a chance to recover, spinning the jagged horn that I had torn from its head in my hand before stabbing it directly into the creature's eye, driving the length of it into the creature's brain. Like a puppet with its strings cut, the devil fell limp in my grasp, all life fading from it as black ichor began to well around the horn's edge. Grunting, I heaved the body off of me, already feeling the otherworldly creature begin to lose substance as the spirit that possessed the body fled its mortal shell.

Grabbing my sword from where I had dropped it, I forced myself up onto my feet, feeling my head still spinning from the devil's earlier attacks. Driving the tip of my blade into the ground to steady myself, I looked towards the inner ring of the ritual circle, seeing both Dorian and Edith standing over Ransom's prone body as they stared at a *grey, diamond-shaped object* floating in the air, directly in the center of a thin pillar of light.

That has to be the artifact! I froze as an eerie sense of *déjà vu passed through me, instinctively knowing that I had seen the object before, but not being able to link a specific memory to it.*

Silently cursing whatever had taken my memory away from me, I took one faltering step forward towards Dorian and Edith, just as a tearing sound filled the air. Glancing past the pair, I saw the pillar of light begin to pull itself away from the artifact, the grey stone-like object beginning to spin faster and faster as the beam of light split itself in two.

I have to stop it! I thought while taking another step towards the spinning artifact, hoping that Dorian and Edith didn't turn around to see me. Fixating on it to the exclusion of everything else as I increased my pace, I saw the two beams of light begin to pull apart from one another, causing a hot gust of foul air to rush into the courtyard.

Gritting my teeth at the smell, I raised my sword high as I rushed into the circle, seeing both Dorian and Edith turn to look at me out of both corners of my eye, surprise written on both of their faces.

Didn't expect me to kill that devil so fast, did you? I mentally taunted as I leaped between the pair and brought my sword down on the floating artifact, channeling every single ounce of strength I had into the blow. A loud cracking sound filled the air as I hit the surprisingly dense artifact, the impact sheering off a chunk of it, causing the twin beams of light to vanish.

"NO!" Dorian screamed beside me in pure terror as the artifact flared with crimson energy, its graceful spin now becoming a wild tumble.

"What the hell did you just do?" Edith shouted, recovering from her surprise and moving to attack me, only to dodge to the side in a panic as a large beam of crimson energy shot forth from the artifact. "Ah!"

"Shit!" I exclaimed as the ground between me and Edith exploded under the beam's power, the shockwave knocking me off my feet and sending me tumbling across the ground.

"You idiot!" Dorian roared at me as he ducked under a stray bolt of energy, the power radiating from the artifact increasing in intensity with every second that passed. "You destabilized it!"

Pushing myself up off the ground, I glanced back at the artifact, watching it continue to spin violently, gradually increasing in speed until it became a blur too fast for the eye to follow. Beams of light poured from the artifact, scouring the inner walls of the courtyard around us and raining debris downwards.

"Lazarus!" I heard Molly's voice shout out amid all the chaos, causing me to reflexively glance towards its source. Spotting her standing in a pocket of relative safety, she beckoned to me urgently, the rest of the party surrounding her as Quinn desperately channeled his force shield in an attempt to keep the falling debris at bay. "Get up!"

Glancing once more at the now blinding artifact, I forced myself back onto my feet for what felt like the hundredth time today, my body screaming at me in protest as I surged forward towards Molly and Quinn's protective shield. I managed to take two faltering steps before I felt a wave of energy slam into my side, the world vanishing in a bright crimson light as an impossibly loud tearing sound echoed through the courtyard.

Then the next thing I knew, I was falling.

TWENTY-SIX

SLAMMING INTO THE GROUND WITH a bone-jarring crack, I felt my sword fly from my grasp as I tumbled and bounced end over end, sliding along the hard-packed ground and throwing up ash everywhere. Flipping onto my back, I gradually slowed to a stop, pain radiating from every single muscle in my body. Coughing wildly through the billowing ash, I opened my eyes and found myself staring straight up into a sky filled with smoke and fire.

That's not right, I thought to myself in a daze as my head pounded violently, making any sort of meaningful thinking impossible. Closing my eyes, I covered my face with a hand, holding it in place until the pain receded, and I took stock of my injuries, making sure that I hadn't broken anything in the fall.

"What the hell just happened?" Sawyer's voice rang out from nearby, followed by a coughing fit. "Am I dead?"

"Ugh," I heard Quinn groan in pain. "I don't think so, but if this is how it feels to be alive, Lord, take me now..."

"Is everyone okay?" Molly asked with a hacking cough. "Did anyone see Lazarus?"

"I'm here," I called out while opening my eyes slowly. Pushing myself up off the ground, I forced myself into a sitting position, realizing that we weren't in the Phineas mansion anymore.

Or Eberia, for that matter.

Glancing around me, I was greeted with the sight of a desolate, rocky wasteland that stretched as far as my eye could see, being broken up by jagged breaks in the terrain. Huge mountains of darkened stone rose up in the distance, with massive columns of smoke billowing upwards from their peaks. As if witnessing the inhospitable landscape weren't enough, I felt a wave of heat sweep over me, sending the dark ash covering the ground billowing up and into my face.

"Where are we?" I asked while shielding my face, joining the others in their violent coughing as the pervasive ash caused my eyes and throat to burn. Waiting until the ash settled, I removed my hand from my face and turned to look for the party, involuntarily flinching at what I saw.

A substantial chunk of the Phineas mansion lay on its side, propped up against a small ridge of stone jutting out of the ground. Looking at it carefully, I recognized it as belonging to the façade that had lined the inner courtyard, appearing as if it had been torn free by a giant hand. Debris littered the ground everywhere as I continued to turn around, spotting the countless fragments of wood, stone, and the partially shredded remains of what I could only assume was once a loveseat.

In the midst of the destruction, I saw the battered and prone shapes of the party, slowly pulling themselves out of the wreckage.

"I...have no idea," Quinn replied as he shifted a pile of debris off of himself and stood unsteadily on his feet, clutching his head. "I remember the artifact exploding...and falling."

"I tried to stop it," I said while standing up and looking around for my sword, thankfully seeing it a short distance away from me, sticking out of the ground. "It didn't quite work out the way that I planned."

"Well..." Molly's voice was tight as she finished extricating herself from a pile of shattered wood and stone. "Hopefully this isn't as bad as whatever Dorian had in mind."

"That's...fine for everyone else." Sawyer grunted in pain as he pushed a large block of stone off of himself, sending the grey slab crashing to the ground with a loud thud. "But what are we going to do? This sure doesn't look like anywhere near Eberia."

"No, it doesn't," Quinn agreed as he surveyed the area, his eyes landing on the remnants of the house. "Maybe the artifact malfunctioned and teleported us somewhere? Looks like it took most of the building with us."

"I wonder where Dorian and Edith ended—" I started to say, before my Perception skill suddenly flashed in my vision and pointed towards a large pile of rubble, a faint voice reaching my ears. "Hey, you hear that?"

"Hear what?" Sawyer grumbled as he tried to brush a combination of plaster and ash from his now grey-red armor. "Something conveniently coming to kill us and put us out of our misery? Because I'm done with this vacation and I'm ready to go home."

"No, I hear a voice!" I pulled my sword out of the ground as I rushed forward. "Help me look!"

That was all it took for everyone to shake the cobwebs from their heads and move to help me as I pointed to the pile of wreckage I'd seen earlier, the faint voice echoing through the air.

"Help," a muffled voice called out from inside the pile. "Someone, help me..."

"Ransom?" Molly was the first to answer as she started to dig through the debris. "Is that you?"

"*Molly?*" the voice replied with surprise. "Please...I'm bleeding out."

Spurred on by a sense of urgency, the four of us clawed through the pile until we saw a familiar blue robe sticking out of the rubble, causing us to slow down slightly as we cleared it away from the trapped half-orc.

"Shit!" Quinn cursed as we lifted a large plank of wood free, revealing the warlock. "He's missing an arm!"

Pulling the Ransom free, I noticed that the half-orc's skin had already gone pale and grey from blood loss, with a massive bloodstain covering his chest from where he cradled a stump of his arm. Wasting no time, Molly reached out and pressed her glowing hand onto the bleeding stump, channeling her healing magic into Ransom.

Looking over the fallen warlock for other injuries, I noticed that his missing arm was only the latest in what seemed like countless injuries and bruises covering his flesh, some clearly having been caused by whatever the artifact did to send us here, but others having lingered for a few days on end. Wherever Ransom had been for the last few days since the heist, it clearly hadn't been a pleasant experience for him.

They kept him hungry so he wouldn't regenerate, I realized, looking at the fresh burns that covered Ransom's head, having seared off the majority of his black hair. *It definitely doesn't look like he was willingly working with Edith and Dorian.*

"Molly, Lazarus, thank God it's you two," Ransom sighed with relief as Molly finished her healing efforts, color returning to the half-orc's face, his wounds and bruises fading as if they had never existed.

"What happened, Ransom?" I asked the warlock, not knowing what else to say. All this time, we had assumed that he had been complicit in both Dorian's and Edith's plans. The only indication that he wasn't a willing participant had been his ragged appearance and how badly he had fought Edith when she dragged him to the ritual circle. "What did Dorian and Edith do?"

"What?" Ransom looked at me with confusion, his eyes shifting to look past me and towards the burning sky above us. Staring upwards, Ransom's expression froze, before slowly becoming one of terror. "Oh, God, we got pulled through. You didn't destroy it."

"Pulled through?" Molly echoed, fear coloring her voice. "Pulled through to where?"

"Avernus," Ransom answered as he forced himself up into a sitting position, cradling the stump of his arm against his bloodstained robes. Contrary to the weakened half-orc that we had pulled free of the rubble, Ransom had made a rapid recovery with the aid of Molly's healing. "One of the planes of Hell."

"*We're in Hell?*" I shouted, feeling a sense of dread come over me as everyone in the party cried out in surprise, each of us trying to process what the half-orc had said.

"I tried to take the artifact from her after you fell, Lazarus," Ransom said, completely ignoring all of our shock, using his one hand to push himself off the ground, and he began looking around as if trying to find something in the distance. "But the second that you touched it...it activated, and both Edith and I were...*twisted.* Anyway, none of that matters right now, we have to find—"

"What are you talking about, Ransom?" I interrupted the warlock rudely, the man's head snapping back to look at me.

"I'm talking about the Arcaneum," Ransom stated with a frown, completely taken aback by my response. "When we tried to keep Edith from the artifact."

I blinked blankly at the half-orc as he stared at me with a puzzled expression. "I don't remember *anything* that happened in the Arcaneum, Ransom."

"What?" Ransom glanced over at Molly in disbelief before turning his eyes back on me and, with a voice tinged with anger, replying, "Come on, Lazarus! Be serious here! This isn't the time to be screwing around!"

"*I am* being serious here, Ransom," I spat back at the warlock, matching his anger. "Something in the Arcaneum caused the game to completely block out my memory. Something that you or Edith did to me."

"You're bullshitting me!" Ransom snapped. "The game can't do that!"

"Do you really think I would do that?" I waved my hand at the surrounding landscape. "Just stand here in the middle of Hell and tell lies?"

Ransom opened his mouth, ready to retort, but paused as my words finally sunk in. "But that's…that's…completely *unethical*, though! How was that ever *approved*?"

"I honestly don't know, Ransom, and given our situation I'm past the point of caring," I told the man, feeling all the frustration that had built up over the day begin to reach a boiling point. "All I know is that yesterday, I woke up in an Undertaker torture chamber with them trying to cut a pound of flesh from me, with Fairfax's body an arm's length away."

"*Oh.*" Ransom looked at me with sudden understanding. "Lazarus, Molly, I'm sorry! I swear I didn't have anything to do with that!"

"That's easy to say without proof," Molly replied, her voice taking on a hard tone. "Do you have *any* idea what Dorian and Edith have done to Eberia in the last day?"

"No, I don't," Ransom admitted, while holding up his one remaining hand. "But whatever they've done so far, it pales in comparison to what they're planning to do next. We need to find them as fast as possible and hope that it's not too late."

"Too late for what?" Quinn asked derisively. "Last time I checked, we're trapped in the middle of *Hell*. This is literally what my grandmother has been warning me about my entire life. How can *anything* be worse than this?"

"Not worse for us, but for Eberia," Ransom explained as he took a deep sigh, glancing between each of us before continuing. "Dorian and Edith are both working with the Holy Ascendancy of Eligos."

"They're what?" Molly hissed as she took half a step towards Ransom. "How? Why?"

"I don't know," Ransom answered, flinching back a step from Molly's sudden movement. "Despite all that Dorian has done, he's still a pawn to someone else. You all saw that strange ghost-man, right?"

"Yeah," I replied slowly, still trying to wrap my mind around everything that Ransom had just said. "Who was he?"

"I don't know," Ransom said with a shake of his head. "But from what I could tell, he's the one responsible for setting all of this in motion. While I was being kept prisoner, I overheard him talking with Dorian and Edith constantly. Their goal was to use the artifact to open a portal into Avernus and to allow the Ascendancy into Eberia."

"*Allow* them into Eberia?" Sawyer repeated with a confused expression on his face before something clicked behind his eyes. "*Shit!* You mean they're going to invade the city?"

"That was their plan." Ransom nodded emphatically at the warrior. "I don't know *how*, but apparently, the Ascendancy sent an army into Avernus, using it as a shortcut so they wouldn't have to fight their way past Coldscar and the Bulwark; if they make it to the portal, they'll be inside the city and past all of our defenses."

"But I thought we were in the middle of—" Sawyer cut in, before his face went pale. "Oh *fuck*, that's why the military left!"

"The talks have broken down," Molly whispered in sudden realization, her eyes going wide. "They're just stalling."

"*The military did what?*" Ransom looked at Sawyer and then Molly in shock.

"They were sent to Coldscar," I replied, taking my best guess at their most probable destination. "They just left this morning without any warning at all."

"Oh, damn." Ransom ran his hand across his now partially bald head, only a few singed hairs remaining. "This is bad."

"No shit," Sawyer snorted. "What are we going to do?"

"We have to try and find the portal," Ransom said as he started to walk forward unsteadily, moving away from the pile of debris that we had pulled him from. Despite being healed, it was clear that Ransom was exhausted, the last few days having taken a brutal toll on him. What he needed, what all of us needed, was a long night of sleep and rest.

But I had a feeling that just wasn't going to happen anytime soon.

"The only thing we have going for us right now is that Lazarus managed to damage the artifact pretty badly and push it out of alignment," Ransom stated as he led us away from all of the wreckage that had come through with us. "Hopefully we can take advantage of that."

"How is that a good thing?" I asked the warlock, waving at the debris as we walked past it. "If I had just let the portal open, we would have had a chance to get to the artifact *without* being pulled into Hell. As it is, I'm pretty sure that most of the mansion was destroyed because of what I did."

"No, we wouldn't have," Ransom replied, shaking his head at me. "We would have been overrun by the Ascendancy the moment it opened."

"What do you mean?" I asked, looking at the warlock and raising an eyebrow.

"Do you know why Dorian went through all the trouble to open the portal in the middle of the House Phineas courtyard?" Ransom countered, waving my question off.

"I thought he was just killing off the nobles, like he did to the Crawridge and Wynbrandt heirs earlier in the day," I replied with a shrug.

"He what?"

Ransom's eyes bulged from his head before he caught himself, shaking his head violently from side to side.

"You know what, never mind, tell me later if we survive all of this. The reason why Dorian fought his way into the House Phineas Estate was because he wanted to open the portal at a *very* specific place in Avernus, but in order to do that, he had to be at specific place in the real world where both Avernus and it matched up," Ransom explained, pausing for a moment, thinking over his choice of words. "Uh, the real game-world, not the real Earth-world. You know what I mean, right?"

"I'm following." I nodded at the warlock, understanding the confusion. It was already hard enough to keep reality and the game separate; adding more planes of existence within the game world wasn't going to make things any easier.

"So if you hadn't managed to damage the artifact and caused it to short-circuit, it would have opened right where the Ascendant army was waiting for it," Ransom told me, miming a slicing motion with his hand. "And they would have started coming through almost immediately."

"Oh," I replied with a hard swallow, realizing just how lucky we had been. Had I been a few seconds slower, Eberia would have been invaded and occupied before it even realized it was at war.

"But since you did damage and knock the artifact out of place, the portal opened off target, and it might buy us enough time to find out where the portal ended up before the Ascendancy army can get moving and go through it."

"Just how off target are we talking about?" Quinn asked from behind us with a worried voice. "Because walking blindly through

Hell searching for a portal that may or may not be there isn't high on my to-do list."

"I have no idea, a few kilometers, maybe?" Ransom replied with a shrug. "I'm not exactly an expert at this; I'm just repeating what I heard Dorian and Edith say."

"Do you have any idea why Dorian chose to open the portal in the Phineas mansion?" Molly asked as we slowly picked our way through the wreckage that littered the ground around us. "Even if he had to be in a specific spot that aligned with the...*real world*, he risked *everything* just to fight into the estate. It would have made better sense to do it somewhere safer and in secret."

"That was the original plan," Ransom said with a shake of his head. "From what I understand, Dorian was planning to open the portal where he was keeping me, in a huge warehouse of some sort. It wasn't supposed to be today, though. Dorian was planning to wait a few more days for better weather before opening it and once the Ascendancy reached where they were supposed to be, relative to where the two planes overlapped."

"But instead, we forced Dorian's hand and he had to open the portal somewhere else, somewhere closer to where the Ascendancy was *now*," I said with anger. "We forced him into a corner where he *had* to attack House Phineas in order to speed up his plans. We just as well killed—"

"*Lazarus!* We had *no* way of knowing what his plans were!" Molly cut in sharply before I could start spiraling. "We were in 'react' mode the entire time. There is literally nothing we could have done differently."

"I *know* that, but I can't help but *feel* responsible," I growled in frustration while rubbing my head. "If I hadn't lost my memory, none of this would have happened."

"And if that happened, then I would have been left alone wondering why the three of you abandoned me," Molly countered. "Because then you would have likely been taken prisoner along with Ransom and I wouldn't have seen you for days."

"I would have escaped—" I started to retort before Sawyer's hand slapped me on the shoulder hard, catching my attention.

"Hey, everyone, remember that army that Ransom just mentioned?" Sawyer said, his voice taking on a nervous tone as he pointed ahead of us. "Well, it's right over there, and it looks like it's coming this way."

TWENTY-SEVEN

SAWYER'S WORDS CAUSED ALL OF us to flinch in panic as we instinctively followed his hand past the remnants of the Phineas mansion and towards the horizon where a shambling blob slowly moved in the distance. Rushing forward, the five of us ran past the wreckage of the building and the ridge that it was leaning against, our feet crunching on broken glass and shattered stone.

"Fuck," I cursed the second I managed to get a better look at the distant army, my elven eyesight easily resolving the blob-like mass into vaguely elf-shaped outlines. "Sawyer's right, they're coming."

As soon as the words left my mouth, a flashing quest update appeared in the corner of my vision with an urgent chime, causing me to bring it up and read through the update.

Due to recent events, your quest [The Heist] has been merged with [No Honor Among Thieves]!
[No Honor Among Thieves] is now a Group Quest and has been automatically shared with your party!

QUEST UPDATED! NO HONOR AMONG THIEVES!

After a brutal battle in storming the House Phineas Estate, you managed to successfully infiltrate the Phineas mansion and confront Thief Lord Dorian in a fierce battle before he could activate the artifact. However, during the battle, the artifact was damaged, resulting in you and the rest of the party being pulled through into Avernus, a plane of Hell.
Regrouping from your transition, you discovered your one-time companion Ransom, who passed on a desperate word of warning: That Dorian and Edith have been conspiring with The Holy Ascendancy of Eligos and have opened a portal to allow them to sneak attack Eberia. Unless you can close the portal before they arrive, Eberia will fall.
Find Edith: 1/1 (Complete)
Find Dorian: 1/1 (Complete)
Find Ransom: 1/1 (Complete)
Discover what Dorian has planned: 1/1
Kill Dorian: 0/1
Recover the Stolen Artifact: 0/1
Close the portal before The Ascendancy arrives: 0/1
(Optional) Recover Memory: 0/1
Difficulty: Very Hard
Reward: Experience, Renown & Infamy

"We need to *move*," Ransom said urgently as he jogged past me, his head glancing around the barren hellscape behind the ridge. "If the portal is still open, it has to be somewhere close by. With the artifact still destabilizing when it pulled us through…the portal would have still been moving before it anchored itself. There's a chance we're not too far away from it."

"I have no idea what you just said," Sawyer grunted as he moved to follow the warlock, his voice starting to sound slightly unhinged. "But it sounds like it makes sense, and I'm willing to grasp at *any* straw that keeps me from being trapped here for any longer than I have to be."

"How do we even know where to start looking?" Quinn asked, moving to follow the Ransom and Sawyer. "This place is full of nooks, ridges, and valleys; we could rush right past it and never know."

"Follow the debris!" Molly shouted, pointing at a trail of wreckage that continued away from us at an angle, vanishing in a cloud of ash as the winds began to stir. "That way!"

With no other encouragement needed, the five of us broke into a jog as we rushed to follow the trail of destruction across the ash-covered surface of Avernus, our hurried footsteps kicking up a trail behind us. Keeping an eye on the approaching army in the distance, I scanned our surroundings desperately, searching for any sign of the artifact before the ash completely obscured all visibility.

Sweeping over us in a hot gust of wind, we ran into the cloud of ash, instantly feeling our eyes and throats catch fire. Coughing wildly, the five of us pressed through the ash, doggedly putting one foot in front of the other as we followed the increasingly hard-to-spot fragments of wreckage.

"I see something!" I called out in between ragged coughs as a crimson flare of light caught my eye in the distance, barely visible through the thick ash that blew around us. "Follow me!"

Taking point at the head of the party, I gripped my sword tightly as I led us in the direction where I had seen the light, my watering eyes trying desperately to pick out any detail they could through the thick haze in front of me. Running through the gloom, it was impossible to see the edge of the ash cloud until we suddenly burst through it, a bright crimson glare causing each of us to squint in surprise.

"There it is!" Molly shouted in a raspy voice, the hot ash having taken its toll on her throat.

Rubbing the back of my hand across my face to clear the ash from my eyes, I saw the rapidly spinning shape of the artifact as it hung in the air a short distance away from us, just in front of a jagged tear in reality that could only be a portal back to Eberia. Blurred beyond easy recognition, all I could see inside the portal was flickering flames and distorted shapes that faded in and out as the artifact discharged large sparks of crimson energy into the ground.

A flash of movement caught my eye as Dorian and Edith walked around the portal's edge and came into view, the thief lord's face scowling in surprise at spotting the five of us.

"Of course it would be too much to wish that you were all killed in the transition," Dorian hissed venomously, his voice still slurring from his damaged jaw as he fixed his attention on me. "But now it no longer matters. The portal is open and stable. All that you have done is waste lives pointlessly."

"Why did you do it, Dorian?" I called out to the man as the five of us slowly approached the portal, our weapons at hand. "Why betray Eberia to the Ascendancy?"

"I am not *betraying* Eberia!" Dorian barked, his face visibly wincing in pain as he spoke. "I am *saving* it!"

"By putting the noble houses against one another's throats? By inciting civil war?" I yelled back at the man. "By killing Fairfax?"

"I went to Fairfax for he—"

"*Shut up, Dorian,*" Edith hissed, her command causing the thief lord's mouth to snap shut painfully. Turning with a shocked expression on his face, Dorian whirled to look at Edith, the woman giving him a smug look. "I know exactly what question is on your mind, and *yes*, I hold your leash as well—I always have. Now, stay put for a moment, like a good dog."

Freezing in place, Dorian's already pained expression intensified as an unnatural stiffness came over his body, appearing as if he was fighting against an unseen force that held him in place.

"What did you do to him?" Sawyer asked as Edith turned her head towards the five of us.

"I think that's self-evident," Edith replied with a dismissive gesture. "I shut him up before his guilty conscience got the better of him. He wants to be seen as a hero *so badly*, it is almost tragic. Well, if he weren't just an NPC, that is."

"You have control over his geas," I stated, keeping a wary eye on Dorian's paralyzed figure, the only thing moving being his right hand trembling at his side.

"Oh? You overheard that bit, did you?" Edith cocked her head at me before looking back at Dorian. "Yeah…seems like King Cyril had some pretty interesting ideas for keeping people in line. All it took was a few tweaks to his old geas and *poof*, a nice obedient minion."

"Why are you doing this, Edith?" Ransom cut in, his voice hard as he addressed his one-time companion. "Seriously, you're going to destroy Eberia by doing this!"

"Oh please, Ransom," Edith snorted as she waved her massive clawed hand in the air while taking a step forward. "What do you think this is? A Saturday-morning cartoon where I stand here and monologue for a half hour? No, I'm keeping my motivations close to my chest."

"Then let's cut to the chase," I said, taking my eyes away from Dorian's rapidly shaking hand and focusing solely on Edith. "What exactly do you want? You wouldn't still be standing here and talking otherwise, especially not when the five of us can steamroll the two of you in seconds."

"You are welcome to try," Edith replied derisively, causing her misshapen face to contort as she scowled at me and pointed at my chest. "But I don't want anything, Cain, though I'll admit it galls me to let you get away with stealing the sigil from me. I have no idea *how* you convinced the artifact to give it to you so quickly or how you locked it afterwards."

I looked at Edith with a blank expression on my face, before turning my head towards Ransom. "What is she talking about? The artifact is *alive*?"

"Sort of," Ransom replied hesitantly, giving me an unsure look. "It...didn't say that much to me while it was fused to my arm."

"*It was fused to your arm and it can talk?*" I hissed at the half-orc, my eyes glancing towards his missing arm before going to the spinning artifact that was still discharging random bolts of crimson energy into the air. "Why the hell didn't you mention that earlier?"

"*With what time?*" Ransom snapped as he gestured towards Edith and Dorian. "I can tell you everything that happened, but we have to close the portal first!"

"Good luck with that," Edith spat with anger. "Cain hit the artifact hard enough that it's not responding anymore." Edith paused, her expression shifting into a grim smile as she began to turn away from us, glancing at Dorian as she said, "But I don't see that as being *our* problem, right, Dorian?"

"*You...bitch...*" I heard the thief lord grind out through clenched teeth, his entire body visibly trembling as he fought the geas. "I... am...not...your...dog!"

"Oh, *Dorian*," Edith said in a weary tone as she admonished the man. "This isn't really the time or the place to be throwing a tantrum. Don't make me have to bring you to heel in front of company."

"I...have...had...enough," Dorian continued, his venom-filled gaze alternating between Edith and the rest of us as he spoke. "Of... all...of...you...damned...adventurers...I...will...kill...you...all!"

As he slowly ground out his threat, Dorian's body began to spasm as the geas began to exact its toll for his continued defiance. Shaking wildly, one of his hands caught on a belt pocket sewn into his waist, ripping it wide open with the sound of tearing fabric. Spilling free from the pouch, I saw a tangle of leather cords fall directly into Dorian's outstretched hand, three familiar shapes swinging in the air. Clenching at the mass desperately, Dorian flicked his wrist, causing the spherical shapes to wrap themselves tightly against the exposed flesh of his arm.

Those are soul shards! A distant part of my brain identified as I instinctively took a step forward, words already forming on my lips.

"Dorian, stop!" Both my movement and shout caused Edith to flinch and take her attention away from the defiant thief lord as she spun to face me, bringing up her massive arm before her in a defensive stance.

"This is the only choice I have left!" Dorian screamed a heartbeat before uttering a word of power, triggering the binding on the soul shards in his hand, causing fire to shoot up his arm as the three bone fragments flared with a blinding intensity.

"*No!*" Edith cried out as she twisted in sudden panic, catching a glimpse of Dorian's burning form a second before his body exploded into a colossal pillar of flame, the shockwave knocking all of us off our feet.

Thrown backwards from the blast, I felt myself slam into Quinn standing behind me, the two of us falling to the ground in a tangle of limbs as a wave of bright light and heat washed over us, causing our exposed skin to blister. Stunned and blinded from the blast, I lay completely insensate for a moment until Quinn's moan of pain snapped me back to the present.

"Ugh, Lazarus, you're heavy," the thin mage wheezed from underneath me. "Please get off me."

"Sorry," I said out of reflex as I scrambled off the mage, rolling onto my knees while desperately blinking the afterimage of the blast out of my already ash-damaged eyes.

It's a small miracle I haven't gone blind from everything that's happened today, I thought numbly as my vision slowly returned, leaving me staring directly at the ash-covered ground of Avernus, the implications of the last few seconds finally catching up to me. *Dorian just activated three soul shards all at once!*

Casting about in sudden panic, my eyes first landed on the singed forms of both Molly and Sawyer, the pair of them slowly recovering from the blast and pushing themselves back up onto their feet. Continuing my scan, I felt my breath catch in my throat as I spotted Edith's blackened body, writhing on the ground in her back in agony, her body completely charred and nearly unrecognizable if it weren't for her large clawed arm. Whining in pain, Edith stared upwards in shock as a massive black claw reached up from above her and lifted her frail body straight off the ground.

Flinching in surprise, I forced my glance upwards, feeling my heart twist in horror as I saw the creature that Dorian had become.

Standing on two clawed feet with a massive tail sweeping the ground behind it, a sleek, black-scaled devil towered high over me as it lifted Edith's body in a single oversized claw, bringing the crying woman closer to its narrow, devilish face. Opening its maw, it revealed countless jagged teeth as saliva poured forth down its chin. Regarding the burned woman with curiosity, two burning orbs on the devil's face narrowed, before a cacophony of twisted voices echoed over the plains.

"*HELLO, EDITH,*" the black-scaled devil purred as it brought its horned head closer to the woman's face. "*I IMAGINE THIS IS AS MUCH A SURPRISE FOR YOU AS IT IS FOR ME.*"

"*What?*" I gasped in disbelief while gaping up at the devil. "I-is that still *Dorian?*"

"I-I d-don't..." Quinn stuttered through his words before trailing off in stunned silence, his feet scratching in the dirt behind me.

"*WHAT, NOTHING TO SAY?*" Dorian's voice rang out as he raised Edith to the side of his head, her choking sobs filling the air. "*AH, YOU ARE IN PAIN. MY APOLOGIES. ALLOW ME TO ASSIST.*"

Bringing the woman down from his ear, Dorian raised a second clawed hand and reached towards Edith, grasping her large twisted arm delicately between two razor-sharp talons.

And tore it off.

"*What the fuck?*" I shouted in shock as a thick gush of black blood erupted from Edith's shoulder, followed close behind by a bloodcurdling scream. Anger shot through me at the violent act, a cold wave of energy pulsing across my chest as the sigil began to stir.

"*GOODNESS! HOW CLUMSY OF ME!*"

Dorian's laugh echoed through the air as he threw Edith's arm over his shoulder.

"*IT SEEMS I DO NOT KNOW MY OWN STRENGTH. HUSH, SWEET CHILD, IT WILL ALL BE OVER SOON,*" Dorian cooed as he brought Edith's wailing form closer to his face, his jagged maw opening wide. "*GIVE OUR MASTER MY REGARDS. I WILL PAY HIM A VISIT AS SOON AS I AM ABLE.*"

Lunging forward in the blink of an eye, Dorian's teeth flashed through the air as he bit down on Edith's head, her terror-filled screams ending with the sickening crunch of bone, her charred body instantly going limp. Chewing through the remains of Edith's skull, Dorian threw Edith's corpse to the ground with such intensity that it bounced twice in the air before coming to a stop nearly twenty feet away.

"Damn," I hissed through clenched teeth, forcing myself up onto my feet as Dorian turned his burning eyes to glare at the five of us. Meeting his eyes defiantly, a tag appeared in the corner of my eye, pointing directly at the creature that Dorian had become.

[Dorian the Soul Eater] – Elite Boss – Level 14

"*THE THIEF AND THE TRAITOR,*" Dorian growled, his eyes brightening as he alternated his gaze between myself and Ransom. "*DO YOU HAVE ANY IDEA HOW MANY LIVES YOUR MEDDLING HAS COST? WHAT IT HAS COST ME?*"

"We didn't make your choices for you, Dorian!" I replied angrily while staring at the black-scaled devil for any sign of movement, the freezing energy of the sigil slowly coursing through my body.

"*THAT IS IRRELEVANT!*" the creature snarled as it bared its teeth towards me and raised its clawed hands in the air. "*BECAUSE OF YOU, I HAVE AN OCEAN OF BLOOD ON MY HANDS! BECAUSE OF YOU, I WAS FORCED TO DAMN MYSELF FOR ALL ETERNITY! YOU MUST PAY FOR WHAT YOU'VE DONE!*"

With a bloodcurdling roar, Dorian powerful legs coiled underneath him as he made to leap forward, the five of us instinctively scattering in every direction. Rolling to the side, I felt the ground shake from Dorian's landing, followed by the sound of scraping claws and talons as he spun to face me.

Acting with the speed of thought, I activated the pulsating Sigil of Rage, feeling the ice-cold torrent of energy surge through my body, slowing everything down before me. However, even with the sigil's power speeding my reflexes, I was hard-pressed to duck under Dorian's oversized claw as he thrust it out towards me. Wildly cutting upwards with my sword, I felt it briefly grind against Dorian's talons before glancing off of them and cutting a shallow wound across his wrist. Not pausing to inspect my handiwork, I rushed even closer to the devil, hoping to find a few seconds of respite deep within its reach.

Damn, he's big! The thought echoed through my mind as I found myself looking straight up at Dorian, his new form being at least half again as tall as I was. Shifting my glance downward for a place to focus my next attack, I found myself staring into a thickly scaled torso with heavy bone growths armoring the creature's side and abdomen. Whatever type of devil Dorian had transformed himself into, I could tell that he was going to be difficult, if not nearly impossible to put down.

"SCURRY AROUND AS MUCH AS YOU WISH, LITTLE RATS!" Dorian taunted, his second claw raking the ground in front of me as I desperately leaped out of its way, only to be clipped in the shoulder by his other claw. "YOU WILL ONLY DIE TIRED!"

Ugh, even with the sigil's help, it's impossible for me to track both claws at the same time! I thought to myself, the pain from the glancing blow causing me to wince.

"I got you, Lazarus!" Sawyer shouted as he charged into the fray, bringing his new axe down onto Dorian's knee, where it bit through the thick scales with a loud crack.

Roaring in annoyance, Dorian tore his attention away from me and swung a massive claw in Sawyer's direction, the nimble bounty hunter easily dancing backwards from the claw's path, having anticipated the attack. Taking advantage of Dorian's distraction, I leaped forward and swung my sword in a powerful slash, carving a long wound across his thigh, which immediately welled up with thick black blood.

"*GAH!*" Growling in pain for the first time, Dorian retreated two steps backwards as his claw reached down to grip the injury that I had just inflicted. Glancing down at his blood-covered hand, Dorian snarled as he glared back at me with his crimson eyes. "*IT SEEMS THAT THE RATS HAVE CLAWS! VERY WELL, SEE HOW YOU LIKE MINE!*"

Raising both claws in the air, Dorian conjured twin balls of fire in his palm, snapping the two of them in my direction as he leaped forward once more. Dodging to the side in a panic, I managed to avoid one of the fireballs, only to have the second slam directly into my side in a burst of fire, its flames washing over the side of my face and searing the stubble from my head. Staggering from the blast, I fell to one knee as I tried to catch my balance, seeing a blinking alert appear across my vision.

[Dorian the Soul Eater] hits you with [Fireball] for 137 points of fire damage!

"Lazarus!" Molly's voice rang out at the same moment a thunderous concussion of magic filled the air as she, Quinn, and Ransom joined the fight. "Look out!"

Looking up, I saw Dorian's claw descending down towards me as he shielded his face from the timely wave of magic that slammed into his head, effectively blinding him for a moment. Rolling out from under the claw as it slammed into the ground, I swung my sword in a clumsy one-handed attack that added another wound across Dorian's forearm. Springing up onto my feet, I saw Sawyer's golden shield out of the corner of my eye as he attacked Dorian's flank, his dull-colored axe already covered in thick black ichor.

Howling from the onslaught of magic, Dorian began rapidly conjuring small fireballs and throwing them wildly around us, in an attempt to disrupt the barrage that Molly, Quinn, and Ransom were laying down upon him. Multiple explosions drowned out all hearing as the fireballs detonated in rapid sequence, throwing burning soil and ash into the air.

Mindful of the sigil's detrimental effects on my body, I made use of the party's distraction and rushed back in close to Dorian's body, landing a powerful blow that carved through the thick, bony armor on his hip and deep into the flesh below.

You [Power Attack II] [Dorian the Soul Eater] for 160 points of damage!

Twisting my blade as I sawed deeper into the wound, I was forced to pull my weapon free as Dorian kicked his clawed leg out in my direction while hissing wildly in pain. Shifting to the side, I darted past the leg and rushed behind Dorian, catching his flailing tail on the edge of my sword.

Nice try, but I learned my lesson with the devourer! I thought to myself as I absorbed the impact of the spiked tail, my glass-steel blade biting deep into it and drawing forth even more blackened blood. Pushing down on the blade, I worked it even further into the wound, until I felt it grate on hard bone underneath.

"*ENOUGH!*" Dorian roared in both pain and frustration as he whipped his body away from me, throwing down two large fireballs at his feet, which promptly exploded in spray of dirt and fire, throwing both Sawyer and I out of melee range from the blast. "*YOU ARE BEGINNING TO ANNOY ME!*"

I groaned in pain as the flames licked over me once more, my body slowly coming to a stop a short distance away from Dorian.

Looking up at the large devil, I saw that Molly, Ransom, and Quinn's attacks had taken their toll on Dorian's upper chest and face, the once smooth scales giving way to bleeding wounds and savage burns caused by the relentless torrent of magic the trio had poured into him. Favoring one side, Dorian leaned heavily on one leg, his lower body completely covered in a patchwork of cuts and bleeding wounds, courtesy of mine and Sawyer's efforts, his thick blood slowly dripping onto the ground below.

"*IT IS TIME TO PUT AN END TO YOUR MEDDLING ONCE AND FOR ALL!*" Dorian howled as he coiled his one good leg and sprang away from me, leaping directly towards Ransom and Quinn.

Diving out of the way just in the nick of time, Ransom barely evaded Dorian's sweeping claws as he threw himself to the ground with a cry of surprise.

Quinn, on the other hand, was too slow.

Catching him fully in the side, all four of Dorian's wicked talons pierced through the thin mage's body, two of the longest claws bursting forth from the mage's chest in a spray of blood. Staring upwards in abject shock, Quinn coughed weakly as Dorian lifted him off the ground and clenched his hand, driving the razor-sharp talons through the hapless mage's body. With a cry of triumph, Dorian savagely flicked his claw, the motion tearing open Quinn's chest as he threw him to the ground.

"*Quinn!*" I screamed at the top of my lungs as I felt his presence fade from the party sense, a heartbeat before his body dissolved into nothingness. All it had taken was a split second, one failed dodge, and we had lost a member of the party.

Emboldened by his success, Dorian raised a clawed hand, casting his gaze downward at Ransom's prone form, the half-orc desperately pushing himself away from the black-scaled devil. Scrambling onto my feet in a panic, I saw the claw thrust itself forward towards Ransom, the half-orc moving far too slow to evade Dorian's attack. Seconds before the claw reached Ransom, I caught the blurred figure of Sawyer leap right in front of him. The edges of Dorian's talons slammed into Sawyer's golden shield with a loud clang of metal, the impact driving the warrior down onto his knees.

Not waiting for Dorian to recover from Sawyer's timely intervention, I launched myself forward, raising my sword high for a punishing attack the moment I entered range. An inky black orb of magic splashed across Dorian's face as I ran, followed by a second purple missile as Molly resumed throwing magic. Hissing wildly at Molly's temporary curse, Dorian swept a blind claw before him, catching both Sawyer and a half-risen Ransom, sending the both of them tumbling back to the ground as his other claw reached up to rub his eyes.

Pumping my legs with every ounce of strength that they possessed, I closed the final distance between Dorian and me, leaping high into the air as I swept my blade downwards, catching the tall devil just under its arm. Both scales and bone parted under my colossal blow, the momentum and weight behind my attack driving my sword deep into Dorian's body. Driven by pure rage as a flare of power from the sigil surged through me, I tore my blade free from Dorian's side before thrusting it directly into his abdomen and twisting it viciously.

Howling in pain from the two attacks, Dorian took a staggering step backwards as he pulled himself off of my sword, the effects of Molly's spell finally wearing off.

"YOU WILL PAY FOR THAT!" Dorian growled, his once powerful voice having weakened since the start of the battle. Lunging forward, Dorian wasted no time in pressing his attack once more, leading with his two oversized claws as he worked himself up into a frenzy, attempting to rend me to shreds.

Forced back onto my heels, all conscious thought faded from me as I descended into the maelstrom of battle. My world shrank to one of flashing claws and gnashing teeth as Dorian and I worked our hardest to kill one another, each of us accumulating even more injuries that ever so slightly slowed us down. We fought with tooth and nail, neither of us holding anything back. A single mistake would be enough to spell the end for either one of us, giving the other a chance to strike a killing blow.

My foot slipped.

I knew immediately when it happened that I was doomed. My foot was slipping off the edge of a small crater in the ground from one of Dorian's earlier attacks. My eyes widened in panic as the tip of Dorian's claw caught me directly in the throat and tore it wide open, followed by a savage kick to my chest that had me tumbling across the ground until I landed on my back, staring up at the smoke-covered sky of Avernus.

Shit, I lost. The realization surged through me as the sigil's power faded, leaving me with a sickening drowning sensation as my lungs began to pool with blood. Coughing wildly as I lay on my back, I saw a spray of blood shoot up into the air, my hand coming up belatedly in an attempt to stem the flow. My vision slowly began to blur as the blood loss caused my head to spin, blotting out the sky above me.

"*Gavin!*" Molly voice sounded distant as she called my name, followed by a blurred shape appearing above me. "Oh, God, this is bad, hang on!"

I felt a warmth surge through me as Molly put her hand on my throat, the spinning sensation slowly fading as I made out her teary-eyed expression looking down at me. A second wave of healing energy coursed through me and my vision began to sharpen, enough to see a large shadow looming in the distance.

"*Molly.*" My voice was faint, barely enough to be heard as my throat slowly reknitted itself under Molly's healing magic. "Look…behind…"

"I can't," Molly said with a sad shake of her head. "You're still bleeding, I need to finish this…before…"

Molly shook her head and blinked tears from her eyes.

"Sawyer and Ransom are out cold. I managed to stabilize them both, but I can't beat him on my own. No. You have to. You have to make sure the portal closes, too."

Realization slowly dawned in me what exactly Molly was saying, and I raised my hand to push her away. "No, don't…"

"I'll catch you on the other side, Gavin," Molly said, giving me a crooked smile as the shadow stood over us. "Don't be late."

"Molly!" I barely managed to get the words out of my mouth before four massive claws burst from Molly's chest, her face straining to hold the smile as she stared into my eyes, the light slowly fading away from them.

And then she was gone. Dissolving into dust like she had never been there at all.

"*MY, MY,*" Dorian's cacophonous voice echoed from high above me. "*IT SEEMS THAT SOME OF MY WORK HAS BEEN UNDONE. THIS IS UNACCEPTABLE.*"

"No..." I stared in shock at the spot where I had just seen Molly, my heart hammering wildly in my chest. I shifted my glance upwards, seeing Dorian standing directly above me, looking down with his burning red eyes.

The moment that I met his eyes, I felt the sigil pulse with an intensity that I had never felt before, an unspeakable cold filling my heart and causing it to spasm with rage.

"*OH MY,*" Dorian said with surprise, seeing my hate-filled expression. "*SHE MEANT SOMETHING—AAAH!*"

Dorian roared in sudden pain as I leaped to my feet with my sword in hand, carving a long slash across his body as I rose.

"You are responsible for so much death today, Dorian," I called out to the black-scaled devil, embracing the numbing cold that surged through me. "I can't think of a better place to kill you than in Hell itself. Whatever soul you may still have left won't have far to travel."

Howling with rage, Dorian quickly recovered from my renewed attacks and threw himself at me in a frenzy, his claws sweeping through the air just inches away from my face as I ducked under a poorly aimed swipe and darted in close to Dorian's body. Moving out of reflex, Dorian flinched, his second claw moving to protect his wounded torso that already bled freely from our earlier battle.

Except that this time, my target wasn't his torso.

"*Rah!*" I shouted with rage as I brought down my glass-steel sword down on Dorian's knee, feeling the ancient relic carve through scales and bone, completely severing the limb in a spray of blood.

Keening in unbelievable pain, Dorian spun his arms wildly as his balance suddenly shifted and he began to fall forward to the ground, catching himself with his two clawed hands. Spinning to the side, away from his fall, I positioned myself directly at Dorian's elbow, my blood-covered blade flashing out once more as it bit into the joint, effortlessly parting it from the rest of his body.

Crashing into the ground as his precarious balance faltered once more, Dorian writhed in pure agony, his roaring cry of pain echoing across the plains. Moving without hesitation, I leaped onto the fallen devil's back as my hand shot out to grip one of the twin horns that sprouted from Dorian's head. Pushing hard on the horn, I forced Dorian's face into the ground, giving the space to guide the tip of my sword into the back of his neck.

Feeling the blade grind against bone and muscle, I ruthlessly drove the weapon straight through Dorian's spine, pushing it until I felt it burst free from his throat and bury itself into the dirt under me. Switching my grip on the horn as Dorian's body began to convulse, I pulled his head backwards with all the rage given strength I could muster, hearing bones snap and crack as I ground them against my blade.

Letting go of the sword, I grabbed Dorian's other horn with my hand and viciously kicked the hilt of my blade until it was flush against his scaled neck. Bracing my foot against the hilt, I then began to pull, slowly bending Dorian's head, closer and closer towards me as I stretched his flesh to its limits.

And beyond.

A tearing sound filled the air as Dorian's head slowly came free from his body, a torrent of blood gushing upwards into the ash-filled air of Avernus. Twisting violently, I tore the last shreds of clinging flesh that tied the thief lord's head to his body, seeing a pair of messages appear in my vision.

You have slain [Dorian the Soul Eater]!
You have gained experience!

It's over, I breathed with a sense of relief as I released the power of the sigil, feeling the seeping cold energy fade away from me, replacing it with a crushing sense of fatigue and loss. Looking down at the large head that I held in my hand, I shuddered at the thought that all of this had been set in motion by just one man.

And not the man whose head I was holding.

No time to worry about that now, I thought as I felt Dorian's body begin to dissolve under me, forcing me to leap off of it. Turning back at the where the body once was, I was surprised to find that everything vanished, except for the head that I was still holding, a single loot sack appearing in its place. Surprised that the head didn't despawn with the rest of the body, I looked at it warily before remembering Isabella's words in what seemed like a lifetime ago, telling us to get Dorian's head at any cost. *I don't think this is exactly what she had in mind, but I'll take it along with me anyway.*

Sighing heavily, I walked over to the loot bag, unable to ignore my basic adventurer instinct despite everything that had happened, and grabbed everything inside of it, grimacing as I added a few of the items to my inventory.

Hellborn Soul Shard Fragments
Quantity: 6
Item Class: Magical
Item Quality: Fine (+10%)
Strength: +1 Agility: +1 Constitution: +1 Intelligence: +1
Willpower +1
Durability: 0/0
Weight: 0 kg
Devil Heart
Quantity: 1
Item Class: Magical
Item Quality: Average (+0%)
Durability: 0/0
Weight: 1 kg

Devil Blood
Quantity: 10
Item Class: Magical
Item Quality: Average (+10%)
Durability: 0/0
Weight: 1 kg
Devil Scales
Quantity: 15
Item Class: Magical
Item Quality: Average (+10%)
Durability: 0/0
Weight: 5 kg
Hellborn Slag
Quantity: 5
Item Class: Magical
Item Quality: Average (+10%)
Durability: 0/0
Weight: 5 kg

Nothing but crafting ingredients, I noted with slight disappointment as I emptied the bag, idly wondering what I could even attempt to do with a devil's heart. *Might be worth money, though, and I'm sure I might be able to make myself some newer armor with the scales.*

"Lazarus," Sawyer's raspy voice caused me to flinch before turning my head towards it.

Sitting on the ground with what appeared to be a broken arm cradled against his chest, Sawyer slowly glanced around the battlefield, his face still in shock. "What happened?"

"We won," I told the man wearily as my eyes shifted to Ransom's still unconscious form.

"Molly?" Sawyer asked as his eyes landed on Dorian's head in my hands.

"She didn't make it," I replied, feeling my heart twist at the words before looking over to where I remembered the portal and artifact being. With a crackle of energy, I saw the still spinning artifact discharge another crimson bolt into the ground, the wavering crimson portal hanging a short distance behind it.

"Shit, we have to go," Sawyer exclaimed as his gaze shifted past me and he began scrambling to his feet. "The Ascendancy...they're almost here!"

Whirling to look behind me, I spotted the once distant army, now barely minutes away from us as they doggedly approached the portal. Dark shapes rushed ahead of the advancing army towards us, no doubt being scouts or mounted riders looking to secure the portal before the army arrived.

"Come on, Lazarus!" Sawyer called back to me urgently, causing me to tear my eyes off the advancing army and back to the bounty hunter as he lifted Ransom's unconscious body onto his shoulders with his uninjured arm. "It's up to you to close the portal, or we're about to get a front-row seat to the invasion of Eberia!"

Sawyer's words spurred me on as the two of us sprinted towards the crackling artifact and portal. Rushing on ahead of me as I slowed to approach the artifact, Sawyer ran directly for the portal with Ransom dangling limply over his shoulder, vanishing without another word as he leaped into the crimson tear.

Reaching out to the damaged artifact, I fought past any reservations I had about getting struck by a bolt of energy and grabbed hold of the spinning object, feeling it stop and come free from its fixed position in the air the moment I touched it.

<*IT IS ABOUT TIME YOU RETURNED!*> a thunderous voice rang through my head with such a deafening intensity that I felt a migraine erupt behind my eyes, my vision blurring from the pain. <*TAKE*

ME THROUGH THE PORTAL AND IT WILL SEAL BEHIND ME!>

"*What?*" I looked at the artifact in my hand, completely dumbfounded, as my stomach clenched viciously, an unexpected wave of nausea washing over me.

<*TAKE ME THROUGH THE PORTAL!*> the voice demanded once again, causing my head to spin. <*HURRY!*>

With no better option at hand, I stumbled towards the crimson tear before me, slowly building momentum with every step I took until it filled my entire vision. I heard a loud shout ring out behind me, a second before something hit me very hard in the shoulder and threw me forward into the portal.

Then everything went black.

EPILOGUE

I AWOKE TO A HARD BUMP that caused my head to leave the ground and come smashing down into the hard wooden floor, making me groan in pain as I slowly regained consciousness.

"Ugh." I tried to reach to grip my head, only to find my hands coming to an abrupt stop as cold metal bit into my wrists. "Wha…?"

"He's coming around," a vaguely familiar voice called out, followed by the rustling of moving bodies. "Lazarus, can you hear me? It's me, Sawyer."

"Sawyer," I repeated the name while opening my eyes to the dark room around me and pulling myself up off the floor, which I now noticed was vibrating as if we were moving. Blinking weakly to clear my eyes, I slowly looked around, spotting Sawyer sitting beside me and Ransom directly across from me. "Ransom? Where are we? What happened?"

"A lot has happened while you were out," Ransom answered, his voice sounding completely exhausted. "Not all of it good."

"Did the portal close?" I asked, feeling a sudden spike of panic shoot through me, as I remembered something hitting me before I stepped through the portal.

"Yeah," Sawyer confirmed, allowing me to breathe a sigh of relief. "Thankfully things aren't that bad."

"Thankfully," I echoed in complete agreement as I recalled my last few seconds in Avernus, remembering the voice that had yelled at me the moment I had touched the artifact. "*Hey*, where is the artifact?"

"Captain Fontaine took it from you after you fell through the portal and had it close behind you," Sawyer said slowly.

"*Captain Fontaine was there?*" I twisted my head to look at Sawyer, who simply continued to gaze forward, since he couldn't see in the dark like I could. "Why was he there?! Wait, where the hell are we right now?"

"We're in a prisoner wagon," Sawyer replied dejectedly. "The good captain and about forty of Eberia's finest arrested me the moment that I stepped through the portal and wouldn't believe a thing I told him…at least not until you fell through the portal with a poison-tipped Ascendancy arrow in your shoulder and Dorian's head in your hand. Right now, we're *guests* of the Eberian City Guard until further notice."

"I was hit by a poisoned arrow?" I said in disbelief as I tested the shoulder that I had felt the impact in before stepping through the portal, not feeling anything amiss.

"That's what they said," Sawyer told me with a shrug. "I just saw you fall out of the portal and throw up the second you hit the ground."

"That may have actually been the artifact," I said with a bit of embarrassment that faded, given the alternative consequences of the portal remaining open. "Speaking of the artifact, Ransom, you were right…it did *talk*. Hell, it *recognized* me the moment I touched it!"

"That's a great deal more than it did to me," the half-orc replied wistfully as he rubbed the stump where his arm used to be. "All it did was keep repeating itself."

"We'll have to find a way of getting it back from Fontaine," I said, my mind already moving forward, despite the sheer exhaustion that I felt. "Do you have any idea what happened to the other thief lords?"

Ransom shifted uncomfortably as he nodded his head towards the far end of the wagon that I couldn't see due to the way that Sawyer was positioned.

"I survived," Stroud's flat voice echoed through the wagon, followed by a rattle of chains.

"Stroud!" I called out to the thief lord, torn between the relief of having him with us and the concern that *he*, of all the thief lords, had been caught. "Did anyone survive the battle?"

"The guilds suffered severe losses, the Crimson Rats especially… after Sable fell," Stroud answered, with a hint of sadness in his voice. "I do not know what happened with Smiling Jade; she entered the mansion before the battle was finished, likely to come to your aid. If you didn't see her, then she must have been caught in the blast that destroyed the mansion."

"Hold on." I looked back towards Ransom and Sawyer. "The mansion was destroyed?"

"Almost completely," Sawyer replied, shaking his head back and forth in the dark. "I don't know what happened when the artifact pulled us through, but it took the majority of the building with it, *much more* than we saw in Avernus…and knocked down the rest. The majority of the thieves outside were buried alive as it fell."

"Did Isabella survive?" I asked, unsure if I wanted to hear the answer.

"I believe so," Stroud answered, his voice uncertain as he spoke. "I was fighting up the main steps of the mansion when it came down on top of me. Isabella was minding the rear of the battle, along with the bulk of the guildmembers. I and a handful of others ended up buried in a pocket of debris and had to be pulled out by the Guard after the fact. I am inclined to believe that once the mansion fell, Isabella pulled back to preserve what numbers we had left."

"Hopefully they did," I replied sympathetically. "If Molly and Quinn can find her, then they should all be able to lead a rescue party directly to us once we stop moving."

Both Sawyer and Ransom took a sharp intake of breath as I mentioned our groupmates.

"Lazarus," Sawyer began with a hesitant voice. "Neither Ransom or I can feel Molly or Quinn via party sense. Not since they died."

"What?" I felt my heart flip as I suddenly realized the same thing. Both of them were still in our party, but I couldn't sense where either of them were. "They could be somewhere where party sense doesn't work."

"Maybe," Ransom said gently. "But try sending one of them a message and see what you get back."

Feeling my heart begin to race, I composed a message to Molly and sent it, seeing a message prompt appear in my vision.

The Player you are trying to message is currently not on your plane of existence. Please try again later.

"They respawned in Avernus," I whispered as I read the message, my blood going cold. "We left them behind."

"We don't know that for sure," Sawyer offered. "There's so little we know about the game so far. They could just be somewhere out of reach."

"But it didn't even go into a queue. It was just a flat-out...rejection," I said softly as I tried sending another message, followed by yet another message, continuing endlessly until there was nothing else filling my vision, the conversation going silent as we continued our ride towards our destination my thoughts spiraling endlessly.

I don't even know Molly's real name to look her up in reality, I thought to myself as I hung my head downward and stared at the floor. *She was so resistant to telling me anything about her real life, despite our relationship. Why didn't I try pushing harder?*

I don't know anything about Quinn's real life either, I continued talking to myself silently as the wagon began to rock back and forth sharply. *Until today, we've just been passing acquaintances.*

What are the odds that I'm going to see either one of them again?

Closing my eyes, I tried to pull myself out of my mental spiral, trying to think of anything to distract myself from the endless rejected messages that filled my vision. Catching a blinking quest alert in the corner of my vision, I brought it up, hoping that it would keep me occupied and off of Molly and Quinn, if only for a little while.

▹QUEST COMPLETE!

NO HONOR AMONG THIEVES!

After an epic battle on the plains of Avernus, you and your companions have managed to defeat Dorian, recover the artifact, and seal the portal to Eberia, forcing the Ascendancy army to turn back in shame! Congratulations!

Kill Dorian: 1/1 (Complete)

Recover the Stolen Artifact: 1/1 (Complete)

Close the portal before The Ascendancy arrives: 1/1 (Complete)

(Optional) Recover Memory: 0/1

Reward: (Granted to all group members)

Experience Points: 14,000

Renown: 1500

Infamy: 1500

Special: Due to your actions, your reputation with The Holy Ascendancy of Eligos has plummeted. Your current reputation level is: Kill on Sight.

Great, now more people want to kill me, I thought bitterly as I dismissed the quest update with a sigh, feeling the wagon shake violently as it hit another hard bump, followed by the sound of a heavy door slamming. A rush of footsteps sounded outside the wagon as someone slid open the lock on the wagon's door and pulled it open, causing bright light to pour into the interior.

"Good, you're finally awake." I heard the familiar voice of Captain Fontaine echo through the wagon as I shielded my eyes from the light. "Get them unlocked and out of there! She is waiting for us already! Double time!"

Before I could say anything, a pair of city guards practically leapt into the wagon and began unlocking all of our shackles, rudely shoving us out of the cart the moment that we were free. Stumbling out of the cart, I found myself surrounded by nearly twenty city guards, all of whom had blood covering their armor. Grabbing my arm in an iron grip, Captain Fontaine chopped his hand forward at the guards before him, causing them to spin on their heels as they led us out of the room.

The next few minutes passed by with blinding speed as Captain Fontaine and the guards led us through a network of hallways and rooms at a breakneck pace. Twice I asked Fontaine what all this was about, but the only response I got was a tightening of his grip on my arm, until the pain forced me to abandon my efforts.

Eventually we burst into a wide-open room, Captain Fontaine and the guards angling us towards a tall, dark-haired woman, dressed in a pure white robe, standing by herself, silently inspecting Dorian's head that had somehow arrived before us and now rested on a stone pedestal.

"My Lady," Captain Fontaine replied formally as the entire retinue came to a halt and forced the four of us into a line a short distance away from the woman. "We have brought the adventurers and thief lord I informed you about."

"So I see," the woman replied, despite keeping her attention focused solely on Dorian's head as she continued to inspect it.

Silence filled the air as we waited for the woman to finish her perusal of the dead devil's head, all of us watching her patiently as she walked around the pedestal, her loose robes billowing behind her as she moved. Minutes passed before the woman was satisfied with whatever she saw in the grisly trophy and turned her attention towards us.

Glowing blue eyes regarded us coolly as she stepped away from the pedestal and began to slowly stalk towards us, her bright gaze alternating between each of us. Lifting a hand away from her billowing robes as she approached, I saw her holding the familiar, broken shape of the artifact, now completely dormant. Part of me wanted to reach out and take it from her, to find out more about the voice that I had heard screaming at me, but the vicious grip that Captain Fontaine still had on my arm made me doubt I'd be able to take a single step forward without his approval.

"I thought there were five adventurers?" the woman asked, her expression unchanging as she fixated her attention on me.

"There were, my Lady," Captain Fontaine replied smoothly, inclining his head towards us. "According to them, two died during the… *incursion*. We have no way of knowing where they may have returned to life."

The woman nodded as she digested the captain's words, stopping her approach less than an arm's length away from me and looking up into my eyes. Her bright azure gaze bored into me with such a piercing intensity that it caused a shiver to crawl down my spine.

"My name is Matriarch Emilia Denarius," she said, her eyes flaring as she spoke. "I have received word that nobles are killing one another in the streets. That the thieves guilds are in open war between one another. That House Phineas has been *completely* destroyed. And most importantly, that the Holy Ascendancy of Eligos has just tried to invade Eberia, failing only by the slimmest of margins.

"All of which brings one burning question to the forefront of my mind." Emilia took a step closer to me as she spoke, bringing her face inches away from mine. "*What the hell have you adventurers done to my city?*"

"AH!" CREATIVITY EXCLAIMED IN PAIN as she ground her teeth together, focusing intently on her task before the opportunity passed her by.

Working desperately, she fought to ignore the biting pain of the black thread as she pulled it loose from the golden strand that it had woven itself around. Glowing blood poured from her fingers as the writhing thread sliced through her flesh and dripped onto the Tapestry below, causing the threads that it touched to grow bright and vibrant.

Stifling a cry, Creativity drew the black thread as far away as she could from its place, her other hand looping a single silver thread to the now exposed gold one. The two threads quivered as she tied the final knot, the silver one beginning to shake defiantly as it resisted its new place in the Tapestry.

"I'm sorry, I know you've been through so much," Creativity said softly as she let the black thread go with a sigh of relief, watching it rewind itself against the golden thread tightly, save for a single gap where the silver thread was now attached. "But this is where I need you the most right now."

Taking a step back from the Grand Tapestry, Creativity brought her wounded hand close to her chest, oblivious to the fact that it had already healed itself as she inspected her work with trepidation.

Things are moving faster than I could have ever anticipated, Creativity thought as she watched the Grand Tapestry weave itself at blinding speed. Every day, there were more and more silver threads joining the Tapestry, which would only cause events to move faster and faster as they shaped the world below.

It was only a matter of time before everything came to a head and chaos took over. Creativity hoped that the foundation she had laid would be enough to keep the Tapestry intact. Only time would tell just how successful her efforts had been.

Giving one final look at the Grand Tapestry, Creativity nodded to herself, satisfied with what she saw. With a gesture, she dismissed the work from her sight and looked out to the starry night that surrounded her.

"It's your move now, sister."

Lazarus's Character Sheet at the End of *Hell to Pay*

LAZARUS CAIN – LEVEL 13 BRUISER

Half-Giant/Half-Elf Male

Statistics:

HP: 800/800

Stamina: 800/800

Mana: 275/275

Experience to next level: 22136/27000

Attributes:

Strength: 79 (92)

Agility: 65 (73)

Constitution: 49 (54)

Intelligence: 10

Willpower: 10

Abilities:

Sneak Attack II *(Passive) – Attacks made before the target is aware of you automatically deal weapon damage +35.*

Bleeding Attack I *(Passive) – Enemies who take sneak attack damage will continue to bleed for 5 seconds, taking 40% of the sneak attack damage dealt.*

Power Attack II *(Active: 50 Stamina) – You slash viciously at the target, putting extra strength behind the blow. Deal weapon damage +25.*

Ambush I *(Active: 60 Stamina) – You ambush your target, striking them in a vulnerable location. Deals weapon damage+125. This ability can only be used on a target unaware of you.*

Kick *(Active: 20) – You kick your enemy for 10-20 points of* *damage and knock them back 1-2 yards. Depending on your Strength/Agility score, you may also knock down the target.*

***Shoulder Tackle** (Active: 40 Stamina) – Stun enemy for 1-2 seconds with chance to knock enemy down based on Strength and/or Agility attribute.*

***Deadly Throw I** (Active: 30 Stamina) – Throw a weapon with extra strength behind it. Deals weapon damage +15. This ability has a chance to interrupt spellcasting if thrown at the target's head, force them to drop their weapon if thrown at target's hands, or slow their movement if thrown at target's legs.*

Skills:

Weapons:

***Unarmed Combat** – Level 12 – 63% (Increases knowledge of Hand-to-Hand fighting and improves related Abilities.)*

***Swords** – Level 13 – 22% (Increases knowledge of Sword fighting and improves related Abilities.)*

***Daggers** – Level 11 – 47% (Increases knowledge of Dagger fighting and improves related Abilities.)*

***Crossbows** – Level 12 – 22% (Increases knowledge of Crossbows and improves related Abilities.)*

***Throwing** – Level 10 – 36% (Increases knowledge of Throwing Weapons and improves related Abilities.)*

Other:

***Stealth** – Level 12 – 97% (Decreases chance of being detected while attempting to stay hidden. Improves related Abilities.)*

***Lockpicking** – Level 12 – 89% (Increases knowledge of lock mechanics, allowing you to pick harder locks.)*

***Wordplay** – Level 12 – 89% (Increases chance to persuade others, resolve differences, and/or get information.)*

***Perception** - Level 13 - 11% (You are skilled in spotting hidden creatures and places. Depending on your skill level, hidden creatures and places will be highlighted in red.)*

Tradeskills:

Blacksmithing *– Level 11 – 12%*

Cooking *– Level 10 – 34%*

Alchemy *– Level 12 – 11%*

Leatherworking *– Level 12 – 17%*

Racial Ability:

Titan's Might *(Giant) (Passive) – Your giant ancestry has given you the ability to wield large weapons in with exceptional strength. All damage dealt by two-handed weapons is increased by 3%.*

Keen Sight *(Elf) (Passive) – Your elven ancestry has given you exceptional eyesight, granting you the ability to see twice as far as normal in all lighting conditions. This ability also grants you Darkvision.*

Darkvision *(Elf) (Passive) – While in total darkness, your vision will have near daylight clarity up to 100 feet.*

Traits:

Sigil of Rage *– A magical sigil written in the Primal Tongue has been carved deep into your flesh, causing it to pulse with an unfathomable torrent of energy. When activated, Primal Rage suffuses your body granting you +10 to Strength and Agility. While this ability is active, you are consumed by burning pain and your body is burned from within, dealing 10 points of damage per second. This ability scales per level.*

Evolving Weapon:

Dormant Glass-Steel Greatsword

Total Experience Gained: 3425/50000

AFTERWORD

Thank you so much for reading Hell to Pay! I hope you enjoyed it!

Please consider leaving a review of this book! Reviews are critical to both help me improve as a writer and to help gain exposure! If there are things that you like or didn't like in this story, please let me know!

You can get in touch with me directly at LyrianRastler@gmail.com or friend me on Facebook! I welcome questions, comments, and suggestions!

Printed in the USA
CPSIA information can be obtained
at www.ICGtesting.com
LVHW091931161123
764155LV00026B/313/J